TRAITOR'S FOLLY

CODE OF THE KEEPER, BOOK 1

MARIE ANDREAS

ACKNOWLEDGEMENTS

I'm so lucky to have so many wonderful writing companions on this journey—artists, editors, beta readers, and readers.

I'd like to thank everyone who has ever supported me, read chapters, edited, let me cry on their shoulder, and/or bought me supporting and soothing beverages. I could never have done this without ALL of you. I can't list you all here, but you mean the world to me.

My editor extraordinaire- Jessa Slade of Red Circle Ink—thank you for keeping the mayhem under a bit of control. My beta readers: Lisa Andreas, Patti Huber, Lynne Mayfield, and Sharon Rivest—thank you so much! Typo hunter extraordinaire- Ilana Schoonover. Any errors or mistakes are completely mine.

And to my very talented artist- Aleta Rafton, another fun adventure for Vas.

Thank you to The Killion Group for great formatting and back and spine cover work—excellent as always!

To all my readers—thank you for enjoying the crazy worlds in my head!

CHAPTER ONE

———

V AS DUCKED UNDER THE BLADE that sliced
toward her head, rolled, and then swung her short
sword up to slice through the attacker. With a leap to her
feet, she spun, and lopped the head off of the one sneaking up behind her. She'd been a bit overzealous, so she
got nicked as the third attacker came charging up. Her
dagger took care of him a moment later.

"Pause," Deven's voice echoed in the chamber, and
the holosuite went gray. "You're still dipping when you
adjust. That works for your longer blades, not these. And
the dagger could have been used for all three, not only
the one you almost missed." He was in the room above
the holosuite, kibitzing—or training, as he liked to call it.

"It doesn't feel right. I'm used to going with my Zalith
blades. This short sword and dagger getup is messing with
me in this fight scenario." She took advantage of the
break to grab a water tube from the side wall dispenser.
"Which is why you chose this setup."

"I'm not one to tell my captain what she needs to work
on. Oh wait, yes, I am. You're getting set in your fighting
styles. Too long doing the same type of fighting repeatedly has left you stuck in a single mode. You can fight
that way with blasters, but not very well with blades or
hand to hand."

Vas sighed. "We were fighting to save the Commonwealth, and possibly other systems as well. I'm not going
to fret if my leg work sucks when I'm fighting for others'
lives."

"Hopefully, at some point we can get back to being

mercenaries and a proper lifestyle. Speaking of which, *they* sent another transmission." The door to the holo-suite opened and Deven strode in. He was dressed in actual workout clothes, including a shirt. As lovers, Vas enjoyed seeing him without clothes. And he usually worked out without a shirt. She appreciated his consideration for her concentration in this case. His green eyes, jet black hair, and pale golden skin were distraction enough. Vas sighed at his comment. She didn't have to ask who *they* were. The Commonwealth politicos were back in force, harassing them even before the buildings on the core planets were rebuilt.

"I'm still not available. You could talk to them, since you're a hero as much as I am." Along with their massively expanded crew, and Marli, a lost and presumed dead Asarlaí; Vas and Deven had fought off some homicidal Asarlaí mutants and saved the Commonwealth. That had been almost eight months ago, and the quickly rebuilding Commonwealth government was not giving up on getting Vaslisha Tor Dain, heroine of the Commonwealth, to become the figurehead leader of the Commonwealth space fleet.

She and Deven had almost died in that last battle, so a nice long R&R on her planet, Home, was perfect for avoiding the politicians. But now both were completely recovered, and the Commonwealth pencil pushers were doubling down on their harassment tactics.

"Not in this lifetime. No matter how many times I come back." Deven called up a few holo weapons, rejecting each after a few swings.

"Nothing from our cyber stalker?" Six months ago, some person, or persons, had punched through all of their electronic security, looking for someone called the Pirate of Boagada. The pirate was a mysterious persona from far outside of the Commonwealth, a position more than an individual. The person bearing the name changed regularly, but the pirate had been connected to some of the largest crimes outside of the Commonwealth and might have been Deven at one time. By the time her crew had patched through the call to Vas and Deven on their beach, the caller was gone. A few random attempts since then made her think they were still trying to get through, but each time they dropped the call before Vas could talk to them.

Gosta, chief navigator and hacker extraordinaire, hadn't taken the technical intrusion well. That he hadn't been able to find out anything about the electronic systems breach during the six months since it happened had left him in a considerably annoyed state.

"Gosta thinks he finally has a lead. The voice scrambler used by the caller was a custom job, but they'd used a base model to start. One from the Zill system." He tested a few more holo weapons before selecting a duplicate of the pair Vas was using.

"Nothing beyond that?"

"Nope. But it dialed back Gosta's behavior a tiny bit. I was ready to ask Terel to tranq him whenever he wasn't on deck." Deven was usually fairly easygoing, and the fact that Gosta's behavior had been annoying him that much wasn't a good sign.

She finished another water tube, dropped them both in the recycle slot, and then raised her weapons. "Shall we?"

"Trianthlin scenario, level four," he called out to the holosuite computer. Vas narrowed her eyes, so he shrugged and flashed a wicked grin. "Make that level six. Someone wants to get her ass kicked."

The suite transformed into a humid jungle, one that appeared to have been untouched since it had been formed five thousand years prior. Vas had been to Trianthlin once on a merc job with a small crew and no other merc teams. The locals, smallish lizard-like beings, hibernated for eighteen years at a time—all at the same time.

They'd not been happy that a wandering pack of Ilerians had moved in during their most recent hibernation.

The battle was short, the place was constantly on the edge of a torrential downpour, and on top of it all, it stunk. Vas had sworn to never take a job from them again. Knowing Deven, and reinforced by the sexy, yet oh-so-sneaky grin he wore, he selected this scenario to throw her off her game.

"Nice choice." She crossed her short sword and dagger in the start position. "Next time someone wants to hire us for a job on one of these planets—you're my go-to guy."

He simply tipped his head, crossed his blades like hers, and flexed his impressive biceps. "Start."

The hologram engaged and troops appeared before them. Vas and Deven were at the opposite ends of the room, and they would each go through a series of fighters before facing each other.

She loved to watch him fight with swords. His moves, even when in the middle of a deadly real-life battle, were graceful and precise. Of course, he'd had a few hundred years to perfect them. He wouldn't completely admit to how old he was, not even to her. But she knew he'd been around for over two hundred years. And didn't look a day over thirty.

She swore as her distraction almost cost her a holographic gut wound. She swung hard, using a move that would have decapitated her opponent with her longer blades. Unfortunately, her short sword and dagger ended up leaving her with a pretty spin and an opponent still coming for her.

"Don't say it," she yelled and moved in to fight the hologram opponent up close.

"I'm watching my own fight, thank you."

She didn't turn toward him, but she heard the smirk in his voice. Bastard. She ran through the first one and made quick work of the next two. Three more fighters flashed into existence and she focused on them to keep from getting hit. No, the holo fighters couldn't hurt her, but the idea behind these trainings was to make sure that a real opponent couldn't either.

It would be embarrassing as hell if she let herself take a holo wound when Deven was with her. The second trio followed the first group into holo oblivion, and she spun to find him standing there, looking relaxed as he watched her. His own opponents had clearly been off the field for a while.

"Ready?" That was an exceptionally evil grin.

She swore. The idea behind this kind of challenge was that the two real fighters would be in a state of fatigue when they faced each other after battling the holograms. She knew she was. Deven looked like he'd just awoken from a nap.

"Come on then, let's have at it." She charged him, a vicious stabbing pain in the back of her head dropped her to her knees.

"Vas!" He released his weapons and ran forward to grab her before she hit the floor. "What's wrong?" Deven was a teke, telepath, but there was no way he would have attacked her like that.

Her weapons vanished into the floor as she clutched her head and curled into a ball. The initial stab of agony was gone but it left brutal smaller waves of pain in its wake.

"I don't know. That was nasty—slammed into me out of nowhere, a stabbing in my head..." She tried to get up, but dizziness pushed her back down again.

"Vas, I'm sorry for that shock, but I couldn't reach you, so I had to punch through harder than intended. We have a problem."

"Shit! Aithnea?" Aithnea, also known as the Mother Superior of the Clionea nuns; a convent of warrior nuns who had all been destroyed almost a year ago by the same bastards Vas and Deven had stopped, was dead. But that hadn't stopped her from being in Vas' head for quite a while after she was killed. She had been instrumental in destroying the mutant Asarlaí who had been doing a damn good job of taking over the Commonwealth. "What are you doing? Where have you been? And why are you back?" Vas kept talking out loud. Aithnea could hear her regardless and she wanted Deven to hear at least part of what was going on. He'd been able to hear Aithnea in his own head sometimes, before she vanished after the last battle, but from the look on his face he wasn't hearing her now.

"That is by design. His not hearing me right now, not your head almost exploding. Again, sorry about that. You can fill him in on my side of this conversation soon. I don't have enough strength to loop him in at this point. I thought I was done with this plane of existence, we all did. Yes, the other nuns are with me. But we're not done by a long shot."

Vas rubbed between her brows and shrugged to Deven. She stayed on the floor in case it moved on her again. "Still no information why you bashed my head open or what's going on." Aithnea had never directly said that the rest of her order, all of whom had died when she had, were with her in whatever form the afterlife took; but it was good to know they were together. When Vas first ran away from the hell she'd called home as a kid, Aithnea and the nuns had taken her in for a few years.

"Always to the point," Aithnea said. *"But a point well taken in this case. There is a problem with the scrolls—the ones you took from the Garmain home world. That you didn't recall taking because you asked me to mind wipe you to protect them. No time for you to get pissed about that again."* She paused. *"I need you and your crew to help us get them back. As for the mind blast, there are some serious mental protections around your ship. Ones that didn't exist before. I assume they aren't*

Deven's doing? His signature isn't on them."

"Deven? She says there are heavy-duty psi protections around the *Warrior Wench*, is that you?"

"No. And no one else could have set them up without me knowing." Deven answered.

Vas laughed as they both spoke at the same time. "Aithnea just mentioned unless they were stronger than you."

Deven didn't answer, but the scowl he gave was enough. In the Commonwealth, Deven would be off the charts for esper powers, if they ever forced him to take a psi test. But there were far stronger races outside of the Commonwealth.

"I feel something from Deven, something beyond annoyance."

"She says she's picking up on something from you. Do you know who might be behind it?"

"No. Maybe. Not a person, but a group. We've figured out that there's more than one person trying to get to us about the Pirate of Boagada."

"Why would they protect the ship? They've been punching through our protections to talk to us—or try to."

"But they keep being cut off. They might be trying to warn us of someone else as much as find that damn pirate."

"He has a good point. Although I'm not happy to hear of people searching for the Pirate of Boagada—it can't be coincidence."

Vas rolled to her feet as the pain in her head lessened. "You're involved with this mysterious pirate figure too? Let me guess, at one time one of the nuns was the Pirate of Boagada?" When you had a persona, who was more than the people who claimed the title, anyone could have been her/him.

"Not directly. Although there was a connection. As far as I know, none of my nuns stood in the place of honor of the pirate. I always thought Therlian would have made a good pirate. Alas,

she gave it up to have a child. And now she's embracing moth-erhood."

Vas snorted. "I think she was in love. And she's the sec-ond in command on one of my ships; that's not sitting around all day making star cookies." Therlian had joined Vas' crew when her own planet had been attacked by forces supporting the Asarlaí. That she'd been a former nun was a bonus in Vas' eyes, and she quickly recruited her to take second-in-command one of the ships in Vas' impromptu fleet—the *Victorious Dead*.

"Neither here nor there. The reason it isn't surprising is that the task I need you and your crew for is on the outskirts of Nhali space. The last stomping ground of the Pirate of Boagada. Sadly, it was literally the last stomping ground. The Pirate was murdered two years ago and hadn't designated a successor."

Vas quickly summed it up out loud and Deven looked as confused as she felt. "So, this pirate is different people, but the most recent was murdered, and now there isn't one? Can't anyone step in?"

"No, the pirate must be selected." Both Deven and Aithnea said at the same time. Deven still looked con-fused, but he'd sounded sure in his answer.

Vas held up her hand even though she knew Aithnea couldn't see it. "One at a time. You echoed each other."

"Makes sense," Aithnea got in first. *"Deven was the Pirate of Boagada very briefly, but it was long ago and before who and what he is now. Once the position of pirate has passed on to another, the memories of being the pirate fade away. However, he'd still have some instinctual reactions from his time. Most likely whoever is looking for the pirate is tracking him."*

Vas quickly repeated Aithnea's words.

"Don't you think I would know if I'd been someone else?" Even though Deven had strongly implied a more than passing knowledge of the pirate and had pretended to the Garmainian officials that he was him, he had never admitted to having been the actual pirate.

"Like when you were a different pirate and also a gahan sex worker? You did forget those for a bit." Not a time she wanted to recall either. But it had happened.

His scowl deepened but he didn't respond.

"The Pirate of Boagada has been around for over nine hundred years. But I don't think it is tied into Deven's prior death, resurrection, and subsequent memory issues."

Vas ran her hand over her forehead. That was one problem with having conversations with someone inside your head, there was no way to glare at them if they pissed you off.

"Then what happens to the position if the pirate doesn't have a successor? And what has it to do with the scrolls I stole for you and more importantly, us?"

"The position is in limbo. And that's not good. The nuns had a connection to the pirate; we began the role, if you would. It will take a fully trained nun to find the new pirate. And the scrolls are needed to assist with that."

"The scrolls will lead us to the last nun?"

"There is no last nun. Therlian can't even reclaim her spot because she broke the bonds. We need to make a new one. You."

CHAPTER TWO

———◆———

"**M**E?"VAS HAD TO AIM her glare somewhere, so Deven got it.

"You what?" He was being patient for only hearing one side of an odd conversation, but that patience was wearing thin.

Vas held up her hand. She wanted more explanation from Aithnea first. "Well? Me what?"

"*You will have to be trained to take the vows. Temporarily, of course. And not the religious ones. The Keeper ones.*"

"The Keeper vows? Those take years, Aithnea, and I couldn't even follow the basic practice. There has to be another option." The Keepers were the fighters of the faith. Considering that the entire order were warrior nuns, that put the Keepers in a unique position.

"*It won't take years. And you learned more than you think during your time with us. Plus, there is no one else. Sorry.*" There was a pause. "*Whatever is protecting your ship is becoming stronger. I will find a way back. Until then, read the blue book in my belongings.*"

A slight popping was the only sound, but Vas knew she was gone.

"That was annoying." She held up both hands. "Yes, I will fill you in on the bits you missed. But on the way to a shower and some food. And a drink down on Home." There was a lot going on in her head, and she had a bad feeling part of it was triggered by Aithnea bouncing around in there. But she quickly filled him in on the issue with the pirate, the scrolls, and the nuns. She briefly summed up the Keeper issue—but didn't go into detail.

She planned on finding a way out of it.

Vas had spent two years with the nuns, doing drudge work to earn her keep, but she also sat in on some lessons. Mostly she lost interest and would sometimes nap.

Then why was she now recalling bits of a hand-combat tutorial? And why did she know exactly what the blue book that Aithnea had mentioned looked like? Aithnea had left a storehouse of weapons, relics, and books on a dead world, then led Vas and her crew to find it. Most of the weapons that had survived the battle against the Asar-laí were with their new owners—members of Vas' crews or her allies. The books, relics, and maps were either in a storage bunker near the captain's quarters on this ship, or in her place down on the planet.

Deven shook his head at the brief amount of information. "I'm not sure what she thinks we can do about any of that."

Vas stood in front of the lift doors, stewing over Aithnea's words until Deven finally pushed the button for their floor. There were a few other crew rooms on the same level as the one Vas and Deven shared—Deven's old room for one. But most of the crew preferred the lower levels, and the ship was large enough that rooms could be left open.

The *Warrior Wench* started out as a loaner, a ship Vas borrowed when an unscrupulous repair dealer stole and parted out her prior ship, the *Victorious Dead*. Then he'd died—and not at Vas' hand, although it had been close. The *Victorious Dead* was eventually found and repaired, but by then Vas was used to the *Warrior Wench,* so she'd handed control of her old ship over to Ragkor, her interim second-in-command.

Two years ago, Vas had one command ship, and was content running one of the best merc companies in the Commonwealth. Now she had eight fully functioning command ships and had saved the Commonwealth.

She liked the old days better.

"What was that sigh about?" Deven keyed open their cabin but put his arm up to block her from going in. "Lost in thought? Sighing? Who are you and what have you done with Vas?"

Vas hit his arm but didn't push. "Funny. The thinking is because of that crazy nun in my head, and the sigh was for missing the good old days."

He lifted his arm, but then looped it around her waist as she passed him. "Do you really miss it?" He gave her a slow kiss. "The good old days when we were just captain and second?"

She held him tight, then stepped back. "Okay, that I don't miss. Nor that horrific esper block on my emotions. But us being mercs without a fleet and a saved-the-galaxy reputation behind us? I miss that."

Deven let the door shut behind them. "I do too, if we're being honest. But this is good as well. We can handle larger commissions. And you always complained the troop movers were too slow."

"Actually, we should probably look into buying some new ones, seeing as the others all got converted to battleships. If we take larger jobs, we can still expand the crew by having troop movers involved. Once the new captains get some more training in, they can take jobs on their own as well." She'd been pushing those thoughts aside for a while, but that didn't mean she hadn't thought about them.

He laughed. "There's the Vas I know and love. Lament the past, but it's better to look ahead."

"That's my saying," she said. "Actually, it was Aithnea's."

"It's still a good one and very much you." He nodded to the shower. "Company?"

She looked him up and down, then sighed. "Not this time. I'm starving, and team showers take too long." She jogged into the shower, finished, then stepped back out to let Deven take one.

They were almost out the door when her comm chirped. "Vas here, what's up?"

"Captain," Xsit's voice was going into the higher trills, not a good sign. "There's a ship coming into the area, full speed, not responding. Grosslyn wants to know if he should shoot it down."

Grosslyn was her commander on Home, the base planet for all of her crew and their families—a bit under ten thousand people lived on the planet or on one of her ships, the last she'd heard. She had people to keep track of that; she wasn't going to. With some help from Marli, Grosslyn had added some pretty heavy protections to Home when the Asarlaí attacked the Commonwealth. A full cloak and a mass of ground-to-space canons that could destroy a ship before they got close enough to see past the cloak. He really wanted to use those massive guns. "Damn it. Tell him to hold. How long until the ship breaches the line with Home?" Vas ran for the lift with Deven right behind.

"Maybe ten minutes, Captain." Gosta's voice was a welcome sound. Xsit was a Xithinal. A prey bird-like race that didn't handle stress well. Gosta was far calmer and rational. Unless it was about people bashing through his tech.

"Thank you, Gosta. We're coming up."

The lift opened on the command deck. Fully controlled chaos at the moment, mostly because they were waiting to see what Vas and Deven did. Her crew was one of the best in the Commonwealth, but they'd gone from fighting for the Commonwealth in a rough and overmatched war to an eight-month holding pattern. Nerves were on edge and would get worse if they weren't allowed to go fight something. Soon.

Gosta waved them over to the console he shared with Hrrru. The two couldn't be more physically different.

Gosta, a Syngerin/human breed, was tall, skinny, and vaguely stick bug-like, with legs taller than Hrrru. Hrrru was a Welischian, a species of short, furry, mostly peaceful people who'd overthrown advanced oppressors of their world by their claws and will alone.

Hrrru was busy tracking something on his screen and didn't look up.

"The ship is unidentified, but the scan indicates a smaller vessel, no more than four or five crew. Possibly a large shuttle with heavier engines."

Vas looked at the expanded image but didn't recognize it. Not surprising considering how many types of ships were in the Commonwealth now. The fight for the Commonwealth had decimated regular planetary fleets, so the worlds that survived were getting ships from wherever they could.

Deven leaned forward with an odd tilt to his head. His eyes narrowed at the screen and then he stalked over to the communications station. "Xsit, let me talk to that ship."

"They aren't answering."

"He will for me." Deven's scowl looked ready to break something on its own and Xsit quickly called up the ship.

Vas gave the screen another glance, but the ship didn't look even remotely familiar. "Who is it?"

"A rat bastard who shouldn't be within five thousand clicks of the Commonwealth." Deven was seriously pissed. Whoever it was they'd pushed some buttons to make her normally balanced second ready to punch someone.

Xsit nodded and Deven hit the comm. "Leil, if you don't answer right now, and start talking fast, we're blowing you out of this reality."

Vas pulled back at Deven's tone. It had almost crossed over to the range the late and unmourned pirate version of him had been. Complete and utter asshole.

"Deven! Thank the abyss. Can I land? We're almost out of fuel."

There was no way in hell Vas was letting any un-verified ship, no matter how small, land on her planet. But since he wouldn't be able to even see it, she assumed he meant docking in the *Warrior Wench*. She looked to Deven and gave a tight nod when he did as well.

"Main docking bay. I'm sending the coordinates. And if you stray even a bit, you'll be shaking hands with your ancestors."

"Understood. Leil out."

Vas came to the communications station. "Friend?"

"Worse," Deven said. "Brother." The scowl that took over his face did not bode well for getting more answers right now.

Vas was surprised but kept it to herself. She might be in love with Deven and share her bed with him, but she knew next to nothing about his life before he came to the Commonwealth. She wasn't fond of her late and unlamented family, and since he never spoke of them, she'd assumed he felt the same about his.

The rest of the crew on deck kept their comments to themselves, but their faces were expressive.

Deven tapped his comm. "Gon, can you meet me in the main docking bay? And bring a large blaster. Or two." He turned back to the lift.

"Oh, I am so coming with you." Vas followed him. "There's got to be something good here."

Bathie had started to get out of the command chair as she was on shift right now, but Vas waved her off. "Nope, that's still all yours at this point. We'll be back soon." Vas had made it a point to keep her command crew on their regular rotation this past month—better to keep them sharp and prepared. Bathie was an engineer, but she had excellent leadership qualities and Vas was making sure she got to use them.

"Can I come?" Mac was halfway out of his pilot sling as he spoke.

"No." Both Vas and Deven said at the same time as the lift doors shut.

"You know he'll find out about him eventually," Vas said. "They all will."

Deven sighed and ran his hand through his thick, black hair. "I know. But out of all of my siblings, Leil is the last one I want anywhere near this crew." He shuddered. "Especially Mac."

Vas laughed. That told her a lot about Leil. Mac was always looking for a quick fix for funds, some magical way to get rich. That con man drive of his had gone dormant while they were fighting the Asarlaí, but she knew he'd been sniffing around for projects the past few months.

She'd make it a point of getting Leil off her ship, and preferably out of the Commonwealth completely before he and Mac could meet.

The docking bay was usually only monitored by a single crew member, currently Marwin, and Gon had been asked to come down. Terel, the ship's medical officer and Vas' best friend, and her assistant Pela had not been requested.

"What are you two doing here?"

"They could be injured..." Terel let the sentence drop, shrugged, and shook her head, sending a ripple through her orange feather mohawk. Her feathers instead of hair and liquid silver eyes were the two most telling things that she was not human. As an exotic, her heritage crossed so many species, no single one could stake a claim. "Fine, as Deven's doctor, I think I have the right to see if this biological sibling of his will allow us to run tests." She nodded to Deven. "You've been through a hell of a lot of changes, you know."

"He doesn't need to know about any of that. If you

want to run tests, and he agrees, and they don't take too long, fine. But don't tell him anything about me."

"Agreed." Terel stepped back as the protection shield came up to enclose them and the entrance to the ship from open space as the docking bay was opened. The smaller ship entered the bay.

Vas watched the ship maneuver, then turned to Terel. "How did you know who was coming in?" Terel had been in her med lab, not anywhere near the command deck.

"News travels fast—especially when people are bored. They need work, Vas."

"I know. I wanted to wait until the new command crews were ready on all the ships. They had a trial by fire, but that's different from running a merc op."

The large shuttle finished loading in and the outer docking bay doors shut and locked. Gon nodded toward the inner barrier and once it dropped, he stepped into the bay ahead of Deven. Gon was big and fierce look-ing—he was also extremely strong but not mean at all. That Deven called him down and had him approach the ship first was interesting and said a lot about his relation-ship with his brother.

Vas' brother had tried to kill her numerous times, even creating clones of himself to come back for more. She really hoped that Leil wasn't on the same psychotic level Borlan had been.

The door for the shuttle swung open. Even if she hadn't known Leil was Deven's brother, there was no mistaking the similarity between the two. He was an inch or two shorter than Deven. He also looked older and kept his dark hair shaved close to his head. But the green eyes were the same.

The green eyes that already looked to be casing the docking bay. Cocky move for someone standing in front of a fully armed Gon.

"Thank you, Gon." Deven stepped past him and approached his brother. "I know you're not alone, so bring everyone out. Gon will search the ship as well."

Leil stepped forward with his arms outstretched for a hug but dropped them when Deven folded his arms.

Leil shrugged and stepped back. "Good to see you, little brother. You look alarmingly well, given the circumstances."

There was a wheedling tone to his voice that Deven never had. Vas narrowed her eyes and wondered what Leil knew. Deven had died, at least once, possibly twice. But Leil shouldn't be aware of that.

"What circumstances would those be?" Deven's voice went from annoyed to bored.

"The fighting you all went through. It's all over the space lanes, even those back home."

Deven stepped back and motioned from Vas to his brother. "Vas, this is my brother. Not as much of an asshole as yours, but close. Leil, this is Vas, the nice captain of the ship you're hiding in."

Leil had turned back to the open door of his shuttle but spun around at Deven's words.

"Very nice to meet you, Captain Tor Dain." He looked ready to shake her hand, but she also folded her arms. It was interesting that he knew whose ship he was on—her full name. But not interesting enough to shake his hand. He gave her an awkward smile, then turned back to Deven. "I'm not hiding."

Deven took another step forward into his brother's space. "Really? I scanned your ship. It's in good repair, has a half-tank of fuel, and is designed for long hauls. You or one of your people inside your ship are hiding from someone. My money is on you." He raised his voice. "This is the second request for whoever is with you to come out."

The entire exchange fascinated Vas. Deven was always

the unflappable one. End of the Universe? Not a problem. His older brother? Major problem. It might not
seem like it to anyone who didn't know him well, but
there was a level of annoyance there she'd rarely seen.

Leil had been keeping his face open and relaxed, but
a flash of anger, and a bit of fear, crossed his face for a
moment as he turned back to his ship.

Three men came out. At first Vas thought they were
human, and then she realized they looked like Deven's
people. Or clones of them. All three looked exactly the
same. And disturbingly familiar, although it took her a
moment to figure out why.

With the number of times questionable people had
been on her ship in the past year, Vas couldn't be faulted
for carrying her sidearm on a fairly regular basis. She
pulled her blaster out and stepped back so she could
better cover Leil and the clones. After Aithnea's cryptic
mental visit, this couldn't be a coincidence.

"Vas? What are you doing?" Deven stayed where he
was.

"Which two of you were with me? Or are there more
of you?" Her brain finally supplied the information of
those faces. Or face. Two of them had been with her on
the vid from Garmain. The mission Aithnea had sent her
on over two years ago and then wiped her memories
of it after. She still didn't recall working with two men
and breaking in, tying up the Grand Council, stealing
some scrolls, and a super-secret ship, but she'd watched
the vid of the robbery enough to know those faces. Or
face. There had been two, but they'd been identical in the
vid the Garmainians had.

Deven shook his head as he got a better look at the
three. He'd possibly spent even more time watching the
vid than she had. "Damn it, you're right." He pointed to
the ship. "That's definitely not the ship stolen from the
Garmainians though."

"You're dealing with the Garmainians now?" The look on Leil's face was disgust with a bit of confusion. The confusion seemed to come from the reaction from Vas. He kept looking back and forth between her and his silent friends.

Deven folded his arms and settled into a solid glare. "You're dealing with clones? Some who might have been involved in a major theft?"

The three clones continued to look ahead. They also stood at parade rest. Although none of them had weapons that she could see, there was no doubt they had them. And that they were trained to fight.

Vas watched them as she used her comm. "Gosta, shut the docking bay interior doors and send down Walvento and some of his crew to stay down here between the docking bay and the corridor into the ship. Our guests might not be what we expected."

"Aye, Captain." The interior security doors slid shut before he finished speaking. Terel and Pela weren't armed that Vas could see, but that wouldn't stop either from fighting. And Vas was sure that Terel probably had some nasty options in her med kit.

"Whoa!" Leil held up both hands. "What's going on? These are my business partners, and they are triplets, not clones. Yes, they are dangerous. Yes, they are mercs. But so are all of you." The grin he flashed at Pela was all Deven. "Except that lovely little lady. You wouldn't hurt anyone."

Pela was short, petite, willowy, and looked like someone's favorite little sister. She smiled, leaned forward, and whipped out a pair of throwing knives from braces inside the sleeves of her shirt. "This *lovely lady* could kill you all before you could pull your blaster out. And that's without resorting to my medical training."

Leil gave a crumbling smile and took a step back.

"Thank you, Pela," Vas said. "As for what's going on, I suggest all of you remove your weapons, and we start over with you explaining what the hell you are doing here. Before I decide to let my med team have at you."

CHAPTER THREE

I F TEREL AND PELA WERE concerned at being used as a threat, neither showed it. The clones, or triplets as Leil called them, all looked to Leil. At his nod, a nice pile of weapons formed on the floor in front of them.

"Great, now talk." Vas had initially let Deven take lead since Leil was his brother. But he seemed fine with her taking over now. At least if the tiny smirk hiding around his scowl was any indication. "I'll get you started. You're not Commonwealth, and since the war, they've been very tight about their borders. We're far enough inside the Commonwealth that you are either authorized, which I doubt given your panicked searching for your brother—who clearly dislikes you—or you're sneaking in." She crossed her arms but kept her snub blaster in her right hand.

"Is there a better place to talk?" Leil looked around the docking bay with a wince. "This seems so public."

"And well recorded," Terel said as she checked some items in her med kit. The one she pulled out was a large, archaic needle. She'd had to use it only once that Vas knew of. On Vas herself when she'd been poisoned. Since then, Terel kept it with her mostly for scare tactics. "I'll need some samples, new ship policy. Whoever doesn't talk is first."

Vas passed her hand over her mouth to hide her laugh. Terel had become more hands-on in the last few months. She was enjoying this.

"I'm good to talk." One of the triplets stepped up. "We're working with Leil. I'm Ome. And lady, I don't recognize you at all." He nodded to Vas. His brothers Pol and Relin each said almost the same thing. Vas knew two of them were the men from the vid of the robbery on Garmain. She just wasn't sure which two. "Are there more of you? Or only you three?"

"Just us. Our parents said we're more than enough." Pol shrugged.

Vas would show them an edited version of the vid later and see if that jogged any memories. Aithnea had wiped Vas' memories at her request to keep the theft secret— there was a chance someone had done the same for the men.

Terel nodded to them, then advanced on Leil with her massive needle held upright. "Well, as Deven's kin, I want your blood the most. This speeds things along."

Leil scrambled backward until he hit his ship. "Hold off! Deven?"

Deven didn't move forward. "What? I agree with her. You've been a con man and a thief since I was a kid. And if you think we're letting you into the main part of this ship, or off this ship, without a full explanation, you're dumber than I always thought you were."

Leil's look bounced around to the triplets. They might be working together, but they weren't friends. At least not judging by the complete lack of support on their faces.

"Yeah, we're not in here legally." He held up one hand. "I thought we were. Like you said, getting into the Commonwealth has been mighty tight since you all beat the Asarlaí. But I have business here. Been running an import business out of Hrylian Twelve for the past few years. My connection for getting into the Commonwealth betrayed me. By the time I realized the codes weren't good, we'd already blown through all the check points." He waved his hand as Terel stepped closer with the needle. "That's all. I knew Deven was out here and figured you could hide us and sneak us back out of the Commonwealth. Or at least to the Rim."

"Fine, you spoke, but you were the last." Terel could move uncommonly fast when she wanted to. Leil was focused on the massive needle in her hand, so he didn't notice the hypo draw in her other. She darted forward, pressed it against his arm, and then darted back. "That should do, thank you."

Leil rubbed his arm where she'd taken the sample, but there was no way he felt anything. "That's illegal. You can't steal my blood."

"She can, and she did," Vas said. "My ship, my rules." She shrugged. There was no way they were going to get rid of Leil and his co-workers without a major hassle on her and her crews' side. The least he could do was donate blood to help determine what all had changed with Deven. Even before he'd died and come back, Marli had mentioned that something had changed in him—but she wasn't sure what or how. Then the dying and coming back into three bodies just compounded the weirdness going on in him.

"Good thing you can't go anywhere. I might need more." Terel put away the needle but after dropping in a new cartridge, kept the hypo out.

Pol shrugged and held out his arm. "I don't care if you take mine. I'd really rather not end up on a Commonwealth prison planet because Leil is a moron." His two brothers nodded and also held out their arms.

Terel quickly took samples. It wasn't really a policy on the ship, but Vas was thinking that might change. They'd been infiltrated by people who were not what they appeared in the past. Perhaps this screening could help avoid that.

Vas stepped back to Deven's side. "This *is* an awkward place to question them about anything. But he's your brother, so it's your call."

The scowl that had been fading came back, but then he let it slide away. "Even as kids, Leil never did anything without fifteen different reasons behind it. He's given us one truth, but there are many more."

"We can put him in the brig. His friends too for the time being." She looked over to where Terel was asking the triplets questions. Most likely family history of some sort by the way she was recording notes. Pela and Leil were having a stare down and Leil was definitely losing.

"As much as I know he deserves it, not yet. And I'm not picking up anything from the triplets. Yes, I've been scanning, but knowing my brother and the type of people he usually associates with, my scanning is justified."

Technically Deven was still wearing his esper bracelets, thin inlaid bands that were designed to block telepathic powers. As Vas had found out not that long ago, they'd never worked on Deven. He kept them on to make others feel better. "He's not an esper as well, is he?" She'd find a special cell for him if he was.

"No. He knows I am but didn't care enough to find out how much. Most of the ones in our family are very low—nothing higher than what would be a two on the Commonwealth scale."

Vas studied her guests. "What about the locked guest rooms? The four on b-deck have coded doors. We can keep them there. Nicer than the brig but without free range of the ship."

"Good idea. We probably want to get them there before Pela tries to rip Leil's head off." But the grin he flashed said he'd probably welcome that.

"It's been decided." Vas stepped forward and raised her voice. "You can stay until we figure out what to do with you. We have secured rooms for your stay. All the luxury of home, but no coming out unless we're with you. We've had a rough time with guests in the past."

The triplets shrugged. At exactly the same time. They

might or might not be clones, but they were freaking Vas out like they were. Leil opened his mouth, looked to Deven, and then shut it.

"Agreed. You'll give us back our weapons when we leave?"

"Probably." Vas motioned for all of them to step around the weapon collection and Deven opened the doorway.

Gon, Walvento, and Marwin stood at the entrance to the rest of the ship. All three had large blasters but were holding them casually. Or what appeared to be so. Vas knew any of them would be ready to fire if needed. Marwin was one of a set of triplets on her ship—all three with extensive combat records. But unlike their new visitors, his siblings didn't look, talk, and act the same. He was watching the trio before him with interest and a bit of distrust. Walvento was her weapons master, and he always watched everyone and everything with distrust.

"Carry on, men," Vas said. "We're going to level three and b-deck." She didn't say anything else, but Gon and Marwin dropped in to follow as they went by. Walvento stayed in the docking bay. Standard procedure now: keep an eye on anything new in the ship.

"Unless you need us, we'll be checking out what our fine friends are made of." Terel patted her med kit as she and Pela turned down another corridor that led toward the med bay.

They had gotten the triplets into their rooms and were walking to Leil's when Vas' comm chirped. "Yes?"

"Captain, we have another ship coming in. Similar to Deven's brother's shuttle, but bigger. Cruiser B class I'd guess based on size. On the same course as the shuttle had been," Gosta said. Xsit might have been freaking out again.

She turned to Deven. "Another brother?"

"No." Deven faced Leil. "It isn't, is it? Pretty sure you're the only one in our family who would even contemplate coming to the Commonwealth."

Leil raised his hands. "No one I know. Similar to my shuttle, you say?"

Deven wasn't that much taller than his brother but he managed to grab him by the collar and lift him a foot off the ground. "Who is it? We're way too far off any space lane for an accidental encounter."

"I don't know." Leil struggled a bit and tried to break the grip Deven had. But Deven was a lot stronger than him. "Okay, I might. It could be some people."

Vas stepped to his side. "Some people? We figured that out. Why are they on the same path you were and in a ship that looks like it belongs with that shuttle you came in on? One I didn't recognize, by the way, even up close." With the heavy destruction of Commonwealth ships from the Asarlaí wars, new ships were being brought in from all over. Not recognizing it wasn't that concerning. Until another one like it came in.

"My ship is stolen. Don't tell the triplets, they'll kill me. I thought we had a legit job and needed to borrow something for a bit. Things fell through."

Deven dropped him. "I say shove him back in the ship and give it to them."

Vas watched Leil as he straightened his shirt. He was lying about the ship. Deven was too emotionally close to pick up on it, but sometimes reading good old body language worked. "Get in the room." She turned to Gon. "Stay here and make sure none of our guests leave. Marwin, go relieve Walvento and have him go back to the weapons bay. We might need to destroy a ship."

Leil had been halfway into his room but stopped at her words and spun with a panicked look. "No, you can't shoot it."

"Want to tell me why?"

There was a battle on his face that finally gave up. "Not a good idea?"

Vas shoved him fully into the room and slammed the palm lock.

"No one in or out. Deven, let's see what your brother brought our way." Marwin had already jogged off to replace Walvento. She didn't know if they were going to have to shoot at anyone, but better to have her master gunner in position.

Deven was lost in his own thoughts as they made their way to the lift, but he shook himself out of it as the lift opened. He strode onto the command deck. "How close is that ship?"

"I was watching the direction our first visitor came from, so I picked them up much further out this time. The route they came from and their projected course is the same as the shuttle we picked up." Gosta flipped his screen to the main front screen. His overlay of the path put it right where they were.

"Xsit, tell Grosslyn he can't blow this one up either." Vas took her command chair back from Bathie. "The course is to us, not Home." She knew Grosslyn would have been tracking the new ship just as Gosta had.

Xsit relayed her command. "He says standing by and waiting, Captain."

Vas shook her head and spun her chair toward Gosta's station. "What do we know about our new friend?"

"It's closer in size to us, although maybe a class above if it had been a Commonwealth ship. But the styling is similar to the shuttle." Mac jumped in. He was the resident ship junkie along with being the primary pilot. There was no piloting going on at the moment since they were circling Home, so he'd pulled up diagrams of ships similar to the one that was approaching.

"Let's move a bit away from Home before we try to contact that ship." Vas rubbed the back of her neck. "Head toward the cluster." The small grouping of odd dwarf stars was Home's nearest neighbor. Not really very close, but distance from everything else was one of the reasons she kept this planet for her people.

Mac swung them away from Home. Once Vas was satisfied that they were in a better location, and Gosta confirmed that the other ship had changed course to follow, she nodded to Xsit. "Reach out to our friends."

Xsit's standard greeting was simple; ship identification and a request for the other ship to do the same. Vas watched as Xsit's yellow feathered bird-like face tightened as she kept sending the call. Finally, she turned back to Vas. "They are bouncing the signal back. The first two went through to them, I know it. Then they started bouncing them back. That's remarkably rude." Xsit wasn't fierce, but she was extremely good at her job. And Xithinals took manners, or lack thereof, seriously.

"Give me the comm," Vas said. Once the outgoing messages had been transferred to the comm on her shirt, Vas hit it. "This is Captain Vaslisha Tor Dain of the *Warrior Wench* calling the incoming ship. Please identify." She kept her voice professional but on the edge of pissed. Xsit was right, not identifying to a hail was rude. And after the Asarlaí wars, it was inexcusable. The paper pushers in the Commonwealth were creating a bill to make it a hefty fine to refuse to answer a hail. Of course, in Vas' book, anyone who was refusing to answer wouldn't really care about a fine.

A brief burst of static, then the line went silent. "Unknown ship, this is the *Warrior Wench*. If you don't know who and what we are, look it up. Refusal to answer will be met with force." She saw, but ignored, the looks from Deven, Mac, and the rest of the command deck. Her reaction was uncommonly harsh, but something wasn't right with that ship. The hairs on the back of her neck were standing up and Aithnea always said to listen to your gut. "You have one minute to reply."

Even if the other ship didn't know who the *Warrior*

Wench was—and after the Asarlaí Wars there would be few in the Commonwealth who didn't—a look at the scan of the weapons she carried should have made the other ship respond, and possibly back away slowly. The other vessel might be a bit larger but had limited weapons. One of Vas' shuttles probably had more firepower.

"Is it running away?" Vas watched as the blip on the screen changed trajectory.

"Aye, Captain. Actually, it's veering toward Home." Gosta was pulling up potential trajectories and flinging them at the front screen as fast as he could.

"Oh no, they're not," Vas yelled. "Mac, cut that ship off. I will blast that asshole from the sky myself if I have to."

"Grosslyn wants to know if he can fire on the ship now."

"No!" Vas and Deven both yelled.

Vas held up her hand. "Sorry. Right now, Home is still cloaked, and I want to keep it hidden. A massive ray of death coming from the middle of space would be noticeable."

CHAPTER FOUR

———————◆———————

"HE'S NOT HAPPY." MAC WAS focusing on pushing their engines as hard as possible and wasn't on the comm himself—but clearly Grosslyn was loud enough on Xsit's speaker that even in the pilot sling Mac heard the noise, if not the words.

"I don't care." Vas kept watching the other ship on the screen. It was still far enough away from Home that she knew they'd be able to cut them off. But she wanted to see whether the other captain actually knew where they were going or was just heading in a general direction. "Gosta, overlay a direct trajectory from the location where that ship stopped to Home." She had a theory, but validation was always good.

"They are going wide."

"Exactly. That ship has no idea where the planet is, they might not even be looking for a planet. Which makes me feel better, but we still need to stop them. They got too close." She hit her comm. "Last chance, unidentified ship. We're not letting you go without knowing who you are. Stand down or we will make you stand down." Normally, giving an opponent knowledge that you were going to fire wasn't a good idea. But as much as she wanted the other ship to stop, she didn't want to have to shoot it this close to Home. She cut her comm.

"Gosta, is there any way to hack in? Maybe we can shut them down or cause some trouble to slow them down?" Hacking into an unknown ship wasn't easy, but if anyone could do it, it would be Gosta.

"I'm not sure, Captain." He switched screens but his

hands didn't slow down as he brought up dozens of attempts.

"Captain, their weapons went live," Walvento called in from the weapons bay. He sounded uncommonly excited.

"Damn it. Take your shot, Walvento. But cripple, don't destroy." Their weapons should come into range a moment or two before the other ship's would, based on the load and ranges on both of them. Vas could see the ranges on the main screen.

"I got in! They're without power!" Gosta yelled.

Three seconds later swearing came through the comm as two bursts of light shot from their ship to the space in front of the other ship but hit nothing. "You shut them down before I could hit them! We wasted two lazerine missiles, Gosta!"

"Excellent job, both of you. It doesn't matter how we stopped them; we did." She turned to Deven. "Find anything about that ship? Even their name?"

Deven had been running things at his science station but looked up with a frown. "No. They aren't showing in the registry, but the Commonwealth did lose track of a number of ships during the war. They had an odd burst of power right before Gosta shut them down. But now I can't pick up anything. Not even life."

"Gosta?"

Gosta pulled away from his screen. "Captain! I would never hack in to kill people…well, unless it was for a good cause and you ordered it. But in this case, I left their life support systems completely intact."

"Okay, we're going to go over for a visit. Mac, move us closer. Deven, you want to get a shuttle crew together? Make sure everyone has suits." She raised her hand to hold off Gosta's comment. "You might not have done it, but something took out their life support or is masking life signs. Either way, it's better we be careful."

"Of course, Captain." He nodded and went back to his

screens.

The lift doors opened and a bewildered Wavian stepped out. A species descended from vicious birds of prey, they always looked ready to attack. Or usually. Right now, Flarik looked confused and annoyed. Her pristine white feathers were all perfect, and as usual, she was immaculately tailored. She had decided to stay in her female state. Wavians could change gender on a regular basis. Flarik had been female for almost two years now. "What happened to my nap?" The long white feathers on the back of her head were ruffled.

Wavians had evolved to handle space travel by hibernating on ships. She'd been asleep for almost a month this time but had planned on at least another week or so.

"Sorry, Flarik. We've had some visitors and one of them tried to cause some problems." Vas pointed to the ship now starting to drift across the screen. "Just how hard did you break into their system, Gosta?"

He shook his head. "I went in through a water replicator system. Everything is really old. It wasn't sealed as well as it should be. But they shouldn't be dead and drifting."

Flarik marched up to the main screen, folded her arms, and glared. "A Pilthian ship? Really? I haven't seen one of those since I was a hatchling. There was a crashed one on our farmland. They were old back then. What is someone doing running around in a relic?"

"Are you sure? They didn't show up in a database." Mac sounded defensive.

"They wouldn't. They were removed from the registry when their planet exploded forty-eight years ago." Flarik narrowed her eyes at the screen but kept the rest of her thoughts to herself.

Vas rubbed her temples. "Adding more mysteries to our already mysterious ship is not helping. Mac, keep us at this distance." They were close enough that the shuttle ride wouldn't be long, but far enough away that they could bug out easily if something went wrong. Vas got out of her chair. "Bathie, resume command. Flarik? You awake enough for a visit to our mystery ship?"

Her sharp black eyes had been a bit out of focus since she came up in the lift, but they tightened now. "I am. Let me go change into my suit and I will meet you in the docking bay." With a quick nod, she turned and left the bridge.

With any other crew person, Vas would have been annoyed at such an abrupt dismissal. With Flarik, it was expected. She was usually a few steps ahead of everyone mentally and worked off the logical assumption that Vas would come to the same conclusion about an action once she caught up. As a Wavian and a lawyer, there was no point in arguing with her.

Vas stopped by her room to grab her suit, but Deven had been ahead of her and both of their suits were missing. She debated swinging by the locked crew rooms and grabbing a quick chat with Leil, but it would probably be useless. It was clear he knew something about that ship, and it was also clear it would take more than the few minutes she had to get it out of him.

Deven had gathered a good variety of people. Glazlie, one of Marwin's triplet siblings, was standing ready and carrying enough firepower that she probably could take on a battalion by herself. Glazlie and her brothers were from a heavy grav world in the Gyolin system, so all three were short and solid. They also marginally followed a death cult and Vas had to periodically remind them that they weren't dying on her watch.

Another woman waiting, Roha, was also a seriously armed fighter. She hailed from the Loaxian system and stood about a foot taller than Deven. She'd rejoined the active crew after a stint on Home before the war and stayed on board afterwards.

And then Terel. The only one already in her suit. She also was heavily laden, but beyond a pair of blasters, it was all scientific and medical equipment. Flarik would also be under armed; most likely she'd have a single blaster.

"All women? Good call." Vas took her suit and put it on. The rest did the same.

Deven nodded. "Flarik mentioned the Pilthians. Since that's one of their ships, and a few of their people survived even if their planet didn't, so I thought it might be a good idea to have our strongest females along."

The Pilthians were a matrilineal society, so his idea was a sound one if they were the ones on that ship. His selection was good regardless. Small group, but all top in their game. Vas preferred to keep away missions to the smallest number of people needed. Just in case they didn't make it back.

Flarik came in wearing her suit. As expected, her only added weapon was a small snub-nosed blaster strapped to her hip.

"I am going to pull medical rank here." Terel did one final check on her kit. "We don't know what's happened on that ship and it could be far worse than a sketchy sensor or life support issue. I go in first, and no one, including you, Deven, takes their masks off until I say so. Understood?"

Everyone nodded, including Deven. Vas completely agreed with Terel. That was the main reason that on any job where there could be health risks, beyond being blown apart by blaster fire at any rate, Terel could override any other command—including one from Vas. There was no point in having experts along if they weren't going to have power behind them.

"Let's go see what's shown up on our doorstep, people." Vas went into the shuttle and took the co-pilot seat. She was a fine pilot, but so was Deven and if he piloted, she had more of a chance to observe the situation as they came in.

The rest entered, locked into their seats, and Deven ran the launch sequence.

Vas tapped her comm. "Gosta, we're underway. If there are any changes to the ship or anything else shows up, report in." A weird feeling hit her. "Actually, if any other ship shows up, warn us, then bug out."

The pause in his response said he was probably wondering the same thing Deven clearly was—judging by his narrow-eyed expression. Bugging out on a shuttle wasn't done unless things were dire. "Aye, Captain." He clicked off.

"Want to explain?" Deven kept his voice low as he checked the launch sequence codes again.

"Not really." Vas sat back after checking the co-pilot's side. Everything was in place. "Just a feeling. I don't like this much activity this close to Home." She ignored his side-eyed look. This wasn't the time to explain hunches.

The ship in front of them was still listing. There were no lights and no signs that any power was running through it. Still, Vas brought the secondary shields up on the shuttle. After the war, she'd had additional layers of shielding put on all of their shuttles. There was no way to know when they'd be in another firefight.

"Secondaries? I really wish I could see in your head right now." Deven kept his eyes on the star field and the ship before them, but he was focused on her side of the shuttle.

"Again, this is all too close to Home. Shut up and fly." Vas watched the ship as they approached. Nothing amazing about it, and no external damage that she could see. In pretty good shape for a ghost ship.

"Captain, I was able to get their docking bay open," Gosta's voice came over her comm. That would make getting onboard much easier. Otherwise they would have to break in.

"Thank you, Gosta." Vas turned to Deven with a grin. "You heard the man, take us in."

He scowled at her, but he was already moving the shuttle into the bay. The ship wasn't as drifty as it first appeared, either that or it was stabilizing.

"Life support is still not reading anything breathing over there, but it could be a glitch. Make sure we roll out armed," Vas said. "After Terel, that is."

Terel smiled, then clicked her suit's helmet on. The rest of the crew did as well while Deven docked the shuttle.

Vas hit her suit's comm. "Gosta, how hard was it to open the docking bay?"

"More difficult than it should have been, Captain." He was not happy about that admission, but it gave her what she needed. He *might* be able to shut it and open it again given time, but if something went horribly sideways on this adventure, they might not have the luxury of time.

"We're keeping that bay door open then. Keep your grav-boots turned on and helmets locked until we clear the docking bay. Actually, helmets stay on until Terel clears us. I won't lie, something about this ship is giving me the creeps." Vas had no idea what was triggering her reaction but something sure as hell was. The Pilthians who had survived the destruction of their home world had mostly left the Commonwealth. Forty-eight years ago. So, what was a ghost ship of theirs doing cruising through Commonwealth space, ignoring her hails, then going dead? And one that might have a stolen shuttle brought into the hold of her ship by Leil?

"We're docked, Captain." Deven tilted his helmeted head as he nodded to the door. Terel was already out and the others were following.

"Thank you." She sighed as the others cleared the doorway. "I was pondering what the hell happened to our nice rest time. I almost miss it."

"Life." Deven waited for her to get up and go to the

door. "We ignored it for a bit, but unless you're willing to retire, and go rediscover the beaches on Home, this is what we have."

Vas shrugged. "I'll retire when I'm too old to shoot someone. Let's go see what the hell is going on here."

The docking bay was clean and there were no signs of an attack. Didn't resolve the feeling that someone had a blaster pointed at her head though. She shook it off but stayed extremely alert as they made their way to the secure door. Terel waited for Vas' nod, then hit the latch. They all quickly entered, then shut it behind them. The secondary seal would keep the air in the ship, but Terel kept her helmet on so everyone else did as well.

Deven ran a scanner along a code on the doorway out of the shuttle bay. "The ship is scanning as the *Fairthien*. I don't know what intel he can find, but I'm sending that to Gosta."

The hallway was clean, like the docking bay, and empty. Vas used her scanner, but she still wasn't reading life signs. If someone was masking them, they were doing a damn good job. There had been life signs when Gosta first spotted the ship. What did they do, kill themselves instead of being captured? A bit extreme.

"Anyone else picking up anything? Terel?" Her medical scanner was far more sensitive than the standard issue ones.

"No...wait." Terel held up her gloved hand, then pointed down a side corridor to the right. "Something down that way, but really faint."

"Deven, you and Flarik stay here. Everyone else, let's follow our good doctor. Keep all blasters on stun for now."

All the lights were on, the engines were still off, but Gosta wouldn't release those without an order from Vas. The corridor was long but had a single destination. A pair of wide glossy white doors greeted them.

Terel ran a medical scan and Vas ran one for explosives. Terel shook her head and Vas' came back negative as well, so she nodded to Terel to test the doors. Vas, Roha, and Glazlie all held their blasters aimed at the doors in case something wasn't showing on the scans. She'd expected them to be locked, given the extreme isolation from everything else on the ship, but they slid open as Terel pressed on the door panel.

The lights flickered, but there was enough to see the rows of cryobeds, and the lights stabilized as Terel and Vas entered the room. Judging from the size of the massive chamber, the stacking three beds high, and the fact that there were six facing them, there had to be hundreds in there.

"Now that is disturbing." Vas fought down a surge of terror. The last cryobeds she'd seen were for the Black Suits. Clones of the Asarlaí bent on taking over the Commonwealth and not caring who they destroyed to do it. "I'm going to look into one. Terel, keep your med scanner on me and those beds; Glazlie and Roha, keep your weapons on the beds." Yes, Terel was in command from a medical aspect, but if there was something seriously deadly in these cryo cases, she needed to stand back so she could save Vas. Vas had no intention of opening one, but they might open on their own.

She kept her blaster in her left hand as she approached the first one. The stacking was done with grav lift shelves, so there was room to see inside each one from the top.

Room wasn't the issue, the heavy fog inside the chamber was. "They're clouded over." She stepped back and motioned for Terel to come forward. "Can we safely clear that without damaging whatever is inside?"

Terel slung her medical scanner over her shoulder and peered in. "It's an old class eight cold sleep chamber. These haven't been made in forty years. But I can clear it for a moment. I should only do it once, who knows how long these people have been inside these. Keep your eyes on the glass." She tapped a few codes on the panel at the head of the unit and the fog cleared.

The man was beautiful. Dark blue tattoos accented his light blue skin. He was slender, judging by the angles of his face and his shoulders. Long blue-black hair vanished down into the shielding for the cryobed. Then the fog came back and covered him again.

"Well? I couldn't see from this angle." Terel was watching the monitors on the side of the cryobed.

"It's a Pilthian. Perfectly frozen in his prime."

"In *his* prime? It's a male?" Terel looked ready to hit the panel again but pulled her hand back.

Vas felt about the way Terel sounded. The Pilthians had males, but they rarely left their home world. Or it hadn't been thought that they did. Obviously, some left before their home world was destroyed.

"Male. Judging by the markings on his face, a high-ranking one." Vas really wanted to clear that window again, but since that was basically pulling back whatever was keeping him alive in there—it wasn't a good idea.

Her comm crackled. "Vas? I think we have some live ones out here. Check your scanner." Deven's voice had a bit of an edge to it; what would be full freak out in anyone else.

Blaster fire swallowed whatever else he was going to say. The doors they came in through slammed shut and automatic bolting mechanisms echoed in the massive room.

CHAPTER FIVE

"DEVEN? FLARIK?" VAS KEPT HITTING her comm as she flipped open the electrical panel for the door, attempting to force it open. If there were any two people who she believed could survive anything, it would be those two. But a possible ambush of some kind wasn't the worst of their problems.

She and the three others were trapped in a room that looked like it might have some serious security around it. It wasn't uncommon to flood highly secure rooms with a deadly gas in case of an attack.

"I'm not picking up anything." Terel scanned the cavernous hold. Roha and Glazlie were watching everything and the grips on their blasters were tight.

The sounds of blaster fire outside of the room stopped, but the doors didn't release their locks.

Vas tried her comm again. "Deven? We're still stuck in here."

"And you will be until you can explain why you're on my ship." The voice came from speakers mounted on the side of the cryobed that Vas had looked into. "You got a good look at me; it would be easier to defend your actions if you came back into my range of vision." His voice was low and melodious.

Vas tilted her head to Terel, and she checked her scanner—then shrugged. "Still not showing a life sign."

"I am alive, I assure you. I'm in a suspended state. However, my bed passes things through the front of this glass to my mind. I wasn't completely aware of you before, but I am now, and it would be nice to see who we are deciding to kill or not."

Vas stepped forward toward the glass. "That's not a good way to win friends, you know." The fog was gone and the face before her was as still as he'd been before. Except for a slight movement under his eyelids.

"Neither is attacking a peaceful ship in non-wartime. The *Fairthien* wasn't doing anything wrong but crossing Cralathian space. Although I don't recall humans being reported in this sector."

The Cralathian star system was about as far away from the Commonwealth as possible and still be within known space.

Vas narrowed her eyes. "Since you have myself and my crew members at a disadvantage, I'll clarify things for you. You're in the Commonwealth. This ship came charging through controlled space and was asked repeatedly to identify itself and to slow down. Your ship ran. We disabled your drives and since there were no apparent signs of life, came to render assistance."

"Come to salvage us, most likely. We can't be in the Commonwealth, we left there months ago." There was a catch in the voice coming through the speaker at the word months.

"I'm Captain Vaslisha Tor Dain, I run a mercenary crew, not a salvage scow. You are in the Commonwealth." She fussed with her scanner to pull up the current location then held it up near the glass. The way he described the sensor anywhere could pick it up, but it felt more natural to keep it near his face.

"That's not possible. We left...Is that the correct date?" The voice went up a bit and the movements under his eyelids increased.

Vas turned the scanner back toward her, glanced at the date, and then held it up to him again. "Yup. When did you leave the Commonwealth?"

The voice was silent for a moment. "Fifty years ago."

The eye movement increased and Terel pulled Vas away from the cryobed as the seal began to open.

Roha and Glazlie both stepped forward with their massive blasters aimed at the slowly rising lid.

"Keep your blasters trained on him." Vas put her blaster away and stepped forward.

The Pilthian moved stiffly as he removed the thin wires connecting him to the bed, but he turned mostly alert lavender eyes toward her. "I think I need some help. We were only supposed to be in here for a few months, not decades." His voice sounded remarkably like the one the ship had been duplicating for him, but rougher.

It took both Vas and Terel to help him out of the bed. Her guess had been right; he was quite slender and looked to be a few inches taller than Deven.

"Thank you. I'm Khirson, Lord Khirson. I should contact my home world immediately. How could they have not noticed we were missing this long?" His question died when he got a good look at their faces. "Something happened."

"A lot of somethings." Vas and Terel guided him toward a bench. He was upright but didn't look like he was going to stay that way for long. "Your home world is gone; a huge chunk of the Commonwealth is gone. Not related. The survivors of your world left the Commonwealth decades ago."

"What? How? Who?" He collapsed onto the bench.

"Pilthia destructed on its own. I'm sure some of my historically minded crew will be able to fill you in in greater detail. The rest of the Commonwealth went to hell a number of months ago when some mutated Asarlaí came back and tried to take it over."

Her comm chirped. "Vas, we have the people who were firing at us under control, but we still can't open that door." Deven sounded annoyed now.

"He's your man, I assume?" At Vas' nod, Khirson lifted

his voice. A series of words in a language she didn't know came out and the locking mechanisms released. Flarik and Deven ran through the barely open door.

Glazlie and Roha had stepped back to the walls so they could keep an eye on everyone.

"You found a friend," Deven said. "We did as well, but ours aren't Pilthians. I assume the people in these beds are Pilthians?"

Khirson glanced behind him and gave a soft smile. "Hopefully. They were when we departed Pilthia, but I've been informed by your charming captain that was a few decades ago."

Vas quickly introduced her crew to Khirson but kept an eye on the wall of cryobeds behind them. Pilthians were known fighters, at least their females were. Judging by the slender yet powerful musculature still evident on Khirson, the males were as well, and they had a seriously kick ass cryo system. Ways to offset muscular degradation in cryo sleep had been improved over the years, but after that long in a bed, he shouldn't look so solid.

"Who should have been out there? Right now, it's an Ilerian and four Garthians—all pirates based on their tattoos." Deven hadn't done more than nod at the introductions. He also stayed near the door.

"There should have only been six of my security team out there. And a non-sleep flight crew, also of six," Khirson said. "But if it's been fifty years, who knows what happened to them." The look on his face was one of confusion and fear. His brain had a lot to process.

Terel nodded toward the beds, but also didn't move forward. "Do I have your permission to scan the rest of the beds? You probably won't want to wake them up until you know what's happening and after we can tell if any of their systems are compromised."

"Good idea, thank you, Doctor." He winced as a spasm hit his left side. "I'm probably going to need a checkup as well. The *Fairthien* woke me to alert me that someone unauthorized was onboard. But that's a sudden jolt and it will take a while to adjust."

Vas put away her blaster and sat down next to Khirson. "Then why didn't it pick up the people Deven and Flarik took down?"

"That's something I'd like to know as well," he said. "They must have had access codes of some kind. Any forced entry would have woken me up."

Flarik had been watching Khirson with narrowed eyes, then nodded to herself and put away her blaster. "I would like to go through your logs if you wouldn't mind. Deven and I might be able to find out some of what happened." If they couldn't bring Gosta or Hrrru on board—and right now Vas didn't want anyone else coming over—Flarik and Deven were the two best to be prowling through a few decades of data.

"By all means. I appreciate your asking these things, instead of demanding." Khirson held out shaking arms. "I am completely at your mercy."

"Like I said, we're mercs not savages." Vas laughed. "Most of us. Usually. I'd like to see the rest of your ship, are you up to joining us?" She wasn't worried about any of the attackers still being on board—Deven wouldn't have come back to get them out unless the ship was clear.

"I can take you all to the bridge, then you may explore as you wish." He got to his feet with only a slight wobble.

"I'll stay here with Terel in case she gets distracted." Glazlie smiled. Secure ship or not, this was still an unknown. There was no way that Glazlie would be lowering her weapon until they were back on their own shuttle. And she had a good point about Terel—an entire hold filled with frozen people from a little-known race? She was already ignoring all of them and it would only get worse as she got further into her investigation. Someone could aim a blaster at her head point blank and she'd only notice if it got in the way of her studies.

"Good idea. Roha, you're with me." Vas nodded to Khirson. "Always good to be prepared." Her instincts said he was who and what he appeared to be. But the odd skin-crawling feeling she'd had when they first spotted the *Fairthien* was still lurking.

She and Khirson went down the corridor with Flarik, Roha, and Deven following behind. Khirson was walking slowly, but he was doing it on his own. Another mark toward his people having had amazing cryo abilities. Too bad they must have vanished when Pilthia had been destroyed. The surviving Pilthians had scattered to various places and most of them went outside the Commonwealth. Vas hadn't heard of them being in large numbers anywhere—and their technology clearly hadn't been shared. There had been a lot of mystery as to how the planet was destroyed, all research pointed to something internal. It was quick, unexpected, and violent; that was the only thing anyone who studied it could agree on.

Bodies of the ones who fought Deven and Flarik were shoved to the side. It would have been good to have had prisoners to interrogate, but considering four of them were Garthians, even Deven and Flarik would have been too busy fighting to stay alive for the luxury of taking prisoners. Hopefully, whoever they were, they'd been on the ship long enough to leave a trail of evidence from when they took over the ship. And how.

Khirson paused at the bodies but kept going without a word. He led them to a good-sized bridge, a bit larger than the *Warrior Wench* but with less technology. The stations had dust on them except the pilot seat and the command chair.

"The history logs will be easiest to access from the two science stations." Khirson gingerly sat in the command chair and pointed to two other locations. He flipped open a panel, made a few swipes and both stations came

to life. "Damn it, someone took out the internal cameras."

Vas pulled out her scanner and checked the settings.
"I'll keep a scan going as we search the ship, but try to get
them back up, I don't like us being blind. Also, we need
to see where this ship has been." She turned to Deven.
"And I think we need to have a long talk with your
brother about the one he borrowed. It has been modified, but now it's clear that it is a Pilthian vessel."

Khirson turned. "You found another? There were three
of our ships with cryobeds. We all left at the same time."

"This was a shuttle. We searched it but no beds would
have fit. It appeared less than an hour before your ship
did. And on the same route."

"I'd like to see the vids of that shuttle, if possible. Later,
of course." There was still hope on his face for the other
missing ships. It was going to take him some time to
come to terms with the massive number of years, and
people, lost.

"That can probably be arranged." Vas held up her scanner and pulled up the ship schematics. Weapons would
be first. The *Fairthien* was sitting around for fifty years,
with all systems going and had only recently been taken
over by hostiles? She wanted to know when, why and
how. It hadn't been wasted on her that aside from the
recent weapon damage, there was no sign of a prior
attack. Of course, if the ship had been left on autopilot
and avoided major space lanes it could have kept going
in a loop through the system even if the command and
security crews died or fled. She doubted it would have
gone unseen for that long.

Deven would be getting that information and a lot
more from his search. With a nod to the others, she and
Roha headed off the bridge.

"Any idea what we're looking for, Captain?" Roha
stayed a step behind Vas but was probably five steps ahead

of her visually and mentally. Before she'd left to raise her
twins, Roha had been one of her primary ground specialists.

"Let's go down two levels. Their weapons bank is
toward the end of that corridor. Be on the watch for
anything unusual."

The lighting system flicked on as they entered each
corridor, but at a fifty percent level. The power appeared
to be fine so it was probably a setting used since most
of the ship would have been dormant. The pirates who
took the ship wouldn't have needed the extra lighting in
most of the ship, so probably never changed the settings.

The weapons room door had already been opened
when they turned down the corridor. Vas unsheathed her
blaster. The life sensors on this ship were off so there was
a slim chance someone got past Flarik and Deven if they
were hidden deep enough.

Roha stepped up alongside Vas and gestured to ask if
she should take the lead. Vas shook her off and motioned
for her to stay at the door as Vas slipped in. Automatic
doors like these could be forced and from the complete
immobility of this one, and the fact that it was stuck halfway at an angle, this one had been.

The weapons room was far smaller than the one for the
Warrior Wench, and most of the consoles had been hacked
open. Since the weaponry itself wasn't in this room, just
the control access, Vas wasn't sure what someone had
been looking for. The damage didn't appear extensive
enough to destroy the access to the weapons, but more
like someone was looking for something hidden.

Vas checked the one console that was still intact. It was
the furthest from the door, and the tools left scattered
along the one next to it told her the person doing the
searching had stopped suddenly.

It took a few moments for the console to come to life,
but a quick search indicated the weapons were still intact.

"What were they doing?" She scanned the entire console area to show Walvento. Whoever had been doing this had a reason, maybe he could take a guess. She had nothing.

Once she'd scanned everything she could, Vas went toward the door. "Let's head toward medical; that might have something. So far all we're doing is raising more questions."

"Agreed. There's something about this place that's making my skin crawl." Roha fell in behind Vas.

"Me too." Whatever had triggered her initial response to this ship was far more focused down here.

The door to medical was shut and didn't open at first. With some force and a quick re-wire to lock the door open, they got the doors cleared. Like the *Warrior Wench*, this med lab had two sets of doors. But the small area between them was completely empty.

The second set opened as they approached. Vas took one step in, then pushed Roha back out and slammed the door. She wished she hadn't set up the outer door to lock but kept pushing until she got them both out to the main hall and down to the end.

Once Roha realized what Vas was doing, she didn't need to be pushed.

Vas hit her comm. "Terel, I need you and Deven down in the med lab immediately. There are bodies in there. Dissected bodies."

CHAPTER SIX

———◆———

D EVEN RESPONDED FIRST. "DAMN IT. I see them
now. We just got the internal cameras up."

"I still don't have access over here," Terel said. "Thanks,
Deven, we have it now. We're coming to the med labs."

"Those are my security crew." Khirson's voice was raw.
"I'm coming down."

"No offense, this is your ship, but we don't know what
killed them," Vas said. "Obviously, they were taken apart
rather extensively, but there's no way to tell what they
died of. I want everyone to get their helmets on now and
recommend Khirson stay on the bridge with the locks
engaged."

"There is wisdom in your words," Khirson said. "I will
be safe up here, but keep all feeds open. I want to know
what in the nine hells happened."

Vas shook her head and pulled her helmet back on.
"We'd all like to know that. Okay, Roha, back we go."

The med lab wasn't as shocking as it had been the
first time, but it made up for that with an increase in
gruesomeness. Like the weapons bay, someone had been
searching for something. Unfortunately, in this case, it
was Pilthians, not consoles they were tearing apart.

Vas wasn't a stranger to injuries or death. As a merc
she was paid to create both. This was beyond that. As she
slowly scanned the destruction, she counted six Pilthians,
or at least six heads. The bodies were so torn apart that
if there were more and a head was missing, they might
never know. The medical machines all looked like they'd
been abandoned in mid-use. Slides were in place where

someone had been running a scan, but all the data of what they had been running was cleared.

Terel would know, but Vas couldn't determine for certain if the victims had been dead when the studies began.

The sound of booted footsteps brought Vas and Roha spinning toward the door with their blasters raised. But it was just Terel, Deven, Khirson, and Glazlie.

Deven held up his gloved hand. "Flarik is staying on the command deck but Khirson changed his mind." The tone in his voice said there'd been a debate about that.

"I need to see what happened to them directly. They were my crew." Khirson looked ready for a fight.

Vas holstered her blaster and shrugged. "This is your ship."

Roha and Glazlie took up positions in the empty outer lobby.

"What were they doing to them?" Terel might be a merc doctor, but she was still a doctor first. Saving lives was an obsession. She ran forward and went from bed to bed, using her much larger medical scanner on them.

"That's what I'm hoping you can tell us," Vas said. "How long ago did this happen? I don't know much about Pilthians, but Khirson recognized their heads, and the bodies still look...fresh." There wasn't a good way to say it, but they were still oozing.

"The lab could have been sealed, but you're right, they still shouldn't look like this. Something did this recently."

"An Ilerian and four Garthians?" Deven shook his head as he walked around the remains. "Garthian guards are muscle and most Ilerians aren't the type to be conducting postmortems—at least not any that leave their home world. Even if the Garthians killed them, there must have been someone else on this ship doing this work. Someone who hasn't been found."

"I agree with Deven," Flarik added through the open comm. "Whoever was here tried to scramble the recordings, but they were sloppy. There's a shuttle missing and there were at least four more people onboard. They were smart enough to manage to avoid the cameras—rather they had facial scramblers that allowed them to avoid the cameras."

Deven froze. "Four?"

"I think we're all thinking the same thing." Vas hit her comm twice to reach her ship. "Gosta, quadruple guards on our guests and their ship. No one goes into their rooms or their ship until I clear it." She didn't think Leil had the brains to do what had been done, but he was Deven's brother. Deven was damn smart and Leil could be playing off his brother's perception of him to make her think he was as stupid as Deven believed. Someone had been doing some serious investigative destruction here, and the shuttle that Leil stole could be from this ship.

"Aye, Captain." Gosta's reply was short, but Vas knew he'd have more guards in place in minutes.

Terel was still walking around the bodies. "From the initial scan of the tissue, they were dead before they were taken apart. But there's so much damage, it's going to take an extensive study to find out how they died."

"I have a full medical staff in cryosleep. To wake them properly will take forty hours. Is it safe to wake my people?" Khirson might be a member of a very female dominated society, but he was the leader on this ship.

"I'm not picking up on any pathogens, nor the remains of any. I think it's safe to wake them. From what I saw, the first row of cryobeds were all functioning normally. I am impressed at your equipment for lasting so long." Terel had two scanners up and was trying to cover everything. Vas noticed that she hadn't said they could drop their helmets yet though.

"They always said it was the best of the best. Of course, *they* are probably dead now." Khirson paused. "I will only wake the senior staff and medical personnel. Then we can decide how to proceed. However, we don't have a place to go at this point."

Vas felt for him and his people, but a hell of a lot more information would have to come out before she offered him space on Home.

"I know a moon, not very populated, that was owned by a late friend of ours," Deven said with a look to Vas. "There are a few refugee groups living there, but until the Commonwealth can find a place for you it might work." Deven was still walking around the remains and pulling up data on his scanner but working on more than one project at a time was sort of his skill. One of many.

Vas knew what moon he was offering. Marli had a number of hiding places, but her private moon had been her most secure. Until she decided to come out and fight against the creatures pretending to be Asarlaí. Deven had the security codes for it and a few other locations she'd left behind.

Khirson smiled. "We appreciate that. It will take a while to gain our bearings and find out where we belong in this universe."

"And what happened to you, both fifty years ago and more recently," Vas said.

A low-level alarm started echoing down the corridors and Khirson's face turned pale. If the med doors hadn't all been open, they probably wouldn't have heard it.

"Get out of the med lab, everyone." He hit a monitor on the wall and the alarm sputtered into the room, then became louder. "Damn it, they left a trap and rigged the alarm to not go off down here so no one would know." He was still weak, but he shoved them out of the med labs. They ran out with Terel bringing up the rear, scanning as she ran.

Khirson kept moving them down the corridor.

Vas hit her comm. "Gosta, move the *Warrior Wench*

back. Something got triggered and we've no idea what it is. This ship could blow." She yelled as loud as she could but while the alarms might have been messed with in the med lab, they were at full strength out here.

"Understood." Gosta might have said more, but that was the important word. The entire reason those people had been ripped apart might have been to draw victims to a trap as much as whatever they'd been looking for. An explosive, a chemical agent—anything could have been triggered to go off.

"This way!" Khirson turned down a side corridor on the right and motioned for them all to duck low. "This is a shelter corridor. As long as the entire ship doesn't blow, we'll be safer here."

They all crouched and stayed against the wall. The alarm stopped. Then nothing.

"Captain?" Flarik called through the comm. "Is everything okay? I've locked down the bridge, but there's nothing on the sensors about that alarm. I don't believe that the ship triggered it."

Vas looked to Khirson, but he shook his head.

"We've no idea. Stay up there and keep the doors locked." She started to say more but a deep boom reverberated through the floor and walls. The vibration was enough to knock everyone off their feet except for Deven and Khirson. Glazlie and Roha scrambled to their feet even faster than Vas did.

"I felt that. What was it?" Flarik didn't sound upset, but there was a tone of concern in her voice. It took a lot to get that tone to surface.

"I have no idea, but we're going to find out." Vas turned to the others. "Roha, stay at this junction, just in case we missed something. The sensors concerning this ship can't be trusted. Khirson, this is your ship but right now I'm running point unless you have a problem with that?"

He shook his head slowly. "Not at all. Right now, I'm

extremely glad you're all here." He stayed a bit behind Vas, but ahead of the others as they made their way back toward the med bay. The vibration didn't appear to have damaged the ship; at least not from what Vas could see.

The med lab was another issue completely. The glass in the front doors was completely covered in fog. Terel pushed the others aside and scanned the door, especially along the seals. Then she very calmly stepped back. "Khirson, is there a way to completely cut off this section of the ship? Immediately? And please everyone, keep your voices down. I'll explain once we get the hell out of here. But we don't want loud vibrations right now." She didn't wait for him to respond but started shooing everyone down the corridor. Her words of terror were discordant with her calm, yet insistent, actions.

"Yes, but there are some important things down here—not to mention our med lab and those bodies."

"Probably not as important as our lives and those of your people in the holding bay. There is a serious contagion behind that door. It was set off but didn't have enough power behind it to blow through the doors. Judging by my initial scans it's a class ten and sound focused. The chemicals can use high frequency to shatter brainwaves in sensitive species. The alarm in the med lab malfunctioning might have saved us all. It was triggered to set the contagion off."

They gathered Roha, then kept moving quickly until Khirson stopped at an even wider junction of corridors. "This is the place. I'll need some help; I still don't have much strength." He tapped out a code on a panel on the closest wall and heavily reinforced walls pulled away from the main corridor. "We need to move these to block the cross corridor. Quickly." They were thicker than Vas' leg and made of steel and some other metals that gave them an odd iridescent gleam. They might be mobile, but it wouldn't be easy.

Deven put down his blaster to take the other side, and Roha and Glazlie were about to do the same.

Vas held up her hand to stop them. "I want you two to stand guard." There were too many unknowns happening to relax at this point. She and Terel took the other massive sliding wall and started pushing. The thing had some mobility—there would be no way even fifty people could have moved these without it—but it was still difficult.

They got the walls in place and Khirson hit the panel again. The walls shook as a tremor much stronger than before slammed into all of them.

CHAPTER SEVEN

———◆———

"WHAT IN THE HELL IS that vibration? Someone set up that *plus* a class ten contagion? Isn't that a bit overkill?" Vas fought the shakes as she looked around. It was as if it rattled through every bone in her body.

"I don't..." Khirson clutched his chest and collapsed to the ground. Terel ran to him.

Deven joined Terel at Khirson's side. "It's a sonic disrupter. Old school weapons that only worked on certain populations, like Pilthians, so most governments gave them up years ago."

"Seriously? Those things have been off the market for over a hundred years." Vas tried to shake it off, but the horrible feeling still lingered in her joints and bones.

"Captain? Is everyone all right down there?" Flarik called on the comm.

"Hopefully." Whatever Terel was doing was helping Khirson. He was slowly stirring. "Did you feel that?"

"Yes. It was most unpleasant. Do we know who did it? Sonic disruptors are unacceptable, and I would like to point that out to them." There was a light clicking sound in the background. Most likely it was Flarik clacking her clawed hands together in annoyance.

Vas looked down to Khirson, but he still was out of it. He was breathing on his own and conscious, but not really aware of his surroundings. "No, we don't. Did Gosta move our ship?"

"Yes. Not far enough in my opinion, but he did move it. Had we exploded, the *Warrior Wench* wouldn't have been impacted. Barely." The annoyance in her voice was getting worse.

"Keep scanning this ship. The sensors are off and most likely were tampered with to make whatever just happened worse. A hell of a lot worse. We'll be up there as soon as we can." Vas looked down to Khirson. "Can we move him? I'm very grateful for this protective wall, but I don't think being down here is a good idea. For a ship that's been missing for fifty years, there seem to be a lot of people out to get them."

"I can move," Khirson said slowly. "Going to need some help though. That imperialist sonic disruptor tore me apart." He held up a hand to Terel. "Not literally. My people are sensitive to them however." His eyes went wide. "My people in the hold! We have to get to them." He struggled to his feet. Or tried to. Deven helped him up, then pulled Khirson's arm over his shoulders.

Terel steadied him from the other side. "They should have been only slightly exposed. The hold is sealed and the cryobeds would offer protection."

"Vibrations can reach everywhere. We need to hurry." Khirson was moving like a little old Ilerian, even with help, so hurrying wasn't an option.

Vas paused when they got to the lift that would take them to the command deck. "I'm going to check on command. Glazlie, you're with me. Roha, stay with them. Just to be on the safe side, make sure to lock the hold when you're inside. Once you're certain they are okay, you probably want to start waking them up. This ship might not be a safe place anymore."

She and Glazlie went up to command. Flarik had unlocked as they approached.

"You two are very loud." She was sitting in the command chair, grimacing at a screen. The door shut and locked behind them.

Vas ignored the comment. She and Glazlie hadn't even

been talking, but when Flarik was in a state, her hearing became very acute. "What have you found? Anything else about where the hell this ship has been or who attacked her?"

"Some. The missing fifty years is easier than who recently attacked her though. Two weeks after they left Pilthia, the captain pulled the ship off course and started visiting rim planets. Not sure what she was looking for or doing. But it appears the ship was docked in an abandoned asteroid mining zone off Vlian-Three after a few weeks of this random traveling."

"Vlian-Three was destroyed in the Asarlaí Wars. The mining belt is still burning." Vas didn't have all the lost worlds memorized, but that one was memorable. The material that had been thought to have been mined out, Cothin ore, was still there as it turned out—just buried. When the Asarlaí planet-killers blew up Vlian-Three, the destruction triggered a reaction in the asteroid belt.

"Exactly. This ship left there three days before the attack. It had been hidden there for almost fifty years."

Glazlie shook her head. "There's no way that was a coincidence."

"My thinking exactly." Vas looked at the screens before her. They'd need time to pull the intel apart. "Please tell me the attack on this ship is not a sign of the bastards we fought off actually still being around."

Flarik shrugged. "No way to say, but I don't think so. I don't follow hunches, as you do. But in this case, it's a hunch that whoever moved them was one of their own people—or a private friend—not *them*." She pulled up a few screens and transferred the images to the front screen. Although a much smaller screen than the one on the *Warrior Wench*, it was still easier than peering at the one on the monitor. Flarik highlighted an area on the screen. "See this? The ship was on auto control when it left the belt. Those people you saw in the med lab were long dead, even if they didn't appear that way. I believe their bodies were a trap, set when the ship was first hidden fifty years ago. Everything was frozen."

Vas looked at the screens but there really wasn't a way to quickly put the clues together. "Damn it, again, no answers, and just more questions. Who hid the ship, what the hell was the command crew doing before they hid this ship, where did they go, and who set the trap? And who moved this thing right before those bastards blew up the neighboring world? Who knew it was there?"

"And who was the trap for?" Glazlie had stayed near the door, her blaster still ready in her hand, but she nodded to the screens. "If most of the crew was unconscious, and would stay that way unless awoken, which is my guess since Khirson should have been the first up and he's been dozing a while; then who set a trap, locked it so it wouldn't degrade, and left the ship?"

Vas loved that her people were always on top of the issues, it made life a lot easier. "All valid points and ones hopefully we can figure out. By we, I mean you lovely people." She gave a half bow to Flarik. "While interesting and yes, I would like to know what happened, this is not directly related to us, our ship, nor is it a merc job. If there's no current threat, I say we get Khirson and his people to that moon, get any supplies they need from Home, and let the Pilthians sort it out."

"I will resolve what I can prior to that time," Flarik said. "In the meantime, I assume we need to purge the section of the ship that became contaminated?"

"I'll check with Khirson since it *is* his ship. But I doubt he wants to keep a class ten contagion onboard no matter how contained it is." Vas hit her comm. "Deven? How are things over there and does Khirson mind if we purge that portion of the ship to get rid of the danger?"

"Things are status quo here. Khirson and Terel are working on the regeneration sequence." He repeated Vas' question then came back. "Hold on, I'm giving him my comm for a moment."

"Captain? There is a way to separate that entire section from my ship. I suggest we do it before we leave the area. The contagion isn't the only concern, the sonic disrupter would have weakened everything on that side of the wall. That part of the ship is too dangerous to keep attached."

Vas widened her eyes in surprise but didn't let it show in her voice. After all, the man knew more about his ship and what had been done to it than she did. "Understood. Do you want to do it? Or tell us how to?"

"I've already found it, Captain." Flarik said, as she brought up a screen with the ship's layout on it. There were red dotted lines across different zones. Considering that one of the lines was right where they'd gotten behind that shielded wall, she assumed Flarik had found a unique aspect of this ship. It could completely cut itself off from any part. The heaviest lines were the section that included the engines, the command deck, and the cryo sleeper hold. If needed, everything but those sections could be jettisoned.

"You can take care of it if you don't mind. I want to stay here with my people." Khirson's voice sounded stronger, but the worry lingered.

"Understood. I have to say this technology would be advanced for now, let alone over fifty years ago. Impressive."

Khirson didn't respond at first. When he did there was a wistful sadness in his voice. "We were the best of the best. Thank you, Captain."

Deven's voice came back. "Anything else for now?"

"Nope. Sounds like we're babysitting until we can get them to Marli's moon."

Khirson's voice came back through the comm, but from a distance, like Deven still held it. "Did she say Marli? Tiny brunette human with way more attitude than size?

She must be extremely old by now."

"How does he know Marli?" Vas waited while Deven repeated the question.

"She used to spend a fair amount of time on our world. A trader of sorts." He paused and his voice became louder. Deven must have handed over his comm. "She was dear to me, and I was saddened that she didn't come to see me off when we went into sleep. I would welcome seeing her again."

Vas shared a look with Flarik. One where both of them were raising their eyebrows. "Marli died during the recent battle I mentioned. She was far more than a trader, and not human. Her sacrifice helped save the Common-wealth." There was no way she was explaining who and what Marli really was right now.

"I am saddened at her loss. Perhaps sometime you can tell me of her final battle. She was a friend to the Pilthi-ans, and her valor should be made into song."

"We will see what can be done once your people are awake and settled," Vas said. "How long prior to your voyage had you last seen her?"

"She had visited me a week before we left. She tried to talk me out of going at first. Then the next morning, she said it was better that I did take the ship, but she would be back to say goodbye."

"And she never came back?"

"No."

Vas processed that. But she couldn't figure out a lot of where and what Marli had done in the time she'd known her; trying to guess something that happened fifty years ago wasn't going to happen. "We will work on disengag-ing the contaminated portion of your ship. Then work out navigation to Marli's moon."

"Thank you, Captain," Khirson said, then closed the comm call.

Flarik tilted her head. "Marli and he were involved?

My knowledge, as limited as it is, indicated Pilthians never bred outside of their own kind."

Flarik's own species, the Wavians, had been viciously xenophobic for centuries. Vas had no idea what the Pilthians' mating habits had been. But it sounded like Marli and Khirson might have been more than friends.

"I'm not planning on asking him directly, but that level of involvement could point to possible answers for a few of our issues. Marli might or might not have hidden this ship, but I'd bet you she got them out before the Asarlaí planet-killers struck that belt—which means she knew where they were. Still no sign of where they've been between then and now?"

Flarik grimaced, but for her it was a grin. "No. And that also leads toward Marli being involved. She must have been moving quickly to re-hide them, but she wasn't sloppy enough to leave a clue. Yet. I disliked her, but she was someone to be admired in many ways."

Vas shook her head at the trouble that woman had caused. But she also saved their asses more than a few times. "Agreed. Now, odd tech aside, do you know how to blow off that section?"

Vas and Flarik spent a few minutes making sure everything looked like it would go as planned. Then Flarik held her hand over the controls. "Would you like the honor, Captain?"

Vas held up both hands. "Nope, you found it, you blow it up."

Flarik shrugged and entered the code. The command deck shook a bit, but it was surprisingly calm for losing almost a sixth of the ship. The only reference Vas had were the decon rooms they had on the *Warrior Wench*. But they were much smaller.

Deven came through the comm. "Captain? Khirson says we can leave now. Since it's going to probably take longer than the originally estimated forty hours to wake his people, we might want to start heading out soon."

Vas took over the navigator's chair. "Agreed. Let me set things up with Gosta and we'll be on our way." She pulled up the nav screens and finally found Marli's moon. Then she hit her comm to the *Warrior Wench*. "Gosta? We're heading out to Marli's old moon. This crew is waking up and I want to give them some time to recover before we contact the Commonwealth about them. I'm sending over a list for you to pick up from Home to get them started. Then follow us over. We'll be going slow."

"That's going to be a bit difficult captain," Gosta sounded calm, but an insistent pinging coming from the command chair caught both Flarik and Vas' attention.

"It's the ship-to-ship vid feed. Gosta's calling up vid connection." Flarik said.

"Connect us."

Gosta winced at the screen as he came into view, then tipped his head to the left as the view panned out.

Leil stood next to him, looking bloody but intact as he held a small snub-nosed blaster to Gosta's head.

CHAPTER EIGHT

———◆———

"WHAT IN THE HELL ARE you doing, Leil? Think long and hard before you answer." Vas kept her voice low. She'd known that bastard was up to something, but taking over her ship? Deven had seriously underestimated his brother.

"Now, this isn't what it seems." Leil gave a weak attempt at a smile. "I need that ship you're on. Intact. Some of your crew has been roughed up, but no one is dead." The "yet" was unspoken but hung there between the ships.

"If you look on the screens, you'll see this ship is no longer intact. We had to blow off a section." Based on the location of the *Warrior Wench* and the side they blew off on this one, he might not be aware of it. He was still breathing heavily, so his coup might have just happened.

"You can't bluff. I will take your ship."

Flarik gave a slight clacking noise with her teeth at his words. She'd caught the same thing Vas did, the use of 'will' as opposed to 'have'. He'd taken the command deck, a major issue, but he didn't have the entire ship.

"If you pull back your blaster from my chief navigator's head, he can show you." Vas folded her arms and kept her face neutral.

Leil looked off camera to someone else on the deck, then nodded and took a step back. His blaster was still too close to Gosta, but at least now Gosta could reach his console. A few clicks and he nodded to Leil to look at the screen.

"Damn it, you had no right to destroy part of my ship."

"Your ship? I have a hold full of Pilthians who are sure

it's theirs. Including the one in charge who is very awake."

Leil paled and his hand shook before he gained emotional control. "That's not possible. They were all dead. The ship was a salvage job. It was rigged to follow our shuttle." He ran his free hand through his short hair and took his eyes off Gosta for a second.

Gosta twisted, grabbed Leil's arm that held the blaster, smashed into that arm, took the blaster, and did a reverse of the original position. He held the blaster at Leil's temple.

"I will destroy him." Gosta's voice was calm and not directed at Vas. It was also a tone she'd never heard from him before. Likewise, neither were the moves he'd demonstrated. Gosta could fight, no one on any of her ships couldn't. But he wasn't one of her ground troops. He'd been practicing with someone, and he was fast.

"Who else is up there? Is it the triplets?"

Whoever was off camera was staying that way, but someone on the command deck widened the range. Gosta tilted his chin towards the far corner. "No. Even with scanning we missed someone on the shuttle. She's running the show, not Leil. But I believe she'd rather not lose this fight right now." As he spoke, Marwin and Bathie pulled out hidden blasters from their consoles and covered the new person. She was a petite brunette with a shocking resemblance to Marli's human disguise.

"What the hell? Marli?" Deven had silently come onto the command deck while the drama with Leil and Gosta had taken Vas' focus. Khirson was behind him.

"Drop your glamour, whoever you are." Vas wasn't as shocked as Deven, but she was pissed. "Or my people will shoot you and shove you out an airlock."

The small woman gave a hiss. If looks could kill, Leil would be a pile of ash right now. She hit a device on her wrist, then changed into an older Pilthian woman.

Now it was Khirson's turn to swear. "Loxianth? You

were scheduled to be put to death fifty years ago. I signed those orders myself."

"You were weak then, and you're still weak. I see you listing as you stand. Imperialist puppet. You and the elites left us to die. Our world died because of you."

"We left to find a better home for all of our people. But not you. Never you. Kill her." Khirson drew himself up straight and folded his arms. He was no longer listing to one side.

Vas held up her hands. "Hold that thought. Marwin and Bathie, can you tie up our friends and escort them to the brig? I assume the others are still in their rooms?" Not that she trusted those three—there was still too much similarity to the two who'd been with her on the vid—but she figured they would have been on the deck had they been out and about.

"Only these two were involved in this adventure. The cams show the others are still in their chambers." Gosta stepped back as Bathie came forward and slapped cuffs on Leil, then nudged him toward the lift. Marwin did the same with Loxianth.

Khirson stayed silent until they left the deck, but he was shaking. "You can't let that abomination live. She was slated to be executed the day after our ships left."

Deven came up to him and put a calming hand on his shoulder. "What did she do? Do you want to sit?" He guided Khirson to the command chair without waiting for a response as Flarik hastily got up.

Khirson dropped into the seat and ran a shaking hand over his face. "She murdered my lifemate and four others of the royal council. There was a rebellion on my world five years before we left. They were stopped but not without great cost." He shook his head and finally looked to Vas. "I don't know how she escaped the execution orders or the destruction of our world. I can understand your hesitancy about killing a stranger on the basis of another stranger's word. But I ask that you turn her over to us. You may keep the one working with her."

Flarik stepped forward. "As the legal counsel for Vas' fleet, I will need to gather all information to document the transfer. Does this ship have a brig? I failed to notice one while looking at the schematics."

Khirson faced Flarik for a few moments. He was coming from a place of pure emotion. As a Wavian and a lawyer, Flarik rarely did so. If he wanted this woman, it would be done properly and with full documentation. Not only would it cover Vas' behind if by some chance Loxianth had living relatives coming to hunt her down, although since she had tried to take over Vas' ship, she was legally allowed to do with her as she wished, but it would give Khirson time to calm down and be rational.

He'd had a hell of a day so far.

"This is a sleeper ship; we don't have a brig. If you would be so gracious as to interview her, and myself, before you leave us on that moon, I would appreciate it." He flashed a sad smile. "I was a legislator for my people. It is distressing that I acted rashly."

"You've had a lot to process recently, so it's understandable," Deven said. "Is there a princess of the realm in your sleeper group?" His voice had dropped and become soothing again, and his hand went back to Khirson's shoulder.

Vas knew almost nothing about the Pilthians, but Deven obviously was aware of their culture.

"There is. She is in the back, to be awoken once we have landed in our new home and set up the palace for her." He looked down at his hands. "At least I hope so. All of the sleeping pods appear to be functioning, but our year-long trip changed dramatically. I will have no idea until all are awakened."

"Captain? What was it you actually called for?" The screen connection was still up and Gosta had been fussing with some things at his station. He looked more attentive now.

"First off, you were very impressive, Gosta. I don't know that I could disarm an assailant that quickly." Vas waited until his blush faded a bit. "I have a list of items that we need to get from Home. We're taking this ship to Marli's moon base. They can set up there until the Commonwealth finds a home for them. But even with the quick builds for a new colony, they're going to need some basics." She stepped back a bit to show Khirson. "Gosta, meet Lord Khirson of the Pilthians. Lord Khirson, met Gosta, my chief navigator and hacker wiz."

"I am very pleased to meet you and am glad that woman did not cause too much harm to you or yours." Khirson gave a bow without leaving the command chair.

Gosta bobbed his head awkwardly. "I am honored to meet you." He turned to Vas. "I've received your list. I assume that ship is okay to fly?"

Vas looked to Flarik who nodded. "Yes. But we'll be slower than you, so head out now." She paused. "Actually, send the second shuttle over before you leave. The heavier armed one. I want that shuttle to play escort, just in case Leil has more friends out here."

"Will do. Safe travels. Gosta out." The screen went blank as the connection was closed.

Khirson nodded. "What now? Your doctor is overseeing the awakenings, but they will still take longer than the normal forty-hour cycle."

Vas got out of her seat. "I think you might want to do an inventory as to what all we jettisoned. I'm taking our shuttle out to do a full surround check of this ship."

Deven opened his mouth to argue, then sighed and shook his head. "I'll help with checking inventory and make sure we have no issues before getting underway, Captain." He gave a tilt of his head and went to the nav console.

Vas knew he had been about to suggest that he take the shuttle out but he dropped it when he saw her face. The itchy feeling on the back of her neck was gone, but she still wanted to be the one to view the damage.

"Captain, Marwin and flight squad B are in the shuttle and heading your way. We're running back to Home."

"Thank you, Gosta." Vas nodded to her people on the deck and left.

"You might want to see this before you head out, Vas." Terel's comment was on a private link to Vas and there was enough concern in her voice that Vas jogged to the hold.

Roha raised her blaster as Vas came in the room but had it lowered before the door even started shutting. "She's toward the back." Roha hooked her thumb toward the cryobeds. They'd been separated with a third of them now on the floor instead of stacked. If there was a pattern to how they were arranged, Vas had no idea. Beyond the fact that they were in five-person clumps, with what appeared to be their heads connected together. A mass of wires and equipment was at the center of each grouping.

"Terel? Where are you?" Vas waded through the beds. She trusted Roha, but kept her hand near the butt of her blaster anyway.

Terel popped up from the furthest clump in the back. She furiously entered something into her data tablet before finally looking to Vas. "This ship was carrying prisoners. Not all, mind you. But at least some. Come see."

Vas wound her way toward Terel. The cryobeds she passed no longer had the mist covering their faces. Bed after bed of blue faces. Some darker, some light, some round, others very thin. All had some tattooing on their faces; a few were elaborate, more like Khirson's, but more were simplistic. Even Vas knew that tattooing had been a major life ritual for the Pilthians when a youth became an adult in their culture. So, there were no kids here—at least none she could see. Maybe this was the advanced group. Khirson had said they were looking for a new home.

"Now what are you…"Vas let her words drop off as she approached the cluster that Terel stood near. The cryobed cluster before her was older than the others, judging by the styling and the extensive wear on all five of them. The first bed she passed was a male, but instead of tattooing he had massive scars across his face—where tattoos had been before he was convicted of a major crime would be Vas' guess. Unlike the others she saw, his hands were crossed high on his chest near his throat. Leaving the heavy manacles on his wrists clear to see.

"I'm thinking he wasn't on the manifest?"Vas nodded to the second pad Terel carried, one she knew didn't belong to her ship.

"No. Khirson left with Deven while I was confirming the names, likenesses, and markings. This is supposed to be an older female scientist." She held up the tablet to verify that the pale blue face on it in no way matched the scarred male in the bed.

"This was a year-long expedition to establish a new world. Scientists, doctors, politicians, builders, military. And at some point, while everyone was being loaded in, five people were replaced with prisoners?"Vas circled the clump. All five, three men and two women had the same scarring and crossed handcuffed arms as the first. She leaned in closer to look at one. "And I don't think they were in there willingly. Look at their faces."

All the other faces she'd seen were relaxed, as if in sleep. These five looked like they'd been locked in nightmares for the past fifty years.

Terel peered down, then added more notes to her pad. "I hadn't noticed that. But yes, that's what appears to have happened. Who would send criminals to a new world?"

"No idea. But I need to get the shuttle out for a recon before we ship out. There was some excitement on the *Warrior Wench* as well." She started jogging around the cryobeds to the door.

"Excitement? More than this?" Terel waved at her prisoner sleepers.

"Gosta disarmed Leil after Leil and a friend tried to take over my ship." Vas hit the door control panel with a smirk as Terel scrambled to call her back.

Vas would fill her in, but she needed to check out the damage to this ship, take some readings of her own, and make sure there were no more surprises before they headed for Marli's moon.

Between them planning on using her moon, that Pilthian disguising herself as her, and Khirson possibly being her secret lover, Marli was extremely active for a dead woman.

She quickly ran through the checks on the shuttle and launched. Now that they had full control of the ship, they would be able to open and close the docking bay. But right now, it was handy taking off. The rear end of the *Warrior Wench* was leaving the area. Mac would have been jealous about her current view. He had a thing for spaceship butts as he called them. Weird, but not the weirdest things about him or her crew.

Vas pulled clear of the Pilthian ship a bit to get a better overall view. No damage she could see, either recent or from the past. Whoever took this ship off its initial course did so from the inside. That's what it had looked like, but always best to be sure.

The damaged section had been cleanly removed. Damn handy in this case, and something she'd look at including on her next ship. The ship below her could break down to engines, command deck, and the hold and would move damn fast if it dumped the rest of the ship. A sleeper vessel designed to get its contents to their destination no matter what. They hadn't counted on an inside threat and spending fifty years hidden in an asteroid belt.

Tracking down more details of where it had gone in the time before being stashed in the belt, and why it was left there for fifty years were questions she'd be curious to learn the answers to. After she dealt with the weird mystical things Aithnea was trying to push her into, that was.

The recent events had pushed Aithnea's words aside, but in the peace of the shuttle, images, words, and incidents were flashing through her mind. Not ones belonging to Vas, but most likely something left by Aithnea when she popped into Vas' head. Sneaky dead woman.

Once they got the Pilthians settled, Vas would contact Therlian. As the only nun, or former nun, alive she'd be the best council. Even with the undercurrent of knowledge floating in her head, Vas had no misconception of her ability to become a Keeper. All of the Clionea nuns were fighters, it was an ancient warrior order after all. But the Keepers were a cut above the rest. Had the nuns been military, Vas would say the Keepers were the black ops of the order. Deadly and efficient, they went on missions behind the scenes—places and events that a nun shouldn't be involved in. Even if her gaining that status was just to find this pirate, or who was supposed to take up the mantle, it was still more than she felt she could do. Hopefully Therlian would have some other options.

"You're welcome to speak to her, but my option really is the only one."

Vas swore as the voice in her head caused her hand to jerk on the nav bar.

CHAPTER NINE

"YOU'RE BACK? AND PROWLING THROUGH my mind without asking? Not a good way to get me to help you."

"*I wasn't prying. Your thoughts are really loud out here without the ship to block them. And it's not about helping me, we're beyond help from this plane. The Pirate was created to balance a lot of injustices. And, if we get the Pirate back, we might get the nuns back. Well, a new order of them at least.*"

"Your order created the Pirate of Boagada, but if we get someone back in that position, it could bring back the Clionea nuns?"

There was a pause, but as had happened before, Vas could tell Aithnea was still in her head. "*And possibly save the galaxy.*"

"Been there, done that, still recovering."

"*No, you helped save the Commonwealth. I'm talking a threat to the entire galaxy.*"

"And me, some person who will be the Pirate, and possibly some new nuns are going to stop it?" Vas had been nearing the docking bay doors but swung wide instead. If she was going to have a nice battle with the voice in her head, she'd do it away from others.

"*All of you will be the catalyst for this.*" Even though Aithnea's voice was in her head, Vas heard a hesitation.

"You've no idea what's coming, do you? Let alone how anyone is going to stop it." Vas set the nav to repeat the same course she'd been on. If anyone asked, she'd say she thought she saw something.

"*I know that something has pulled me back into this plane.*

I'm in limbo, not alive but not dead. I'm feeling something is wrong, but yes, I can't find the exact cause. I know the galaxy needs the Pirate and I know a new order of nuns will be needed. It could be for something that happens a year from now or a hundred."

Vas watched as she circled the ship. "If I do this, will you be free?" There was a sadness in Aithnea's voice when she mentioned still being in limbo. She and her order had sacrificed themselves to keep Vas and her people hidden when the Asarlaí clones were trying to find them. But that wasn't where the sadness came from. The nuns believed in the afterlife as their reward for a battle well fought and a life well lived. That they were all denied that was a damn good reason to try and help them. Saving the galaxy was good, too.

"I believe we will be." Her voice was low, but clear.

Vas didn't pause. "We're dealing with this sleeper ship, but once that is done, I'll look into doing what you ask. I promise, we'll find a way to set you free."

Again the pause. In life Aithnea never wanted anything from anyone. Vas knew her spirit was having trouble now with asking. *"Thank you. But it really could be crucial to saving the galaxy."*

Vas laughed. "An added bonus."

"I'll be leaving for a bit. The strain isn't as bad as when you're in your ship, but it does make me tired."

"Gentle rest, dear friend." Vas said automatically. It was how the nuns said good night to each other—something she hadn't said for over twenty years.

"To you as well, dear friend." Aithnea's presence was gone.

"Captain? We're in position, anything we should watch for?" Marwin's voice cut into her thoughts. Most likely the other shuttle had been trying to figure out what exactly she was doing for the past few minutes.

"Not that I know of. Sorry, making sure we don't have anything to worry about. We should be ready to leave in a half hour. Stay to the rear in case someone wants to see what an old cold sleeper like this is doing puttering around the space lanes." She looked on the scanner. The section of ship they'd blown off was still intact, just sitting there. "Do you have a tag and recording buoy?" The *Warrior Wench* had three shuttles: the one she had was the smallest. Marwin and his crew were in the largest, best armed, and best supplied.

"Aye, Gosta resupplied us."

"Excellent. Set one up with a warning for a class ten contagion. Also set it on full record sent to both your shuttle and Gosta's station on the *Warrior Wench*. Thanks." She clicked off and brought in her shuttle. There was way too much weird shit going on with this ship. She trusted her people, but she wasn't completely certain that whoever set up the trap in the med bay did it fifty-plus years ago. If whoever was behind this knew protocol for the Pilthians, they would have expected Khirson to jettison the section. Someone might have wanted that part of the ship.

Deven waited behind the shield with the controls for the docking bay, then came out once the doors to space had locked and sealed. "We decided flying around with an open bay probably wasn't the best idea. You took a long time, see anything?"

Vas locked up the shuttle out of habit then went to him. "I had a visit again; it was easier for her without whatever is interfering on our ship. She thinks there is a threat of some kind, but it's vague. At least vague beyond we need to find the new Pirate and somehow that person will start a new order of the nuns." She held up her hand and shook her head. "Yeah, I know. Vague *and* problematic. But more importantly, I think we need to find this pirate so the nuns can leave limbo. They are stuck there, and she didn't say it directly, but I got the feeling Aithnea thought once she'd helped us free the Commonwealth, they'd be

free. Hasn't happened though. They died to save us and
the Commonwealth; they deserve their reward."

Deven nodded as they headed out of the bay. "You
don't have to convince me. The least we can do is set
them free. That's why you were out there so long?"

Vas stopped right before the door into the hallway.
"Part of it, but also something still doesn't sit right. I'm
not sure, but I think someone wanted us to jettison off
that chunk. I had Marwin tag the wreckage with a warning and recording drone."

"You could be right, but there's been an awful lot of
hunches coming from you."

Vas glared at him as they went toward the command
deck. They'd had this discussion before—many times.
"They are completely respectable hunches based on provided information as processed by my mind based on
past events. Not telepathic."

"Thank you, *doctor*. But in this case, Nariel could be
wrong."

"She's not." Vas picked up speed. She had been having appointments with Nariel, her ship's mind doc, since
the battle with the Asarlaí. Part of the issue were these
hunches. Nariel explained them to her in a nice rational
manner. Deven thought it was some form of latent telepathic abilities. Vas was sticking with Nariel. She wasn't
as teke hysterical as she had been most of her adult life. A
mental block had been placed in her mind when she was
a kid—one Deven and his telepathic skills broke through.
But she wasn't up to becoming a telepath herself.

They entered the command deck and Deven dropped
the issue.

Flarik and Glazlie were the only ones there. The rest
were probably dealing with the newest mystery in the
cryo hold. "Are we ready to go?"

Flarik had resumed the command chair. "I believe so.
Terel called Khirson down about her find. It is only the

five prisoners she showed you, but Khirson was furious when she told him."

"We'll prepare to leave but wait until he gets here." Vas went to one of the navigation stations and Deven took over weapons. Not that there were many on this ship, but something was better than nothing. The navs weren't too different from older ships she'd been on, so getting used to them wasn't difficult.

"Flarik, is there a manifest of everything that would have been in that section we jettisoned? Beyond the med bay?" Vas couldn't ignore that there might have been something else going on that wasn't on the surface.

"There should be. I can find it once we get underway. Anything specific that I'm looking for?"

"Not really," Vas said. "I'm having them keep an eye on the segment through a buoy. It would be good to know if someone wanted us to separate that section off."

"She sensed something." Deven didn't even look up as he said it and Vas didn't respond.

Vas changed direction. "What happened to the bodies in the walkway?" She knew Terel would want to examine them, unless Khirson's own med team wanted to when they woke up. Of course, they no longer had a med bay to do that in.

"Roha and Glazlie moved them to a cold locker near the sleeper hold," Flarik said. "Khirson thought it best his people didn't wake up to random bodies in the halls. The truth of their current situation will be jarring enough."

The doors to the command deck opened as Flarik was speaking and Khirson came in. "And the level of betrayal." Khirson stalked onto the command deck.

Flarik rose from the command chair and stood next to it as Khirson took his seat. He was moving better than he had been. He was recovering quickly from the abrupt cryo awakening and his reaction to the sonic disrupter.

"I take it you figured out who those five bodies in the

sleeper hold are?" Vas asked.

"Yes, unfortunately, and I think we have an idea as to why Loxianth was after this ship. They were are the five others convicted of leading the rebellion that she created. All should have died immediately after we left, at the same execution that Loxianth should have been killed at. The only reason I haven't spaced them is because I need answers. However, they won't be woken until we are settled."

"Then you're okay with us getting underway? The *Warrior Wench* will meet us en route and our shuttle escort is ready." Vas entered the route to Marli's moon. She was certain it had an actual name, but she'd never heard it. Now it was a fitting tribute to keep calling it after Marli.

Khirson was silent for a moment, then shook himself out of his dark thoughts. "Yes, I believe so. But a simple shuttle as an escort? If we need something, wouldn't a ship with weapons be more appropriate?"

Vas laughed. "Oh, all of my shuttles are fully armed and heavily shielded—including the one in your docking bay that we can also use if needed. I made a few changes after our last battle—to all of my ships."

They left the area slowly, with Marwin staying in the flanking position. Vas knew the shuttle could go much faster, but this ship wasn't in great shape. Judging by what she was pulling up, aside from the recent run when it was tied to the shuttle Leil had, it hadn't moved at all in almost a year. When someone moved it from the asteroid belt right before the belt was attacked.

Khirson seemed more relaxed now that they were on their way. "I got the idea from talking to your charming doctor, that you aren't used to having more than one ship?"

Vas smiled. "Nope. Had one, then lost it. Then had two, and now I've somehow gathered a fleet. It's not too bad, but I hate the paperwork."

"That you mostly shove off to me or Gosta." Deven leaned back in his seat.

Fair assessment. She knew they were better at it. When she did it, she either started throwing things after a few hours, or got drunk and started throwing things after a few hours. "Eh, we all have our skills. I have to say, it is weird having extra ships. What about you, Khirson? If you don't mind my asking, who were you before you went to cryo sleep?"

He paused and a wistful smile flashed. "I was a secondary leader in the royal cabinet. Mostly I kept track of supplies and products. I was made the leader of this expedition because the Queen felt I would be best at organizing it." He laughed. "Maybe if things get rough once we try to find a place to fit in, I can hire myself out to overworked fleet commanders. To do their paperwork."

Vas laughed. "I might take you up on that. You have no idea what went wrong?" She kept scanning the files as they talked. Nav was set, she just needed to make sure nothing came up to throw off the pre-set course. Meanwhile, she was looking for any evidence of the ship traveling about during its missing time.

"With this ship or my world destroying itself?"

"Both."

Deven, Flarik, and Glazlie were all quiet, but Vas knew they were listening. Conversations had been lax when he first woke up, but the fact was Khirson was a leader, and Vas was one as well. Any serious conversations would start between them.

"Sadly, no. My head of security might have a better idea as to what went wrong, once she is awake. But everything seemed fine the day we went to sleep. The rebellion had been repressed for a few years. We were looking to start a new world, but that had as much to do with Commonwealth policies as anything else. Things were getting too crowded and we wanted to branch out. The Commonwealth refused to let us. But nothing that would have indicated we would be so horrifically taken off course. Nor how we managed to destroy our world." His voice dropped a bit. "How many of our people were saved before it was destroyed?"

Vas turned to Flarik and Deven. Both were history buffs and Deven would have been alive during the events.

Flarik's face was grim. "Not many, from what I read as a hatchling. Your people had isolated themselves the year prior to the destruction; not a lot of information coming out from your world. Whatever happened appeared to be sudden per the history vids. But in the year prior they had been slowly getting people off planet, no explanation. The Pilthians left the Commonwealth for the most part. They might have been looking for this ship and the settlement you were supposed to create."

"Or one of the other two ships," Khirson said. "Would it be too much to ask for a current data download? Is the Commonwealth library still in place? I don't want to try and contact the Commonwealth directly until we are in a better situation."

Based on her assorted dealings with the Commonwealth government both current and prior, Vas agreed with him on that. "I think we can set something up. I'll have to speak to Gosta, but we should be able to get you access to more information without connecting directly. I agree, until you're certain that it was only Loxianth who was after you, staying low is a good idea. The current data system might not have a lot of information about your people if they closed themselves off those last years though."

"True, but hopefully something will be there. And maybe some mention of what happened or is believed to have happened to the other two ships." His melancholy returned and a scowl crossed his face. "We all left together. If we went as far off target as the information indicates, then where are the other two?"

"Unless all three ships were betrayed?" Glazlie stood at parade rest; she'd been military on her home world.

"Or someone found a way to make the other captains think this ship had been destroyed," Flarik said. "Would the other captains have turned around if one of the ships were lost?"

"Honestly, no. Our sleepers were all redundancies to each other. We each had the right number of different skills to start a new colony. If one was lost, the others would have gone on."

Vas kept looking through the locations where the ship had been as Flarik and Khirson discussed aspects of his world. As far as she could tell there was nothing of importance in any of the worlds the ship had stopped at before the crew abandoned it. However, there was no reason it had been bouncing around the Commonwealth when it should have been far outside the rim within a few weeks.

"Any signs as to who hid it?" Deven kept his voice low as he came and leaned in behind her. "Since we can guess who moved it away from danger. It would have been not long after she found her way back here when we were trapped outside of the Commonwealth."

"Not that I can tell. Whoever did it was good and cleaned the ship's logs. But only a week's worth. The original crew didn't log much, but their logs were intact. These are gone. The crew left the ship at Denaril Eight three weeks after it left Pilthia. It appears a timed auto pilot was left in place. Two weeks later all movement stopped. The ship was hidden somewhere in the asteroids until a little over a year ago."

Deven sat at the console next to her. "There must be some evidence. Something showing who hid it, even if we don't know why."

"Khirson, in exchange for access to a completely

Commonwealth connection-free library, might we have copies of your logs? All of them? I have a few crew members who might be able to solve some of this." Vas had enough things on her plate, but she didn't like mysteries sitting around. Especially ones that might be related to Marli. She knew that Gosta wouldn't begrudge making a copy of his library in exchange for a fifty-year-old mystery.

He tilted his head, then nodded. "It would be a fair trade. I am disturbed that my people had stopped being open with other worlds before they destroyed our planet. Our problems with the Commonwealth were not based on any disagreements with individual worlds." His grimace was close to a smile—a dangerous one. "That won't continue under the new queen." He shook his head, and the sadness filled his eyes. "Maybe we did destroy ourselves. The people on the three sleeper ships were thousands of our best, brightest, and most forward thinking. Maybe we didn't leave enough behind."

CHAPTER TEN

———◆———

THE TRIP TO MARLI'S MOON took a few hours since there were no functioning gates to it nearby. Vas didn't want to attract more attention by taking a mysterious Pilthian ship off course just to go through a distant gate and save an hour. The *Warrior Wench* joined them at hour three, but no other vessels in the area appeared to even notice they were passing through. Gosta had agreed to the information trade with Khirson, and Deven was gathering copies of all the ship's data he could find. After the first hour, Khirson and Flarik had joined Terel in the hold to see how the cryo awakening was going.

Vas called down to the cryo hold and Khirson as they came closer to the approach. "This ship appears to be capable of entering an atmosphere and landing, are you okay with me setting her down? We can shuttle your people and the supplies down if you prefer, but it will take a few days." She really hoped he wouldn't pick that option—there were almost a thousand people on board, and judging by her scans of the other holds, they came with a lot of supplies.

"Thank you, Captain," Khirson said. "But this ship is actually going to be the center of our colony. We will have to build a new medical bay obviously, and a few other things. But if you could land it in a suitable spot that would be acceptable."

Marli's moon had gravity and a breathable atmosphere. Of course, it was also larger than some planets, so that helped. Vas suspected that some planet modification had taken place when Marli first moved there a few hundred years ago. Marli didn't agree with the actions of her people, but she did use their technology when it suited her and wouldn't be used against others. Unless they deserved it.

Vas scanned the moon, then adjusted. "I'm going to set down in a wide field in the southern hemisphere. Most of the refugees that we relocated there have found permanent homes, but the few that remain would be in the far north. You and your people shouldn't be disturbed unless you want to be."

"Thank you. This is going to be a rough adjustment for my people. It might take some time before we know what we're going to do."

"Not a worry. Marli left all of her possessions, including that moon, to Deven and me. Stay as long as you need." That had been a fairly recent development—not what she left them, the date on the will was eighteen months ago—but Vas and Deven had only found out two months ago. Marli's lawyer had been dawdling. Until he met Flarik. The property and everything else were put into Vas and Deven's names immediately after Flarik spoke to him.

If Marli and Khirson had been lovers, and she had been involved with saving them, she'd appreciate that his people would live on her moon even if only temporarily.

"She must have thought very highly of you both. She was well known to our people, as shown by her image being duplicated by Loxianth. But she was never that generous when I knew her."

Deven laughed. "She mellowed out over the years. Especially the last few. Prepare for landing, everyone."

Vas and Deven readied the ship to enter the atmosphere. "Gosta?" Vas called over the comm. "Still no one paying attention to us?" The moon was masked, but it was subtle, not a full cloaking like Home. If someone had a reason to think there was something there, like they saw a ship vanishing into what appeared to be empty space, they would eventually be able to see it. Vas didn't see any ships close enough to pick them up, but the *Warrior Wench* had much better sensors.

"No one that we can pick up with our long-range sensors. I have Xsit scanning as well." The sensors for communications could pick up things beyond the rest of the ship's sensors.

"You heard the man, Deven, let's bring this thing down." Vas was still navigating, leaving Deven to handle piloting.

For a ship as old as this one was, it made a fairly good landing. A bit of a jolt as the missing section caused it to be a little unbalanced.

"Did the landing gear just adapt to make up for the missing section?" Vas asked as the ship stabilized itself. She was so going to have this feature added to her next ship. She'd say add it to the *Warrior Wench*, but this type of design had to come from the bones of a ship.

"It did. Fairly well too. No instability detected at all now."

Khirson cut into their admiration. "I take it we're down? Might we tour the area? My people still shouldn't wake up for another forty hours or more."

"Aye, let me run a few more scans first." Vas ran the outside monitors, then called Gosta. "Still nothing?"

"Nothing at all. The final refugee encampment even left two weeks ago."

"Thank you. Keep scanning both above and the surface. We're going to tour the area." She turned to Deven. "I think one of us and a guard should stay behind, but I don't care who. Your call."

Deven got up and stretched. "If you don't mind, I'll play tour guide. Could use a walk."

"Glazlie, you stay with me, Roha, go with Deven and Khirson. Flarik and Terel, do what you wish." Vas didn't like ordering her people if it wasn't needed. And this wasn't needed. She'd guess that Flarik would go on the walk and Terel would stay monitoring the cryobeds, even though Khirson had explained there wouldn't be anything worth monitoring until a few hours before they woke up.

Flarik, Deven, and Roha led Khirson on a tour of his people's new home. For now, anyway. Vas didn't really mind if they ended up staying here, but she knew Deven was emotionally attached to Marli's actual home. It would remain locked and sealed, and Khirson's people would be instructed to stay away from it.

"I'm going to go check on Terel. Call me if anything weird pops up," Vas said to Glazlie and left the command deck.

Terel looked up as she entered, then went back to shaking her head and scrolling through something on her screen.

"That's never a good look, even in a hold of frozen people. What's wrong?" Vas peered in a few cases as she went by, but to her they all looked the same.

"I think those five criminals weren't loaded before this ship took off. There's more than just a difference in these cases. There's a discrepancy in their cabling, the timing of when they were brought into the system, a number of things."

Vas moved over to look, but she'd take her word for it.

"See? Look at this." Terel held up her tablet. She'd run an age analysis on the connectors. Something Vas really wouldn't have thought of. Apparently, watching people wake up from a deep-frozen sleep was as exciting as it sounded—even Terel had been looking for distractions while she waited.

"Then, they weren't executed when they were supposed to be, but years later they were frozen?"

"Nope," Terel said. "Well, you are correct that they

weren't executed, obviously, but they have been in cold sleep almost as long as the others. Maybe even a bit longer. But their beds didn't start out on this ship."

Vas waited for more information to follow. Her crew was very bright, but sometimes things they noticed, while interesting, weren't pertinent. "And this means what for us?" she finally asked.

"Nothing for us specifically, but it is part of the mystery." Terel smiled and went back to flipping through things on her pad.

Vas shook her head. "We have to get a real job soon. You're really stretching for things to find interesting."

Terel shrugged. "Yes, but we're here, so we should at least figure these things out."

Vas' comm chirped before she could respond. "Vas here."

"Captain?" Gosta sounded too excited for this to be good. "We have visual on a ship trying to grab and haul the separated section of the Pilthian vessel. It's a shuttle identical to the one Leil had and is having problems. It's too small to move it."

"What? Damn it, this better not be another one of Deven's family." She tapped her comm over to Deven. "How many shuttles are missing from this ship?"

"One. Khirson said they only had two and one is currently in the docking bay. Why?"

Vas filled him in and heard swearing from both he and Khirson. "That property belongs to Khirson and his people. But the shuttle out there is too small to retrieve that piece on its own."

"Either Leil's ship or the one there now could be from this ship. One of the other ships that left when this one did could also be out there," Deven said. "But I'd doubt they'd come out of hiding only to get that section. While that shuttle alone might not be able to haul it, something this size could. I'd think they wouldn't just send a shuttle if they had a larger ship."

"I give you complete rights to that salvage. Not sure what you'd want with it though." Khirson's voice came through Deven's comm.

"I think it's more important that whoever is trying to get it, doesn't. A true salvager would have tagged it. I wouldn't worry about an actual salvage except I still have an odd feeling that someone wanted us to expel that section for a reason. Not to mention, how many Pilthian ships are roaming around?"

"From what you have told me, not many," Khirson said. "This can't be a coincidence. I think my people will be fine here. But would it be possible to hire some medical personnel when you leave? It would be for a few weeks as my people recover, and I would pay a fair merc fee to them and you."

Vas looked to Terel. Vas knew Terel would want to stay here, but the resignation that crossed her face said she wouldn't.

Terel narrowed her eyes at Vas. "I think I need to stay with you all—who knows what trouble you'll get into if I'm gone. But Pela studied the Pilthians in graduate school. I trust her implicitly to lead things here. Grifion is advancing as a strong doctor as well. Both will welcome the chance."

Deven must have handed his comm over to Khirson as his voice was louder. "I will welcome any assistance you can offer, Captain. It will take my medical team a while to recover."

"Excellent." Vas switched her comm back to Gosta. "Have a shuttle bring down the supplies from Home for the Pilthians. We have the ship's data, so you can transfer down the library copy as well. Have the shuttle also bring down Pela and Grifion I'm temporarily assigning them to the Pilthians on contract. We leave orbit in two hours." She'd also leave the smaller shuttle with Pela and Grifion.

Normally, she wouldn't but something told her it might be a good idea. As of right now, that Pilthian shuttle was having trouble moving the section of ship. Hopefully, that wouldn't change before they got there. She had no idea what in the hell they were going to do with the section, beyond getting it away from the bastards who might have sabotaged their own people. They'd sort out more details later.

"Should I call out a hauler from Home? Any idea where we'll put that section once we retrieve it?" Gosta was thinking clearer than she was.

"Yes. Have a hauler head out now as they'll be slower than us. As for the where? I think first we need to poke some holes in it and get that contagion out of it. Then we can drag it back here. Maybe Khirson's people can use something from it." There was always the chance that by poking a few holes in it, they might blow it up.

There were way too many mysteries here. While she was glad they really weren't hers to solve, she was happy for something to stir up her crew. She hadn't seen this much interest from them for over six months.

"Aye, Captain. Shuttle is on its way. We will be ready to leave once both shuttles return." Gosta signed off.

Vas turned to Terel. "Anything you want to set up or leave here for them? If not, let's get ready to go."

Terel kept fidgeting with her tablet, but finally shook her head. "No. I've left copies of my observations for Pela, Grifion, and whoever Khirson has for medical. This has been exciting though." She picked up her things and marched to the door.

"How many papers do you think you'll get out of it?" Vas asked and nodded to Glazlie who dropped in behind them.

"It's not only about the academic accolades, you know." Terel spun and flashed Vas a grin. "But I'd say at least a dozen."

Vas knew academic papers were like gold to Terel. She was always looking for new things to shove down the throats of the academic powers in the capital of the Commonwealth. Vas shook her head and prepped the shuttle, then went to help unload the one from the *Warrior Wench* that just landed. Mostly what she'd ordered were food stuffs and basic emergency shelters and supplies. Khirson didn't seem worried, but if his people weren't going to be waking up for a bit, he might need to be ready for some massive disorganization.

Deven, Flarik, Khirson, and Roha came up as they finished unloading.

"Thank you, Captain. This is extremely generous. Deven showed me where was off limits and while the protections I saw around it will keep my people away, I will also make it forbidden. Rather, our new Queen will."

Terel introduced Khirson to Pela and Grifion as everyone not staying on the moon prepared to leave. Vas handed a comm over to Khirson. "This is a limited one. It will only hail our ship directly, not any individual. But if something goes south and Pela and Grifion can't reach us, use this. Hopefully, we can bring that missing piece back to you."

Khirson clasped her arm at the elbow and gave a short nod. "Thank you again. I will make sure my people know what you have done for us."

Everyone jogged back to their shuttles and lifted off. Vas let Deven pilot again, but she didn't need to navigate. "Anything more about Leil? Oh yeah, did Khirson want that woman back once we're done questioning them?"

"No." Deven's face darkened. "And I don't think I should be involved in the questioning. At least not of Leil. As for Loxianth, Khirson didn't mention her again. I think keeping her as far as possible from the frozen bodies of her companions should probably be our goal."

Vas watched as he took a few deep breaths to calm down. "I get it, he's your brother, and you two have bad blood. He and I have bad blood now and I just met him. But this reaction is unusual for you." She'd rarely seen him this out of sorts, and the few times she had it had been more warranted.

He ran his fingers through his hair. "And unlike your brother, Leil didn't even try to kill me. Yeah, I know. Growing up, Leil was a con man and left everything he touched in shambles. I hate what he tried to do. He threatened Gosta of all people. I don't know what to do with him besides shoving him out an airlock."

"I take it that unlike you, he probably wouldn't come back from that?"

"Not that I know of. My people do have different abilities than most, but what I did was unique even for us. Leil hasn't ever shown any abilities of that sort."

They got the shuttle into the *Warrior Wench's* bay. The bay doors closed, and everyone headed out.

"I've been thinking," Terel said as she walked alongside Vas. "I'd like to be in on the questioning of our two prisoners. Are we still treating Leil's other companions as prisoners?"

Vas sighed. "Yes, in that they stay where they are until this is sorted. And I am able to figure out why at least two of them were on that vid from my missing time with the Garmainians. Beyond that, I don't think questioning them will help." She led the way to the lift. "But yes, I'd like you along. Deven's out on this one."

"I, too, would like to be included. Legal reasons, of course." Flarik clicked her teeth and few people besides herself would call the look on her face a smile.

"Good idea." Vas turned to Deven. "Could you work with Gosta on sorting the data from Khirson's ship? We'll make much better time back than we did out. I'd say without having to go so slow, we should be back within an hour. I'd like you two to have a plan for dealing with that section of ship without blowing it up."

Deven smiled. "And if we can't?"

"Then we blow it up." Vas, Terel, and Flarik took the lift to the brig while Deven went back up to the command deck.

"Which one first?" Flarik stood outside of the brig. There were two large cells, and four smaller ones all of them sealed and soundproof. Leil and Loxianth were in the two singles at each end with two empty cells between them. The sides facing toward each other and the main room were darkened so that they couldn't see out.

"Leil is the weakest link. Even without knowing any-thing about Loxianth I can tell that." Vas walked over to his cell then paused and motioned for Flarik to enter first. "I scare some people, but you scare *all* people. After you."

The feathers on the back of Flarik's neck flared up to almost become a hood and her eyes narrowed. She also looked far toothier than she had a moment before. "Gladly, Captain."

CHAPTER ELEVEN

———◆———

TEREL RAISED AN EYEBROW AS Vas gestured for her to follow Flarik, but she went in. Terel didn't look scary, but Vas had noted Leil's unreasonable fear of blood taking. Might as well make herself look friendly in comparison to the other two. At first.

Leil had been laying on a narrow cot, that and a latrine with a sink being the only items in the cell. He rolled to his feet as Flarik entered. Then backed up as far as he could into the corner. Vas was glad that he'd picked the corner without the toilet.

"Where's Deven? I'm sure he wants to talk to me." He was looking behind Vas, but she pulled the cell door shut behind her.

"He actually doesn't." Vas leaned against the door. "See, I have a policy of interrogating before killing. Right now, he's having a problem with that. Actually, so is Flarik. She's particularly fond of Gosta and doesn't like her friends being threatened. But while I can control Deven, no one controls Flarik."

As Vas had been speaking, Terel had stayed to one side, looking at Leil and consulting her tablet. Flarik on the other hand, had lowered her head and was pacing back and forth, watching Leil like she was trying to decide which part of him to rip off first.

Vas had to cover her mouth to keep from laughing. Flarik was pissed, yes. And she could rip him apart should she wish. But she was going all out for the fear element.

"I would advise you to start talking quickly. She was pulled out of hibernation early, in part thanks to your stunt." Vas stayed against the door. Not that he would have a chance of getting out, but it gave her a view of Flarik's act.

Leil looked ready to pee his pants. "Okay, I will tell you. Just make her leave."

"No. Flarik is also my legal counsel and it's a good idea to have her here in case I need advice. She will only hurt you if she has to loosen your memories. Start with where you met Loxianth."

Leil looked to Terel, who had moved closer to him but was still adjusting things on her tablet.

"Medical support in case something goes...wrong." Terel gave him a look up and down, then nodded to Flarik. "Things happen."

Flarik said nothing but hunched into a crouch.

"I'd start now." Vas folded her arms.

"I met Loxianth outside of the Commonwealth five months ago. At a bar on the Leta Six space station. Said she had a big job, would pay millions of credits. Needed three more people, smash and grab types. Took me a while. Found the brothers. Picked her up in that shuttle I came in on. Problem—couldn't find the ship she wanted. Then we found it. She had another crew, and they took control of that ship, slaved it to the shuttle I had. But then they rebelled against Loxianth. I guess she wasn't paying them enough. They killed the connection she had on the big ship. We ran, but the shuttle and the ship were still linked so they could follow us. Saw you, knew Deven was here, and hid Loxianth in the shuttle. The other ship showed up." He paused to take a huge gulp of air. Vas was grateful this would be recorded by the cell itself; he was talking so fast she could barely understand him.

"You went over there. Left us locked up. Loxianth got out of the shuttle since no one knew she was there, then found me." He lifted his shirt. "She'd imbedded a tracker in my chest right here when we signed the contract. Can you take it out?" He turned to Terel with his shirt still held up. He dropped it when she scowled. "Maybe later. Anyway, she got me out of my room, said we had to get that ship." He paused. "Not that it matters, but I'd no idea she was one of the blue people."

Flarik shook her head as the excessive speed and quantity of words got to her too.

"You're an idiot. A serious, serious idiot. I want you to slowly, very slowly, expand on everything you told us. Simply say it to this room. It will record you as well as your heart rate and breathing to see if you're lying. I don't want to talk to you anymore." Vas turned to the door to leave, but Flarik still hadn't moved.

"She can't stay here." Leil's voice was similar to Deven's but she'd never heard his voice go that high.

Vas looked to Terel who consulted her tablet. "He's right, his blood pressure is so high he'd probably die in less than an hour. Flarik wouldn't even need to touch him."

"Fine. But she will be right outside the door," Vas said. "And if Flarik doesn't get you to talk, Terel will. She'll also be right outside, listening to every word."

Leil's eyes were still unnaturally wide, but he nodded. "Everything I can recall. I swear."

Vas watched him with narrowed eyes for a few moments, then nodded to the other two and opened the door. Once they were out, she coded the front of his cell to go even darker. He could have seen shapes outside before, but now not even that, and she made sure the system speakers were working. None of them were going to be out here, they needed to speak to Loxianth. But he wouldn't know that. Fear would hopefully make him slip and give away something useful.

"You had too much fun with that." Vas turned to Flarik.

The grin was still toothy but more smile-like. "That was enjoyable." She tilted her head as the speaker from

Leil's cell started to burst out with his rambling. A bit slower than before and more details—but still rambling and non-linear. They could go through the recordings later. To be honest, he seemed like a thug for hire whose job went horribly wrong.

"Now our Pilthian guest." Vas walked to the second cell but paused before unlocking it. "Did Khirson give you any more information on her? Beyond wanting her dead?"

Flarik shook her head. "He knows her, obviously, but I gathered it was only after she and her rebel cohorts attacked. And after she'd been assigned to be executed, he didn't think about her. Their concept of revenge is different from ours."

"He looked fairly pissed off and vengeful when he saw her," Vas said.

"Yes, but that was because she was still alive and threatening people. I gather that the Pilthian culture doesn't hold for going after revenge once an outcome has been decided. Had she died when she was supposed to, he wouldn't have thought of her again."

Vas stored that away. Knowing how a culture processed things like grief and revenge could be helpful in understanding their motivation. "I think this time, I'll go in first. Flarik, play it as scary as you deem necessary. Terel stay back, but step in if something pops up." Vas keyed open the cell door. Loxianth didn't get off her cot but looked up as they entered.

"I wondered when someone would come get me." She slowly rolled to her feet and flashed into Marli's human guise.

Flarik growled and flexed her fingers.

Vas scowled. "I'd drop it if I were you. Marli was a friend...and an adversary. Either way, wearing her form is a good way to get killed."

Loxianth tapped her arm and reappeared as herself, then

sat back down on her cot. "I figured Marli was immortal and using her likeness might help." She pointed to the section of her wrist with a tiny bump. "I could only pick one form when I got this. I guess I picked the wrong one."

"You did. I'm sure I can help you remove the temptation to use it." Terel peered at the wrist before Loxianth rolled her hand back and kept it out of Terel's sight. "Whether we do it with pain meds depends on your answers." The grin she flashed was a great mimic of Flarik's—minus the excessive teeth.

"Answers? Aren't you turning me over to Khirson? He can't be happy about me being alive, nor what happened to his ship."

Vas smiled. "No. He just wants you dead, but we have far better tools to achieve that after we've found out what in the hell you were doing. Your best option is to talk and talk quickly."

Her dark gray eyes darted between all three of them but lingered on Flarik. Vas hadn't noticed but at some point, Flarik had dropped into the same crouch she'd done with Leil. While Loxianth's reaction wasn't the same as his, she also wouldn't look away from her for long.

"This has nothing to do with you or your people." But the confidence she'd had before was fading.

Vas took a step closer. "You tried to take over my ship. The last bastard who did that was spaced. Tell me why we shouldn't do that to you?" Granted, he'd spaced himself after his mind was broken, but full details weren't always needed.

"I was desperate. My people were stolen, put in cold sleep, and placed on that damn ship. Do you know how hard it was to find them? It took me fifty years." Real emotion passed across her face. A brief combination of fear and sorrow. For the first time, she looked decades older than Khirson. Then her hard shell came back up as she faced Vas.

"You were all supposed to be put to death. You tried to overthrow an entire world. Just being alive is something that should be corrected, according to Khirson."

Loxianth spit. "Khirson, that sanctimonious jackass. He was on our side; did he tell you that? He gave us the details to get into the council chamber. He wanted the ruling party out as badly as we did. But his wife wasn't supposed to be there that day. He tried to stop the attack when he realized she was and he couldn't reach her, but we couldn't stop once it was in motion. When it was over and his wife had been killed with the others, he turned us in. The few of us who survived. I had three hundred people with me, six of us survived. When I found out that the others had been sent off on a sleeper ship, I fought to find them."

CHAPTER TWELVE

VAS WATCHED HER CLOSELY. OUT of the corner of her eye she saw Terel tap quickly on her pad. Loxianth didn't appear to be lying, and there would be no reason to lie to Vas about Khirson. If Vas had her killed, it would be for trying to take her ship, not for anything she might have done on a long dead planet.

Terel must have been running a biofeedback scan on her pad; she glanced over to Vas and gave a slight shrug. Nothing conclusive.

"Why were the six of you spared from execution?" She wasn't sure if she believed her story or not. But there were a lot of holes. "And why were the others put into cold storage with Khirson and his crew when they left your planet?" Terel believed they'd been put on board at a later point, but this way she could find out more of what Loxianth knew.

Loxianth adjusted the way she sat, she was still trying to keep the arm with the glam-tech hidden from Terel, and it didn't look comfortable. "I don't know about the others. They kept me separate. One night my cell was unlocked, so, I took off. I got out of the capitol and hid, certain that once my escape was noticed the news feeds would blast my image all over." She shook her head. "They didn't. Not a word was said publicly anywhere. Then the *Fairthien* and the other two sleeper ships loaded and left under huge pomp and ritual. Five days later our executions were broadcast. The fact that I was supposedly in the same room as the other five when we were killed gave me hope that they were alive as well." She reached for a water tube from the wall dispenser and finished it before continuing. "I stayed in a small cottage in the farmlands for a month. Then one day a message was left on the front door—it said the other five had been locked into cold sleep and sent off somewhere. I assumed they'd been put on board one of the sleepers when they left."

"There is a lot of information still up in the air, that's why we're asking questions." Flarik straightened out of her crouch. "And you have no idea of anything concerning your friends beyond that? You do realize how improbable your story sounds, correct?"

"Trust me, I know. But even after fifty years of searching, I still have no idea who did any of it. I thought all of the sleeper ships had gone out of the Commonwealth, so I spent most of that time in the outer worlds looking for them—but no sign."

"Did you find the other two colony ships?" Vas oddly believed her. But it didn't absolve her from any of her actions.

"No." Loxianth's face hardened. "There were rumors, before the ships were even built, that the entire escapade was a ruse by the government. The *Fairthien* was dormant and hidden somewhere for almost the entire time; I found that out once we found her. The people I had on there once we found her sent me the readings. Or did until they killed my captain and took over the ship. The other two ships have never appeared anywhere. Not even in the areas they were supposed to be."

They already knew that the *Fairthien* had been dormant, Vas even knew where the ship had been. She hadn't known about the other two. Judging by the interest, Flarik might be joining Gosta in trying to solve the mystery.

"Moving on," Vas said. "Why did you threaten my crew?" There was no doubt that there were some serious issues going on in the Pilthian government fifty years ago. But the planet in question wasn't even around anymore, which made it hard for Vas to want to spend much more time on it.

"I want to free my people. That was the best way to do it."

Vas shook her head. "Before we went over to the *Fairthien*, we had no idea what or who was over there, you could have asked for help from us. Leil had no problem asking."

"That man is an idiot. He said his brother would help us. I heard everything that was said in your docking bay. His brother hates him. Kill me if you want, but I stand by my actions." She folded her arms and sat back.

"Captain, I'd like to run some samples of the prisoner if you don't mind. Verify who she is and compare her to the people from the ship."

"Agreed. We've had a problem with shape shifters before, and since you've already shown one disguise, we will need to check."

Loxianth pulled back at first, then relaxed and leaned forward. "For good or ill, you and your people are the only reason I'm still alive." She held out her arm. "Take what you want. You can even take the glam device out. Don't think I'll want to pretend to be her again."

Vas' comm buzzed, and she turned a bit away from Loxianth. "What do you need?"

"We're at the rendezvous." Gosta sounded distracted but knowing him he was doing eight things right now.

"I'm coming up." She turned to the others. "I'm needed on deck."

Loxianth started to rise, then dropped back as Flarik stepped toward her. "What about me?"

"Right now, Terel and Flarik will be taking care of you. Once we figure out where you're going, you'll be told." Vas palmed the door release and left. She knew Terel didn't need Flarik there, but it would make things easier if Loxianth changed her mind about cooperating.

Vas tapped her comm as she headed for the lift. "How are our friends in the shuttle doing?"

"They are not having a good time. They started pushing their engines harder once they picked us up on their sensors, but they aren't large enough to move it."

Vas entered the command deck in time to see for herself. The Pilthian shuttle was trying to keep the sheared-off section between themselves and the *Warrior Wench,* but judging by the energy reading running along the bottom of the screen, they were also still trying to move it.

Vas went to her command chair while she watched the screen. "Isn't that our hauler I see approaching? Wouldn't the shuttle notice it?"

Deven looked up from his station. "Yup. They're ignoring it and us. We've been hailing them the entire approach."

Vas watched the shuttle's antics for a few more moments then shook her head. "Inter-ship comm to me please." A light on the arm of her chair flashed and she punched it. "Pilthian shuttle, you are severely outgunned. Leave that wreckage alone now or we will remove you." A feeling of having this conversation before hit Vas. Especially when the shuttle didn't answer.

She turned to Gosta and Deven. "Can you tell if that shuttle is from the *Fairthien?*"

"I was already looking into that, Captain." Gosta held up his left hand as the right one did a few more calculations. "Based on the age of isotope decay on that shuttle it is not from the *Fairthien.*"

"Great." She hit the comm again. "I'm not in the mood for games. If you feel you have a legitimate claim to this wreckage, we can talk about it. Otherwise, take off before we blow you to bits."

The comm light flicked, went out, and then came back. "This is the shuttle *Arthaie,* we are claiming this wreckage by rights of it belonging to the Pilthian people."

"Shuttle *Arthaie*, you do not have a salvage marker out, and we are working with the Pilthian ship that section came off of. There is a deadly contagion on board. You're going to lose this fight. Back off and go home." Vas cut the comm and turned to Gosta. "Can you paint a tracker on them? Only a tag for now, then when they leave hit them with a drone? They shouldn't notice the drone when their shuttle is accelerating."

Gosta grinned. "Excellent thinking, Captain. They might lead us to one of the missing sleeper ships."

"That was my thought. Although it can't be coincidence that two of them showed up after being missing for fifty years." She hit the comm to the shuttle open again. "*Arthaie*, I'm not a patient woman. Do we have a problem? I have to tell you that even my hauler has more firepower than you do. And I have a lot of little fighter ships that are waiting to come out and play." The Flits weren't waiting, but they could be ready quickly.

"You're lying. The ship this section belonged to has been missing for fifty years. It's ours."

"I have things to do. We'll be firing now. Nice to have known you." Vas cut the comm and shook her head as she turned to the others. "If they don't back off, shoot the section. Preferably over the med bay. If we're going to haul it anywhere, we need to vent that contagion anyway and the shuttle can think we missed."

Deven called down for Walvento to scan for the best target.

"Wait! We can make a deal!" The original voice made an 'oof' as if someone had hit them, then a second voice came on. "Thank you, we'll be leaving now."

The shuttle took off, Gosta released a drone, and Walvento fired at the *Fairthien's* med bay. He was usually sparing with his weapons, but either he was frustrated at not being able to shoot much for a long while or not being allowed to hit the *Fairthien,* but the entire rear of the section of the ship was sheared off by a batch of small missiles.

"I said if they didn't leave, Walvento." Vas wasn't angry. They were going to have to do something to vent that section anyway. The fact that he of all people was wasting weapons told her how badly her crew needed a job to focus on.

"I wanted to make certain they understood why they were leaving." His voice was a bit lower than normal, usually that only happened if he was embarrassed.

"Both the painted tracker and the drone are sending back information. First guess I'd say they are heading for the jump gate." Gosta had been so subtle with painting the tracker, a form of tracking another ship through an ultralight scanning shot, that Vas hadn't even noticed when he did it.

"Keep tracking them. If we can trace them to one of the other Pilthian ships, Khirson would be grateful." She turned to Deven. She'd noticed that he'd been running a number of scans on the wreckage since they got close enough. "Is there any reason for us to keep it?"

"Not that I can tell. However, there was a tracker embedded in it. It's old and barely working so most likely was for the entire ship."

"Can you get it contained and removed?" She didn't think Khirson would really be happy if they brought back someone who had been trailing them to the moon. Even if the Pilthians didn't stay on the moon for good they would need to stay there a while to recover.

"Yes, it's really ancient tech, far more so than the ship." Deven wasn't looking up but kept adjusting things on his screen.

Gosta came over to look as well. "It's not Pilthian? I assumed they would have tracked their ships. Although had they tracked it, they wouldn't have lost it."

"It's not...wait." Deven started pulling information

from the station next to him. "It *is* Pilthian, or at least part of it is. I'm sending a containment drone out there to get it." He launched the new drone out toward the wreckage, then swore.

"Is there a problem?" Vas looked over but he hadn't moved any of what he was working with to the front screen.

With a few more swear words, he sent the information up to the front screen so she could see it. "The other signature on that tracker is Fothan. Those bastards must have been working with the Pilthian government when the *Fairthien* launched." His voice dropped. "No wonder Marli hid them. Although, the tracker is disabled it looks like, she wouldn't have taken the chance if she hadn't been able to remove it."

Vas had been looking at the screen but spun back to Deven. "That tracker is telling you Marli hid them? Pretty sure she was the one who saved them from the belt explosion, but why would she hide them?"

Deven stayed silent as the drone removed the tracker. "No one in the Commonwealth knows much about the Fothans, count yourselves lucky. They are as vile a species as anything out there. They are slavers, vultures, and murderers. They don't care who or what they destroy. If they were tracking the *Fairthien* there was only one purpose—they were going to harvest the Pilthians on board as slaves or for body parts to sell on other worlds." He stared at the screen for a few seconds. "Permission to destroy that tracker. Disabled or not, I don't think anyone wants that near them."

Vas glanced to Gosta. Not that Deven couldn't be right, but he was also extremely emotional for him right now. Gosta nodded and the pale green color of his face said that while most in the Commonwealth might not have heard of the Fothans, he had.

"Do it. Then if there are no more issues to deal with,

scan a few more times to make sure there are no more trackers or signs of contaminant, and tell our hauler to hook it up." Vas watched as Deven sent the drone to explode the tracker. The result was so small, it was only a tiny flash, but the drone came back without cargo.

CHAPTER THIRTEEN

——◆——

DEVEN RAN THE SCANS HIMSELF and sent the orders for the hauler. Vas hadn't planned on escorting the section back to the moon, but since it had already gathered unwanted interest, she thought it best to go along to make sure no one else decided to fight for it. She hadn't been lying, her hauler was armed, but it *was* still just a hauler.

Once they were underway, she motioned to Deven. "Can I talk to you in my ready room? Gosta, you too." She knew Deven was still thrown off by his brother, but she needed to figure out why a tracker put on a ship fifty years ago was upsetting him now.

Both men followed her into the room and Deven shut the door behind them. Vas sat behind her desk; this might take a while. "Okay, spill. These Fothans sound like people we're glad aren't in our part of the galaxy, but that tracker was placed fifty years ago." She paused as a thought struck her. "It *was* fifty years ago, right? Not some new addition?"

Gosta took one of the chairs facing Vas' desk, but Deven remained standing.

Deven ran his hand through his hair. "Yes, the tracker showed enough wear that it had been on there for at least that long. Khirson told me the ship was two years old when they launched. The tracker could have been put on then."

"I go back to my original question—why the hell are both of you so upset about a very old tracker?" There were enough things to worry about in this time, they didn't need to be running back fifty-plus years.

"It's not the age that's upsetting, captain, at least for me," Gosta said with a quick look to Deven. "It's the fact they had any contact that deep in the Commonwealth. In every history book or vid I've seen, they never crossed the line into the Commonwealth, not even within a few systems of here. If they were involved in this who knows what else happened. While the Fothans were never as widespread as the Asarlaí, they were more destructive to other races. The Asarlaí wanted to rule everyone, but the Fothans just wanted to destroy everyone."

Deven shook his head and slid into the chair next to Gosta. "More like the Fothans want to be in control of everyone in their section of space. They care about only that which will increase their own value and power, which is a lot like the Asarlaí used to be but on a smaller scale. But the Asarlaí didn't participate in the slave trade—or the black-market body part trade."

Vas watched them both, thankfully Deven was calmer now. Gosta was still a bit pale, but it was probably more from him not knowing that these Fothans had ever been in the Commonwealth rather than anything else. Lack of knowledge disturbed him.

"Fine, so we're good to move on? We need to dump that wreckage and get a real job." Vas got to her feet and was heading for the door when the alarms started.

She ran onto the command deck. "What's happening?"

Bathie was off shift now, but she was still at a station. "Incoming fighters, Captain. They're charging the hauler." The main screen flipped to show three unknown fighters, a little larger than her Flits, on a direct attack course to the hauler.

"Mac, move to block them, and I need Squad A out there in their Flits immediately. Squad B stand by in case I need you."

The fighters had wisely picked the side that the *Warrior*

Wench wasn't on, but the *Wench* had better maneuverability than many larger ships.

Vas tapped her comm to call to the hauler. "Fire if you feel you need to. We're coming around, and the Flits should be out...now." As she spoke, she saw five Flits leave the bay and head toward the incoming fighters.

"Captain, six more fighters coming in." Mac swung them around.

"Damn it, those aren't long range fighters. Is anyone picking up their base ship?" Vas swore as she kept scanning, but she wasn't seeing anything. Her Flits were now engaged with the initial fighters, but the second round would be there in moments.

The hauler rocked as it fired at the enemy fighters and one got off a return shot.

"Damn it Alia, disengage, let that wreckage go." The fighters were trying to get to the hauler, and while armed, the hauler crew couldn't keep up a long fight.

"I think we can hang on." The captain of the hauler was young, but he should know they were outgunned.

"That is a direct order, Alia, get back. They must have a base ship somewhere."

A pause, then the hauler pulled free of the wreckage. "Moving clear." Alia, like many of her crew, was stubborn, but he wasn't stupid.

The lack of a visible base ship for those fighters was making the hairs on the back of her neck stand up. After the Asarlaí Wars, Vas had upgraded all of her ships' sensors to levels beyond anything on the market. They should have picked up something.

"Should I fire if I get a clean shot?" Walvento asked from the weapons bay.

Vas kept watching the front screen as she answered. "Not yet. We have too many Flits out there. Keep scanning for where these fighters are coming from."

The Flits were holding off most of the fighters, but

it was a numbers game. If the other side got more out there…she hit her comm. "Flit Squad B, go out."

"I can't identify those fighters." Deven kept pulling up screens.

"Gosta? Hrrru? Anyone? No identification, no base ship?" As she spoke, she picked up a large shape at the far end of the sensor range. Because it was so far out there, details were limited. But if what she could see was accurate, it was massive. "Are you seeing this?"

Another group of enemy fighters came into range.

"I see it, Captain. No idea on who or what that ship is." Gosta wasn't happy about that admission.

Vas knew her crew was good, and so were her ships, but a massive, unknown ship with a lot of fighters? Over a piece of wreckage that wasn't even hers?

"Everyone back off. Only fire if the others engage and get behind us." Bringing the Flits inside might be safer, but she'd need them out and ready to fight if that ship wanted more than the wreckage.

Two enemy fighters continued after the hauler as it moved away from the wreckage. "Walvento, if you have a clear shot, take them out." There was no way they hadn't noticed that the hauler was backing off.

"Aye." A moment later, the closest enemy fighter exploded. The second pulled back at the last moment and while it took a tumble, it was still intact. Two Flits shot out from behind the *Warrior Wench* and chased the fighter.

"Okay, it's far enough out, everyone pull back. Any idea on the incoming ship?"

"Not yet, Captain," Gosta's voice was distracted as he tried every manner possible to identify it.

"Everyone keep pulling back." Vas wasn't sure what that other ship was. She didn't recognize the fighters, but she didn't want to risk any of her ships. "Xsit, can you reach the main ship yet?"

At first there was a bunch of high-pitched swearing from Xsit, finally she looked up. "I think it's going through now."

Vas hit her comm. "Unidentified ship, we have claim to this wreckage. Please identify."

The way the day had been going she was surprised when a voice answered. "We are the Lethian Assembly. That ship belongs to the Pilthians who are members of the Assembly. We have permission from the Commonwealth to reclaim our wreckage."

Deven came to Vas' side when she cut the comm. "The Lethian Assembly? They're from beyond my home system and rarely travel beyond their own borders. The other Pilthians could have ended up there, I suppose, but why would any of them be here? And how would they have known about the ship?"

"Captain? That ship is tracking us and powering their weapons." Gosta was extremely calm considering that the Assembly ship was twice their size.

"Assembly ship, we're leaving you the wreckage. Power down your weapons."

"Negative, *Warrior Wench*, we cannot allow that." The voice was different from before. There was no doubt that this man planned on destroying all the ships who were out here.

Vas cut the comm. "Shit. Distance?" She looked to Gosta. This had changed radically and for no reason she could tell. She had to get her people out of here.

"Still tracking, but they are out of range for a clean hit."

"All Flits and the hauler get into the docking bay. It's going to be tight with the hauler, so stay in your ships once you're inside. Mac, pull us clear of the wreckage. Walvento, as soon as we're clear, destroy that wreckage."

Deven nodded. "Probably a very good idea. I'm gathering as much sensor data as I can about the Lethian Assembly ship, but we are seriously outgunned."

"I assume I should use as many weapons as needed to make as large an explosion out there as possible?" Walvento wasn't as happy about shooting something down this time; he knew he'd be shoving out a lot of ordnance to cause a mess for the other ships. They might not be able to out gun the Lethian Assembly ship, but they weren't going down without a fight.

"As always, right on the nose. We can't take out the big one, but we can hurt them. On my command." Vas watched the screen closely. The larger ship was visible on the scanners now and she knew every bit of data they gathered about it would be torn apart and analyzed by Deven, Gosta, and Hrrru. Right now, she needed the ship to worry more about its own survival than coming after them.

"Their weapons are about to go live, Captain."

"Now!" Vas yelled. Walvento must have had the firing system half-released, as that single word wasn't fully out of her mouth when a massive display of firepower hit the Pilthian wreckage. The enemy fighters were too close to it and added to the chaos as they exploded. Vas didn't think the larger ship would be affected, but then a second barrage came from the *Warrior Wench*, deflected off the exploding mess, and engulfed the enemy ship. It didn't hit hard enough to destroy it, but it got a few minor explosions burning on the larger ship.

"Is everyone inside our bay?"

"Aye, Captain," Bathie yelled.

"Then let's get the hell out of here. Mac, do not head for Home or Marli's moon, other than that I don't care where we go. A few gate jumps might be a damn good idea." Vas dropped back in her chair. Her hands were shaking. That was too damn close and for no reason she could see. If the Lethian Assembly ship had been sanctioned to enter Commonwealth space, they should have claimed the wreckage and left. Which meant they'd not been approved to cross over, and the Commonwealth hadn't noticed them yet.

She'd wanted to get back in the action. Aithnea always said to be careful as thoughts can become reality far too easily. But she didn't think it would be over some wreckage. They weren't even getting paid for this.

"Whatever stunt you pulled there, Walvento, I applaud it. Please make excellent notes so we can share that technique with the rest of the fleet." She'd never seen weapons use an established explosion like that for a longer-range strike—she knew the reach of this ship and that was further than it should have gone. Focusing on the impossible stunt settled her nerves.

"Aye, Captain," Walvento's voice was subdued. If Vas had to guess, he hadn't been sure that would work. Good guesswork on his end though.

"The Lethian Assembly ship isn't following, Captain," Gosta said. "It appears to have taken some serious damage in two of its drives."

"Bastards. I hope it takes them months to limp home. Mac, come back to this quadrant from the Lixia gate once you've hit a few others." While that gate was technically in this quadrant, it was so far from everything it was rarely used. It was also on the opposite side of Home from their current location.

"Do you want me to contact Pela and have her let Khirson know what's happened to his wreckage?" Deven was still running scans and it looked like he was monitoring at least one drone over the Lethian Assembly ship. They had drones they'd picked up in battle, ones that had been re-wired but could never be traced back to Vas' ships. Deven used them on his own judgement to gather data without risk.

"Yes, and let them know that we might have found where some of their people went, but I wouldn't recommend trying to find them yet." The Lethian Assembly was a draconian collection of worlds; the other Pilthians might have joined them against their will.

Vas watched as Mac led them through a tricky collection of jump gates. She hit her comm. "Flarik? As our official legal counsel, can you gather information about what just occurred, omitting who that wreckage belonged to for now and submit a complaint against the Lethian Assembly ship to the Commonwealth? I'd like to know if they were really in the Commonwealth legally." Judging by their quick to try and blow them up behavior, she'd guess they weren't.

"Agreed," Flarik sounded a little groggy, so she might have dozed off again. "I'll contact you when I've filed our concerns."

"Where to now? I've jumped eight times." Mac sounded like he'd been having far too much fun, but eight was enough. If anyone had been tracking them, that number of jumps would have left them lost.

"Head for the Lixia gate and let's go home." The gate was far enough from their original location, that even if the Lethian Assembly ship came back, it wouldn't notice them.

Mac sent them through, and they came out at the far end of the quadrant. "It's going to take a few hours to get back to Home."

"And you can keep things nice and steady and stay out of trouble, right?" There wasn't much out this way, it was all Commonwealth, but the lack of habitable planets made it less than popular. There shouldn't be any trouble, but she knew if there was, Mac would find it. "I mean it, Mac. Get us to Home calmly and peacefully. I have some things to look into. Deven, you have the bridge."

Deven nodded but stayed at his station. He was obviously working through something to do with their recent adventure. If Vas had to guess, she'd say he was trying to see if there was a connection between the Lethian

Assembly and the Fothans. From what he and Gosta had told her, she really hoped there wasn't.

Vas left the deck and headed for the small storage area near her room. There wasn't anything to do about the Pilthians, or the Lethian Assembly at this point, but there was still that vague command from Aithnea floating in her head. She needed to find that blue book.

The *Warrior Wench* had a lot of storage, most of it hidden. Very hidden. This spot near her room was not only hidden extremely well, but it was also extensively alarmed. Most of her valuables were hidden in her safe in her room, or at the house she had back on Home. This storage spot was for things that needed to be close by, but still needed to remain hidden.

She pulled off the first two panels, then used the palm of her hand on the lock panel to release the third. The space inside was about the width of her ready room, but only four feet high. Most of the items inside were things she'd removed from the collection that Aithnea had left hidden for her. There was still a large room in her house on Home that had more items, but the ones that seemed most personal, Vas kept on board.

It took a few moments to crawl back to where the book was, but it was where she'd seen it in her mind when Aithnea brought it up. It was a good-sized book, and the writing and images were small and dense.

"This is going to take forever," Vas muttered to herself as she backed her way out of the storage area with the book.

"*Not really.*" Aithnea's voice popped in her head, but without the splitting headache of the first time. That was a start.

"I do have a few other things going on, you know." Vas got back to the corridor and shut all three panels. "I said I will help, and I will. But this book is huge." An unhappy thought hit her. "There are more, aren't there?"

"Yes, but I think you'll be surprised at how quickly you get through them. Had I realized that all of the current situations were going to take place, I would have had you start during your rest period on those beaches."

"You were around for that?" Vas trusted that Aithnea wouldn't spy on her, but there were a lot of extremely private moments between her and Deven during that time.

"No. I actually thought my sisters and I were on our way to the beyond, to our true death. It was only in the last week that I realized the new problem and that we were still stuck."

Vas thumbed through the book. There was no way this was going to be fast. "I still think it's going to take a while to get through these books, let alone learn the skills." Vas wanted to help the nuns, but she really didn't have the time for serious study. Nor the inclination. She studied things; the history of some planets fascinated her. But this book looked dry.

"I can make it faster, all of it. But it will be tricky." Aithnea went silent for a moment but Vas could tell she was still there. *"I will need you to go into your holosuite."*

Vas started to ask why, then shook her head and walked toward the lift. "How is it that you're not having as much trouble getting through this time?" She hit the floor number in the lift for the holosuite.

"I'm not sure. It's not as if the interference went away, but as if it's been mitigated by another. Something or someone is weakening the block."

Vas scowled as she let herself into the holosuite. While she was appreciative that her head hadn't been cracked open lately, she still wasn't sure if whatever had blocked Aithnea's visitations had been good or bad. Whoever had been trying to find the Pirate of Boagada hadn't tried in a while and it might have been because of that mystical block.

"We'll worry about that later. I'm in here, what do you

need me to do?"

"*Go to the control panel and select operation 05-02.*"

Vas paused and wished she could see Aithnea. "What in the hell is that? And why and how do you know of something on my ship, that you were never aboard, I might add."

"*I had some time to study it during the final battles. And I only now realized that this could be used in this manner. The operation is not designed in the way we're going to use it, but I believe it will work. Might make a large drain on your engines however, so good thing you're close to Home.*"

Vas paused as she popped open the panel. "How much of a drain? You might not have been around for it, but there was a big ass Lethian Assembly ship trying to destroy us over a piece of wreckage. I think we've lost them but if there's a chance this will cause a problem, we're waiting until we reach Home."

"*Not that bad of a drain, at least not for what we're doing right now.*"

Vas took a deep breath, then entered the code. The large blue screen to the right of the control panel flared to life and prompt arrows appeared. "What now?"

"*This is going to be tricky,*" Aithnea said. "*Hold the book up to the screen. Open it and hold it up. Doesn't matter which page.*"

"How is holding a book up tricky? And how is doing so going to help me read it?" Vas hadn't held up the book yet, but she had her fingers holding a page open.

"*It has to be at the right angle, might take some moving around. Explaining how this will hopefully work would prob-ably take as long as it would be for you to read the book. Hold it up.*"

Vas felt an odd tingling in her arms. "Is that you? Seri-ously? You're going to try and take over my body now?" She was drawing the line at that.

"*No, that's the most I can do, just motivation and guidance.*"

Vas shook her head and raised the book. With subtle and disturbing prompting, she finally got it in the exact position needed. "Now what?"

"*Now focus your thoughts on the screen.*"

"The one I can't see."

"*Yes. Focus your thoughts on pushing through to the screen. I'm going to push as well, and this might feel odd.*"

A moment of pressure, power, and light flowed through her and all her nerves flashed with pinpricks of pain.

Then she woke up on her ass, sprawled across the floor of the holosuite. The book was still with her, although she'd grabbed it so tightly that the edges of the cover were bent.

"It worked! Even better than I thought."

It took Vas a moment of laying on the floor to figure out that she'd heard Aithnea both inside her head, and in the room itself. She gingerly rolled to her feet. "What the hell happened and how are you in my holosuite?"

"*I am in both places right now, but that's a little disturbing.*" The voice in her head vanished. "There, for now I can talk this way. Oh! Maybe I can even…" The voice in the room vanished. Vas walked over to the blue panel, where lines of code were processing too fast for her to glimpse any of them individually.

"I did it!" Aithnea sounded like she was standing right behind Vas.

Because she was.

Vas stumbled back into the control panel, but it was Aithnea standing before her. Same short cropped gray hair, lean scarred face, but young eyes. Standing in her holosuite. "What in the hells? I know that was never taught in nun school. No one can do that."

The joy on Aithnea's face was wonderful to see, though. "I know! Rather, I don't know. It was simply a test of a solid seeming theory, and I proved it. This is most peculiar." She looked at her hands and then around the holosuite.

"Captain, we had a massive power surge from down there. Is something wrong?" Bathie called down via the open holosuite comm.

Vas looked to Aithnea, who shrugged and started walking and watching her feet. "Was it only once or is the drain continuing?" It might be handy having Aithnea out of her head and in a place where she could face her while they talked, but not if it was going to damage her ship.

"Gosta said everything is fine now, but that was a sharp drain."

"I'll explain later. Just let me know if there are any more." Vas turned off the comm, then closed the control panel, and entered a scenario.

A peaceful lavender lake appeared surrounded by massive dark green and deep blue leafed trees. "And two chairs." She spoke to the suite and two lounge chairs appeared. "How about we sit while you tell me specifically what you did?" Vas normally wouldn't be calling up relaxing scenarios, but it was late on an insanely long day, and relaxing sounded good. Besides, this would be something Aithnea would do.

"Well done." Aithnea settled in a chair. "This is fascinating. I know my body is naught but space dust now, but I can feel things through this. Very interesting."

"Yes, it is, and I'd like to know what you did and what you getting a holo body has to do with the book. Or my ability to read it faster."

"Well, I can now train you in person, so to speak. As for the book, it's in the holo matrix as well. Open a page and place your hand on it." Her grin was far too excited for this to be anything good for Vas.

Vas let out a long-suffering sigh and put her hand palm down on a page. And was sent flying across the room again. She flung the book away from her and scrambled to her feet. "What in the hell was that?" As she spoke, images and thoughts flowed through her head. She completely understood the page she'd touched.

"How…" She ran and grabbed the book, flipped open another random page and placed her hand on it. She was expecting the burst, so she only staggered this time as the images slammed into her head and a few pages flowed through her mind, not just the one she touched.

"That is amazing. Can this be done with any form of knowledge?" This could be a huge game changer in the education field. And upgrading all of her crew in background skills.

Aithnea sighed. "I doubt it. The books of the Clionea are specially treated. They are real old-fashioned paper books, but there are lines of coding inside each page. They are meant to be able to be used with high-end scanning devices, but I had hoped that your holosuite would work."

Vas flipped the book shut. "Will I need to be in the holosuite to do this?"

"No, once the book is triggered, the change is in it, not in this suite." She looked down at her holo body. "Unlike me, I'm afraid. I'll only have a body in here. Can this room be left running without a person in it?"

"Yes. You want to rent my holosuite?"

"Only for a while. If we tie in Gosta's library, I can do some investigation into what is going on with the Pirate, whoever is trying to get through to you, and your new Pilthian friends."

Vas tried to fight a yawn but failed. "It's been a really long day. I'll tell the crew the holosuite is being used for a project and lock the observation area as well." She slid aside an inner panel and pulled out the workstation inside. "You can get to the library from here, it's on the ship's system. I'll see you in the morning."

Aithnea looked like an Ilerian with her first pile of money. She waved one hand toward Vas and descended on the workstation.

Vas shook her head and then left, tapping her comm as she went down the corridor. "Bathie, can you lock the holosuite doors, the observation lounge as well? I'm running a study in there."

"Aye, Captain. Gosta wants to know if that's what the power drop was."

"Tell him yes, and I'll explain later. I'm going to sleep now." She knew they'd wake her if there was an emergency.

She carefully held the blue book closed so there was no chance that she'd accidentally touch the pages. She wasn't sure if she needed the full-page contact for the effect to work, but she really didn't want to trigger it unexpectedly. Especially in this narrow hallway. She'd been slammed into these walls before, and it wasn't fun.

Their room was empty, most likely Deven was still lost in his own research. Which was probably for the best; she really wanted sleep, and if he were here that would be less likely to happen.

She hit the low-level lights, dropped the book on her nightstand, and then went toward the shower. Sleepy, lost in thought, and feeling safe in her own room, she screamed when someone grabbed her from behind.

CHAPTER FOURTEEN

———◆———

"DON'T MOVE AND DON'T YELL again. Where is the ship? Where are the scrolls?" The voice was low. One arm was around her shoulders, the other around her waist. Someone who didn't know her very well, obviously. She kicked back as hard and as high as she could. She wasn't sure if it was male or female, but that kind of kick would hurt a woman too. Then she dropped out of her attacker's arms and rammed her elbow into his face.

It was one of Leil's triplets. He dropped to the floor trying to hold his balls and his nose at the same time.

Vas pulled out her blaster. "No idea which one you are but I will blast you apart and figure it out later if you so much as make one false move. Am I clear?" She could call for back-up but that would take too long and be more of a hassle. He'd caught her off guard, but that wasn't going to happen again.

He gave two short nods.

"What in the hell are you doing?" She sat on the edge of her bed, but kept her blaster aimed at him.

"You were there…Where are the scrolls?"

"From the raid on the Garmain home world that you said you didn't recall?" The bastards. Here she'd thought they'd been mind-wiped like her.

He sat up stiffly but stayed on the floor. "My brothers were, not me. They had their memories wiped at my insistence once they got back." He shook his head but that made his nose bleed faster. "I'm Ome. I worked with Mother Aithnea on a project that would help both of our people. You got the scrolls for her; I recovered the stolen ship from my brothers. Both are now missing."

"If the nuns got the scrolls, how do you know they are missing?" She leaned forward. "And although you look like Deven's people, you're not, are you?" There were subtle differences; the two races might be related, but not the same.

"I know the nuns died. Mother Aithnea had someone take the scrolls for analysis before that happened. It was a planet in the Nhali system. The scrolls are gone and so are they."

She'd have to confirm with Aithnea. She could call her, but it might be more confusing than helpful right now. "And your ship? While I don't recall taking it, the Garmainians were very upset about it being stolen."

"I'd heard their home world had been destroyed?"

"It had, but they'd already found me. They had no advanced ships from what I saw."

He wiped his nose, but the bleeding seemed to have stopped. "They shouldn't have had that one. It wasn't theirs." He looked ready to say more, then shut his mouth.

Vas shook her head. "No, see, you're on my ship, you broke into my room, and you *will* tell me everything."

"It's a long story. My people are the Etia and we have issues with a nearby system, the Daila. A gang of Daila pirates attacked a hidden facility, stole a secret prototype ship we were building, and they sold it to a high-ranking Garmainian." He grimaced. "That ship was a prototype that would change space travel as we knew it."

That was interesting. The Garmainians had acted as if they had built the ship. Then claimed it had been stolen and all the documents concerning the building of it were taken as well. It went far to explain why they were so pissed at losing it though. The ships of theirs that Vas had been on were below most Commonwealth standards. "And then your brothers got it back. Over two years ago. Where did it go? How was it lost?" She folded her arms so that she wasn't aiming her blaster at him directly, but she watched him carefully. This one, Ome, was definitely going into lockup after this. She was deciding if his brothers should as well. Might be a good idea since the locked crew rooms obviously weren't holding worth crap.

"We brought it to our Emperor. It was kept under lock and key, or so we thought. To be honest, we've no idea who stole it, nor exactly when. Our government went through some conflicts. I came out to the Commonwealth based on a rumor that it had been seen during your recent war. My brothers travel doing odd jobs and this time I went with them. They have no idea about the ship or their part in it." He rolled his eyes. "And we sure as hell weren't involved with Leil's crap and that woman. I was using that job to get us inside the Commonwealth."

Vas watched him for a few moments, then hit her comm. "I need Gon and Marwin to come down to my room and relocate a prisoner to the brig. Deven might want to come down too." She got to her feet. "I'm going to have my Wavian lawyer talk to you. Later. Right now, I am locking your ass up. Going to do that to your brothers as well." She held up a hand when he started to protest. "I might believe you, but the fact is, I want you all under heavy lockup."

He struggled to his feet, still partially hunched over. She had kicked him hard.

"Captain? Is everything okay?" Gon's voice was welcome to hear from outside her door.

"Come in, Gon." Vas raised her voice.

Gon entered in full thug mode with a massive blaster raised and aimed at Ome. Marwin was behind him. On a ship full of mercs, it really didn't make sense to have designated security people, since everyone on board was fully trained. But Walvento, Gon, and Marwin seemed to enjoy it the most.

"I have a visitor. Please escort Ome to the brig. Then also secure his brothers. Those locking crew rooms aren't staying locked very well."

Gon grabbed Ome and shoved him toward the door. "Are you okay?"

"Thank you for your concern, Gon, but the day I can't get out of a simple grab is the day you all need to bench me." She yawned. "I really do need some sleep now though, so if you could make him and his brothers uncomfortable? Thanks." She herded them toward the door as Deven came running down the corridor.

"Hi Deven, I had a visitor, he and his brothers are going to the brig."

She must have looked exhausted. Deven ran his hand alongside her cheek. "I know what you'll say, but you are fine, right?" The worry in his sharp green eyes was touching, even if unfounded.

"I am. He came out of our encounter far worse than I did."

He watched her a moment more, nodded, and took hold of Ome's arm roughly. "You sleep, we'll relocate." He smiled at her, then shut the door.

Vas waited a moment, just to make sure there were no other surprises. When no one came pounding on her door, she took a quick shower, and fell into bed.

"*I found it.*" The voice in Vas' ear was insistent, determined, and actually coming from inside her head. It had that exasperated sound of someone who might have been trying to get her attention for a while.

Vas's brain finally latched on to who was talking to her. "It's the middle of the night, shouldn't you still be playing in your holo body?" Aithnea obviously could switch back and forth between Vas' head and the holosuite.

"It's mid-morning, according to your ship. Don't you want to know what I found?"

Vas nodded, then remembered who she was talking to. "What did you find?" Sleeping in wasn't common for her, but she'd had strange, disjointed dreams and hadn't slept well as a consequence.

"I found who took the scrolls, and how." She sounded far too smug.

"Great, can you sum it up for me?" Vas rolled out of bed and stretched. Deven's side was untouched. Most likely he'd stayed up all night researching something. He could go for days without sleep, then manage to fall asleep standing up if need be. Vas loved him, but that was a bit of an annoyance.

"You have no sense of academic adventure. At any rate, they were stolen from the last Keeper by a band of pirates who had been hired by someone—most likely the Alitar. It was only about a week before those damn Asarlaí bastards killed us. I figured it had to be close to that event or I would have been notified. Unfortunately, the Keeper died at that time as well."

The Alitar were a group of worlds that mostly kept to themselves. They also wouldn't have been playing with pirates in a normal situation. They were located on the edge of the Nhali system, however. Vas changed but waited to leave the room. "What was on these scrolls anyway? The Garmainians thought them sacred but had no idea how to read them. The description of who left them did sound like some nuns I knew." The High Counsel had been very pissed about her stealing them, but even though they had been in his domain, he really knew nothing of them. They were a part of that office that got passed down through the years.

"They were ancient secrets that went back to the beginning of our order—the very beginning, long before my time. I wanted to study them, but even at that point it was clear there was something else far more dangerous brewing. The Keeper was the best

person to protect them." A tone of sadness ran through her mental voice. The last Keeper must have been someone close.

"Why was she the last Keeper?"

"It was part of our cycle. New Keepers were already trained when the end came, but they were all still in the compound when we were attacked. The point is, I believe we know the area of the people who killed the last Keeper—possibly the Pirate of Boagada as well—and stole the scrolls. Rather they hired pirates to steal them."

"Do you know the pirates who were hired? I don't see my crew taking on the entire Alitar sector."

"No, but I'm narrowing…oh dear. Something is blocking me again. I—" The empty space in her head told Vas that Aithnea was gone. She left her room and headed for the holosuite. Whatever was blocking Aithnea might or might not also be impacting the holo version of her. There was more shielding on the holosuite even than the upgraded shields on the rest of the ship. Vas hadn't upgraded the holosuite though—it had come to her with that addition. One more oddity of this ship.

"Aithnea?" The holosuite looked the same as she had left it and the library connection was still up. No sign of her friend though.

Then a shape got off the floor. "Okay, that was very odd. The connection with myself on the other plane is gone. But I am still here."

"You're real? Or here as in still in a holo body?" Vas walked up and swung her hand through Aithnea. "Holo body. But you can't feel yourself in that other plane at all?"

"No. But something is scanning your ship. I can't leave this room, but you need to get to your command deck. Now."

Vas didn't question, just turned, and ran. Even stuck on a holo deck Aithnea was a voice to listen to.

She hit her comm as she ran. "Gosta? What's going on up there?" They should have made it to Home while she was sleeping. They also should have woken her up when they got there. Judging by the sound of the engines, they weren't at Home.

"We're not sure. We were approaching Home about an hour ago when all forward movement was cut off. We're being pulled back toward the Lixia gate at an advanced speed." He didn't sound freaked out, but his words were freaking her out.

"What in the hell? Why wasn't I woken up immediately?" She hit the lift and punched the button for the command deck.

The command deck had both the late crew and the morning crew. All stations were full, but Bathie got out of the command chair at her approach. "We didn't realize what was happening at first."

Vas took her seat and pulled up the past time logs. "Has Grosslyn contacted us?" There would be no way that he wouldn't know exactly where this ship was.

"We can't reach him," Xsit said from her station. The night communications crew member was standing behind her. Obviously that shift wasn't leaving until they found some answers.

"Damn it. Can we reach anyone on Home?" She looked around. "And where's Deven?" She'd expected that he'd been off doing research, but he should have noticed their current status. Then again, she hadn't, and wouldn't have if Aithnea hadn't told her something was wrong.

"He was down in the library access on the medical level," Gosta said.

Xsit trilled as she kept hitting communication failures. "I can't reach anyone off ship and Deven's not responding either. It's as if all attempts are echoing back at me."

Vas drummed her fingers on the arms of her chair. What in the hell was going on? "Gosta? Anything coming through in those reports of yours? Mac? I assume we have been fighting against whatever is pulling us toward the gate?"

Mac was keeping up a solid low-level swearing which told her the answer, but he responded anyway. "Aye, Captain. Whatever has us isn't letting me push the engines to fight back. We're moving, but not the direction we want. If I try to switch directions our ship ignores my command."

"No reports of anything. It's like Xsit and the communications. I'm getting ghost results, but nothing real. Just echoes of the commands I put in." Gosta didn't even look up as he kept trying to break through whatever was blocking him.

"Deven? Please respond." Vas knew he could get lost in research, but this was worrying her.

"Vas?" Terel sounded concerned through the comm. "Three of our crew with telepathic abilities have collapsed. I'm not sure when they went down. Others found them and brought them in."

"Damn it, can you check the library access near your lab? Deven was last seen there." She turned to Gosta and Mac. "How long ago did you say the ship started being pulled back?" Aithnea got cut off less than ten minutes ago.

"About an hour ago. That's when we also noticed we couldn't get through to Home."

"And again, you never notified me, why?" She'd wanted them to think before they contacted her, but this would have been a justifiable time.

"We did. You responded that you were on your way." Gosta's face went pale. "That wasn't you?"

"I was asleep. Damn it, Aithnea's been in the holosuite, she could have thought she was doing me a favor." She noticed the raised eyebrows at her comment but ignored them. "Nothing new in the last fifteen minutes?"

"I don't know up there, but that was about when the first unconscious telepath was found. Wasn't worried until now, when two more were brought in." Terel had kept her link to the command deck open. "And Deven was in the library access down here. We brought him to the med lab and he's slowly coming to but he was unconscious when we found him."

Vas got to her feet. "Everyone keep trying to break free. Xsit, keep trying to punch through on those communications. If something is bouncing things back to us, then change frequencies, do whatever you can to get through. I'm going to the holosuite then the med lab." She knew Gosta especially wanted an explanation of the holosuite, but there was no time. Some force was pulling them back to a distant gate, they had to break free before they got pulled through. If they had no control of the gate entrance the ship could be destroyed the moment it entered. Thanks to the ship pulling them through, they had absolutely no control.

Vas ran down the corridor as soon as the lift got her to the holosuite level. Hopefully Aithnea would have some answers.

"Aithnea?" First glance she wasn't there, then she reappeared two feet in front of her.

"Sorry, I was testing if I can go back. Succeeded in putting myself into the holo buffer." She tilted her head. "I take it from your face, there's more wrong than just me being stuck here?"

"Something is sucking this ship back through the gate we came through. We can't fight back, we can't pull away, hell, we can't even communicate with anyone. And our telepaths are unconscious or recovering from being so. Including Deven." Vas was concerned about Deven and the other tekes, but she needed to check to see if Aithnea had any clues first.

Aithnea started pacing, something she used to do when

she was alive. It was more disturbing when she walked
through the hologram furniture while she did it. "It
sounds like a Hive ship. You probably aren't picking them
up because, like everything else, your sensors are bouncing back at you." She paused. "They *are* bouncing back?"

Vas nodded. She'd not heard of Hive ships, which probably meant they, like so many of her headaches the last
day, were from outside the Commonwealth. The damage
from the attack of the mutated Asarlaí was longer lasting
than anyone thought. Worlds were being rebuilt, but new
threats from other sectors were still seeing the Commonwealth as easy pickings.

"They have you completely blocked. This ship will
be forced through a gate ill-prepared. When the *Warrior
Wench* is critically damaged, they will swarm and take
what they want." Aithnea nodded. "Yes, I believe you
have a Hive ship on your hands. Or rather a pair of them."

Vas stared at her friend for a few seconds. "It's great that
we know what is going to kill us, but how do we stop it?
What do they want? Where are they from?"

Aithnea sat in a hologram chair. Vas wasn't sure how
sometimes she went through things, and others she didn't.
But the sitting wasn't good. That was the hard-thinking
sit and if what Aithnea said was true, they really didn't
have time for hard thinking.

"What they want is everything. Whatever is not
destroyed by the gate, they will take. Where they are from
is the Outer Weithia system, part of the Lethian Assembly. I've never heard of them coming even remotely near
the Commonwealth before though." She looked down.
"And I have no idea how to stop them."

Vas nodded. "They are blocking everything, all our sensors. They don't seem to be blocking internally though?"

"No, just sensors, communications, ability to navigate.
In theory, your weapons would work if you could take
out the lead ship. There will be a pair. The first will be

holding the power that is cutting your ability to control yourselves, the net if you will. The second is pulling you to the gate."

"Can they stop a ship from flying out of our bay?"

"No, but I don't think... You still have a Fury, don't you?"

"We have one. If they can't see internally, I should be able to get out. Hopefully that ancient flying bastard will have enough juice to take out that net ship."

Aithnea vanished and reappeared at the library console. "Possibly. The Hive is powerful. Make sure you aim for the one that looks like this." Her hands flew over the panel and a sleek warship appeared. "This is the net." She tapped again and a more vicious-looking, and much larger, ship appeared. "This is the club. It looks like you should take it out first, but don't. Once the net is disabled, your people on here can fight back, and stop being dragged into the gate. Your crew should regain control to fire at the larger ship once the net is taken down."

Vas studied both ships, nodded, then ran into the corridor, hitting her comm as she ran. "Terel? How's Deven?" Her initial plan had been to go to the med lab but there wasn't time for it. Plus, if Deven was even a little awake, he'd try to take her place. She wasn't sure what about the net hit the tekes so hard, but right now wasn't the time to find out.

"He's still mostly out of it," Terel responded. "Aren't you coming down?"

"Not yet. Bathie will take command until I come back—or Deven wakes up more."

"Come back? Vas, where are you going?"

"Later." Vas cut the comm and took the lift down to the bay. "Gosta, Bathie, I've got some intel on our captors. It's a pair of ships from the Hive. See what you can find out, but right now, I'm launching the Fury at them. One ship has a net on us, and the other is pulling us back through the gate. Have Walvento ready. As soon as the net drops, you'll see the second ship. Blast it out of existence." She cut him off as well. Her comm beeped with either the med lab or the command deck trying to call her, but there wasn't time. There were mere minutes before those Hive ships pulled them through the gate.

Whether going through unprepared would crush them completely, she wasn't sure, but she knew they would not be coming out of it the same way they went in. Easy for another crew to pick off what they wanted from what was left.

She hit the bay and nodded to her guard. "Marwin, we have a serious situation, and I'm taking the Fury. Lock this door behind me until I'm out." It wasn't that she didn't trust her crew, but they often wanted answers. Time was slipping away and answers could kill them.

Marwin opened his mouth to say something, probably asking for answers, then shut it and slammed the lock closed behind her.

She ran to the Fury. It was kept in the back of the bay since she'd not flown it in months. The funny thing was that she'd been pissed when Deven first brought them on board, but now she was wondering if she and he could fix up a few more from Marli's collection.

Furies were the most insanely powerful small fighters ever invented. They were also the most unstable and equally likely to explode themselves as destroy their enemies. But there was nothing in the world like flying one. Sheer power hummed through every part of it the moment the engine was engaged.

Vas strapped herself in and fired up the arm that would swing the fighter into launch position. The internal shields were up, and the bay doors open. She left the bay.

An odd force pushed her back toward the ship. Nothing she could see, but since they were still inside the net it must be affecting the Fury. She pushed the engines hard and broke away quickly from the *Warrior Wench*. Then she was outside of the net.

Of course, she'd been pushing so hard that the Fury shot off course once the pressure of the net released. She slowed down, made the corrections, and spun back toward the *Warrior Wench*.

The attacking ships were easy to see now. A massive one was pulling what looked like a giant bag behind it toward the gate. The second was sitting on the top of the bag with extensive lines of net spinning around it.

The gate was now seconds away.

CHAPTER FIFTEEN

VAS IGNORED THE FLASHING COMM in the Fury and the one pinned to her shirt. She would have one shot at this and couldn't wait for anyone else. The net ship might not be the power threat that the larger one was, but based on the size, it would be a serious match for even the firepower of a Fury. Neither ship had reacted to her; most likely they were focusing on getting through the gate.

Vas armed the first bank of missiles, then went ahead and flicked on the second. Forty missiles of massive power should do the trick. If they didn't, there wasn't anything else she could do.

Of course, full firing seriously increased the likelihood that the Fury would blow up once it disbursed all the weapons. Not a great thought, but as often the case, the only option on the table.

Vas turned the Fury toward the net ship, locked in the target coordinates for firing, and let the missiles go.

The Fury spun as it fired, which was what it was designed to do for a full discharge. It also started shaking and slipped off course—that wasn't good. The weapons had all hit the net ship before Vas drifted off course, but she needed to get control back before she slammed back into the *Warrior Wench*.

The net separated into strands as the net ship exploded. The second, larger Hive ship was almost through the gate when it happened. They tried to pull back but got slammed between the gate itself and the weapons fire from the *Warrior Wench*. The larger ship exploded much better than Vas would have thought. She'd have Gosta and Hrrru look into the impact of the gate being that close to the Hive ship for future battle scenarios. Maybe they could add it as a strategy.

Vas wasn't sure exactly what had happened, as she was still spinning, but the amount of firepower that Walvento used was impressive. Between that and their encounter with the Lethian Assembly ship, there couldn't be anything left in the weapon banks.

She tried to control her spin, but so far, the Fury wasn't responding. Of course, it also hadn't exploded, for which she was extremely grateful. She hit her comm to the command deck. "Nice shooting, Walvento, and excellent work everyone. The Fury and I are having a bit of a problem."

"That's what you get for doing it without me," Deven's voice came on the line. He sounded a bit out of it but was fighting to wake up.

"Then you would be out here instead. Oh wait, you were unconscious." Vas tried changing the direction, but nothing—the Fury was in a spin and had no intention of coming out of it until it smacked something larger than itself. Great. "I need some help, folks."

"Cut the engine, then restart once it stabilizes," Mac responded.

Mac had never flown one of these, but he was a serious ship junkie. Still, Vas knew Deven had heard him as well, so she waited for confirmation. Groggy or not, Deven was the Fury expert.

"Try it," he said.

Vas shook her head but cut the engines. The remaining spin sent the ship tumbling worse, but at least it was away from the *Warrior Wench* instead of at her.

The spinning was more of a drift now, residual, not being caused by anything. She hit the engines. A brief moment of swearing followed when they didn't engage.

Followed by some well-placed punches. The engine kicked in. "Got it. The ship is still wobbly as hell, but it's working. Coming back now."

There was more rattling inside the ship than when she went out, but that could be fixed. Still, she came in slow. The tendrils from the Hive net ship were sparking as they drifted away. "Gosta, can we safely grab a few of those lines? The non-sparking ones preferably. If this Hive is coming into our neighborhood I want to know how to defend against that net. This is the second incursion from a species that is part of the Lethian Assembly in two days—we need information now."

"I believe so, Captain. We will send a shuttle with a decon box. Oh, and Grosslyn has been trying to reach you."

Vas sighed. He could speak to anyone on that deck, but sometimes Grosslyn had to go to the top. "Fine, patch him through."

"Captain? Are you all okay? Shall I send ships?"

"We're fine now, Grosslyn. Don't send ships but keep an eye on us in case those things did some long-term damage. When we get down there, I'll give you a full report." The Fury was rattling more, and she really didn't have time to discuss what happened. She needed to keep her focus on the flying ball of bolts she was piloting.

The pause on the other end told her she was right; he wanted more information. Patience wasn't one of his strong points. Finally, he cleared his throat. "Aye, Captain, we'll be watching you." He cut the call.

Vas navigated the Fury into the docking bay, secured it, and made her way back to the command deck. One of the shuttles was still out gathering net threads.

"Damage report?"

"One slightly rattled Fury and pilot, we're out of weapons, and there was an engine reaction once the net failed that I think we need to look at." Deven looked up from his station with a smile. "And some still shaken telepaths. Whatever that net does, it hits hard."

Vas nodded then mentally reached out to Aithnea. "*Are you back?*" The silence in her head wasn't welcome. "I'll be back, and I will explain things, but right now I need to go to the holosuite." She ran off the command deck before anyone could throw questions at her.

Mentally, she kept reaching out, but Aithnea wasn't there. She hit the door to the holosuite to find Aithnea's holo-self sitting at the library doing research. "Back for more? I'm not really sure how to shake the Hive ships. Our contact was minimal. But you must have slowed them down as we're intact."

"We blew them both up," Vas said. "But you still can't reach yourself on the other plane?"

Aithnea shut down what she was looking at and turned with a scowl. "No. I can't feel anything. If that net is gone, I should be able to get back."

"Can you sense any of the other nuns? Maybe get back that way?" Vas had no idea what else to suggest; as far as she knew no one had done what Aithnea had been doing.

Aithnea was silent for a moment and she closed her eyes. Finally, they opened and she shook her head. "No, I can't. Looks like I'm stuck here in your holosuite. At least for now. That net ship changed something. We need to find out what."

"I'll have the others work on it as well. Maybe I'll also send Deven down, he might pick up things we're missing." Vas would be more disturbed by the situation except that Aithnea clearly wasn't. Being upset wasn't the way of the nuns.

"That will work. In the meantime, I am thoroughly enjoying the library access." With a grin she went back to her screen.

Vas nodded and went back to the deck. The trip to

Home was slower than normal, but Mac was concerned about the state of their engines and Vas wasn't going to argue. If there were experts, it would be stupid not to listen to them.

"Welcome back, Captain," Grosslyn called up on the comm as they came closer to Home. "Ground landing?"

Most of their fleet could land on a planet, but it was easier to leave them in orbit. Vas looked to Mac and at his nod, responded. "Aye. There's some damage to the engines that might need more work than an orbit docking repair can handle. We'll be down in ten minutes."

The ground landing wasn't hard but involved a lot of different stations and people doing things. Vas mostly stayed out of their way. She wondered what in the hells had happened that all of these non-Commonwealth ships were coming into their space. Damn it. Now she had two incursions to report to the Commonwealth council. Even though they wanted her to be their figurehead, communications with the Commonwealth were still a pain in the ass.

The *Warrior Wench* landed, not gracefully, but landed. Vas opened the ship-wide comm. "I know we were only out a few days, but unless you have a project that needs you to stay on the ship, you have down time. We have to figure out what happened and find a merc job." The last few days had been more than their share of weird, and they still had no job. Of course, getting the word out there that her crew was up and running again hadn't been going terribly fast. Most of the merc teams had been hurt or decimated by the Asarlaí war and the entity that kept them organized—the legit ones anyway—wasn't much better. Vas didn't want to go rogue and take non-sanctioned work, but they needed something soon.

"You've been busy, Captain." Grosslyn met her as she came down the ramp. He was a huge man. Vas wasn't short, but he topped her by a head.

Hopefully, he had a sanctioned job ready for them. Preferably something they could tie Aithnea's scrolls, nuns, and Keepers project to. Nhali was far from the Commonwealth rim, so it wouldn't be easy. But even if the fate of the Universe was not actually at stake, Vas owed it to the nuns to get them to their promised peace.

"And none of it earned us a dime." Vas shook her head as she reached him at the bottom of the ramp. Then she saw his huge grin. "Wait, we have a job?"

"Aye! Okay, you need to have an open mind." He led her to his office in the landing area.

"I'm not going rogue, Grosslyn. Not unless there is absolutely no choice. Even with the messed-up Commonwealth right now, we don't need that headache." Once a certified merc company took a non-sanctioned job it was a bitch to get back in the good graces of the Commonwealth. Going rogue meant the actions of the merc company could be taken to court—something far scarier than fighting for your life. She'd seen a few companies be legally destroyed and end up having to disband. That was one of the primary reasons she'd brought Flarik on board years ago.

His grin grew wider as he held open the door to his office. "Nope, I verified. It's an odd job, but fully certified."

Vas sat down and folded her arms. Grosslyn didn't go on jobs anymore; hadn't once she'd realized what a good administrator he was years ago, and she put him here. His concept of odd was different than hers. "I'll bite, what is it?"

"Now hear me out. There is a company, Dackon Industries, that is desperate to find out what has been happening to their ships. They are being lost to pirates without a trace outside of the Commonwealth. But they are throwing enough money, both at us and the regulatory agency of the Commonwealth for us to go out and solve it." He pointed proudly to a map of the system the ships were vanishing from. Not that far from the edge of the Commonwealth, but once out past the rim, they could find a way to get to the Nhali system—after their job was done.

Vas gave him a few seconds to spill the rest, then tilted her head when he didn't. "I didn't hear a merc job in there. Is there someone to fight?"

"Once you find them there will be." He was way too pleased with himself. The pay must be huge.

"It's a glorified retrieval mission? Not very exciting, but it's better than nothing and we need to get back out there. I'd like the engines of the *Warrior Wench* checked out before we go though. That Hive net did a number on them." Vas needed to light a fire under Grosslyn and his people to finish the training for the rest of the captains and start getting them out there as well.

Grosslyn's face fell. Vas wondered how he did at cards, since everything showed up on his face. "About that. You can't take the *Warrior Wench*, too well known now. They don't even want any of our other ships, since they were all documented in the Asarlaí war. This has to be a stealth mission."

"That's the catch," Vas said. "I'm not buying and fitting out a brand-new ship for a single job. There's no way they are paying us that much."

"Actually, they are. They are including a ship, speed-ster class, along with your upgrading up to half a million credits. And we keep the ship once we're done. On top of the half a million they are paying."

Vas had been getting to her feet, they could find a better job somewhere, but she fell back into her seat at the number he mentioned. "These amounts are confirmed?" Along with sanctioned jobs saving a merc company's ass in court, they also required confirmed and agreed-upon payments. The numbers were about what she would make in a year.

"Yup." He fussed with his monitor, then turned it to face her. The official document for the job appeared on the screen. "We are limited in the ships we can get; they want us to go in as smugglers. Pirates, if you will."

Vas scowled as she read the specifics. She was all for a little role-playing, but that class of ship would limit her crew to about half. She ran with a lean fifty on the *Warrior Wench* right now, and it was handy. She'd have to carefully winnow down her crew and make sure the ones left behind knew it was temporary. Her crew were serious fighters, but they could be whiny if given a chance.

"What's our timeline? And how close is the nearest ship we can buy?"

His scowl etched itself deeper. "That is the thing. They want you on your way within seventy-two hours. There are a few ships in that class available that aren't too far. I sent the details to your pad."

Vas nodded. She'd want to look over her options in private, but the truth was they didn't have much time. "I'll be in the office. Call if you need me and don't forget we need a serious check on the engines, even if the *Warrior Wench* won't be on this trip."

The job was solid, and the more she looked, the stronger it got. Not an exciting job, even if they should get a good fight out of it once they found the pirates behind the thefts. But the pay was great and the risks relatively low. And it would get them out past the rim to track down Aithnea's scrolls and whatever else she needed in order to save the Universe and move on to the next plane of existence.

She switched over to look at the available ships.

The speedster class wasn't her favorite; they were sneaky ships, but not large enough to be taken seriously on their own. And the nearby options weren't good. She finally pulled up one that might work, *Traitor's Folly*. Not an auspicious name, and legal titles weren't changeable in the Commonwealth, but it would work. In this case the title might even help. She pulled up its record and started laughing. It had been used as a school runner for kids from small worlds before the Asarlaí attacked. She could make up a story if anyone cared enough to check the background.

It had done some regular courier work before that. And the routes were suspicious enough to look like potential smugglers. Excellent. Taking on a job with a subset of roles meant making sure things looked legit. Dackon Industries wouldn't be dishing out this number of credits for a simple job. There were layers under it that were still hidden.

"Grosslyn, check out the scans on the *Traitor's Folly*. If it comes back solid, buy it."

"You sure? You could check them out."

"I'll trust your scans; those can't be faked. I think we want to have time to do some upgrading before we leave." Vas always trusted her gut, now more than ever. But this time it was experience that was kicking in. She liked the job, the money, and a new ship—she knew those things came with a price.

Deven came in as she went through a few more of the specs, but nothing was jumping out at her.

"Heard we have a job. What are we going to do with our prisoners and locked-up guests?" He was moving stiffly, whatever knocked him out had been strong. Deven was the king of not showing an injury.

Vas rocked back in her seat; she'd forgotten about them. "Loxianth can go into lockup here, she can sit for a few months. I'd say your brother and Ome as well." They had a planetary jail, of sorts. It usually wasn't used long term, but right now she didn't want them out in the Commonwealth prison system. "I think the other two brothers can be dropped off somewhere on our way out.

I'll leave it to you as to where."

The other two really seemed to have no idea what Ome had done. She wanted to question them about their adventure with her, but they supposedly had no memory and she actually believed Ome on that.

Deven nodded, then stretched. "I'm going to go to my home for a short bit. Terel threatened to lock me up in the med bay for a week if I don't get some rest." He shook his head. "Better I get out of her sight for a while."

"I'll catch up with you. Still have some things to go through."

Deven nodded and left.

Vas was looking through schematics and the original contract to see what was hidden in it. She'd sent a copy to Flarik as soon as she got it, but it was always good to see for herself.

"Captain? There's a call coming in from Pela for you." Grosslyn stuck his head inside her office.

"Thanks, switch it here." It might be nothing, but aside from her newfound tendency to brandish knives at annoying people, Pela was very stoic. She wouldn't call just to check in. "Vas here."

There was a lot of static on the line, but eventually she could hear Pela. "Captain, we were set up. The Pilthians are awake and planning on going to war. Grifion was killed, along with a few Pilthians who were against the new Queen. I'm in our shuttle, I destroyed their extra one and have a lead on them, but they are coming after us in the *Fairthien*."

CHAPTER SIXTEEN

⸺◆⸺

"**D**AMN IT. KHIRSON BETRAYED US?" Vas would grieve for Grifion later. This hadn't been a life-threatening job. Or so she thought.

"No, Captain, he and three other Pilthians helped me get away. They are with me. Sorry, didn't have time to ask about bringing them along." She paused. "The weapons on our shuttle were sabotaged."

Vas swore under her breath. "Don't worry about it. Go toward the Kackli system. We'll be there."

"Aye, Captain."

Vas ran out of her office. "How are the engines on the Wench?"

Grosslyn had been looking at some schematics and jumped when she ran out. "In pieces? Sorry, even though you won't be taking her, I thought it best to fix them quickly."

"Crap. Where's the *Victorious Dead*?" Her former flag-ship, captained by her former second in command, wasn't as fast as the *Warrior Wench*, but since Marli's upgrades, it was damn close. And it would still get them to the quadrant she'd sent Pela to in time.

"Ragkor is coming back from a training with two of the newer captains. They are coming into orbit and were going to land."

"Belay that." Vas tapped into the *Victorious Dead*. "Rag-kor? We have an emergency situation and the *Warrior Wench* is out of commission. Commandeering your ship."

"Anytime. As you keep saying, these are technically all your ships," Ragkor said. He was a seven-foot-something former marine and fully dedicated to the cause. Whichever cause there was at the moment.

"Excellent. I'm taking a shuttle up now." Vas nodded to Grosslyn and ran toward one of their Home shuttles. "Get ready to head out toward the Kackli system. Have all weapons ready. We're going to be rescuing one of our shuttles from a Pilthian ship. I'll send you the specs on my way up."

She launched the shuttle and pulled in the information as to where best to match the *Victorious Dead* in orbit. Damn it. That was what she got for being helpful. One crew member killed and a second on the run.

"Vas, where in the hell are you going?" Deven called in on the comm.

"We've been betrayed by the Pilthians. Well, most of them." Vas filled him in as she brought in the shuttle to land in the *Victorious Dead*'s docking bay.

"Okay, but I'm beginning to think you're taking off without me on purpose. I'll see you when you get back—and be careful."

Vas felt a twinge at the words and the tone. She didn't mean to keep leaving, at least not consciously, but part of her felt he would slow her down. Another thing to work through with her mind-doc—later. "Sorry, needed to run. Keep an eye on things." Vas ended the call and left the docking bay. True to his word, Ragkor took off as soon as the bay doors shut. She knew part of him still wanted to wait until his superior officer was on the command deck, but she was slowly breaking him of his military training.

The *Victorious Dead* had been her ship for fifteen years. And although it had been torn apart and rebuilt, it still resembled the original enough to pull at Vas' heart as she strode to the command deck.

"Good to see you, Captain." Therlian saw her first. The former Clionea nun was now Ragkor's second in command. She was almost as tall as Deven, and usually had a don't-make-me-have-to-kill-you look on her face, even when happy. It wasn't there this time, just an honest smile. "The information you provided on the Pilthians is interesting."

"Yeah, we all thought they'd left or died. Saved some, and it turns out they're murdering assholes." Vas waved Ragkor back into the captain's chair. "Stay. I'm borrowing your ship, nothing more. We had a run-in earlier and the engines on the *Warrior Wench* were damaged."

Ragkor nodded. "Gosta sent us the specs as to what to look for. I can't say I like all of these non-Commonwealth ships suddenly showing up."

"Me either. We have a small job; Deven, me, and about half of the *Warrior Wench* crew will be heading out of the Commonwealth for it. I want you two and this ship to command the others while we're gone." Vas was figuring out that having a fleet meant more than simply ordering ships around. There needed to be a figurehead.

Ragkor gave a stern nod. One thing about that military training, he obeyed orders. Therlian looked ready to question them.

Vas walked over to her. "I have something separate to talk to you about. Can we talk in your ready room?" At her nod, Vas turned back to Ragkor. "Notify me the moment we get within visual range and keep all sensors at full alert."

Therlian didn't sit once they got inside, so Vas didn't either. "Aithnea is back." Better to cut to the chase. Therlian was one of the people who believed Vas from the beginning since she'd known Aithnea when she'd been a novice nun.

"In your head again? I thought she'd finished what she needed to do. We won the battle."

"She thought so as well, but apparently not. She was in my head, just showed up yesterday with some mysterious warnings. Then she managed to put herself in my holodeck as well as my head. She got locked into the holodeck when the Hive appeared."

"And you're not taking the *Warrior Wench* on this job."

"Nope, we can't. I need someone to check in on Aithnea from time to time. I'll talk to her once we get Pela and her new friends back, but this job is time-sensitive."

"I'll keep an eye on her." She tilted her head and narrowed her eyes. "That wasn't the only thing though, was it?"

"No." This was harder. "Aithnea feels there is another threat and it's somehow involved with the Pirate of Boagada. Or rather, the fact that there is no Pirate right now."

Therlian rocked back and nodded. "And no Keeper to find a new one. Damn. That's not good."

"You caught on to all of that a lot faster than I did when she told me. She's selected me as the candidate."

Therlian laughed, then covered her mouth. "You're serious? Eh, you probably would have made a crap nun, but the Keepers were another class completely. Rules didn't pertain to them. Which is sort of your MO." She walked around Vas slowly. "How will you be training?"

"I was hoping to tap into you and Aithnea. But I'm afraid you'll both be in the Commonwealth and we're not going to be. There's a time limit on this, and also on the things Aithnea wants me to look into. And we've still had someone trying to track the Pirate through us." That was one nice thing about this job: whoever kept trying to contact them would hopefully keep trying with the *Warrior Wench*.

Therlian thought for a moment, then nodded. "I have my training modules. It won't cover all of the Keeper training, as I never finished, but I'll send them back with you. Not as good as hand-to-hand, but a holo program should help. This is tied to your new job?"

"It will get us to the right area of space to start searching, and maybe I can also find out what in the hell is causing so many non-Commonwealth ships to enter our space."

Ragkor called from the command deck. "Captain? We're in range. The Pilthians are gaining on our shuttle but not within firing distance yet."

"Thanks, let's keep it that way." Vas left the ready room. The main screen was filled with a star field and two ships. He was right, the Pilthians were gaining.

"You have some Flits ready?"

"Always." Ragkor looked hurt that she might think he wasn't battle ready at all times.

"Therlian, you're with me. We can get there faster than you'll get in range. We'll go after the Pilthian ship and hopefully draw their fire." The Pilthians didn't have a lot in terms of their weapons, but Vas had seen what was left and it was enough to make things rough for a shuttle with disabled weapons.

Vas and Therlian ran down to the Flit bay; not as much fun or firepower as the Furies, but they were still good fighter ships.

"Only distract? No full attack?" Therlian's voice came through the ship's comm as she readied a second Flit.

"Oh, they killed one of my people. I intend to do as much damage as possible." Vas finished her check. "Which should be very distracting for them. Ragkor should be close enough to keep them backed off anyway."

They launched and headed for the Pilthian ship. "Pela, veer toward the *Victorious Dead*, Therlian and I are going after the Pilthians."

"Thank the goddess you're here, didn't think we were going to make it." Pela moved the shuttle as Vas and Therlian shot past to engage the larger ship.

"Stand down, Pilthian ship. This is your one and only warning."

"We are simply trying to reclaim our missing people.

The people in that shuttle kidnapped them. The shuttle is not from your ship."

"Wrong. I'm the one who saved your asses when you were frozen. How do you repay us? Killing one of my people? Stand down immediately. The ship closing in on you is mine also. You are completely outgunned. Stand down." Vas shook her head; she'd talked too much already.

"They're not standing down. Let's show them what these little ships can do," Vas said to Therlian. Then she swerved in and fired along the side of the Pilthian ship. Right where they'd had to dump that section. She also fired a tracker to stick to the other ship's hull.

Therlian took the other side, leaving a nice trail of explosions in her wake.

The Pilthian ship turned and fled.

"Shall we pursue, Captain?"

Vas was about to say no, she was hoping the tracker might lead to where they were heading. Obviously, Marli's moon was now off limits to them. She'd make sure to have Ragkor and crew do a thorough clean-up of anything or anyone they left behind and set up more sensors. "Yes. I want to make them work to get away. And if we do more damage, good." She was pissed about Grifion. Losing people in her command wasn't uncommon—they were a mercenary company—but he'd been on a mercy mission, trying to help.

She punched the Flit forward and started firing as she got within range.

Therlian might not be able to see what was in Vas' mind, but she adapted quickly and took the other side.

Two Flits wouldn't have a chance of taking this ship down. But they did some damage before the larger ship left the area. Flits weren't designed for long flights, unless modified, and these two weren't.

Vas turned and led them back to the *Victorious Dead*.

Pela's shuttle was already onboard but she, Ragkor,

Khirson, and two more Pilthian males were waiting behind the shield.

Once the outer doors were shut again, Vas and Therlian joined them.

"I'm sorry about Grifion, Pela. What happened?"

Pela looked ready to hurt someone badly. "We were ambushed. We'd gotten the primary crew awake and moving about sooner than expected. The new Queen called us to her cabana. She said we were a risk and had to die. Her guards shot Grifion before he could get his hand on his sidearm. I threw my knives, then shot at least three before I dragged Grifion out. He was already dead. Khirson and a squad of his people came running and were immediately under fire from the Queen's guards." She pointed to the other two Pilthians. "These are the survivors from a squad of ten. The guards murdered their own people without question."

"Damn it, Khirson, what happened? That *was* your Queen, right?" Had they somehow switched people? They had been floating around for over fifty years.

Khirson had a bandaged arm and looked like he'd been in some fist fights as well. He also looked embarrassed. "I'm not sure what happened, not really. But that both was, and was not, our new Queen. It was her body; but the mannerisms, speech patterns, bearing, and ideas were not her. It was as if someone replaced her. Swapped her mind with another."

"Did your people have that type of tech?" As far as Vas knew no one could body swap. Outside of cheap vid dramas, anyway. But the Pilthians had shown some exceedingly advanced cryo tricks that weren't around even today. Who knew what else they had?

"No, we didn't. Which means someone else developed it and managed to swap not only the Queen but all of her guards. Either that, or we were all fooled into accepting her as the new Queen fifty-plus years ago."

Pela started heading toward the med lab and everyone followed. The other two Pilthians were roughed up but didn't look in bad shape. Vas knew Pela would want to check them all out before they went anywhere. Terel had trained her well.

"Where's the *Warrior Wench?*" Pela asked. "Not that we weren't glad to see this ship come to our rescue." She flashed a smile to Ragkor and Therlian.

"Ran into some unexpected problems and Grosslyn is repairing the engine drive. If you're all good to head to medical, I'd like to get some things from Therlian."

Ragkor nodded. "I'll be back on deck heading for Home. Do you want us to track that beacon for you?"

"Good spotting." Vas laughed. She hadn't said anything, but Ragkor was a master of details. Hopefully, the Pilthian ship wasn't as thorough. "Yes, please keep an eye on them. I have an itchy feeling we haven't seen the last of them."

Pela and the Pilthians went toward the med lab, Ragkor went to the command deck, and Therlian led Vas down to her quarters.

The room looked like the nuns' rooms had back in the day. Therlian might have left the calling, but it was still a part of her. Maybe that was why she and Ragkor got along so well. They both came from regimented backgrounds but had left what should have been their life's calling.

Therlian reached into her closet and without looking pulled out a slim box. She took out a smaller box from inside it and handed it to Vas. "All of my training is there. I would start with file 2.36, that'll put you right in it."

"Thanks. I won't lie, if you had been able to do this instead, I would have pushed you into it immediately."

"I might have not argued." She grinned. "I do miss the nuns and my commitment to them. But my life has taken another direction."

Vas clapped her on the shoulder. "So has mine. I'm not sure how much contact we'll be able to make. But I will as I can. Keep an eye on Aithnea as best you can."

They got back to Home and readied Pela's shuttle along with the one Vas had come up in to go to the planet. Before she got in though, she pulled Ragkor aside. "Don't take the *Victorious Dead* to ground, stay in orbit. I trust you to keep things together, but I would suggest that any jobs that come our way go to one of the other crews. Stay near Home."

"A hunch?"

"Yeah, been getting more lately. But there's been way too much activity in our neighborhood to be good. Oh, and report the attack of an unidentified ship, looking to be of Pilthian design, to the Commonwealth. Send them any images you can scrub our fighters out of." She really didn't have a lot of faith in the Commonwealth. But like the attack by the Lethian Assembly ship, she felt someone should know. Telling them about the Hive ship might be pushing it. She'd confer with Flarik for the best way to report it but keep the Commonwealth eyes off them. Three strange attacks in a day and a half and even the Commonwealth would come out looking. "You know what? Delay the report until we're a day out. I don't want to give them another reason to come hunt me down."

"Understood. Have a good journey." Ragkor didn't salute, but Vas swore she saw his right hand twitch.

"Thank you. Take care of my company." Vas closed up the shuttle.

The trip back to Home was uneventful, but Deven and Grosslyn were both gone when she got there. And Terel was in Vas' office in the hangar and looked annoyed.

"Why are you at my desk and where is Deven?"

"I wanted to make sure that I didn't miss you. We are going after those bastards, you know that, right? You don't kill people on a peaceful medical mission." She shook out her shoulders. "Deven and Grosslyn went to go get the ship you picked. They took Bathie and Mac as well."

Like Vas, Terel had lost more than her share of friends, even other med team personnel, but not in a situation like this.

"Good, we'll need to modify it some before we leave." Vas' tone softened. "I've got a tracker on that Pilthian ship. They won't get away. Ragkor is keeping an eye on them."

"I want to find them and make them pay." Terel rocked back in the desk chair and folded her arms. She could be more stubborn than Vas when she tried.

"Then I'll be taking Pela and Tris as medical on this mission?" Vas stood and watched her friend. She needed to get some more guidance from Aithnea. It wasn't going to be fun trying to become a Keeper even with Aithnea's and Therlian's help; without help while in a strange ship was going to be a major pain in the ass.

Terel shook off her scowl. "What? Damn it, no. I want to get back out there. I do wish our new job wasn't outside of the Commonwealth, and with my comfortable med bay. But I looked over the scans. For a ship its size, the new one has a decent med bay. I'll make it even better."

"You'd better move fast. I want to be out of here as soon as we can." Vas turned to leave the office but stopped and turned back. "I have a unique situation, and maybe you can help me with it. Come with me back into the ship." There was a chance that Terel might have some ideas about Aithnea. Vas had no idea what being stuck in a holosuite would do to a person whether or not they were dead, or in limbo.

She explained it to Terel as they crossed the hangar and went into the *Warrior Wench.*

"I can't say I've ever heard of a disembodied spirit transferring itself into a holosuite, let alone getting stuck there. But I'd love to talk to her."

The ship was empty beyond a few crew working on the engines as they walked down to the holosuite.

The lights came on as Vas entered. A bit disturbing since they'd been triggered by Aithnea's presence to stay on before. "Aithnea? Are you here?" Even with the engines off the holosuite had been left powered.

No answer. Vas walked over to the computer console. It was on and a single key was flashing. The enter key. Vas looked around the suite once more. Then she hit the enter button.

"Hello, Vas," Aithnea's voice come from the computer speakers in the wall.

"Crap, you're in the computer now?"

Terel came up to the console as well. "Hello, Aithnea, I'm Terel. Nice to meet you."

"Ah! Excellent to meet you as well. Can you explain to Vas here, why my being in the computer itself as opposed to the holosuite program only is a good idea? She's bright but sometimes takes longer than necessary."

Terel laughed. "I like you already. Vas, it's a good thing. She's mobile this way. Download her program, such as it is, and take her to the new ship. It does have a small holo emitter per the posted specs. Transfer her to that and you'll have her with you."

Vas rolled her eyes. She would have sorted that out— she was just trying to put together too many pieces. "Fine. But you don't know how to get her out of the system?" She held up her hand. "Yes, this is handy and all, but the fact is that you are still trapped in a computer system. Wouldn't it be better to be reconnected to whatever plane you were on before? I might not know anything about being dead and cruising around, but I'd think being cut off from your other plane of existence would be bad."

Aithnea's sigh coming out of the wall of the holosuite

was a bit disturbing. "Well, it's not ideal, I will say that. But I still have hope that once you find the new Pirate of Boagada, my nuns and I can go to our reward."

Vas tapped a few commands into the console. "I'm downloading you onto a disk, so stay put." The disk the console spit out was the size of Vas' thumbnail, but she clipped it into her comm for safe keeping.

"That's settled." Terel shrugged and led the way out of the holosuite. "Since you're itching to go, I think I'll go get some work done in my med lab before heading home for the night."

Vas followed her out, but then turned around to the hangar. She wanted to see this new ship as soon as it came in.

She stopped by a small food stand next to the hangar, grabbed a sandwich, and went back to her office. There were a lot of details of their new job that still needed to be sorted out.

A few hours later she was tired, cranky, and annoyed. This job paid damn well, but it was harder than she'd thought at first. They were going to have to keep their cover very close to the vest. The good news was that Flarik hadn't found anything legally questionable. She heard voices in the hangar and closed everything up.

Deven, Grosslyn, and Bathie were coming out of the distant landing area and into the hangar. They didn't look happy.

"Do we have our ship or not?"

All three looked up, but only Deven kept walking toward her. "There's been a complication."

"With the ship? Then pick one of the others."

"Not with the ship. It's fine, or it will be with some more work on it."

"Work we've started right away." Grosslyn yelled from halfway across the hangar. Not a good sign that he wouldn't come closer.

"Talk to me. Now." She folded her arms and shot a glare at them. Mac was probably hiding.

Deven held up his hand. "It was no one's fault, not really. But we probably want to leave earlier rather than later."

"What?" Why was it that the worse things were, the longer the information got dragged out?

"On our way back from picking up the new ship, the Commonwealth made an announcement that they were looking for whoever blew up a Pilthian vessel. Two small fighters were seen going after it and they are working on who those ships are registered to. The information they had was sketchy and there was only a long-distance vid."

"We didn't blow it up. Therlian and I thought about it, but when that ship took off it was intact." Vas rubbed the back of her neck. "Where was it destroyed?"

"Past the Alara system."

Vas held out her hands. "You know there's no way any Flits could travel that far without support. I am pissed that someone destroyed them before Terel and I could have a talk with their new, now late, queen though."

"Someone is trying to set us up," Deven said. "Rather, set you up. The vid they had definitely looks like a pair of Flits, but it doesn't look like the Alara system of space. Of course, it's such a bad recording that it's hard to tell for sure."

"Someone knows you were out there, they destroyed the Pilthians, and now is subtly pointing toward you." Grosslyn stayed in the center of the hangar. He was still not taking chances on her annoyance level.

"I don't think that I would call a secret release to the Commonwealth subtle." Bathie walked closer to Vas. "I'll look into it, but it looks like whoever did it was watching everything from the start. They were waiting at your meet point with the shuttle."

Vas rubbed her eyes. Sleep wasn't going to be an option.

Someone was setting her and the crew up. They needed to get the *Traitor's Folly* loaded, updated, and out of here on a legitimate job before anyone could stop them. Yes, she and Deven were favored by the Commonwealth right now, at least until they decided they didn't need them as figure heads for the new Commonwealth space military. And their favor was fickle. If they traced the Flits, they'd lead back to her via the *Victorious Dead*. She returned to her office and brought out the cart with her belongings and other items she wanted off the *Warrior Wench*. "Let's go. Grosslyn, I have a list of the people I want with me on this job. Get ahold of them and tell them we leave tomorrow so they need to get back here now."

Deven stepped in alongside her. "That was quick."

"Do we have a choice?"

"Not so much," He paused. "They will eventually track it to Ragkor."

"I know, damn it. I can't send him away from here. I need him to keep the company in line." She mulled over her options until she saw her new ship.

She'd once had a derelict ship called *Defiant Ruin*. A previously crashed cruiser rebuilt out of odds and ends. It served its purpose and helped end the Asarlaí menace. It was also, formerly, the ugliest ship she'd ever seen.

Now that dubious honor belonged to the vessel on the landing pad before her. It was smaller than the *Victorious Dead*, but larger than the *Defiant Ruin*. The long nose looked out of place on anything larger than a fighter, but it was a conceit of the designers. They'd been trying to combine speed, stealth, and firepower and ended up with one of the oddest ship classes around.

And this one had been through hell and back since it hit the space lanes.

"Everything checked out?" Vas paused in front of the ship's ramp.

"Everything is fine. It's not as pretty as that gilded tart

we've been running around in." Deven took her cart and went up the ramp.

His point was good. When she'd first taken on the *Warrior Wench* its glamour had been one of the things that had annoyed her. "As long as it stays sound, we're all good." She followed Deven up.

The inside was in surprisingly good shape, which told Vas this might not have been its first deception voyage. Someone had wanted it to look bad on the outside. Most of the consoles on the command deck were within three or four years old and had been higher end at the time.

The crew quarters were decent, but a quick peek told her that her crew wouldn't be looking forward to a long trip. Like her, the size and variety of crew rooms on the *Warrior Wench* had left them spoiled.

Deven and the cart rounded a corner at the end of the hall, so Vas followed.

The captain's quarters were smaller than even the one on the *Victorious Dead*, but serviceable.

Vas looked around as Deven started moving stuff out of the cart. "What do you *really* think is going on?"

He turned away from the cart. "I think something big is happening, too many little things all pointing the same direction. All right after we come out of R&R? And how did they, whoever they are, know where you and the *Victorious Dead* were? The Pilthians, my brother, the Lethian Assembly…the Hive for crying out loud?" He ran his fingers through his hair. "There is something massive taking place, something that involves a leak among our people, or we've fallen into a vortex of unnatural coincidences."

"Which, while possible, is unlikely." Vas put her stuff away. Deven's things were already there. "What do we think? Someone was waiting for us to come out? The Lethian Assembly really seemed more focused on the Pilthian wreckage rather than us. Destroying observers to an illegal salvage wouldn't be that unthought of if they weren't supposed to be in the Commonwealth to start with. The Hive ship was specifically after us though."

"I've no idea." He flopped back on the bed. "I'm thinking we might as well stay onboard since there will be a lot of work to do if we're leaving in the morning. Is Aithnea still in the holosuite back on the *Warrior Wench?*"

Vas dropped down next to him. "Nope. She went into the main system and I have her here." She tapped her comm. "Need to get her installed on this ship. That's another thing, what in the hell cut her off from her other plane of existence? Okay, so we know most likely the Hive's net did, but why can't she get back? I'm not sure how much help she'll be on this job, but I'll need to be working on my Keeper training and it'll be handy having her for that."

Deven nodded. "I know my esper talents have been a bit off since that attack and it could be something that is affecting her. No one in the Commonwealth knows a lot about the Hive unfortunately."

Vas thought about them just staying in bed, but if Deven thought the ship needed work before it could go on this job, then they needed to make sure things got done. She leaned over and gave him a slow kiss. They'd gone from being together all the time, to barely having time alone. "So, to work we go?"

He ran his hands up her back then sighed. "Yup. I'll leave you to the holosuite, and I'll start working on the command deck. Gosta and Hrrru should be here soon to update the computer and add the library." He rolled off the bed, pulled her to her feet and kissed her longer. Vas sighed after they separated and forced herself to walk away.

She had to look at the layout twice on her way to the holosuite. For a small ship it was extremely convoluted. The holosuite would be better named the holo-closet.

But similar to what she'd seen on the command deck, the quality was good. Honestly, a holo-anything on this class of ship was a rarity.

She removed the small disk and slid it into the wall outlet. Nothing happened. "Aithnea? Are you there?" Still nothing. She started to take the disk back out, but then a hand dropped onto her shoulder. She didn't scream, but she did jump.

"That was worth the effort it took." Aithnea was behind her looking very solid.

"You're completely solid now?"

"Only if I focus. Since holo-beings are solid or not depending upon their program, I appear to have more control over that than I thought. And something is bothering you?"

Vas told her about the recent updates and her concerns.

Aithnea agreed there was a setup of some sort going on but couldn't figure it out either. Vas left her with a promise that she'd be back to start her Keeper training once they got underway.

The work on the command deck was in full swing. Mac, Deven, Gosta, Bathie, and Hrrru were upgrading and adjusting everything. Even Xsit was fussing with her communications station. Then some swearing came from an unseen person behind the nav station, and Khirson stood up, rubbing his head with his good arm.

"Not that I don't appreciate the extra help, but you're not on my list for this trip," Vas said.

"I wanted to talk to you about that, Captain." He came around the station he'd been swearing at. "I think I need to go with you." He held up his hand. "Not to find my people, or anything, but I believe that your recent issues are tied to finding us. I have a full background of almost all of the cultures in the quadrant of space you're going to. We thought that was to be our new home and the intel was fed to me while I was in cryo. I can help you."

Vas was already shaking her head. This was a small crew and adding a rare being to the mix was going to be difficult. Khirson's people weren't common anywhere.

"I've done some study," Gosta said from his mess of a console. "There are at least a few communities of Pilthians not far from where we're eventually heading to in the Nhali system. Having him with us on our pirate job could make our ruse of being from that area more plausible. In fact, the pirates we're meeting with have a Pilthian in their ranks—the woman leading this conclave. I might have already communicated to them that we had one as well." Gosta had found a place for them to start looking for whoever was behind the Dackon Industries thefts—a bi-annual gathering of pirates under a flag of truce. They convened to discuss problems within their scattered ranks.

Vas looked from him to Deven to Khirson. They'd planned this. Not sure when, but they had.

"Logically presented. Fine. Make up a viable cover story as to why you joined this crew of pirates and have Terel put a stim cast on that arm; less noticeable than it being in a sling." She held up her hand. "But keep in mind that finding information on the Pirate of Boagada as well as who has been robbing our clients are the two top priorities."

An hour later, Vas had finished setting up the small captain's ready room as good as it could get when her comm pinged. Grosslyn's pissed-off voice wasn't what she'd expected.

"Captain, Leil and Loxianth escaped lockup and took off in that derelict star jumper ship Mac found a few months ago." Grosslyn was so pissed she could hear the growl in his words.

"What? How in the hell did they get out? And that ship wasn't able to fly unassisted."

"We think they planned it; they knew about that ship.

Someone got them out of jail, then three of them got on the ship and took off."

On a ship that had been found months before any of this started. A chill hit Vas; that put everything into a different level of not good. "Who was the third?"

"Not sure. They knew enough to scramble our cameras."

"Shit." Someone had a longer-range plan than they thought. Did they plant a beat-up ship near their airspace on the chance that Vas' people would bring it in? That was scary planning. "Are the brothers still locked up?" Ome was in heavier security, but so had been Leil and Loxianth. The other two had been in a holding tank until she figured out where to send them.

Grosslyn came back a moment later swearing. "Ome is missing. Most likely he's the third, but he knew an awful lot about our systems to do what he did."

Vas rubbed her temples. He'd been the one behind his brothers working with her two years ago getting that ship and the scrolls. He obviously had abilities. Damn it. Deven might have seriously underestimated his asshole brother—but even when he threatened her life, she'd underestimated Ome.

"He played me."

"Captain?" Grosslyn asked.

"Nothing, simply chewing myself out. That star jumper ship was old, it should be easy to track even if they modified it. Find it."

Vas went to the deck and told her crew what happened.

Grosslyn came back a half hour later. "I've tracked what gates they went through, but it's worse than we thought, Captain. They broke into our system and downloaded copies of our data on the planetary defenses—both the guns and the cloak. The information is still heavily scrambled; Marli laid massive security codes on it, but if they keep it, they can take their time breaking it." He sent over the info on the gates they'd gone through—well, the first three, after that tracking was impossible. Directly out of the Commonwealth and toward the Nhali sector.

"Damn it, we have to go after them. Replicating those weapons and Marli's shield could be horrific." Marli had modified the guns enough that they wouldn't be mistaken for the original Commonwealth ones, and the shield was her invention. If either were mass produced it could mean a quick demise for entire quadrants.

"We have that job," Gosta said half-heartedly.

"That is in the same general direction." Vas held up her hand. "Look, I know we have a job, and Aithnea has her own thing we need to do, but right now we need to catch those three."

"I agree," Deven said. His jaw was still so tight it looked ready to snap, and he was probably making a permanent dent in the back of his chair where he was grabbing it. "We need to stop my brother. I misjudged how far he would go. We need to get him before more people are killed."

Vas knew he was probably more upset at his own misjudgment than he was about Leil. It was one thing to think your brother was a con man, another to think he might be behind something much nastier.

"We need to be out of here in an hour max. I want all security increased on everything in the shipyard and the ships themselves. Plus, put the two remaining brothers in high-risk lockup. We've no idea if there were other contingency plans in place."

A little under an hour later, the *Traitor's Folly* was decked out and heading toward the Lixia gate. Vas hated rushing prepping time, but they'd been caught by something larger and messier than she expected, and they needed to get those plans back.

Mac had the ship at full speed—not as fast as the *Warrior Wench*—when an alarm broke out.

"Captain! We're taking fire!"

A sideways rattle shook the ship and more alarms sounded. "Mac! Get us to the gate now!" Another blow hit the ship and the lights flickered.

CHAPTER SEVENTEEN

VAS SWORE AS THEY CAME out of the gate. Whatever that damn ship had fired at them had come too close. She wasn't sure whether it had been aiming at the *Traitor's Folly* or the gate—either could have been horrific.

"Stations?" The lights on the command deck were on emergency low and the way the ship was bouncing and rocking meant the dampeners were off as well.

One by one the crew checked in. Xsit sounded the most upset but she sounded more pissed than injured.

"Med is okay, tossed about, but intact," Terel called in.

"I assume whatever just happened was not the normal behavior for this vessel?" Flarik called up from her quarters. "I am okay, however."

Deven and Gosta worked on the main console and got the ship lights to hold and the bouncing to stop as all of her people responded.

"Do we know what in the hell attacked us?" Vas knew the sensors on the ship were far inferior to those of the *Warrior Wench,* but they still shouldn't have been that blind. They had barely picked up the ship before it fired. The fact that nothing followed them through the gate could mean they thought they'd destroyed the *Traitor's Folly* or the gate. "Did they have some sort of cloak?" Cloaking technology was still an infant science and no one except the Asarlaí had been able to make it work. That didn't mean that hadn't changed. The fact that she had a hidden planet meant it was possible. Of course, the planet didn't move beyond rotation. All prior tests of cloaks failed once the cloaked item moved significantly.

"I don't think it was a cloak, Captain." Khirson responded, as he studied the screen at his console. "They jumped into our viewing range quickly, but we didn't pick them up until they fired. It was based on speed."

"I agree," Gosta said. If he was upset at someone else getting the jump on him about information, he didn't show it. "Plus, there are odd limits on the tracking systems for this ship. Things I hadn't noticed previously." *That* he did look upset about.

"I need you to figure out what's messed up with this ship, and who attacked us." She tapped her comm to hit the relay to Ragkor. They wouldn't use it much once they got further out, but she needed to touch base. "Ragkor? We were attacked on the way out. They either shot at us directly or the Lixia gate."

Ragkor was silent for a moment, or mostly. He kept his swearing under his breath and hard to hear, but it was there. "We'll head out and look at the gate, but sensors aren't reading any extra ships in the area. We can scan the buoys and see what information we can get, but they aren't that close to the gate."

"They aren't, but they might have recorded something. We didn't even pick up on this bastard until he was on top of us. Make sure to send out regular recon, far enough out from Home that it's not clear what they are protecting but keep eyes out." She rubbed the back of her neck. "And have Grosslyn keep a gunner on station at all times. I might be paranoid, but I don't like all this recent activity around our corner of the Commonwealth."

They needed to make a few more jumps, but because she wanted them to appear to be coming from anywhere other than the Commonwealth, they needed to use different gates. Never assume that someone wasn't watching you. That paranoia had kept her and her crew alive a lot longer than many.

By the time they were ready for the last jump out of Commonwealth space, Deven, Gosta, Bathie, and Khirson had figured out the odd glitch. Or rather, glitches.

"Then the range was deliberately modified?" Vas looked at their results. There were limits in the range of sensors, weapons, and audio. None of which had kicked in until five hours earlier. If she wasn't worried about this being a setup before, she sure as hell was now. They'd gone over this ship too well to have missed that. Granted, time was rushed, but her crew was good.

"That's what it looks like." Deven pulled up another schematic. "Delayed coil degradation. Five hours ago this coil disintegrated, which led to a cascade of events. None of which were good."

"Damn it. I need everything fixed and a full diagnostic on each system. Gosta, if you were going to destroy this ship, how would you do it? I want you to check everything that you can think of. We should assume this ship was a setup as well and might have been connected to the job offer, or the intel that was passed along." He was her best hacker, so hopefully if there were any other sneaky gifts left behind, he'd find them. "Deven, ready room. Rest of you, run more checks on your systems."

Deven followed her in. Like everything on this ship, the captain's ready room was small. But there was a desk, two chairs, and more importantly, it was cut off from the crew. One of her private checks had been to scan for listening or video devices in the ready room and their quarters.

"How in the hell did someone know we'd be buying this ship? How did someone know where we'd be meeting Pela's shuttle?"

He ran his hand through his hair. "No idea, but we've definitely got a leak."

"I trust the people who were with us on the *Warrior Wench* with my life, let alone the portion of them who are here."

"I do as well. But someone very close to us is leaking information."

"And we'll find who it is. But who is it being leaked to? We've been out of things for months. And before that, the entire Commonwealth was going to hell. Why is someone coming after us now, and how?"

"Considering that most of our issues so far, even the Pilthians, were not from the Commonwealth, I'd say we attracted some unwelcome attention outside of the Commonwealth."

"Agreed. But when?"

"Could be when we picked up the Pilthians? Our prisoners?"

"I don't think so. We would have picked up any devices on our scans. Could we have someone who isn't who we think?" She raised a hand. "Yes, hiding like that is difficult, but not impossible, even with our current scanning. As our friend Loxianth showed. Her tech wasn't picked up when she came into the ship. Hell, *she* wasn't picked up."

"True," Deven said. "I looked at her bracelet. Old-school masker. Very limited, only could be used by one person to mimic a single person. I tried working on it to see if I could make it change me, but no. It's so old our system didn't scan for it."

Vas found a few more select swear words. "Someone could have been on the *Warrior Wench* not as themselves." It wasn't a question. They had a spy, and they might still. Ome might have been the one who got Leil and Loxianth out, but there could have been someone else involved. She hit her comm to call Terel. "We have records of full blood work for everyone on board, right?"

"Odd question, but I assume it relates to our recent attack? Yes, I do. Even Khirson, from my first tests."

"Good. I'm going to have everyone report down

there—tell me if anyone acts oddly or something doesn't match. Or if markers indicate a clone." Thanks to the prior engagement with a few real clones, Terel had the ability to track the subtle differences in cloned blood. Vas cut her comm and turned to Deven. "Pretty sure it's not you or me, but we lead by example." She held out her arm. "After you."

He tipped his head and went out to the command deck.

Vas did an all-ship call. "We have word of a possible contagion onboard. Things were damaged in that attack that might cause a risk. We've locked it down, but I need everyone to report to the med lab. Terel will call you down as she's ready. Deven and I will go first."

Gosta narrowed his eyes but nodded.

Vas and Deven went down to the med lab.

"Welcome to my little home." Terel motioned to the three med beds along the wall and a bank of older machines. Newer lab machines that Vas knew she'd brought in from the *Warrior Wench* crowded out into the hall.

"Can you put all the crew's blood profiles on the screen?" The only bare wall was almost entirely covered by an old-school medical screen. It could project anything from the connected machines.

Terel shrugged but did so. The profiles meant nothing to Vas, but it would be clear if either Terel's or Deven's blood didn't match immediately.

Vas took a hypo and held it up to Terel. "Sorry, but please draw some blood, and run it through the scanner." She had a hard time believing anyone on this crew wasn't who she thought they were, but it would be worse if it was Terel or Deven.

Terel held her look for a second, then nodded, took a hypo draw, and sent it to the scanner. All in a single motion. She didn't even watch as the numbers showed on the screen. An exact blood match.

Vas let out a breath then held her arm up. The numbers of the blood samples matched.

Deven did the same. Again, his blood matched.

"Now can you tell me why we're doing this?" Terel set up rows of hypos each labeled with a crew member's name. "It would be helpful if I knew what to look for."

"We have a leak. It could have been someone left behind on Home, and once I've cleared this ship, I want you to send a coded message to med assistant Tris on Home. Have him scan a sample of his own blood first while you watch; make sure who he is. Then have him test everyone who was on the *Warrior Wench* but didn't come with us." She broke down what had happened.

Terel didn't swear much, but she was increasing the frequency and creativity. "I agree, someone isn't who we thought they were. But if our ship was going to explode, what kind of person would hide themselves on it?"

"A zealot," Deven said. "I agree they probably aren't on this ship. But we need to be sure. Things we didn't think were related now appear to be so. We're not sure how."

Terel took a few deep breaths to settle herself into her normally neutral medical persona. "Who will be next?"

"I want to hit the people with the most access first. Gosta, Flarik, and Mac will be next. And Khirson, I want him looked at quickly. Then call the rest down until you get everyone. Oh, keep Flarik here once she's cleared. Just in case we do have a zealot who's unhappy about not blowing up."

Terel nodded and Vas and Deven left.

"I know you don't like to talk about him," Vas said as they walked to the lift. "But is this behavior even remotely like your brother? No offense, but he came across more as sniveling con man than spy."

Deven ran his hand through his hair. "He never was bright. Either he suddenly gained some brain power, or someone is good at manipulating him. My money is on the latter. Ome and Loxianth were clearly not what they appeared."

"Agreed. But what do they have in common?"

"Power? Revenge? Loxianth was pretty bitter. I reviewed the vid of you questioning her—she was sincerely upset."

"Ome is our wild card. He knows about the job his brothers and I did. He probably knows more than even Aithnea about what went on. And the fact that both the scrolls and the ship are missing isn't good."

"True. I'd say he was lying but Aithnea said the same about both." The lift opened on the deck where Mac, Khirson, and Gosta switched place with them to head down to the med lab. None of them looked happy, but none of them looked like a deranged zealot either.

Deven waited until the door closed on them. There was no one left on the small bridge. "What now, boss?"

"I think once we've made sure the leak isn't one of our crew, and get a few more jumps under us, we try to find out where those assholes went and what is going on with the pirates." She got into the command chair. It wasn't bad, fairly average for these chairs, but she already missed her specialty one back on the *Warrior Wench*.

Deven settled into his station. "And get your Keeper training in."

Vas grimaced. She well and truly wanted to set Aithnea and her people free, let them go to their reward after death. There was no doubt they deserved it. But she was not looking forward to going through the training—even if it was extremely expedited.

The door opened and Mac and Gosta came back on deck.

"Where's Khirson?" She hadn't heard anything from Terel, but she'd expected him to come back up.

"Terel had to redo his stim cast. His metabolism is still off from the cryo, so it was already cracking. She said to tell you all of us were fine." Gosta didn't look to her as he went to his station, but Vas could feel his unspoken questions.

"We have a leak," she said, which got both to turn to her immediately. "There's no other way to explain what's been going on. We're not sure where it came from but Loxianth had been using crude shifter tech to look like Marli—tech we never picked up—we're checking the blood work of everyone."

Mac raised an eyebrow.

"Yes, including Terel, myself, and Deven. Flarik stayed in the med lab?"

"Once her results came back, Terel insisted. She told her after we left, right?"

"I would assume so. This is a small ship, so we need to keep it down until everyone has been checked. Now, is there anything you can do to make us look more like pirates? We need to track Leil as best we can right now, but the persona for this job will help keep us under the radar while we do that." The last bit was directed at both of them and even Gosta smiled at that. Vas knew he wasn't upset at having to be tested, but he wanted to have known about it. A new job would get him back on track.

"I can make some of the external functions look more hodgepodge, build up a history." Gosta was already doing it as she watched. Pirates were all different, obviously, but there were some shared traits that would let other pirates know what they were. Those changed all the time so that authorities of various worlds couldn't also find out who they were, but Vas had faith in Gosta's searching abilities.

Mac leaned back. "We'll also need to look like pirates in person though. This gathering is in person, on the planet, not on ships, right? I have some ideas." He started pulling through files on his second screen.

Vas leaned toward Deven before he could speak. "Yes, I get to wear an eye patch. No, you can't stop me."

He laughed. "I was afraid you'd go there. Fine, but I'm not following suit. Some tats might be nice though."

"An eye patch?" Gosta looked up at their conversation.

"Back in the old days, when health-care was rare, pirates made do with whatever injuries they got along the way. Eye patches were common." Vas started pulling up her own records. They might as well get ready here. They had gone through enough gates that if anything did come through their original gate after them, they would have a hard time following.

"I know, Captain. But why are you so excited about getting to wear one?" Gosta was still entering information into his system but was also looking very confused.

Deven beat her in answering. "When we first met, she'd been wearing one because she thought it made her look fierce." He laughed. "I convinced her it wasn't necessary. It was right before you joined us, Gosta."

Vas held out her hands. "I was young, it seemed like no one would take me seriously."

"The eye patch worked?" Mac looked up dubiously.

"No. Just made her look like a little space princess playing dress-up." Deven gave her a wink.

"Okay, it might not have been the best idea. But I am wearing it on this job. I'm bitch enough to back it up now."

Khirson and Flarik came back on deck. His stim cast was a bit more solid now. Made it more noticeable, but hopefully he wouldn't crack through it again.

"According to Terel, the crew is all who we think we are." Flarik took over the science station she'd claimed as her own. She was a lawyer, not a trained scientist, but she was smart enough to take any station she wanted. "I presume we are running a full debugging?"

"Once I was certain we didn't have an imposter on board, that was next on the agenda." Vas turned to Gosta. "Please run any and all forms of scans, debugging pro-

grams, and anything you can think of that weren't part
of the initial run. Send a coded message to Grosslyn as
well." She sent over the message she wanted sent. Grosslyn would be instructed to call her back in ten minutes
on her private comm. She'd be in the med lab and make
him do the test live. Once he was clear, he'd go after the
rest of her crew.

There was a connection between the events of the past
few days, if only she could figure out what in the hell it
was.

"We've lost Leil's ship." Xsit had been tracking for him.
"They came through here, but I can't tell where they
went after that. There seem to be trails to both gates."
There were two gates in the system they were in, but it
wasn't a difficult trick to loop through and leave multiple
trails.

"Thank you, Xsit. Everyone keep scanning. We'll go
toward the pirate gathering and find out who is taking
out Dackon Industries ships. Unless we get a bite on
where Leil and the others went."

Mac broke her out of her thoughts. "Are we ready to
keep jumping? I have a great set of gates lined up, and
there's no way anyone can figure out where we're coming from." He was practically dancing his fingers on the
control pad. While there wasn't the pilot sling that the
Warrior Wench had, the pilot station was exceptionally up
to date.

"Not until we're certain we're bug free." She held up
her hand when Gosta started to complain. "I know you
would have searched initially, but someone fooled us
with that degrading coil. We can't chance that they did
something else too."

"I don't understand what they were after. They set us
up to take this vessel, then had it rigged so that we would
take a fatal hit when we went for the first gate?" Flarik
scowled. "Why not put a bomb on board?"

"We'd detect the bomb," Deven said. "We wouldn't have been looking for something that was literally designed to break-down at a set time. The cascade impact from that coil was impressive."

Khirson had been silent but he didn't look happy. "Do you have the specifics of the degrading coil as you called it?"

Deven nodded and sent the image to the main screen. Vas wasn't one to go taking things like that apart, but what it did and what it was designed to do was impressive. And not something she'd heard of before.

Khirson walked closer to the large screen, shaking his head as he did. "We called those Daling devices. They were designed to do as you said, but could do so much more." He waved toward the bottom right corner. "This isn't good. See here? Not only would it kill any system you connected to it on a delay, but it would also continue going after systems if it failed." He turned to Deven. "We have to get this off this ship. I recognize the pattern on this one. I know who designed it." He ran to the lift. The specs clearly showed the device had been put in the engineering side access.

"Who did this?" Vas asked as she followed.

He held the door for Vas and Deven to join him. Flarik joining them hadn't been his intention it appeared, but she darted in as well.

"I don't know who installed it. But I know who created it." His face was grim as he looked at them all carefully. "Me."

CHAPTER EIGHTEEN

VAS HAD HER BLASTER OUT and aimed at his head. "Do you wish to clarify?"

Neither Deven nor Flarik had pulled out weapons. The lift wasn't big enough if they all had. But they didn't need them.

Khirson took a deep breath. "I didn't place it on this ship. I have no wish to die, thank you. But I made that specific one. As I looked at the version on the screen, I saw one of my marks. Before my wife died, and I was selected for the colony, I was an engineer."

Vas lowered her blaster but kept it out. "And someone is using your fifty-plus-year-old toy to try and take us out?"

"I think we can guess who: our friend Loxianth. But again, we're back to what was her purpose?" Flarik shook her head. "It can't be to destroy Khirson since you joined us at the last minute. So there's something about this specific crew she wants to remove."

"Or if they planned the theft of our cloak and gun specs, she wanted to make sure we couldn't stop them." Vas swore. There were too many things going on, and many of them appeared to have been planned while she was still resting on a beach.

"I'm afraid I have no idea as to her true motivation. And she'd be the only one I can think of who would have access to one of these devices," Khirson said.

They reached the engineering level and Vas held open the lift doors. "And you didn't have to tell us that was your mark. Now if you can get this thing off my ship, we'll be ready to move forward."

Khirson moved out of the lift but let Deven take the lead down the corridor. Vas and Flarik followed.

"I think we should be able to disengage it." Khirson waited until Deven opened the access corridor before he looked in. "Well, except for that." He stepped back so Deven and Vas could see inside.

There was the device—it looked exactly like the image Deven had picked up from the internal cameras. What the cameras didn't show was the bomb attached to it. Whoever planted it knew exactly what the camera's range would be.

"*That* is definitely not one of my designs." Khirson stepped further back and stayed there.

Deven moved in closer. "It's a Jolian mine. Converted to work off a ship's systems and the coil device." He pointed to where the mine was tied to the small Pilthian device. "Damn that bastard."

Flarik leaned in to see, then pulled back. Vas took his word for it. Jolian mines were outlawed in the Commonwealth for being too dangerous and unpredictable. The transport of them caused more deaths than the use of them did.

"Leil?" Vas was beginning to wonder if Leil was going to turn out worse than her own brother. He still had a way to go on that, but he was trying.

"Probably. Or your friend Ome or his brothers. And this thing is old; not as old as Khirson's creation, but it is old. It would have come from outside the Commonwealth most likely." He looked back at them. "I'd say to stay back but if I can't disarm this it won't matter."

"And you know I wouldn't do it anyway." Vas stayed where she was.

He flashed her a grin. "That too." He took a few deep breaths, then went back into the corridor.

Vas could still see him although most of what he was

working on was blocked by his body. Each movement he made was measured and slow. She noticed that his breathing had also slowed down, something she'd seen him do when he meditated. Clearly, she might need to reconsider meditating.

It felt like an hour, but the chrono outside the corridor said only two minutes had passed. Even so, Deven had a fine sheen of sweat on his forehead when he turned to them.

"The mine is neutralized." He stepped away and motioned to Khirson. "This part is all yours."

Khirson nodded and took Deven's place. He worked silently but took longer than Deven. Finally, he came out holding the device. "We need to space this immediately." He looked far more worried than he had been going in.

Vas ran to the lift. Khirson followed but kept a slow measured pace. "Is something else wrong?"

Everyone quickly got into the lift with Khirson in the middle.

He licked his lips. "This was intended for me. I don't know how they knew I would be joining you on this trip, but this was added with haste and with the intention that I would try to disconnect it. You not only need to send it into space—I need to go as well."

"What?" Vas looked around him, but he was protectively holding the device.

He lifted his arm a tiny bit but kept everything else still. "It was coded to me. Either it would destroy this ship, or it would destroy me." One of the wires from the device had stabbed itself into his good arm. It had to have hurt like hell when it happened, yet Khirson hadn't even flinched.

"An attack bomb? Why would you have made something to do that?" Flarik looked both fascinated and disturbed.

"This wasn't my design and it's so old I didn't even

think to look for it. Long ago, before we became civilized, my people were very good at finding new ways to destroy each other. These were called kill leashes. If someone succeeded in disarming a weapon, they would still be killed." He looked to Vas. "You will have to space me with it, or this ship will be destroyed. There's no other way."

"There has to be something." Vas looked to Flarik and Deven, two of the three smartest people she knew. Neither looked hopeful. "You two escort him to the hatch, but do not let him out until I say so." She held up her hand when Khirson looked ready to argue. "My ship, my rules. I'm going to ask Gosta. You three will wait." She put a lot of emphasis on that last word.

Flarik nodded. "I'll make sure they do." She narrowed her eyes at the men as if daring them to go against her.

"Thank you." Vas got off the lift at the command deck and the doors shut behind her.

Gosta and Mac were debating something but stopped when she came on the deck.

"Are we safe now?" Mac was anxious to impress everyone with his creative gate hopping. Vas hoped they got to do it.

"Not at all." Vas went to Gosta's station. She could have called him on the comm, but she wanted to be able to talk honestly about the situation without Khirson hearing. "We have a serious problem. Can you pull up the cameras outside the engineering corridor and inside the lift? Grab the recordings from a few minutes ago. Focus on Khirson, his arm, and that thing sticking into it."

Mac got out of his chair and came over. He stayed silent but there were a million questions in his eyes.

Gosta quickly and silently pulled up the camera vids. Then he started swearing. It was low, and in a language Vas wasn't familiar with, but he was definitely swearing. "A Pilthian kill leash? Really? How archaic." He pulled up data on two monitors at once, switching between those two and the small replay of the camera in one corner of a screen.

"Anything?" Vas knew Flarik would keep Deven and Khirson from doing anything stupid, but that device could explode at any time. Not even the iron will of a Wavian could stop that.

"Not yet...yes." He looked up and gave her his very scary success smile. Because of the sharp angles of his long face, he always looked on the edge of mania when he was extremely happy.

Vas never told him that.

Gosta tapped his comm. "Deven? We need to get a helmet and tether collar on Khirson immediately. Then shove him and the device out the airlock. According to my research, space will cause the leash to immediately retract. Then you grab Khirson and bring him in before he dies, or it explodes. I'm certain that Mac will be able to get us far enough away before that device blows up."

"We don't have the arm on this ship." Vas knew they would be missing the perks of their former ship. The *Warrior Wench* had an arm that could reach out and grab things in space.

"I know," Gosta paused. "Someone will need to go out with him in a full suit obviously. Then both will be pulled in by the third."

Both Deven and Flarik said "I'll go" at the same moment.

"It makes more sense that I go, Captain." Flarik sounded like she was already putting on a suit. "Deven would be better equipped to pull us in if there are complications."

"Vas—"

She cut him off. "Sorry, Deven, I agree with Flarik. Besides, she probably beat you into the suit."

A loud sigh. "She did. I've got Khirson in the helmet and tether, Flarik is fully suited and also with a tether. I'm stepping behind the shield and getting my own suit on."

A few moments later an alert on Gosta's screen indicated an open airlock.

Vas heard noises but none of them sounded deadly, so that was good. Two minutes later, the airlock showed shut. "Are all of you inside?" Mac was back at his station waiting to hit the command to get out of here.

"Yes. Go. And we'll need Terel down here for Khirson." Deven must have had to work to get them both in; he was uncharacteristically out of breath.

Vas nodded to Mac. "You heard the man. Just get us out of this space. No gates yet if you please."

Mac shrugged and they took off.

"I'm on my way down there, Captain," Terel called up. "If you'd asked, I might have found a less risky option."

"In the minutes that we had?"

Terel's silence was her surrender. Vas knew Khirson would have taken some damage; exposure to space without full protection was fairly detrimental to most oxygen-breathing life forms. But while Deven sounded winded, he didn't sound like things were worse than expected.

Vas kept the sensors on the location where they'd left the bomb. It exploded a lot faster than she would have hoped.

"Any damage from debris?" The device was a tiny thing, but even the smallest bit of metal could bring down a starship if it hit it wrong.

Bathie called up from engineering. "Nothing that I'm seeing."

Gosta was now watching three screens at once. "It doesn't appear that anything came this far. But it was a near thing."

"Too near. If Khirson hadn't recognized it, we'd be back there in bits."

"If he hadn't been here, they might not have tried to

blow us up," Mac said.

Vas shook her head. "I'm not certain. Even I didn't know he was joining us until right before we left. The use of his own weapon might have been convenience as well as irony. That leash could have attacked any of us who tried to disarm it. We can't assume."

Gosta nodded then went back to gathering data as Mac zipped through gates. "Agreed."

Deven and Flarik came back on deck a half hour later, neither looking worse for wear.

Vas looked up from the plans she had on her screen. They would proceed with their job while keeping an eye out for Leil and Loxianth. The quality of people they would be with at this pirate conclave might help with that. And tracking information on the last Pirate of Boagada and who might have killed him. "I take it that since we are all still here, including Khirson, everything went as planned?"

Flarik looked to Deven but went silently to her station.

"It almost didn't," he said. "Khirson fought being brought in. Flarik had to strike him before I could pull them back. As soon as the leash released, he tried to head out into space."

"What? Why? That's suicide." Vas had seen people near the end before, where they felt that was their only option. There were usually signs, ones she hadn't seen with him. "Do you think it was a reaction to cold sickness? An extremely delayed reaction?"

Cold sickness was one of the drawbacks of cryosleep. It could impact cognitive functions in different ways. But usually not this long after being woken up.

"I'm not a doctor; mind, or body, but I would say no," Flarik said. "He seemed fine as we readied ourselves to go out there. It was when I went to take hold of him after it released. I've rarely seen that look of terror on anyone's face, but it wasn't directed at me. I grabbed him, and luckily Deven was able to pull us in. But Khirson fought it."

Vas hit her comm to the med lab. "Terel? How's our patient?"

"Unconscious. His vitals are slow, but there. I've got him in the controlled bio-bed to try to bring everything back up to normal. That thing did a serious number on his arm. He might end up being in two casts."

"That won't make for a good pirate, and thanks to Gosta we should have a Pilthian on crew. Let me know when he wakes up. Oh, and keep restraints on him. He may recover and be fine, but there was some odd behavior on his space adventure. He seemed to be terrified and was trying to get away from the ship. I don't want that to be an issue later."

"That would be an extremely delayed reaction, but then he was in cryo for over fifty years. I'll keep an eye on him, restraints and possibly a guard. I'll keep you updated."

Vas turned to the deck crew. "People, we aren't off to a good start on this job. We don't know where the leak is coming from, we don't know what Leil and Loxianth's real plan is or where they went, and I really have no idea where the location of the last Pirate of Boagada is." The job they'd been hired for was becoming lower on the list at this point.

Deven nodded. "We need to wait and see what's happened to Khirson, although I think we need to have a plan if he can't go in. I'm not blue, but I can fake it. There are chemicals that Terel can mix that will make my skin blue, and add hair extensions. We can mimic Khirson's tats as well. And I am non-Commonwealth so can answer many of this pirate's questions. They never asked to speak to Khirson nor about where he came from, when we got this job."

Vas let out a sigh. "That's a damn good backup plan. But I was counting on both of you to be enough non-Commonwealth for the pirate leading this meeting. Humans are everywhere, but we're more found in the Commonwealth."

"There is a flock of my people, rebels and misfits, who have lived on a large moon out in the Alitar sector for a hundred years or so. I can claim allegiance with them," Flarik said thoughtfully.

Although Flarik was a deadly fighter, Vas was planning on her to be the legal power behind everything. But having her out front as a rebel Wavian might help.

"Can you not look and sound like a lawyer? Because that would be a giveaway."

The feathers on the back of Flarik's head ruffled up and she lowered her forehead so her narrowed eyes were looking up and half lidded. "I sound how I want." There were odd guttural stops that Vas had never heard a Wavian use.

"That works."

"That is amazing." Gosta was wide-eyed as he watched Flarik shake off her transformation. "That is the Carathio dialect exactly. Where did you learn it so well?"

Vas had no idea who the Carathio people were nor what their dialect was symbolic of. She liked that Flarik didn't sound like a lawyer.

Flarik resumed her seat and primly folded her hands in front of her. "I grew up a bit rougher than what you see today. I might have run with some Slig gangs."

Now Vas' eyes went wide. "What? The Sligs are some of the worst pirates out there. They kill everyone." The fact Flarik had that in her past would come in very handy when dealing with the people who were hiring them for this job. It also scared the hell out of her.

Flarik shrugged. "Not as often as they let people think. Many people they attacked weren't nice to begin with. Anyone found who was an ass, but not a complete waste, was given a partial mind-wipe and left on one of the agro planets. It was a short rebellious phase." She looked at her hands and scowled. "I'll change my feather color, however. White feathers would be far too noticeable on any sort of Slig mission."

"What color did you wear when you were in the gangs?" Vas was very curious as to how Flarik was going to look once she got into character. Like most merc companies, Vas knew the background that was immediately pertinent to the job she was hiring someone for. And what they felt like disclosing. This was a side of Flarik she never knew existed.

"This." Flarik held up her arm and the feathers turned to a heavy green with dark purple along the shaft of each feather. The result was striking. Flarik finally shook her arm and the feathers went back to white.

"That is very impressive," Deven said. "I know it's not easy to change like that."

"It is not. We're all born a dusky brown color. White was my hatchling house, so I reverted to that out of ease. It will take me a few hours to change my feathers completely, so if you don't mind." She stood, nodded to everyone, and left the deck.

"You never really do know people, do you?" Gosta still seemed stunned.

"No, you don't." Vas turned to Deven. "Worst case, you fill in for Khirson, and Flarik steps in as our second exotic."

"Probably wouldn't be a bad idea for me to plan on going Pilthian either way. Even if we can get Khirson up and with at least one arm. Having two Pilthians would probably make the woman behind the pirate conclave very happy."

"How far are we from the gate, Mac? Let's get a few hops in, then get our gear on and head in to meet these pirates."

"Not far at all. And I have the perfect place for us to

rest and get ready, too." Mac set the coordinates for getting into whatever elaborate gate hopping plan he had.

Vas went over the data on the coil device, the bomb, and the leash. Normally she'd go into her ready room where she could think about these connections in private. But the ready room on this ship was so small she didn't feel comfortable in it. Working at it from her chair was easier, especially with the large number of images. Gosta had scanned every single angle of the event at least a dozen times.

There was nothing unique about any of them, aside from their age. Not only was Khirson's invention over fifty years old, but the leash was also of similar age and the bomb had been almost as old as Deven. And all of them looked to be in perfect shape. She'd seen a stockpile of perfectly protected and very old weapons a year back. Aithnea had led her to a stash from the nuns. Right after she'd been killed.

She looked up as the night shift came on deck. She hadn't noticed the time while she was thinking. Mac had locked them into orbit around a nice desolate moon. Good enough for her. With a wave to Bathie, Vas left the deck.

Deven was already gone from their room, but she recalled him saying he was going to visit Khirson and study his markings. Vas wanted to speak to Aithnea before heading for bed.

The holosuite was too closet sized without a program running so Vas called up a forest scene. Lots of trees clumped together made her nervous if they were on a job, but on their own she found she enjoyed them.

She'd figured calling up a scene would bring Aithnea out, but nothing stirred beyond the hologram leaves in the made-up wind.

"Aithnea? Can you come out?"

Silence. Vas pulled up the computer panel and entered a

few commands that should bring Aithnea out. Still nothing.

"Hrrru? Can you scan the data system for the holo-suite for any abnormalities?" She'd almost asked Gosta but if he was still up there, she was going to ignore him. He needed to take sleep breaks too and often worked through his down time.

"Aye, Captain." From the pause in his voice, Hrrru was questioning why she was calling him instead of Gosta, which meant Gosta was still on the bridge.

"And tell Gosta to get some rest. Captain's orders." She knew he loved getting caught up in mysteries, they both did. But they were also heading into a job and she needed her people at their best.

"But, Captain, I think I've found some interesting connections." That tone didn't bode well for him sleeping at any time soon.

"Gosta, is it related to anything that will try to kill us while you get some sleep?"

Silence, then finally, "No. But it is interesting." He sounded like a petulant schoolboy having to put away his favorite toy. Which wasn't too far off the mark.

"I know, but it's crucial that you are at your best tomorrow. With Flarik going in as a fighter, you get to confirm our contract for the conclave." They were already checked and rechecked, but Vas always liked Flarik to make an appearance in official lawyer form at the start of a job. Gosta wasn't a lawyer, but he probably knew about laws in various systems almost as much as Flarik did.

"Understood." At least his tone was resigned. He would never risk the lives of the crew, even if it meant he had to go sleep.

Hrrru came back on. "The holo system looks fine now, but the logs show it had a burst of energy, then shut off for a few seconds right when we took those hits. All the systems are running. Do you want me to clean the system?"

"No, thank you, not right now." This wasn't the time to explain who was theoretically undead and living in the holosuite at this time. There was no way to know what a system purge could do to her.

"Understood." Hrrru's voice dropped. "And Master Gosta has left the deck as you ordered. I believe he might have even yawned." Hrrru and Gosta shared a number of interests, with mysteries and puzzles being first and foremost. But Hrrru clearly agreed with Vas' assessment of Gosta's need to sleep.

"Thank you, Hrrru."

Vas started to run a lower-level check, one using the frequency that Aithnea had been on when she was on the chip in her comm.

"How am I here?" Aithnea's voice from behind a few holo trees startled her.

"Aithnea?"

Aithnea drifted over through the trees looking more than a little confused.

"Yes, how am I here? Where am I?"

This wasn't good.

"We're on the new ship, *Traitor's Folly,* in the Nhali system. I talked to you a few hours ago."

Aithnea's hologram was wispy, as if she wasn't holding it together. "I don't recall anything. It's fuzzy."

"Can you sense yourself in the other plane?" This was worrying. Aithnea needed to help her become a Keeper so they could find the Pirate of Boagada, and for that she needed Aithnea to be functioning.

"Of course I can. I can't figure out why I'm in this machine instead of in your head."

Vas ran her fingers through her bangs. "You'd found a way to get into the holo system on my ship. Then we were attacked by a Hive ship with a net and you were cut off. I was able to move you to this ship." She narrowed her eyes but Aithnea looked a little more solid. "You do recall almost exploding my head and the fact I have to become a Keeper to find the Pirate of Boagada so you and your sisters can all get out of limbo?"

Aithnea was definitely more solid. She started pacing around the trees instead of through them. Although even as a solid hologram she could have gone through them. "I do. Well, some of it." She waved her hand and sat down in the chair that appeared. "Now, that is handy." She looked down at the seat. "I recall being in your head, but there is something or someone who has interfered with my other memories. Or they weren't mine."

"I was there, so were you. Of course, they are your memories."

She shook her head. "They may not be. I feel as if I was pushed aside. If I had been a program, I would say taken offline. I was not completely here in those times you speak of."

Damn it. She might have found their leak. "Tell me something that only you would know?" The other Aithnea, the one she'd been talking to for the last few days, had seemed to know her. But she'd mostly talked about information that could have come from a book.

"When you first came to us as a child, you could barely read and write." There was a softness to her eyes that hadn't been there before.

That brought a flood of memories. Because she had been constantly trying to keep out of her brother Borland's way growing up, she stayed out of school. She recalled the painful embarrassment she felt when Aithnea realized her new foundling was functionally illiterate.

"That'll do. Thank you again for correcting that situation. But we have another one." Vas quickly went through what had happened and what she believed Aithnea's unwitting part in it had been.

"They linked in through me? How did they even

know I was here? I do recall transferring myself into the ship. And a vague feeling of loss, but most everything is dimmed. I believe I was there, but whatever spy program they slipped in overrode me. This is extremely disturbing."

"This was part of a longer game than we thought. I have a feeling that might have been the purpose of the Hive ship. There was no reason for it to try to harvest us. And to do it inside the Commonwealth?" Vas shook her head and walked through the forest. "They destroyed two of their ships, simply to get their spyware into you." That was the weird thing. She personally hadn't heard of the Hive, and she was sure if there had been historical records of them crossing into the Commonwealth and trying to salvage a functioning ship, she would have heard about that.

Aithnea nodded. "It makes no sense for them to try and get spyware into my system, or block me, if they were planning on pulling you through the gate. Unless their tactics and the gates have changed, they would have destroyed your ship."

"Which would make it sort of stupid to sneak a digital spy on board." Vas shook her head. "I think I liked things better back on my beaches."

Aithnea laughed. "That, I have a hard time believing. Okay, you were recovering from nearly dying, with the man you love who also almost died, so I guess you might have enjoyed it for a while. But anything beyond that? Mark my words, you will fall in battle. Probably as a cantankerous old woman."

"I always did look up to you as my role model." Vas dropped the smile. "But how can we be sure the spyware is gone and what if it happens again?"

"I honestly don't know. I'd suggest cutting this holosuite off from the rest of the ship. Just leave my connection to the library, would you?"

Vas tapped her comm. "Hrrru? Can you sever all connections to the holo room? Leave a sealed version of the library, no computer access beyond that."

"Aye, Captain." He signed off.

That was one reason she really liked Hrrru; he was one of the few members of her crew who did what she asked without badgering her endlessly about the reasons behind it.

Her comm pinged. "Vas here." Maybe Hrrru had been hanging around Gosta too much and was now questioning her.

"Captain? We have an issue." Hrrru's voice was softer than before.

"What?"

Another voice cut off Hrrru. "There's a ship coming into this star system, still a bit out, so maybe they haven't seen us," Bathie said. "Hrrru picked them up. It's the ship Leil and Loxianth stole."

CHAPTER NINETEEN

———————

"WHAT? DAMN IT, WE NEED to follow them. Who's in the pilot chair right now?"

"Divee. And he would gladly offer it up should you wish to take over." Bathie wasn't laughing but Vas heard the tone in her voice. Divee was an odd one. He had potential, but he liked to stay in the background. He only had a piloting shift because she made him.

Normally, Vas would make him ride it out. He needed to become confident in different areas. He was an engineer and damn good at that, but her primary crew people needed to have a variety of skills. If they needed some fancy flying right now though, he wasn't going to be the one to do it.

"I'm on my way. Keep an eye on them and drop all external tech except for Gosta's sensors." Starships were always sending out sensing signals, usually low-level ones that couldn't be detected. But there were ways to expose them. Gosta had added the method to do so to the *Warrior Wench* a few months ago—he also did so to this ship first thing.

"Aye, Captain, they appear to be slowing down near a smallish moon on the edge of this system. The analysis of this entire system said it was lifeless."

"Gather as much data as you can without drawing their attention. Vas out." Vas turned to Aithnea. "I hope we've done enough to keep both you and us safe. I'll be back in the morning."

Aithnea had drifted to the computer pad in the wall. She was already calling up the library. "Thank you."

With a nod, Vas left the holosuite and locked it. A command lockout would keep any curious crew out. They needed to figure out if Aithnea had truly been the leak and how to catch it if it happened again.

She ran for the lift and almost smacked into Deven coming down a cross corridor. "Looks like your brother is easier to find than we thought. Any ideas of anything that might be in this system that might cause him to come here?"

Deven punched up the lift. "Not a thing. This system has been dead and abandoned longer than I've been alive. He's got something planned, or the people with him do."

"They could be looking for a place to hide. Especially if they know we're after them." Vas shrugged. Even she didn't believe that.

"Not in any world we know of. He's a bigger asshole than I thought. Just in case there was any question, if we need to kill him, I'm okay with it. I'll even break the news to my parents."

Vas pulled back in surprise. "I didn't know they were still alive." She'd spent six months alone with this man and felt like she didn't know him at all.

"Yes, and they will be glad he's gone too. They disowned him eighty years ago."

The lift door opened to the command deck before she could ask more.

"Anything?" both Vas and Deven asked as they came on deck. Vas went to the pilot seat and Divee went to a science console. Deven took his regular station.

"Nothing," Hrrru answered. "They don't appear to be doing anything, but they did land."

Bathie turned toward Vas. "And there's no indication they've picked up on the cloaked sensors. But as soon as we get close to them, they will notice us."

"Damn it. Ideas? Any indication what they might be after? I seriously doubt they ran out here to land on a deserted moon for no reason."

"I think I have something," Deven said. "There's an old mine on that moon. Jonlario ore. It was mined out long ago and one of the reasons this system was abandoned. There's really no planet here that makes for happy living. The ore at least gave them something to sell."

Hrrru looked worried as he pulled up a few screens. "If there is still a sizable amount, even if it isn't easy to get out, which would be cause for abandonment, then that could be a source of danger." He was as close to babbling as Vas had heard in years. He used to become almost insensible when seriously stressed out. He was close right now.

"He's right," Deven said. "I don't know how it could be used, but the moon would be unstable if there was enough ore left in it. But only if the people on that ship did something stupid."

Vas tilted her head. "This is your brother we're talking about."

"I'm hoping the people he's with are smarter than he is."

"Vas? Oh, this is different than being in your head." Aithnea's voice came through Vas' comm. "You need to leave now. Immediately. Doesn't matter where but go. How do I know? We were right, those bastards were using me as a spy. I trapped them as they tried to access me again and fried some of their circuits. They are on that moon and about to do something really stupid. Get out of this system."

"Understood." Vas cut the comm. They'd deal with how Aithnea took care of the intruders later. "Hrrru, plot a course after we get through this gate." She started up the engines. "And leave a drone behind."

Hrrru had barely got his agreement and confirmation of the drone's launch out when Vas shot them through the gate. Mac had left the rest of his planned gate hops in the system, so Vas followed the first two.

"What do we see from the drone?" Vas knew her people were watching the feed carefully, but she couldn't right now unless it went in front of her.

Hrrru pulled up the drone's camera to the main screen. Even flying at full speed, the drone would take a while to get to the moon. It was only halfway there, sending back any data it gathered, when the moon exploded.

The drone was slammed with data, and bits of moon, then exploded.

"Damn it, did we get anything we can use?" Vas stopped hopping gates; the system they were in wasn't heavily populated, so they might as well wait here. Not that anyone should be looking for them, but stranger things had happened. Had continued to happen if she looked at the past twenty-four hours.

"Yes, I believe so. I can run through the information, and then relate it all to Master Gosta when he awakes." Hrrru was nodding furiously. Most likely he'd planned on calling Gosta immediately, realized she wouldn't like that, and changed his direction mid-thought.

"Did your they just destroy themselves?" That behavior really didn't go with what she'd seen of Leil. But if he and those with him weren't aware of what was in the moon…accidents happened.

"I don't know." Deven looked through the screens. Most likely even though Hrrru said he would go through the images and data, Deven had downloaded it to his monitor as well. "I don't believe what we are thinking happened." He held up one hand but still watched the screen. "They blew it up all right, and that ship they set up and stole is almost certainly gone. But look here." He sent an image to the main screen. It was extensively magnified, but even so Vas wouldn't have noticed anything if Deven hadn't pointed it out. There was a tiny flash of the distant sun on metal. After the explosion. It was hard to make out clearly through the debris of the destroyed moon.

"Something survived? What in the hell could survive that?" It could be nothing, just a reflection off the floating debris. But something indicated that wasn't it at all—there was a shape beneath that debris.

"I'm not sure. Something far stronger than most substances certainly. We must go back."

Vas stared at the screen then finally nodded. "Not looking forward to dealing with a ship that could survive that, but if by chance they did survive, we still need our plans back."

Damn it, that's why simple things were often best. Having fancy weapons now led to people trying to duplicate them. Which raised the question—Leil and crew were all in lockup when they approached Home; so how did they even know about those guns? Simple answer: they knew about them before they were captured.

Vas tapped her comm. She wasn't sure exactly how Aithnea got through, especially since she was electronically cut off from the rest of the ship, but she called out to the holosuite.

"Aithnea? Can you hear me?"

"Yes, and it's odd being on the receiving end as well. You saved the ship, excellent work."

"Yes, we thought so. Thank you for the warning. Can you sense the ones that caused the explosion?" Granted they were quite a few systems away, but that probably wasn't a problem since the ship using Aithnea to spy wouldn't have been close to them from the start.

"No, nothing. But it is unusual for dead people to be up and talking. My own company excluded. You don't think they died?"

"There's a debate on that. Just wanted to see if you still felt a connection to them. Sit tight, I'll fill you in once we find out what's going on." She dropped the comm call.

"Let's go back. Deven, I want you and Hrrru using every sensor this ship has to monitor for information." With nods from both, she reversed course and went back through the two gates.

The system entry was rough, but since the gate wasn't that far from the moon that had exploded, it wasn't too surprising.

What *was* surprising was the shiny, asteroid-sized ship that was floating in space where the moon had been.

"Any guesses, gentlemen? Bathie? What is that?"

"Vas?" Aithnea's voice was back in her comm and sounded worried. Something rare when she'd been alive and usually only when there was danger to others. "I know you're blocking my access, but can you send a link to what you're seeing? Something is very wrong."

Vas nodded toward Hrrru. "Patch though a link from the main screen to the console in the holo deck."

Hrrru silently followed her command.

Aithnea's swearing was loud and well-educated. "How in all that is holy did they do that?"

Vas counted to ten, then verbally shook Aithnea out of wherever she was mentally going. "Do what?"

"That is the ship you helped steal from the Garmainians, the prototype ship that Ome's people created, or it was before they modified it somehow. I saw the copies of the specs; it was impressive to start with, but now... Has it moved since we got into the system?"

Vas had never seen a ship that even remotely looked like that. It was covered in an almost fluid metal looking substance. "No movement we've seen aside from the fact the skin moves. I'm sure it saw us come back into the system though."

"Good. Maybe they destroyed the engines."

Aithnea's words had just been spoken when the silver ship took off at a speed Vas had never witnessed. There was an asteroid belt out at the distant end of the system and Vas waited for it to slow down, but it didn't. Explosions could be seen without magnification as it tore through the field. Literally. The asteroids exploded as if they were made of air.

"How in the hell is it doing that? All of you smart science people—start talking." Vas found she couldn't take her eyes off the front screen. The silver ship kept looping through the field and destroying asteroids.

"I don't know, Captain, but we might want to leave," Gosta cut in on the comm. "Yes, I should be asleep and yes, I can see the main screen on a viewing port in my quarters, but this is not good. What if that ship goes through us next?"

Vas would chastise him later. "What is making them able to do that?"

"The Jonlario ore from the core of the moon. I'm not sure how, but that ship is literally coated in ore."

"Crap." Vas hit the engines and turned back toward the gate. The last asteroid popped like a soap bubble.

"They are turning toward us," Deven said. He was extremely calm; the dead calm he got when they were in serious danger.

"We're out of here. Hang on, I need to lose them." Gates could go to any number of civilized systems; the older ones went to completely uncivilized ones. Vas wasn't sure which option would be better, she just needed to get the hell out of there. "Hrrru, drop another buoy." They needed to leave, but they also needed data on that damn ship. "And leave one in each system we go through—set self-destruct on them if compromised." Those things were expensive and while they'd brought most of the ones they had on the *Warrior Wench* with them, she had hoped they would last longer. But that silver ship was terrifying.

The crew was silent as they did their jobs and she got

them out of the system. She stayed long enough to drop a buoy, then went to another system. She found one that had three different gates. Went through the most remote one, then found her way back and went through a second one. After ten minutes, she picked one system and waited. "And the results from the buoys?"

"The one we left in the system with that ship has some specs and data. But it's mostly images. That coating of theirs is blocking a lot of our scans. They destroyed the buoy." Hrrru pulled up a screen and data and images flooded by. For something that couldn't pull in much data it was doing a good job. She'd have Gosta and Hrrru pull out what they could and give her the summarized version.

"And the others?"

"Still scanning. The ship didn't follow us." Deven sounded as confused as she felt.

"What were they after? They wanted us to leave, but didn't care where we went?" Vas looked at the vid images of the ship as the brief flight from the asteroid belt to the gate and the destruction of their data buoy played out over and over.

It was an insanely tightly designed ship to begin with, but those twin gun ports on the front weren't like anything she'd ever seen. And the surface really did look like the ship was encased in a liquid metal. It wasn't just an effect of the movement causing it to look that way.

"We need to know what exactly that ship has become, how it happened, and how Leil of all people knew it could be done."

Deven snorted. "There is no way my brother is the brains of that group. Even I've never heard of something like that."

The lift doors opened and Khirson stood there watching the clip in horror. "I have." He slowly stepped onto the command deck but didn't take his eyes off the main screen. "I might not be as old as you are Deven, but I have heard of a Ralith ship. The name is Pilthian, also known as zombie ships, because they come back from the dead and are indestructible. They use the center of a dying moon or planet, one high in certain classes of ore and other requirements. A chemical explosion is begun. In theory, if done correctly, the ship is transformed on the exterior. A few idiots on our council set up a test once. They used a dying mining planet. It killed the twenty scientists on board and obviously failed to prove the hypothesis." He looked pale but it was hard to tell if it was from seeing the ship or because he wasn't yet recovered from his spacewalk. Both arms were now in stim casts.

"Can you tell us the mechanics behind it?" Deven shook his head at the screen. "I have no idea why that ship wasn't destroyed the moment the explosion started."

"Sadly, I don't have much information. Two of my good friends were involved in the experiments, planetologists of the highest order. They were forbidden to speak of the specifics. As it was, even general information of the experiment was kept hidden. The government blamed their deaths on a lab accident gone wrong."

"There's really only one purpose for such a ship." Hrrru tilted his head toward Khirson. "That ship is designed to destroy things." Hrrru's people were peaceful. They would defend themselves, but something like that ship, destruction just for power, was foreign to them. But Hrrru had been part of a mercenary crew long enough to recognize it for what it was.

Khirson slid into an open station. "That is the truth, Hrrru. My people were trying to leave the Commonwealth, to start anew somewhere they would have more freedom and room. But there was a dark faction of my people that wanted to take what they wanted. They claimed it was a defensive ship. Clearly it's not."

"Okay, so the assumption being that Loxianth or Ome has the knowledge and made it work. I need ideas on how to stop it." Vas hit her comm. "That goes for Gosta, Aithnea, and anyone else who is still awake and has ideas." She didn't hit ship-wide, so only people with their comms open would hear her. If she ever wished that Marli wasn't dead, this was one of those times. Although the idea of her with that kind of ship was terrifying. She rubbed her arms at the shudder that caused.

"Are you okay?" Deven was next to her before she even noticed.

"Just had a thought of what would have happened if the Asarlaí clones had that tech."

Deven's eyes went wide and he echoed her shudder. "Thank you, now I won't be sleeping for a while. The thing is, the original Asarlaí sort of did that with their transformation of the planet Mayhira. Underneath was pure trithian. The two chemicals aren't that different. I am surprised they didn't think of it."

"Maybe my people are actually worse than them in some regards. If that is a true Ralith ship, there is nothing that can stop it. It can go through anything." Khirson kept watching the replay. "Do you have vid of how it came to be?"

"Not much." Deven changed the screen to the explosion. "Only what we caught off the buoy as we left."

"Can I have these sent to my quarters for study? I am exhausted but would like to see if there are clues. It's been a brutal few days for me."

Vas could only imagine. Being in cold sleep for over fifty years, being betrayed by the person you were supposed to serve, and now evidence that some of his people had successfully created this monster. "Everything will be available from your console. Go rest."

"Thank you." He held up his arms. "I'm not sure how much I can help you with the pirate conclave, if you're still going."

Vas got out of the pilot station and nodded for Divee to take it back. "We are, and you're not. Whatever is going on with Leil, Loxianth, and your people is important, we won't lose sight of that. And one way or another, we need to get those plans back. But we also need this job. I need to track down this Boagada character, or rather information on him before he died. The last people he was with are supposed to be among the folks we'll be meeting for the conclave. But we're going to dye Deven blue. You can help tattoo him, and we'll have our Pilthian as we previously stated." She walked with him to the lift. "I'll ride down with you, and you're welcome to go through all of the vids, but sleep would be good as well. Tomorrow, I'll introduce you to someone else who's also staying on board."

Khirson yawned as he got off the lift and Vas bid him good night. She hadn't really introduced many to Aithnea, though she knew her crew had an idea who she'd been talking to. It was a small crew; it wouldn't take long to spread. Besides, her plan was to leave Hrrru on the ship with Aithnea and Khirson when they went down to the planet. Hopefully, the three of them could resolve some of the how's regarding that Ralith ship. She still wanted the specs they stole, but that new ship was worse than them having access to Home security.

She made sure to turn on all the lights before she entered her quarters, it made her feel better. She intended to go through some of the specs for the job but fell asleep instead. When a warm body crawled in next to her, she knew that Deven finally made it in—and was as exhausted as she was. She curled up next to him and snuggled into his chest.

CHAPTER TWENTY

DEVEN WAS GONE THE NEXT morning, not unexpected with what was going on, but still disappointing. She showered, got into her pirate garb, including her eye patch, added her two Zalith blades and went down the hall. The patch was for appearances only and she'd modified it. Not only could she see perfectly fine out of it, but it also had extra scanning abilities. Nothing too outrageous, nothing that would set off tech sensors. But she could record and replay events, see through lighter items, and a few other things. The rest of her garb was tight and dark. The pirate accents were the slashes of bright color running through the flat black fabric. Her boots came mid-thigh but were flat heeled. They each also had two knives in them. The one in the top was barely visible, while the second was a pressure blade that would shoot into an opponent if she kicked them. She was feeling pretty good until she strode onto the command deck and saw her crew.

They made her look like she was playing a weak dress-up. Flarik had done all her feathers in that wild combination of purple and green and looked even fiercer with her back feathers ruffled, steel points on her claws and a long leather jacket. Deven was now a reasonable version of a Pilthian. A Pilthian who happened to also be a trained assassin. He wore a vest rather than a shirt, and it made an excellent frame for his very well-muscled arms and chest. It was open to the front as well and Vas was reminded that they'd had no real time together since they came back from their R & R. This wasn't the time, but she was regretting that soundly.

Khirson was directing Xsit, who looked suitably fierce in dark brown leather, on applying the liquid that would stand in for the Pilthian markings on Deven's face and torso. One specific mark caught Vas' eye. A circle and slash with a hand on it sat right above his left pectoral muscle, and was noticeable when Xsit stepped back as she finished.

"Do many of your people have that mark? It stands out but I'm not sure why."

"They didn't before I went to sleep, but the world has changed since then. It is the assassins' guild. Normally no one would see that until they found a body. By having it so visible it should give the other pirates something to think about."

Deven flexed his pec and grinned. "I knew I needed some tattoos." He got to his feet and turned slowly around for all to see. His hair was dyed a deep blue, darker than Khirson, but still within the range of the Pilthians she'd seen.

"You look quite dramatic. But what about his eyes?" Vas had only done a brief survey when she realized they were again running into Pilthians, but there was no mention of green eyes.

"I'm taking care of that." Terel came in through the lift. "I recently finished these so don't lose them." She handed a case to Deven and he went to the mirror Xsit had been using. "They will not only change his eye color but enhance his vision. Like your cute little patch, but better."

Terel was far too smug for this not to have been her own invention. There were augmented eyes, but nothing that she knew of that could be popped onto the eyes.

"And these are your prototypes, aren't they?" Vas laughed. "Deven is your test subject."

"Well, that sounds harsh. I had been working on something like them but fortunately this came up and I was able to modify them to help the cause."

Deven turned back from the mirror and Vas nodded in appreciation. The lenses made his eyes almost glow with a rich purple-blue. They also finished the job of making him look very Pilthian.

"I'd say you will pass well." Khirson walked slowly around Deven, nodding in approval. "You look like one of us who has been living on his own for a long time, which is what you want. There could be a colony of Pilthians out here if our other ships ever got away. It's going to be easier to pass off the lack of societal norms if he was on his own since he was young." He looked around at everyone watching him. "You did say you wanted back story, right? That's what I was going to use."

"That is actually brilliant, and leaves things open for me to deviate from what might be standard Pilthian behavior." Deven came up to Vas. "You ready to serve in this pirate's war?" Vas would be going in as Deven's second in command. Originally, Khirson would have been Vas' second, but with Deven, Vas didn't have a problem with him leading.

"Wherever you're leading, I'll be right behind." She turned to Khirson and Hrrru. "We have an hour before we meet, and I want you to meet someone." Gosta was hovering on the edges. He wasn't outrageously dressed, but he'd work as the legal end of her pirate gang. He didn't look happy though and clearly wanted to be included in whatever she was off to do. "Gosta, you too. You should see this, but you are still going with us to the meet."

He ambled alongside of them, looking a bit less dour.

"Let's get to the rendezvous point." Mac was already in the pilot station, but he started getting things ready.

"You have the coordinates, take your time switching gates to get there. They won't expect anyone to directly come in."Vas led the way to the lift. "We'll be back up in half an hour."

"Might I ask who we are meeting who has not come to the bridge?" Khirson was being polite; her normal crew would have been blunter.

"It's a very long story, but I have a dear friend who died a while ago. But her job on this plane wasn't finished so she hasn't been able to leave. We thought her spirit had been freed once we defeated the Asarlaí clones, but we were wrong."

"Aithnea," both Gosta and Hrrru said at the same time. The tone was different though, Gosta's was intellectually curious, Hrrru's had a sad tinge. His people were very spiritual and trapped souls disturbed them. Vas hadn't thought of it before, but if they resolved this current problem and Aithnea and the nuns still couldn't move on, maybe she could convince Hrrru to send some of his people to help.

"Yes. But she's not in my head this time." Vas sighed. This was going to take longer to explain than she wanted to spend. "I'll send you all more details, but right now, just know she's in the holosuite. There is a belief she was compromised by those bastards in the silver ship. We think she's no longer compromised, but I'm still keeping her offline from most programs." She finished as they hit the holosuite door. "I've been keeping this door locked, but you can each have the code. I don't really want other people coming in here."

The door opened and Vas motioned the other three in. It was even more claustrophobic with all of them inside, so she again punched up the forest scenario. "Yes, I know the space in here did not increase, but this makes me feel less crowded."

Gosta smiled. "I wouldn't have said a thing, Captain." Hrrru and Khirson nodded.

"Aithnea? I've brought guests."

Aithnea's hologram seemed less confused than before. "Excellent. You never let me meet anyone new." She strode forward. "I recognize Hrrru and Gosta from my prior engagements. I am the late Mother Superior Aithnea."

"You saved us many times. It's nice to meet you, so to speak." Gosta paused, then bowed. Hrrru did the same.

Khirson stepped forward. "I am Khirson. I must say I have never met a late anything, let alone a Mother Superior of the Clionea nuns."

Vas watched them chit chat. This was part of what she had hoped for by introducing them. If something did happen to her and Deven during this fight, she wanted others to be aware of Aithnea. "Aithnea, can you fill them in on what we're looking for? They will be up here during the conclave, and maybe together you can find more clues beyond any we find on the planet." Technically, Gosta would be going planet side, but he'd spend most of his time back up here.

"Good thinking," Aithnea said and stepped back. "Although I do enjoy your forests, I think something more conducive to conversation might be in order." Immediately the room changed into a conference room that Vas recognized from the old nunnery.

Vas smiled. "I'll leave you all to it. Gosta, come back up in fifteen." Her tone reminded him she'd come find him if she had to. The sheepish look on his face said her reminder was a good idea.

Vas swung by medical on her way back to the deck. Terel was in gear as a pirate but far more subtle than most of the others. But she was packing some serious edged weapons.

Vas whistled in approval, then walked around Terel slowly. There were even more weapons than she thought. "You do realize this is a conclave, right? A time of truce, sort of, for these pirates?"

"Oh, I know." Terel grinned as she pulled out three smaller, and concealable, blasters. "I also have my field med kit, never worry."

Vas watched her old friend. "What is all this?" Terel usually had weapons on her; it would be foolish to be in a battle unarmed. But she was rarely on the front, and she never looked quite so ready to kill.

"I'm trying to look the part." Terel held her innocent look for a few moments, then dropped it. "Fine. After the war, and you almost dying—a few times, mind you—as well as others I care about, I decided I wanted to be more involved in defending our crew. I'm tired of people not coming back." She looked far fiercer on the final word. "I know this shouldn't end up with a fighting situation, not down there anyway. But I think it's better to be pre-pared."

"Well, you were technically overseeing medical for nine ships, so you couldn't have protected them all. And we were in space."

"We lost people on the ground too. I stay in my med lab and wait for the dying. I am tired of doing that."

Vas shook her head. "You're our best doc. I will order you to stay on board if I think there is the slightest chance that you are going to pull some stupid heroics."

All of them had changed in the past two years, but she hadn't noticed it in Terel until the past view days.

Terel's shoulders dropped a bit. "You don't need to. I intend to stay near the back if there is any fighting. But if needed, I want to be ready. I am a merc too, you know."

Vas laughed and patted her shoulder. "Trust me, no one would ever say otherwise. Meet at the docking bay in fifteen."

"We aren't landing?"

This ship was even better at planet landings than one the size of the *Warrior Wench* would be. And usually bringing the ships to land meant they couldn't be off firing on the enemy so was often required for questionable gatherings. "Not this time. Which means most of the crews involved will leave their ships spaceside. I'm not leaving us grounded if things get ugly."

Terel held up her hands. "I'm not arguing. Do you want Pela to fly one of the shuttles?" Someone from medical had to stay onboard and Terel had nominated Pela.

"That might be a good idea. We'll need all three. I was going to have Gosta fly one back once he finished the official paperwork. But this way we can leave one on the planet." And hope they didn't need to get off planet quickly. It was that or risk leaving two on the planet to be destroyed if things went bad. If things went bad a single still flying shuttle could save the day. Pirate conclaves like this one could simply be places for pirates to gather and share intel for a price. Or they could be explosions waiting to happen.

Terel went back to adjusting things in her med kit and Vas took that as the time to leave. Things were quiet and empty on her way to the command deck.

"Good timing, Captain. We're approaching the system for the gathering." Gosta had beat her back up here.

"Let's get into character, folks." They rarely went incognito on jobs. It was frowned on by the Commonwealth and part of the reason they got jobs was because of their reputation. This time they got to reinvent themselves.

She started to go for her captain's seat, then turned toward Deven. "I believe that is yours." She took his former seat once he took her chair. She had to admit, he looked very impressive blue and half-naked.

He suddenly looked at her and grinned. She must have been thinking about him a little too clearly. It had faded over the last six months, but sometimes they could pick up each other's thoughts. His wink told her it was back, to some degree.

"We're being hailed, Captain...what are you going by

again?" Xsit's voice went up in a trill, she was getting flustered. This happened sometimes before when she'd first joined the crew but not in a few years. However, it had been two years since they'd last had a merc job. Vas would watch her closely.

"Captain Fhailson," Deven said as he flashed a grin. "Khirson said it was a dangerous family name."

Xsit swallowed and nodded. "Captain Fhailson, call coming in."

Vas watched Xsit for a few more moments, then focused on Deven.

"Fhailson here." He switched the call to open so the entire deck could hear it but kept the mic only to himself. He also kept the deck screen off. Smart crews could gather information from an open screen. Smarter crews never gave anyone the chance.

"Captain Fhailson, well met. Your specifications have been recorded. The conclave begins in five hours. Please land at these coordinates and you will be assigned a camp area."

Deven watched the screen as the location appeared and his upper lip went up in a snarl. "What are you playing at? You were informed that we would not be landing the *Traitor's Folly* and where you've marked is a location for a full ship. And too close to at least three other ships."

The pause on the other end was short but noticeable. "Ah, I apologize. We do have you noted as landing. But that will be fine. Your shuttles can land here instead."

Vas looked at the location that came through. Now they were too far away from the official conclave—it would make them appear weak to the other crews. Deven obviously saw the same thing.

"That won't work either. What's wrong with coordinates 562.47?" The perfect spot in relation to the conclave center.

The pause was longer this time and when the voice

came back on it was more strained. "Impossible. However, we could give you 564.85."

Deven looked to Vas and shrugged. "We will accept that. Fhailson out." Deven scowled at the comm for a few seconds after he cut it off. "There's something wrong."

"As in, we abort? Or as in we watch ourselves down there?" Vas would go with it if he said abort. His teke powers had never let them down before. It would mean starting from scratch with searching for the pirate, but better that than dead.

Deven's pause was enough to make her order Mac to get them out of there. Then he shook his head to himself. "No. Just that we watch ourselves there. There's a lot of things that aren't what they seem. There's a trap being set, but I don't get the feeling that it's for us."

Vas watched him for a moment, then finally nodded and opened a ship-wide comm. "Crew of *Traitor's Folly*, if you are going down to the planet with Captain Fhailson and myself, please make your way to the docking bay now."

Hrrru and Khirson came back up to the deck. "Hrrru, please take the pilot chair, but you are in command until Gosta returns to the ship. We're leaving Pela, Khirson, and Xsit here with you."

Xsit had been getting herself ready to go down but she still looked nervous. Vas wasn't going to risk her crew—including Xsit—on that newly re-found sense of nerves. "I'm sorry, Xsit, but I need you to stay on the ship. I know you were looking forward to engaging with the pirates, but this ship really needs three crew to man the command deck. Gosta will take over when he gets back, but for now, just do what Hrrru asks."

Xsit's face was schooled into a look of disappointment but Vas watched as the tension left her shoulders. "I understand, Captain." Then she turned to Deven. "Captains."

Deven smiled as he passed her. "Captain Fhailson is disappointed that you won't be joining us but is grateful that you'll be up here watching out for us."

She chirped and started pulling up more screens. "I'll keep an eye and ear out on the incoming chatter, Captains." She looked so content; Vas wondered if she'd need to force retire her to Home after this. Xsit was extremely good at what she did, but there were times when the entire crew needed to go into battle.

Vas shook her head as the crew not staying went down to the docking bay. That was a worry for another time.

Pela was already in her shuttle, Gosta had taken the second one, and Deven led the way to the first. He paused in front of it and looked down at her with a crooked grin. "Does Lisha, second in command to Captain Fhailson, wish to pilot?"

Vas thumped him in the chest as she went into the shuttle. "Captain Fhailson better watch himself. And yes, Lisha very much would like to pilot the shuttle." The shuttles were deceptively small on the outside, but they'd been stripped down to seats and weapons, so they were much larger on the inside than they looked. That was another advantage of Grosslyn's adaptation work—he'd made them to haul lots of crew and carry more firepower than any shuttle aside from the ones on the *Warrior Wench*. Vas originally insisted they take the ones from *Warrior Wench*, but the design would be too hard to modify in the short amount of time. And she had to admit these fit in much better with *Traitor's Folly*.

The crew automatically divided themselves into groups of three. Once the shuttle was loaded and everyone was belted in, Vas queued up the starting sequence.

Pela's shuttle left first, with Gosta following behind at a precise distance. He wasn't a flashy pilot, but he was a very accurate one.

"Captain? There's someone coming into the sector."

Xsit didn't sound happy.

"Please tell me it's not that silver ship?" Vas' plan to deal with that ship was to avoid it until they found a way to take it down.

"It's not the silver ship," Xsit said. "It's a Hive ship."

Deven's swearing beat hers by a full ten seconds. "Where? Is it coming this way?" If those two Hive ships had been specifically after Vas, then other ships of theirs shouldn't realize this was her new ship. She hoped. Of course, there was no confirmed reason for why those ships had crossed into Commonwealth space and attacked the *Warrior Wench*.

"Captain Fhailson? Are we still going down?" Pela called on the comm, but kept heading her shuttle toward the planet.

Vas watched the Hive ship. It wasn't one of the two attack-class vessels that they'd seen in the Commonwealth, this was a smaller fighting ship. And it quickly and precisely landed.

Deven hit the comm. Part of a good ruse was maintaining the lie even when you didn't know if anyone was watching. "Keep going. Take your time though."

Vas called to Xsit. "Thank you for the report, keep an eye on it and note all ships that come in and whether they land or stay in orbit." Maybe she'd have to rethink the idea that some of her specialists didn't need to also be fighters. Someone else might not have noticed the Hive vessel and that wouldn't have been something she'd want to find out about when she was on the ground.

They made a slow approach and watched the crew from the Hive ship disembark. Vas had been expecting that the ship would go back up and maintain an orbit position, but it didn't.

Some crews were already there with about half in orbit. None were ones she recognized.

A chirp from the ship's comm took her out of her

thoughts. "Lisha." Hrrru had a pause as he said the name, but he recovered. "The Hive ship's data is coming across as stolen. The intelligence out here is not as good as ours, but that ship is definitely stolen. Or so they say."

Which meant it probably wasn't from the Hive worlds or the Lethian Assembly. Or it was, and they were doing the same thing she was; going in there as something other than what they were. "That's okay. I'd wager most are. Including ours." She really hoped that no one was eavesdropping, Gosta and Hrrru swore they had tightened up the system to where nothing could get through.

"True. It's unusual for a Hive ship to be taken." His quick recovery to the fact the lines might not be completely secure earned him a smile he did not see.

"Which could mean we have some heavy players on board. At least they're on the same side we are while the conclave is in place." A truce between all parties who gathered under the flag of conclave held until the leaders called it off—supposedly with a warning. Vas wasn't sure how true that was.

"Aye. We will keep watching. *Everything.*" Hrrru sounded fiercer than he usually could manage on that last bit. He disconnected the call.

"Do we think it's really a stolen Hive ship?" Deven arched his left eyebrow.

"Are you looking for a wager, my captain?" Vas brought the shuttle in as Deven pulled up closer views of the Hive ship and their crew.

He let out a long breath. "I'd say that would be a fool's bet. Know any pirate or smuggler crew who marches in perfect formation, even when they are obviously trying not to?" He opened the screen. Vas could still see enough of the field for landing, but she could also see a very bad attempt to hide military precision marching.

"Why though? If they were trying to go undercover, wouldn't they have realized that was a dead giveaway?"

"The Hive doesn't deal with outsiders except to destroy them and take their raw materials. They probably think they are extremely clever."

"Another thing to watch out for. At least we won't be landing near them, but I do wonder why they are keeping the ship on the ground."

Vas watched as her first two shuttles landed easily. Then she brought around her shuttle. And started swearing. She motioned to Deven to look, then called back to the ship. "Khirson? Are those two fighters Pilthian?" She'd never seen the style before, but the markings looked a lot like what had been on the cryoship.

It took a few moments for the response, probably for them to see the ships. They were on the ground, two sleek fighters—neither looked like they would have much room for crew but plenty for weapons. Sort of suspicious for an event that was just for meeting.

"I don't recognize the design, but those are our markings."

"Thank you, Khirson. That's another couple of ships we'd like you all to watch." Vas started rubbing the back of her neck. There was something weird happening. Something she wasn't seeing.

"Connect Aithnea to the vid. Ask her to shout out if she sees anything." The odd feeling lingered. As if the devils of the abyss were playing with her nerves.

"You okay?" Deven was watching her. She'd accuse him of trying to get in her head again, but she didn't want to deal with gossip from the crew.

"I have a weird feeling." She held up her hand. "A *feeling*. Not anything more."

"About it being a trap." It wasn't even a question and Deven didn't look happy about stating it.

"Yes. But I don't get it. It feels like I'm seeing it, but it's not aimed at us."

"That's what I felt on the *Traitor's Folly*. I didn't ask

before, as I figured we'd be keeping my real abilities hidden. But what level of engagement, *Captain?*"

Vas watched the landing area as the ground came up to meet them. He was asking at what level he could use his esper powers. Usually, it was little to none—too dangerous to use them in the Commonwealth. But there was definitely a skin-crawling issue going on right now. "Whatever level necessary." She felt his eyes on her but was busy landing the shuttle. "I mean it, even if this trap isn't set for us, it doesn't mean we can't get caught in it. Besides, we're not in the Commonwealth, so there's no one to report your higher-than-average esper abilities to."

In the Commonwealth, espers, or tekes were closely monitored. Most powerful ones, that weren't currently on antipsychotic meds, were no higher than a three on the Commonwealth teke scale, higher than that and they went crazy. That's what Deven officially appeared as. He was closer to a ten.

"Understood."

"Vas?" Aithnea's voice was now coming through the comm. "There is something familiar about those ships."

"Considering there are about ten down on the planet, you'll need to be clearer on that."

"Those deep gray ones, the big ones. Not on the planet, but in orbit."

Vas brought the shuttle down, then looked to the sky through the scanners in the shuttle. "I don't see them. Where are they?"

"They're right over the landing area. You should be able to see them."

Vas motioned for the crew to stay in the shuttle. She didn't see any ships like that. Deven shook his head, he didn't either.

"Hrrru? Can you see what she's seeing?"

"I'm trying to find them. We all are." He didn't want to admit failure, but he obviously wasn't having any luck.

"Aithnea, are you sure you're not picking up a glitch?"

"No, but you all might be. Try adjusting your red filter by .0856. Being dead must change the spectrum a bit."

Deven made the changes, and from the gasps on the open comms, so must have Hrrru, Gosta, and even Pela.

"How are they hiding like that? And who are they?" Pela got the words out first, but they were the same ones Vas was thinking.

"They're Racki? That can't be right." Deven was more talking to himself than anyone else as he started pulling up close ups of the ships. He continued to adjust the focus on something on the hull of the closest ship.

Vas leaned over his arm to try to see better. There were two and they were awkward looking ships, almost round and a far cry from many of the sleek fighters in attendance. Where most of the pirates gathered had attack ships, this one looked like a bunch of rich dilettantes wanted something to bob about the systems in. There was no way that thing could move fast.

"Damn."

Vas gave him five seconds to expand on that. When he didn't, she hit his arm. "Damn what? Gosta? Do you know of some people called the Racki?" There was no way Deven's earlier mutter carried over the comm.

"I do not, Captain, but I'm sure Hrrru can find them in the library."

"Not necessary," Aithnea's voice cut in. "Although probably only Deven and I recognize them without that library assistance. Even though I couldn't recall their name. They are not good news. Nor would I believe they have anything to do with pirates, except to possibly hunt them. I would recommend leaving as soon as you get the information we need."

Deven nodded. "If it weren't that this intel is crucial and can possibly only be found here, right now, I'd suggest leaving sooner. And how in the hell are they hiding outside of the standard spectrum like that? They weren't nearly that advanced a hundred years ago."

Aithnea laughed. "That's why it's called advancement."

"Captain, I believe we do want to leave soon. Those ships are dangerous," Hrrru called down over the comms.

Vas leaned over and looked again. Nope, still roundish balls of metal. "Seriously? Where are their gun ports? For that matter where are their engines? Hiding outside of the normal visible spectrum is great but what are they going to do, bump another ship to death?" Vas knew that sleek designs didn't necessarily mean the ship was fast, but those ships were ridiculous.

Hrrru again responded faster than the others. He did have direct access to their library after all. "They have smaller multi gun ports along the entire surface. And the system Ome and his brothers came from is part of their quadrant."

Both of those facts caught Vas' attention. Smaller ports over a round surface could mean extremely rapid firing like grenade bombs; they would hit anything near them. "Their people are with these Racki people? Damn it, this is really not good." That changed things. Shifting out of normal vision, rotating gun ports, and now a connection to at least one of the bastards behind the silver ship? "Shit."

"Now you see why I was swearing." Deven leaned back in his seat. "We need this job to get the intel we need to find where the last Pirate of Boagada was when they died. But there are a lot of things pointing to get the hell out of here." His voice was calm though. He was clearly laying out the issues, but even though he wasn't happy, he wasn't completely freaked out. That told Vas a lot.

"Okay, I need everyone, and I mean everyone, to be watching everything. No daydreaming. Constant awareness and we stick together. We'll get the command tent up first and meet there in thirty. *Traitor's Folly*, keep all sensors on high alert."

CHAPTER TWENTY-ONE

THERE WAS AN AIR OF subterfuge that loomed over the area where she parked their shuttle. Not their location specifically, but the entire zone. It could be the result of a bunch of secretive people all gathering. Vas and her people might do some questionable work occasionally, but she'd never taken a pirate job before. In the Commonwealth, merc companies who tried to go rogue, to work outside the rules and regs the Commonwealth required, usually ended up as pirates. That was why, as much as she disliked the Commonwealth and their rules, she made sure they followed them.

Fortunately, those rules and regs vanished the moment their ship left the Commonwealth. Unless whatever you did was so heinous that news got back to them, the Commonwealth didn't want to know what went on outside their rim planets.

Vas rose, secured her weapons, and nodded to Deven. "Lead on." They went outside and gathered their people near the shuttles.

Deven addressed their crew. "Set up camp. Like Lisha said before, keep your eyes open and your mouths shut. We have a job to do." Their job was to find out who was stealing the Dackon Industries' ships. But it was more importantly looking for clues as to who knew what happened to the Pirate. And where. Knowing the star system they had been in was helpful—but it was a damn big system.

Vas watched the camps being set up around them as Deven spoke. He had a bit more to say, mostly general talk. There was a chance this conclave could explode, and the crew needed to be on high alert. There didn't appear to be anyone near enough to hear, but technology could take care of that. His speech sounded general enough that while their people would get the points he was making, others wouldn't.

His speech also gave her a chance to watch the other crews while supposedly supporting her captain. The patch she wore was pulling in a lot of data and because of the way it worked she could see in a wider panorama than normally. And she didn't have to move her head much. The Hive-not-Hive group were almost more obvious down here than they'd been from space. She bet that if she measured the placement of their tents, she'd find they were all spaced exactly the same distance from each other—down to a microdot.

The crews were an odd mix. If they hadn't already seen the Hive ship folks, the fighter Pilthians, and the mysterious Racki, she'd feel it by the other crews. They didn't feel like what she would call normal pirates.

"Shall we go talk to the people running this show?" Deven finished his talk and Pela was already in her shuttle, ready to launch. Vas almost wanted to keep her and the shuttle down planet side. It was a toss-up as to whether risking the shuttles on the ground, or her crew being trapped was the larger risk. But if she needed to, they could fit everyone in the two remaining shuttles. Gosta wasn't going to be pleased about having to stay down here, but it would be good for him to get some groundwork done. Or ground observations, at any rate.

Gosta ambled over, looking a little awkward in his rougher pirate clothing, but he kept a swagger to his walk. "I have all letters of treaty and negotiations, Captain Fhailson."

Deven nodded and pounded his right fist over the assassin mark. Must have been something Khirson told him to do as she'd never seen him do that. He also had a serious loose-hip swagger as he led them to the command headquarters.

Vas dropped a bit behind Deven and Gosta; both to reinforce her role as the second in command who would protect her captain and to scan the area via her eye patch. The master quarters were a large, constructed dome. They'd entered the wide doorway, but at first there was no sign of anyone. Then a thin curtain toward the back moved.

"Captain Fhailson, it is good to see a fellow Pilthian." The woman's voice came out moments before she did. A Pilthian woman, but one with all her facial tattoos removed. Badly. The scarring disfigured her face, but Vas was pretty sure she had been born with that snarl.

Pilthians had their markings removed when they were sentenced to death. That seemed to be a non-functioning threat from what Vas could tell based on the woman in front of her and the people found on Khirson's cryo ship. They kept threatening to kill their criminals but seemed to have a problem with follow-through.

"Sedari Laque, I presume?" At her nod, Deven turned to Vas and Gosta. "My second and negotiator, Lisha Darkwin and Klic Rancon."

Sedari's face grew haughty. "Human and hybrid, interesting choices. It is an honor to meet you." The tone of voice said it was anything but an honor. Vas wanted to get through this, do what they needed to do, and get out. Hopefully, all in one piece.

Sedari kept looking to Deven's chest. While Vas knew that it was a fine chest and nice to look at, she had a feeling it was Deven's tat she was sneaking looks at.

"I have the letters of treaty and the additional confirmation of negotiations." Gosta was taller than any of them if he stood completely straight. He rarely did, but Vas was surprised to see he did so now.

Sedari nodded. "Thurnil, attend me."

The curtains blocking the back moved and another Pilthian, male this time, came out. He was shorter than Sedari and upon closer inspection, appeared to be part human. Something almost unheard of before the Pilthians left the Commonwealth. Unlike Sedari, he had tattoos, but they were thinner and far fewer than any she'd seen on the cryo ship's Pilthians. Perhaps a way of acknowledging that he wasn't pure Pilthian.

He bowed and stayed a step behind Sedari.

She sighed and rolled her eyes. "When I call for you, you may approach me all the way, not hovering back there like a pet. These are from the *Traitor's Folly*. Please meet with their negotiator, and make sure the proper documents have been cleared."

"Klic, please see to the needs of our crew." Deven gave a slight bow. That was an old-fashioned wording. Not Pilthian, but something that would have been common fifty years ago.

"Yes, Captain." Gosta kept his back straight and his steps short to walk alongside the shorter Thurnil.

"I would like us to chat, Captain Fhailson." Sedari looked pointedly at Vas.

Vas folded her arms and gave her a dead look.

"My second stays with me. But I would like to talk as well. You can speak freely."

Sedari was clearly torn between an interesting Pilthian and having his second there. That she really didn't like humans, or non-Pilthians in general, was obvious.

Her lip only curled slightly this time. "That is fine." Sedari clapped her hands and two Pilthian men came out with tables and chairs.

Vas waited to sit until after the two captains had.

"That is an interesting tattoo you have," Sedari said as she poured heilina, a strong liquor, into three glasses.

"It was part of my job."

Sedari said nothing but raised an eyebrow in question. Deven's smile was deadly. "I'm retired, you could say."

"I've never heard of any retired assassins." She took a long sip of the golden drink and nodded to both. "Please enjoy. We've had to set back the start of the conclave until tomorrow. Some important crews couldn't be here today."

That was interesting. Vas took her glass, but kept her right index finger, and more importantly, the ring on it, over the mouth of the glass. The ring was one of Gosta's inventions that really hadn't gotten much use—it could detect poison.

The gem in the ring flashed a subtle green—it was clear. Deven's ring was on his thumb. The spark of annoyance that briefly crossed his face as he glanced at his ring wasn't good.

"I would like to know more about this conclave. We are new to this." He sat down the glass but was watching Sedari, so it landed on the lip and tumbled off. His move to catch it looked legitimate, but Vas had seen how fast he could move. Had he wanted to actually catch it, he would have. He picked up the now empty and cracked glass from where it had bounced on his foot. Or rather, where he'd placed his foot. There was a fair amount of liquid on his boot now that could be studied later. "Do forgive me. It was a long trip here."

Vas had been watching Sedari while Deven dumped his drink and saw a glint of something, whether it was anger or fear she wasn't sure, as his glass fell.

"Let me order you another glass." Sedari schooled her face and turned to call one of her people.

"It's fine, he can have mine. Both of us never drink at the same time." Vas reached over and handed Deven her drink.

He held his thumb over it for a brief second then took a sip. "Thank you, Lisha, thoughtful as always."

"I can have another brought out." Sedari looked at the drink being soaked up by the dirt and sand she'd packed in as flooring.

"I think one is enough." Deven took a longer sip. "We prefer not to drink at the same time. Helps keep people from trying things they shouldn't." He watched Sedari for a few seconds then sat down his glass. "We were talking about what this conclave is meant to do?"

They'd found out as much information about the conclave as they could once she'd gotten the specs for their job. Being a bi-annual gathering of pirates, that hadn't been much. Except for the fact that tips on hot items and where to buy them were common behind the scenes.

But that lack of prior knowledge and the fact that Sedari was clearly interested in Deven, gave them a good reason for a longer discussion.

"This is a chance for those who normally work alone to gather and share intel on the various systems." She nodded to Vas. "You have two Commonwealth species high in your ranks. That indicates you have done work there. Such information could be useful for other crews. You can barter items, but more than that, information. It lasts five days from the start. I decide when we start."

"Interesting, so why take this chance? You don't know my crew; I'm thinking you don't know most of the others either."

Sedari smiled. "But I do. I did a lot of research on you, the other crews as well. Very impressive."

Vas was busy scanning the area in the back, whatever her eye patch could pick up. It would be interesting to hear what Deven said. He and Gosta had created such a wild history for this team that she wasn't sure how he could add to it.

"We've been busy. I like to stay occupied in my retirement."

"That's one thing I don't get. The assassins' guild is very

old school and very secretive. If you don't mind me saying so, *that* is not either." She nodded to his chest and the tattoo.

Deven flashed a sexy smile and flexed his chest. "It's not supposed to be. I was an assassin, the best. I decided I wanted more. This is to remind anyone who comes after me that I lived, and they won't be able to say the same if they go against me." His tone was at odds with his smile.

Vas half-listened to the rest of the small talk, mostly about the rich idiots that Sedari had robbed in the past. Vas focused her eyepatch and its receiver toward the back of the area. There wasn't much to see, but she was now picking up something with the receiver. People behind the curtain had moved closer to it and were now in range of audible pick-up.

"She will be furious that the drink wasn't consumed."

"It wasn't my fault he's a clumsy oaf. She'll have to seduce him the old-fashioned way."

"What she wants, she wants."

"A fighter with an assassin's mark? Even if she had drugged him, I wouldn't have waited around."

Vas sighed. They'd still run a test of the remains sitting on his boot, but she'd much rather have had Sedari simply want to have sex with Deven than something more permanent. Of course, Vas would make sure she paid for that attempt, but she couldn't blame her.

CHAPTER TWENTY-TWO

THE SPEAKERS IN THE BACK moved away so Vas turned her attention to the people passing by the open front of the massive tent-like structure. Deven could report back if she missed anything from Sedari.

The people going by didn't seem to be paying attention to anyone other than whoever they were with. Their conversations were either designed to be boring and useless, or they were actually that boring in their lives.

"I told them they needed to wait. There are too many missing." It was the fury of the voice more than the words that caught her attention. The speaker was barely within range for her receiver to pick up, and was out of visual completely.

She got to her feet and stood at parade rest behind Deven. This put her a bit closer to the outside.

"Is there something you need?" Sedari barely looked away from Deven as she spoke.

Deven responded before Vas could. "She's protecting me as she's supposed to. There seems to be more people moving around and we can't be too careful, can we?"

"Everyone who has landed has signed a peace accord. Are there specific people she is looking for?" Again, not even looking Vas' way.

Vas turned herself a bit more. Deven could handle it and she could listen to both conversations.

"I said, not now. Damn your Finglian hides."

Damn it, the voice was moving away from the tent. Vas automatically took a step to follow, then realized she'd need an excuse.

"Lisha, could you return to our shuttle and bring back a tablet with the images of those interesting ships we saw?" Deven's voice was calm, but he was suddenly tense. "The ones our communications officer found." Damn, he wanted her to bring back images of the ships Aithnea and Xsit found? She knew he'd have a good reason for it, but it made her nervous.

"Aye, Captain." She gave a slight bow then moved out of the tent.

"The accords were for all landed crews, yes? And the ones who haven't come down yet?"

"All of the ships have representatives on the planet, that's how they work."

Vas left the tent. She seriously doubted that the ships in question had a ground crew down on the planet, but something made Deven trust Sedari enough to share what they had. And he'd given her a chance to follow the voice she'd heard.

She tried to look like she was on a mission as well as listen to everything around her.

She stopped herself an instant before she crashed into a tall, furred creature—one of the Hive, or rather, pretending-not-to-be-Hive crew. "Beg pardon, gentle sire." She flung out the most non-Commonwealth accent she could find as she steadied herself.

"Be careful." The creature growled at her. His voice was different than the one she'd heard before, but she realized that like her, he was trying to hide his real accent. Considering he was one of the Hive-not-Hive crew, she wasn't surprised.

As he moved past her, he also returned to his argument. At first, she thought it odd that he was talking out in the open, clearly with what was his natural accent and loud enough that people could hear.

Then she saw a small noise shield on his shoulder. Cheap piece of work and obviously Gosta's toys had no problem busting through it. She stepped out of his sight and pretended to be working on her scan pad as she listened into his conversation.

"—it's too dangerous. If this doesn't work, we're stuck for another six months. Damn it, stop talking over me. The heretics must die and if we can take out the rest, that's good too. But we need them to be here." He either cut his call or moved out of range as the conversation ended.

Vas waited twenty seconds, then came out from behind the ship she was standing near. He wasn't in sight. Nor was his intel very useful. Knowing that someone might do something at any given time was sort of standard operating procedure in Vas' world. This was a bit more concrete as to who was behind it. And if she had her people record all the ships that came in after this point, it might give them a partial intended victims list. But it wasn't enough to determine the threat level, if any, to her own crew.

One final check to see if he'd returned within range, then she went to their shuttles. A large, hard-sided tent was set up next to their larger shuttle and her crew were organizing their things. The crew would stay in the tent, Deven and Vas would take the shuttle. If Gosta stayed down planet-side he could sleep in his, but she had a feeling he'd want to leave as soon as possible once his part was done. She'd decided against keeping two shuttles on the ground.

"How did it go, Lisha?"

Vas heard the catch in Divee's voice as he almost said Captain. "Captain is still in talks. There looks to be a delay, so the official conclave won't be until tomorrow at the earliest, just picking up a few things for him." She ducked into the shuttle and downloaded a single scan of the Racki ships both with and without the right filters on them. Deven might have his reasons for wanting to show Sedari, but Vas saw no reason to give her too much information.

She left the shuttle, but her crew was too quiet for comfort. "What's wrong?" They were all standing around. Except two. "Where are Mac and Flarik?" While she, Deven, and Gosta were keeping their real names hidden, she wasn't worried about the first names of her crew.

Terel stood slowly. She was furthest back in the tent and already had a med area set up. Vas would have reminded her that this was a fact-finding mission—a peaceful gathering; but she knew it wouldn't matter. On either topic.

"Mac saw someone he knew and then when he didn't come back, Flarik took off after him."

"Damn it if anyone can find trouble it would be him. How long ago did they leave?"

"I saw Mac take off about five minutes after you and the captain." Gon did better about recalling who was who than Divee.

"And Flarik took off about twenty minutes ago."

Terel's tone echoed what was going through Vas' mind. If Mac got into trouble, Flarik would have gotten him out of it immediately. "This isn't good. There is something going on besides this gathering." She wasn't certain if Deven had sent her on this mission to give her a chance to follow whoever she was listening to, or he truly wanted to show Sedari the ship. But he usually managed to combine goals, so she needed to get the tablet to him. She also needed to find out where in the hells Mac and Flarik were. Comm use was supposed to be limited, but neither responded when Vas sent out a code to them.

"Gon, take this to the captain. He's meeting with a Pilthian named Sedari in the large tent down the way. Tell him I had an issue with our pilot and needed to punish him. I don't know that we want them to know we are missing people."

Gon took the tablet and nodded. "I'll keep an eye out

as well."

Terel adjusted her sidearms. "I'm coming too. There may be injured. Especially if someone got in Flarik's way."

"Bathie, you're in charge until the captain comes back." Vas glared around the tent. "No one else leaves."

Once they looked as agreeable to that as she knew she'd get from them, she and Terel left.

"Flarik went south," Terel said as they left the tent. "How is the woman leading this event?" She kept her voice low.

"Interesting. A scarred Pilthian and she has at least one mixed breed one working for her. She is very interested in our captain, but it could just be slim pickings of fellow Pilthians out here." Vas filled her in on what she'd heard but Terel wasn't impressed either.

"That's not much to go on, and we already knew something was off about those Hive pirates." She had been speaking very low but swallowed her words as a one-armed Glatherin staggered a bit too close. Good to know some pirate myths were alive and well; he'd been drinking for a while to get as bad off as he was.

"Sorry, ladies." His words were enough to make any-one around him drunk. Vas pulled out her blaster when he almost tripped into Terel. "No shoot. Leaving." He stumbled off and Vas watched him vanish behind a ship.

Terel stood there with an odd look on her face.

"What's wrong? Did he hurt you?" She didn't see any-thing, but Terel was patting down her side.

"No, but let's move a bit out of the way." She had her hand closed around something and all but dragged Vas around a cargo ship with no crew visible.

"He was faking it, doing a damn good job too, but no one as drunk as he was pretending to be could have gotten this under my blaster belt like that." She unfolded what was in her hand, a note.

"Old school, most people use chips. What's it say?"

"That the writer doesn't write much and has horrible penmanship." Terel looked up and then back to the note. "From what I can translate, our people are at the Cothin cave three clicks due south from here. Also, 'thanks for Anteria five years ago. Thager.'" Her look this time was even more confused. "Anteria? Thager?"

"Five years ago?" Vas started walking south but held out her hand for the note. The writing was horrific, but Terel had been right about what it said. "Five years ago, we *were* fighting on Anteria. Messy battle and there were some real assholes on our side. Remember that company from Hasihen? I figured they'd start killing us next."

Terel scowled. "Our crew injuries were as much because of them as the people we were fighting against. But what has that got to do with our mysterious note writer?"

Vas started to shake her head, but then stopped as a thought hit her. "I sort of recognize the name, this has to be him. After the fighting ended, and the other side was surrendering, three Hasihens started killing them instead of taking their surrender. I caught a few about to kill a Glatherin. He was on his knees, no weapon. They wouldn't stop, so I shot them." She looked up. "In the legs, just in the legs. I brought in the Glatherin as a prisoner and that name sounds familiar."

They started walking again.

Terel shrugged. "And he obviously got free and became a pirate. Hey, for once doing a nice deed paid off."

Vas laughed and pocketed the note. "Not that we do a lot of them, normally. But yeah, this one paid off. It was mostly because I wanted an excuse to shoot the Hasihens. An entire species of assholes." She looked back but Thager was out of sight. "Wish he'd stuck around a bit though. I'd like to pick his brain about things." Like the fact he had known who she and her company were even though they were disguised.

"And find out why he already had that note on hand

when he found us?" Terel looked back as well.

"That's one thing. He might have been heading toward our tent and planned to give it to whoever he saw."

"Or he's setting us up," Terel said.

"Exactly. The story of our lives. But since I gave direct orders not to leave until after our meeting, and Flarik would only break that for a very good reason, we need to take the chance." Vas wasn't too surprised about Mac leaving. Just a whiff of a secret deal somewhere and he'd be gone. But Flarik leaving was an issue.

The path led down a slope toward a small lake. The ground was rocky and had large enough hills to hide a cave, but they still had a way to go to travel three clicks. Nevertheless, Vas peered around the closest hills as they passed.

"Who lives on this world?" Vas was certain it had been in some of the documents she'd received, but this had happened so fast that she'd focused on the items involving the conclave and the possible people here. Aithnea felt this would be a good place to start looking for contacts of the last Pirate of Boagada, and it looked like a likely start for finding who was stealing from Dackon Industries. Their job might be a cover for them, but it was still her name on a contract. She'd see it through, after they got what else they needed.

"Not many. It's owned by the Caseaz Company. A conglomeration out of the Triven province. There is a small population of Ilerians living on the southern continent, but they aren't native. If there were native populations, they died out or left long ago."

"This company rents out their planet to a bunch of pirates?" Vas knew this conclave had been going on for years, and always in this sector.

"As far as we can tell. Pirates are still not really a positive influence for most star systems, but I think they rent the space to anyone who has the money."

Vas walked around a hill, but still no cave. "Then who is paying for this? They never asked for money."

"According to Flarik, the larger pirate companies do. This benefits them as they get a better idea of who is doing what. Some smaller companies don't come back which tells me this might be a recruiting trip for the big ones."

Vas nodded. There were some merc companies who tried to pick new crew from the smaller companies. They wisely left Vas and her crew alone. Of course, she didn't have that reputation riding behind her here—or rather, Captain Fhailson didn't.

Did someone try to pick off Mac, and Flarik couldn't stop them? That was an unsettling thought.

Terel paused and held up her hand. Her hearing was better than Vas' human ears, but after a few moments she heard it too. Bickering. Not loud or angry enough to be an actual fight, but the annoyance level was high in both voices. A man and a woman—neither happy.

They started jogging toward the voices. The man was Mac, but the woman was not Flarik. Bickering wasn't Flarik's style.

Vas moved ahead of Terel and pulled out her blaster. She doubted that Mac was in a life-threatening situation; even he wouldn't argue like a twelve-year-old with someone trying to kill him.

The voices were coming out of a cave all right and still no sound or sight of Flarik.

"This wasn't my fault. You always blame everyone else. I'm stuck here because of you." That was the woman, young, probably human. Vas might not recognize the voice, but she knew the tone—she often had it when dealing with Mac.

"I wanted to see if that was you. How did I know you were bait for a trap?" Mac sounded like he was struggling, so both were likely tied up. Vas couldn't figure out why they hadn't gagged them though. She would have.

Terel pulled on her sleeve and pointed up a ways from the cave mouth where a low hill sat. A single white feather hovered and then drifted down. Flarik wasn't taking a chance that anyone would find one of her changed feathers. Vas went for her comm, but only had faint static on the other end. Whatever block had kept her from Mac and Flarik was now keeping her from anyone outside this area. Mac and whoever he was arguing with seemed to be alone, but the fact that Flarik was holding back said she was expecting someone.

Vas held up a hand to let Flarik know they'd seen where she was, then tried to make sense of the arguing inside the cave.

"What are you doing here? Aren't you driving luxury liners somewhere?" Mac had a healthy dose of bitterness there.

"That fell through. I am here for a job, but I guess I arrived early. I'd heard that your crew were killed months ago. So, when I saw you, I sort of freaked out. Trust me, I had no idea that you'd follow or that some jerks were waiting to grab you. And me."

"They could be after you, you know."

"I drive a dozer, Mac. A clean-up-after-all-the-excitement-is-over dozer. No one is going to be after me. They grabbed me because I was with you."

"Aw, geesh, I'm sorry, Janx. Don't cry, okay?"

Mac was obviously close to the woman or had been at some point in his life. Vas leaned to speak into Terel's ear. "Keep your blaster out and watch Flarik's location for clues. I'm going to get Mac and his friend back." Not the brightest idea she'd had lately, but she couldn't wait for whoever grabbed them to come back.

At Terel's nod, she slipped down to the cave mouth.

The woman sniffled a bit. "It's been a sucked year, ya know? I tried to be what they wanted, but nope, not glamorous enough. Who needs a pilot to be glamorous? I'm living in a hovel on Dethi Five, have no freedom, not really, because I can't afford anything."

Vas peered into the cave. Mac was tied to a chair, one that had seriously seen better days. Across from him was a woman with shoulder-length blond hair. She was also tied to a beat-up chair and looked like she'd been roughed up before she got tied to it. Vas couldn't see much of Mac's face, but his bright red hair looked tousled.

Unfortunately, the woman saw Vas, with her blaster held high, before Mac did and screamed. Mac hopped and turned his chair toward her.

"Va—Lisha. Thank you! It's okay, she's with us." His smile had a bit of a bruise to it.

"So, not just you. *None* of your people died?" The woman tilted her head.

"Some did. This is Lisha, our new second in command." How Mac could succeed at being a con man when he was such a bad liar, Vas had no idea.

"I know who that is, now." The woman blushed. "Sorry that I screamed, but you have to admit you don't look like you right now."

"And who might that be?" Vas holstered her blaster, then moved forward and freed Mac. "Are there any traps? You probably could have broken these damn chairs and gotten free, you know that, right?"

Mac rubbed his wrists and shrugged. "No traps that I saw. Things happened fast and I got distracted. Oh, this is my cousin, Janx. Janx, meet Lisha."

Janx shook her head. "If you want to be Lisha, I will address you as Lisha. But I also know who you are. You're on wanted posters."

Vas had been about to untie Janx but stopped and took a step back. She also pulled out her blaster again. "No one has wanted posters for me. Now, what are you doing here? And to let you know, cousin or not, I take care of my crew."

Janx held still but dropped her voice. "I know you are Vaslisha Tor Dain, captain of the *Warrior Wench* and the leader of a band of mercenaries. I know that you were killed along with your crew almost a year ago. At the same time, I know there is a reward out for you. Providing you weren't already dead. I didn't know Mac was alive, let alone here." She lifted her chin. She might have broken down in tears about her life in general to her cousin, but she would face potential death with a chin held high.

"I like you. But someone used you to get to Mac, which means to get to me." Vas kept her blaster out, but it was more because of the feeling of a trap closing on her than concern about Janx. She motioned toward Janx. "Mac, untie your cousin and let's get the hell out of here. I think she has a lot to tell us." She added a smile to keep things from seeming too threatening. But she wasn't letting Janx out of her sight until she found out what was going on.

Terel and Flarik came running into the cave as Mac freed Janx.

"We have company." Flarik was the queen of understatement but the feathers rising on the back of her neck told much more.

They were in trouble.

CHAPTER TWENTY-THREE

"DAMN IT." VAS LOOKED AROUND the cave. It wasn't very defensible with little to no coverage to hide behind. She jogged toward the back. A stone corridor went out the rear of the cave, but this wasn't the time to see where it went. Aside from making sure no one could come in that way. "Terel, I need you to keep an eye back here. Might be a dead end, might be our way out, or another way in for them. Whoever they are." She looked to Flarik, who was watching out of the cave.

"No idea. I counted ten that I could see. I saw who tied up these two, and these aren't them." She didn't have her blaster out but flexed her talons. "These look to be more standard military rather than pirates. Not sure whose military though."

"Mac, I'm assuming neither of you have weapons?"

Janx held out a very sad looking folding knife. "Only this."

"I had my snub blaster, but they took it."

Flarik handed him her blaster and Vas handed over her snub blaster to Janx. She really hoped this cousin of his was on the up and up. At this point, there wasn't much to go on and they needed everyone here to be able to fight. Janx didn't look like a trained fighter, but she did check out the settings on the blaster correctly and seemed comfortable with it.

"We want the red-headed woman, the rest of you can go." The voice was low and guttural and Common probably wasn't one of his first five languages.

Vas shrugged to the others. "Go where? Away from

here, so you can kill them? And what do you want with me? I have done nothing to you." She was tossing that out there, but she might have. If they got through this, she needed to see this wanted poster. The Garmainians had one on her, but that shouldn't still be active. Not to mention that the Garmainian home world was blown to bits.

"You've done enough, Vaslisha Tor Dain. We know you attacked many of our ships and then fled here to hide. We aren't fooled."

Vas dropped her voice and turned toward Flarik. "Shit. Are they Lethian Assembly?"

Flarik had been listening with her head tilted, but finally turned to her. "I believe so. The speech pattern is not one of their primary worlds, but the Maelian province is part of the Lethian Assembly and this sounds like one of their people."

"Damn it." Vas didn't know much about the Lethian Assembly or the Maelians, but this didn't look like a time to find out.

A blaster shot went past her as she was about to yell back. But it had come from inside the cave. She ducked and spun. Janx had fired.

"Look." Mac pointed out of the cave. A large body lay a few feet from the cave mouth with a blaster shot still smoldering through it. Whether he'd been the speaker or not, Vas couldn't tell. But he'd obviously been sneaking up to the cave. His thero-blaster, about the size of her leg was thrown out in front of him.

"Good shooting, Janx." Vas nodded to her, then faced the cave mouth again. Like all of her people she was against the cave wall and staying low. But that thero-blaster could have taken them all out. "You can keep coming and we can keep picking you off. Back down. I'm not surrendering and don't trust that you'll let my people go even if I did. The rest of my crew will be here soon."

"Lisha? I have one of Gosta's toys." Mac crept toward her and held out the small ball he held in his hand. "I had it with me to try and modify it to be more specific, but we could use it?"

The thing, which Gosta had never named, acted like an EM pulse and wiped out all powered weapons. The problem was, it took out everything in the immediate area, not just the enemies' weapons. She looked at the thero-blaster in the dirt beyond the cave. If more of them had those monsters, there was no way they were getting out.

"Aside from Janx's knife, how many edged weapons do we have?" She kept her voice low. Terel had two, Mac had none, and Flarik raised her talons. Vas had two blades. Both were a bit longer than Janx's, the ones in her boots would help if things came hand-to-hand, but not before that. The odds were still better than a blaster fight in this case.

"Set it off, Mac. Everyone drop your blasters." She kept her voice even lower, but everyone in the cave put down their blasters. Janx looked confused, but at a nod from Mac she put down her borrowed blaster.

Vas gave Mac a nod and he set off the gizmo.

"You don't have a chance of surviving. Toss your weapons on the ground and come out slowly." The voice was annoyingly confident.

Vas turned to Mac. He pressed the button on the ball a few more times.

"My people will be here. Why should I give up?"

"The comms won't reach out here; you couldn't have called them. You won't—"

Crackling sounds came from the hills around them along with swearing and a few minor explosions. Vas' blaster smoked a little but didn't explode. Gosta had made some improvements in his toy, it looked like.

"That won't save you." The voice was pissed now.

Vas smiled and nodded to the others. Angry people made mistakes. Angry, injured people made more. Anyone who'd been holding their weapons as the pulse went out was in pain right now.

"Come and get us."

They had been closer than Vas thought, but she'd been expecting the charge. Eight fighters came running into the cave. Three were immediately pushed back by Flarik's claws and she followed them out. She was in her element and was enjoying it.

Vas blocked a strike from a wide Dracil with a short blade, then she spun and jabbed up as he went for another try and got her dagger right under his ribs. He staggered back and she pulled her dagger free as she kicked him in the head and out of the cave.

Mac had one of Terel's extra blades and was fighting back-to-back with Janx. Granted that knife of hers was small but she was short and fast. Her opponent already had three leaks in him.

Vas spun as another attacker came into the cave, managed to get a slice in on her upper left arm, then danced out the back of the cave. They thought there had only been ten, but there was always the chance they were wrong, or they had reinforcements. Vas followed him out but sped past the cave wall. Yup, two more fighters were hiding there.

"They're coming in the back!" Terel yelled, but a quick glance told Vas that Terel was handling them. The tunnel there was narrow; few people would mount an attack from there.

Vas focused on her own attackers. Her charge had confused them. If she had to guess, even though they were acceptable fighters, hand-to-hand wasn't common with them. Vas ran for the hill that Flarik had been behind and hoped they would follow.

They did without hesitation. She was faster than they were and got to the spot well ahead of them. This kept them from being able to join the others and gave her more room to fight. She would kill for her Zalith blades right now.

The first one was faster than the other two, but still not quick. Vas waited for him near the top of the hill.

He ran and lunged, he had a full sword and used it like he knew what to do. Vas dropped and swung low with her legs knocking him over. As he went down, she stabbed his sword arm. He dropped the blade and she grabbed it. Now this at least felt better than only having a dagger. He staggered to his feet but was having far more problems than he should. He stumbled around, almost like he was drunk. Then he dropped to his knees and collapsed face first at her feet. The other two were approaching but breathing heavily. She didn't know anything about their planet, so maybe it had a different atmosphere. They were acting as if they weren't getting enough oxygen. They both swung at her, from at least three feet away, then fell over.

Vas kicked them. They weren't dead, but definitely unconscious. She started down the hill toward the cave when the world started to tilt. She tried to speed up, but found her feet barely moving. She wasn't sure at what point she dropped her stolen sword, but she noticed when her dagger fell from her fingers. She dropped right after it.

CHAPTER TWENTY-FOUR

DEVEN'S VOICE BROKE INTO VAS' slumber. Her head was throbbing too hard for her to even think about trying to open her eyes.

"Thank you, Sedari, I believe we can revive them. It's good that you have drone surveillance running."

"And that our drones are weaponized. We will remove the Dracil from the conclave. From what I saw, they captured two of your crew and held them to bring in the others."

Vas assumed Sedari was pointing to Mac and Janx, and that Deven would roll with their new crew addition and ask questions later.

"I appreciate that. However, given this situation, I believe I must decline your dinner invitation. Please give my regards to the other captains."

Sedari paused before answering and Vas heard the annoyance that she was trying to hide. "I understand. I will send for you and your crew when we are ready in the morning."

Vas waited until the footsteps crunching through the dirt and rock vanished before opening her eyes. "That was fun." She let out a long breath and tried to get her eyes to focus. "What in the hells did she hit us with?"

"My guess would be Iogutha powder in some sort of spray form. Nasty stuff." Terel was sitting up on her cot but didn't look happy.

Flarik rolled into a sitting position and dropped to her feet. "I agree. However, they could have simply killed us all and sorted it out after. Fighting is against the accord of the conclave."

Gosta had been out of eyesight but he stepped forward. "It is. But the captain and I were with Sedari when news of the attack came in. She didn't seem surprised, but she did act quickly to get those drones out."

"What in the hell happened? Gon gave me the pad and said you had an errand. By the way, Sedari has never seen a ship like that and no amount of searching could make it visible to her equipment. Then her people start yelling about an attack. Turns out it's you all, with a new friend." He pointedly looked to Janx, who was slowly sitting up and trying to remain unnoticed.

Mac pushed himself up but didn't look like he was going to try for more than the edge of his cot. "This is my cousin, Janx. She found me here, but thought we were all dead. She freaked and ran; I took off after her. We got grabbed." He dropped his head into his hands. The drug the drones carried wasn't fun.

Flarik shook out her shoulders, but she looked like she was ready to snap someone in half. "I went after Mac when his comm didn't respond. Not only do they have drones, but they also have comm dead zones set up out there."

Vas filled Deven in on the rest up until she blacked out.

"You think they were trying to get you for a warrant?" Deven shook his head. "Whose?"

Janx had only nodded when they'd been introduced but she seemed to be arguing with herself. She finally spoke up. "It hit the waves yesterday. I figured it was a hoax since the last we heard the *Warrior Wench* was reported lost with all hands." She pulled out a small pad and started searching. Finally, she held it up and handed it to Deven. "See? I was curious because Mac may be a pain, but he used to look out for me when we were kids." She turned to him and shook her head. "I've been grieving you for the past year."

Mac gave a crooked smile. "Thanks, I guess."

Deven swore at the pad, then handed it over to Vas.

"Damn it. Why can't they use flattering pictures?" This one was a few years old and taken right after a two-month ground siege. She hadn't bathed in two months and looked it. It said she was wanted for crimes against the Lethian Assembly. Nice big reward, but no specifics on the crimes. She handed the pad back to Janx. "You don't live in the Commonwealth, do you?"

"No, I'm from Dethi Five. I work out of there and most of my jobs don't take me into the Commonwealth. Stories are saying the entire place was destroyed."

Vas shook her head at Deven. "Someone has to do a better job with the intel. Mac, I'll let you update her, but the Commonwealth is alive and more or less well."

"Someone recognized you and set a trap to get you. I don't know that being in the middle of a bunch of pirates is a good place for you to stay." Flarik looked a bit less murdery than before, but Vas almost felt sorry for those idiots who attacked them if she ever caught them. Or not.

"I can help disguise you," Janx said. "The hair will be the hardest, but we can cover that as well." She shrugged. "I used to work in live theater on the cruise liners before I made it up to pilot. I still have a full make-up kit on my ship."

Deven nodded. "We really do have to disguise you, or you go back up to the ship."

"I know." Vas turned to Janx. "Is your ship down here?"

"No, I was contracted to be here in a few days, but ended up being early." She shrugged. "They weren't happy, so told me to stay far out of orbit. I have a two-seater shuttle pod down here."

"It would be better if you two went to her ship, changed Lisha, and then landed further out when you come back. Lisha will go up to our ship with Gosta and a new second will come down. I'll tell Sedari you had a bad reaction to the gas the drones used." Deven was fussing with Janx's pad. And scowling. "Gosta, when you get up to the ship can you do a check on this warrant? We need to figure out what's going on."

Gosta was so happy at getting back to the ship and his beloved computers that his neck bob bounced. "Aye, Captain. Shall we get a gurney out to the shuttle for our ailing second?"

"Nice touch," Vas said. She really hated hiding, but they were right, it was that or stay up on the *Traitor's Folly.*

Terel made up an empty gurney that was heavily wrapped and looked enough like a body that no one would wonder about it. Vas knew Sedari's drones would probably be watching their area closely. Not so much to protect Vas or her people, but to cover their own asses. From what Gosta had read up on about this gathering, safety for all participants was crucial. If it got around that someone had broken that, Sedari could be in a world of hurt.

Gosta lifted off and they all went back into the tent.

"The *Warrior Wench* is up there?" Janx asked. "I scanned the ships in orbit, I kinda like seeing them and doing cleanup doesn't really give me much chance. I didn't see her."

"Nope, the *Warrior Wench* had some issues, so we left her in the Commonwealth." Vas narrowed her eyes. "What is it you do again?"

Janx blushed. "I'm a dozer pilot. I was contracted a few weeks ago to clean up space rubble in this system. In three days."

"Really? Anything said about what was going to cause the rubble? Do you know who hired you?" The hairs on the back of Vas' neck were standing up. Three days would have been when this gathering was over—if it hadn't been pushed back.

"I'm grunt labor, my ship is a giant space trash collector, they don't tell us much. We get hired through a contractor, we're never told who paid for the clean-up." She fished around in her pack and pulled out a smaller tablet. "This is a fairly standard cleanup contract. It does say that six other crews have been hired, which is a lot for what we do."

"Six?" Flarik stepped forward with a bit more aggression than Janx clearly felt comfortable with. "How many are normal?"

Janx stepped back and moved closer to Mac. "It depends. When the Garmainian home world was blown up, we had twelve. For most sanctioned battles we might have four."

"And they ordered six? That can't be good." Vas wasn't sure what they'd gotten into, but they might have to find another way to track down the last Pirate of Boagada as well as whoever was stealing shipments from Dackon Industries.

"This contract is too vague to be of use." Deven handed both pads back to Janx. "I think we need to get you changed and keep a tight watch down here tonight." He tapped his comm. "Hrrru? Gosta is on his way up there, but I need you to move further out of orbit once he gets there. And keep someone monitoring communications at all times."

"Aye. What are we looking for?"

"We have no idea but watch for anything." He clicked off the comm. "This conclave has been happening for over fifteen years, yet the year we come in hell breaks loose. That can't be a coincidence."

"No, it can't." Flarik tapped her claws together. "I think we do need to get our wanted poster girl out of here though. I hear booted feet, a number of them in unison, coming this way."

Vas hopped off her cot and grabbed a blanket. She

wrapped it tightly around herself and hunched over. "Janx, can you escort me out the back way to your pod? You've got an old former pirate who wanted to relive her glory days."

Janx grabbed her pack and took Vas' arm. "Right this way, Old Mother."

They made it out the back and zig-zagged behind a few other camps. Vas couldn't see the main road, so she wasn't certain if whoever those booted feet were had been heading toward their camp, but better to be safe. Things were crumbling on the edges. They weren't hellish yet, but they would be soon if they didn't change direction.

Neither Vas nor Janx spoke, and no one appeared to question her blanket-covered self by the time they got to Janx's pod. She wasn't kidding about the size; two people could fit if neither were large.

Vas unwrapped herself from the blanket once they lifted off. "How long have you piloted a dozer?" They were large ships, but usually only manned by one or two people. Their entire purpose was to remove space debris, so they weren't fast, flashy, or defensive. They were shaped sort of like giant rocks.

"The last three years. The cruise line I worked for got shut down for smuggling and we all lost our jobs. None of the crew were involved, but still couldn't find a job after that. I don't love what I do, but it is freeing being alone."

Vas nodded. She'd been debating on asking Mac if his cousin might be a good fit for their merc crew, but disliking being around a lot of people wasn't a good fit.

"Where'd you learn to knife fight like that? I only saw a bit, but you are fast."

Janx laughed. "Believe it or not, Mac. He used a stick, but he taught me how to fight. We were close growing up. I'm glad he's not dead."

"So are we." Vas watched the stars as the pod passed larger ships. "You know, if you hadn't come down and seen Mac, we might not have known what was going on." She could tell the younger woman was feeling guilty about what happened.

"You still don't know, though, do you? And now your cover has been compromised." Janx maneuvered the small pod toward a massive block of metal. Standard dozer.

"Actually, you helped us realize it was compromised. My team would have found out about the warrant eventually, but we're not from out here. It takes a while to build up data-gathering."

"True. And that wasn't on the open frequencies. I check the less used lanes for places that might need my services." She looked embarrassed at the admission.

"You realize that all those people back there in my tent, including your cousin, are mercs. We are always looking for ways to turn things around to our advantage. I call it being business smart."

They docked into the dozer and once the docking bay was sealed again they left the little pod. Vas wobbled a bit getting out.

"Are you okay?" Janx sounded terrified.

"It's the result of being heavily drugged and being in that tiny pod right after waking." She tilted her head. "You were fine facing those attackers, but you're awfully worried now." Vas didn't think Janx meant to hurt her, but she was on the edge of freaking out.

"It's...okay. I sort of followed the adventures of all of you, right up until a year ago when you vanished. Then the Commonwealth cut itself off from everyone else and no news came out. You and your crew are kinda special. I'm a huge fan of yours." She looked a lot younger than she had before.

"You're a *fan*?" Vas knew vid and music stars had fans. Didn't think a merc crew would. Janx was silent for a few minutes as they walked down an industrial corridor. There was nothing fancy or even welcoming about this ship, or at least this part of it.

"Yeah. You have such an exciting life. Even before I became a dozer pilot, my life wasn't exciting." She shrugged. "Plus, I'm not good around people. Mac was always the mouth when we pulled off things." She pushed open a heavy door that clearly led to her personal space. This was decorated, not fancy, but filled with pictures of places. And a few of the *Victorious Dead* and *Warrior Wench*.

"How long have you been a fan?"

"Since Mac joined you. I was already off planet, but he posted to me to say he was becoming a merc. I was envious."

Vas turned around from the photos. "Do you want to become a merc?"

Janx shook her head so fast her blonde hair was a whirl. "No way. No offense, I really enjoy the records of what you do, but killing people isn't my thing."

"And you don't like a lot of people."

She laughed and pointed to a chair with its back to a large mirror propped up on a table. "That too. Now come sit over here and let's make you someone else completely."

Vas watched as Janx pulled out a serious collection of make-up pans, wigs, and what looked to Vas like moldable explosive. "Ummm, what is that?"

Janx quickly created a nose. "Moldable skin. I can change your features, then we put make-up on, and you will fool any facial recognition scan in the galaxy."

"Scans can see through that stuff."

"Not this quality." Janx's grin reminded Vas of Mac. "I got that cruise ship to pay for it before they got busted. Explained we really needed it to make the actors seem more real. They bought the top-of-the-line stuff."

"Kinda understand why they turned to smuggling."

She shrugged. "Yeah, not sure what they were really doing, but money wasn't their strong point."

Vas nodded. Or tried to. Janx grabbed her chin. "I need you to hold very still. This stuff can be tricky, and we want you looking different, not like a monster."

"I will stay still." Vas had been undercover before, but it was usually simple changes. Of course, she wasn't trying to fool scanners—or drones. It was disturbing how quickly Sedari got her weaponized drones out there. Why have a comm dead zone that far out?

"Can we pause for me to call Gosta? I thought of something I need him to look at."

Janx nodded and put her materials down.

Vas hit her comm. "Gosta? Are you on the deck?"

"Captain, yes I am, but I can barely hear you. Is something wrong?"

"Not immediately with me, but can you do a scan on the area surrounding the camp compound? A bit past where we found Mac and Janx? Look for comm dead zones. But do a low-level scan since we have no idea what tech Sedari is using."

"Will do. Will you be coming here when you are done there?"

"Yeah, if Janx doesn't mind taking me over. It would be better if Lisha's replacement comes from our ship."

"Good idea. I'll report what I find."

Gosta clicked off.

"You don't mind running me over to the *Traitor's Folly* after this? That's our new ship."

Janx shook her head. "Could I check it out a bit? I'm not as much of a ship junkie as Mac, but I do like to see them intact, instead of the way I normally see them on my job."

"Sure, stay as long as you want. I'll be taking the shuttle back down." Vas sat back in the chair as Janx reassembled her molds. "When you get a contract for a job, how much information do they give you?"

"Not a lot, just where, what we'll be hauling away, and what other dozers are in on it. We all must report unauthorized dozers—sometimes scavengers try to come in."

"If you're hauling the stuff away to be dumped, what would it matter?" Vas knew that probably after every ship battle that she and her crew had been hired for, a dozer or two was brought in afterwards to get rid of the remains. There were dump processing stations on the outer rim of the Commonwealth and many systems out here had them.

"True, but if someone's paid for us to dump it, it gets dumped. There could be security issues that they don't want found."

"What were you contracted to remove here?" There was no debris in orbit around this planet—but there were a lot of ships.

"Ships." Janx kept her voice low. "When I got my days messed up and came here early, I noticed that all the ships seemed to be intact. There isn't going to be an official, contracted space fight here, is there?" The dread in her voice was clear. Her life might not be exciting, but she didn't really want it to become so.

Vas clenched her fist. "No. This is supposed to be a gathering, not a fight. Is it okay for me to move enough to contact my ship again?" Janx had been working quickly, but Vas wasn't sure she was done. Gosta needed to confirm what they feared. Before Janx could answer, alarms echoed throughout the ship.

"Someone broke my seals." Janx ran to a dark monitor and hit the buttons along the side.

Vas followed her over. Eight heavily armed and armored troops were coming from the opposite corridor than she and Janx had. "What's down that way?"

"They're coming from the port to the holding tank;

smaller junk gets put inside. The big stuff I get a beam on and pull."

"How did they get in?" Vas still had her two blasters and dagger, but she seriously doubted that she and Janx, with her small knife, could stop them. They looked dangerously well-prepared. And covered. Full helmets meant she couldn't see who they were, and she didn't recognize the armor.

"I don't…crap. They blasted it." Janx changed screens and angrily tapped where a dark sleek ship sat attached to hers. "Look at those edges they made. That is going to take a lot to repair, damn it."

Vas spun her around. "Janx, those people are killers. We have to get out of here."

"Oh, we'll see about that." Janx ran to the back wall of her room and hit the corner. The panel slid down and a lovely selection of weapons appeared.

"Where did you…" Vas found herself in awe—that collection would make Walvento weep.

"Single-person ship, some folks think I'm easy pickings. I try to convince them otherwise." Janx grabbed a thero-blaster and handed it to Vas. "It's modified. The walls on my ship will deflect the energy. Want a sword too?" She held up a nice long blade. Vas holstered her two blasters and took both weapons.

"As for their ship." Janx went back to the viewscreen and pulled out a keyboard. "First, seal the hole. Then blast it out to space. Mac would love this."

Before Vas could say a word, the dark ship was forcibly ejected from the side of the dozer.

Which meant she and Janx were now trapped with eight, heavily armed, and now very pissed attackers.

CHAPTER TWENTY-FIVE

"THAT WILL SHOW THEM!" JANX looked far too pleased with herself to have really thought it through. She was definitely related to Mac.

Vas hit her comm but all she got was static. On the chance anyone could hear her, she told Gosta they were under attack and now trapped with their attackers.

Janx didn't look upset. "This way they can't get reinforcements in."

Vas checked the thero-blaster again and shook her head. "Good point. And I doubt we could have chased them back to their ship anyway. What's to stop them from latching on again though?"

Janx had loaded up on a number of blasters and a smaller sword, but she tapped the viewscreen. "Betsy has a few tricks." She gave a crooked grin. "That's the name of my ship. After a beloved aunt. Don't tell Mac."

Vas watched as the dark ship stayed a bit away then started back. Explosions launched where it would have attached itself to this ship, then spread and it stopped dead in space.

"That was impressive." Vas didn't know what else to say. Janx was far more than she seemed.

"Again, a girl's gotta do what a girl's gotta do." She pulled up a few more screens. "The invaders are heading to the command deck, but I have all of my controls routed down here and one other even deeper room. I want to get their numbers down before we attack." She spun. "Actually, what would you do? You are the mercenary captain after all. I'm a dozer pilot."

Vas laughed. "You're a damn tricky dozer pilot. You seem to have faced this before, and this is your ship. I always defer to the captain of the vessel."

Janx smiled. "Not exactly like this, but yeah, again, people are stupid." She turned back to the viewscreen. "I have a trap set right before the command deck. Why are they moving so slow?" Her hand hovered over the keyboard.

"Because they are looking for traps? I would be. That much muscle and armor isn't for taking a dozer. I have a feeling I have a few unwanted fans."

"Yeah, usually I don't get professionals, just drunk idiots. What did you do to the Lethian Assembly? They are really pissed."

"I have no idea. Okay, they came after a piece of wreckage that wasn't theirs and weren't going to let my ships go when we let them have it. We might have damaged one of their cruisers. Then a pair of Hive ships came after us. And someone is trying to blame my crew for the destruction of a Pilthian ship far from where we were." Vas scowled. "Those could be it. But they started it. I don't even know why they were in the Commonwealth."

"The Lethian Assembly has gotten more aggressive in the past year. As the Commonwealth had more problems, they crept closer to it. This isn't Lethian Assembly space, it's a no-mans' space of non-associated systems. But more and more Lethian Assembly and Hive ships come through here. The big ones. Ha!" Janx hit a few keys and the viewscreen expanded on a narrow corridor. Three of the attackers were in it and they dropped to the floor twitching.

"What was that?" Vas watched as the spasms stopped and they went still.

"Electric shock through the floor plates. Only good for one round before it must be reset again, but we took three out."

Vas was impressed. Janx was as tricky as Mac, without the apparent con man tendencies.

The cameras were more extensive than Vas would have suspected on a dozer, but made sense. This was an open area of space, there really was no one to call for help. Being prepared for the worst could save your life.

"It looks like one got a partial zap." Vas pointed to the screen. The remaining five were backing away from the corridor, and one was dragging his leg.

"That'll slow him down at least." Janx jumped as a blaster shot hit the wounded man and he collapsed. "Why did they shoot their own?"

Vas looked closer. The one who shot the injured one took his weapons and pushed him to the side. "He would have slowed them down. Damn. These aren't mercs. They're assassins." The wanted poster for her hadn't said dead or alive, but Vas had a feeling it was implied.

"Betsy still has a few more tricks." Janx muttered to herself as she flipped through a few more screens. Then she hit a button and a second screen with a keypad appeared. "I can do this by myself if needed, but it's easier with two."

"They're testing out your corridor." Vas would have looked at other areas of the ship as well as the command deck, but Janx's electric shock greeting probably reinforced them thinking she and Vas were in the command deck.

"Yeah, they always do. That's one thing I don't get, why have your command controls where people would think they would be? Seems like a serious target."

Vas laughed. "I've thought of that as well, but I try to keep my ship from being boarded. When we get through with this, I'd like it if you could come up with some plans for the *Warrior Wench* and the rest of my fleet."

Janx looked up. "Fleet?" She waved her hands. "Later. But yes, I'd love to help. Okay, when they get in the corridor this time, you and I hit this key combination. Two-two-five. I'll call it."

Vas was curious but figured seeing what this did in action would make Janx happier. And she really did want her to do some specs for Vas' ships.

"Now!"

As they both entered the code on their keypads, a cloud of white hit the screen and the corridor doors locked shut.

Blaster fire came through the speakers and the two remaining fighters outside were pounding and yelling. One put a small explosive on the door, and they both stepped back.

Alarms rang out and were swallowed by the explosion. It wasn't large; if you didn't want to blow a ship up, large explosions were a bad idea.

When the screens cleared. The door was buckled and the white mist had vanished. The bodies in the corridor weren't moving.

"And this one was?"

"Snow drift, my own invention." Janx grinned. "Not stable in large amounts, but very effective in close quarters. They froze to death."

"I seriously need you to talk to Gosta and Hrrru about adding some of these defenses." Vas watched the final two as they pulled out a small gizmo. They both pointed away from the command deck and started making their way toward this end of the ship.

"Damn, they have a tri-scanner." Vas swore as she recognized the item. She didn't want to get trapped in this small room but most of this ship appeared to be small rooms and narrow corridors.

"I have a scanner blocker." Janx scowled and furiously typed in commands.

"And the tri-scanner busted through them. Those things aren't stable, but they have a lock on us now. Most likely it took this long for the scanner to break through your blocker." They needed somewhere they would have a fair chance.

"That's not good," Janx said.

"It happens. Tech always is finding ways to break tech."

"No. That. They have a second ship and it's heading for the docking bay."

Vas looked at the outside screen. For a moment she thought it looked like a Flit and maybe Gosta had heard her after all. Then the ship turned. She didn't recognize it, but it wasn't a Flit.

"How far are we from that storage area you mentioned?"

"Not far, but there's not much in there. I have a few smaller parts from my last job that didn't get dumped, but otherwise it's a big open space."

Vas added another blaster to her collection. Blasters didn't have unlimited power and there were ways to take them out. So far Gosta was the only one to completely wipe the weapons out, but who knew what toys these assassins had with them.

"Empty and spacious is better than closed in and trapped. Let's go." Vas tapped open the door, looked down the corridor then motioned for Janx to lead the way.

Janx took a deep breath and jogged out into the corridor. Vas stayed right behind.

The route was twisty, and these corridors would make Vas claustrophobic in a few days. Alarms shrieked out again. They'd breached the docking bay.

CHAPTER TWENTY-SIX

JANX MOVED FASTER AND DUCKED down an extremely narrow corridor. She swore as she saw the door had been blasted open.

The storage area was a massive hangar and while Janx said only a few things were in there, there were piles everywhere. Sorted piles.

Janx worked on trying to reengage the door and Vas looked around. Ship parts were far too carefully sorted to be going to the dump.

Janx looked at a screen in the wall. "I shut it the best I could, but there are at least five more and they're coming our way. I can't blast their ship off since they are in the bay. And my other tricks won't work from here." She grimaced. "I've never had this serious of an attack before."

"Sorry, I'm afraid this is all because of me."

Janx shrugged. "Things happen. I offered to help you."

They both crouched behind piles of ship parts. Janx was across from Vas, but Vas heard the sigh she gave.

"These weren't junk."

"Nope. But I can start collecting again."

Boots came down the narrow corridor and sounds of the door being broken—again—followed.

Vas dipped around the pile she was behind and kept her thero-blaster aimed at the door.

The first one came through close to the floor; he was smart enough to expect them, but obviously low enough on the pecking order that he was sacrificed. Vas expected that approach and her shot took him cleanly in the head.

"We can stay here all day picking you off. Help is coming and we did nothing to you. Get off our ship," Vas yelled as Janx picked off the next one through the doorway.

"We want Vaslisha Tor Dain. You can keep your ship."

This was where they tested Janx's make-up work. "Send a camera in. There's no one here by that name. We're dozer pilots, nothing else."

"What are you doing here then?" He didn't sound agreeable, but a small camera flew in. Vas nodded to Janx to cover her and stood up. Her hair wasn't finished, but it was blonde instead of red.

"The other one, you stand up too."

Vas dropped behind the cover and motioned for Janx to stand. The camera scanned her as well and left the room.

"Well, neither of you are her. But you did kill a bunch of my folks, and I can't use a dozer in my group. Sorry, ladies, you're done." The booted feet started heading away from the doorway and a small bomb was tossed in.

"To the back!" Janx yelled, as she ran toward the far end of the room.

Vas seriously doubted that would be enough distance to save them, and those bastards could leave a trail of them once they got out of the docking bay. The good thing was they didn't think she was herself—bad thing is they didn't need either of them.

Janx dove behind a larger pile of parts and started pressing buttons on the wall behind it. "Hurry!"

Vas dove to join her right as the bomb went off.

As she lunged over the parts, a thin shield came up behind her and deflected most of the explosion. But she still felt where shrapnel hit her side. Blood seeping through her shirt told her more pain would be coming.

"You're hurt!" Janx put down her blaster and turned her over.

"Yup." Vas winced. "But still alive. Nice trick with the

shield."

"It's a small personal shield I found on a job. Sorry it didn't stop everything."

"We aren't dead yet, so that's good." She hit her comm again. Still static but fainter. "Gosta, do you read? The dozer is under attack. Hostiles leaving docking bay. May blow up this ship." She repeated the message to Deven, same static and no response.

The floor beneath her rocked as an explosion hit somewhere on the ship.

"Vas? Are...there?" Deven's voice came through the comm. Well, part of it did. There was still something causing havoc with the comm system. He was breaking up badly.

"We're under attack. Where are you?" Static greeted her so she turned to Janx. "Is there another way off this thing beside your pod? We have to assume that if your docking bay isn't shot to hell yet, it will be."

Janx chewed her thumb then tugged on something hidden by the nearest pile and a camouflage cover. "This. But it has really crap engines and navigation. I was building it."

Vas shook her head as she realized what it looked like. "Is that a mini-Fury?" As far as she knew they came in one size, with a lot of weapons. This was stylistically similar but about a quarter the size and with no weapons she could see.

"Yeah, sort of. The design on them is fascinating. Mac sent me specs when he was trying to repair them."

"Can we both fit?" Vas winced as movement told her the pain from her injuries was kicking in.

"It'll be close." She moved it toward a blast door. "This will open everything to space. But if we drift out with the debris and your crew is coming for us, we might make it."

There were far more ifs there than Vas liked, but their

other options were zero. She repeated their plans to both Deven and Gosta's comms but got nothing but static again.

"Let's do it." Another rumble rocked the ship. There was no way to know if it was from the people trying to kill them or trying to help them.

They climbed in and the interior made Janx's pod look huge. Vas didn't care as long as they got off this thing before it blew up under them.

Janx sealed the small ship and blew the blast doors. They tumbled out with the collection of junk.

"Keep the engines off until the junk breaks away. Let's drift with it." Vas watched as the second ship flew free of the docking bay and turned toward them. Same design as the first, she looked for any identifying marks. They didn't fire yet but were taking up position to hit the dozer first. Vas had no illusions about the drifting debris becoming a target if their attackers thought they were hiding in it.

"Stay there." Aithnea's voice came through Vas' comm and the *Traitor's Folly* came into view.

"Attention ship attacking the dozer, back down. She's part of our crew." Deven's voice coming through the open hail was a welcome one.

The enemy ship fired up their weapons, but either didn't respond to the open hail or only did to Deven.

Traitor's Folly fired on it a second later.

The other ship was close enough to the dozer that the explosions pushed the dozer and the debris field away from the ships.

"This might be a good time to hit the engines." Vas held her injured side as they tumbled about.

"I'm trying," Janx said. "It's not engaging." She started a nice Mac-level of swearing and took out a wrench and started smacking the console.

The engines clicked a few times, then came on. Vas was sure there were pony carts that could move faster, but it was enough to move them clear of the tumbling dozer.

"Vas, are you okay?" Deven's voice was still buried in static, but she could hear him.

"Yup, we're in this odd little ship pulling free of the debris field. You might need to come get us." She turned to Janx. "No offense, this did save us after all."

"None taken."

"We're coming around. The docking bay is open." The *Traitor's Folly* came as close as it could without hitting debris. Janx gunned the engine and the tiny ship puttered into the docking bay. Vas swore she heard it sigh as it shook, and the engine went off.

The docking bay doors shut and Deven was down there before Vas got completely free of the ship. Unfortunately, she hit her injured side and stumbled as she was getting out.

Deven grabbed her before she hit the ground. "Damn it, you didn't tell me you were injured." He hit his comm. "Pela, we need a gurney, immediately. Vas is injured."

"I can walk, just some shrapnel from those bastards." Vas tried to stand and push him off, but neither happened.

Deven held her close to him. His voice was calm but there was fear in his eyes. "You'll ride in that thing and do what they say. Your side is covered in blood."

"Yeah, yeah, yeah. But more importantly, how do you like my new look?" She tried again to stand on her own, but her body wasn't having it.

"You look better as you. But, admittedly, no one else would recognize you in this." His smile was tight, but at least he gave one. Him being worried made her more worried.

Pela and Khirson came into the docking bay with a gurney.

"I don't know what they used, but there were a lot of parts flying about," Janx said.

"We'll do a scan. Something must have gone in deep."

Pela glared at Vas as she started to sit up on the gurney. "Terel wouldn't put up with that and neither will I." She turned and started back to the med bay. The gurney followed behind with Vas staying flat.

Khirson and Deven stayed alongside, and Vas figured Janx was trailing along behind.

"Who attacked you?" Khirson seemed more focused on that than her injuries.

"Not sure. They were wearing heavy armor and fully shielded helmets."

"I can show you." Yup, Janx was somewhere behind their little parade.

Janx stepped into Vas' range of vision and handed her pad to Khirson. Deven looked curious, but he was staying as close to Vas as he could.

"Enforcers. That was a modified Pilthian fighter we blew up and those are definitely their uniforms. That's bad. If they are anything like they were in my day, it's amazing you both survived."

"We survived because Janx here is a wise and tricky woman." Vas turned to her and smiled. "Thank you."

"And here is where you all leave my patient." Pela might be shorter than Terel, but she copied the attitude with ease.

"I'm staying with her." Deven folded his arms and glared down.

Pela narrowed her eyes, then finally nodded. "You only. Nice to meet you, Janx. Now if Khirson could escort you to the command deck I will work on saving our captain."

Vas watched Khirson and Janx, who both clearly had more questions, cower under the glare of Pela.

"We'll be on the bridge." Khirson turned around and they left.

Pela kept Vas on the gurney as she ran a med scan over her.

"Deven, I'm going to need you to help me keep Vas

calm." Pela was the champion of calm, but there was an edge to her voice now. She ran the scan two more times.

She hit her comm to go ship-wide. "Level one lock for the med bay. Clear everyone from the level."

Vas tried to sit up again but Deven held her down with two fingers.

"What is it?" Vas asked as she tried to see anything from the gurney pillow.

"There are nanites in the shrapnel," Pela said. "Evil bastards. If they weren't already blown up, I'd say we hunt them down and kill them. These little things are trying to tear up Vas' insides and also build something. Most likely a bomb."

CHAPTER TWENTY-SEVEN

"ARE THEY PILTHIAN?" VAS FELT remarkably calm considering the circumstances. But then she noticed Pela had slipped an IV into her arm and Deven was holding her hand and appeared very focused. Good thinking. Having things moving inside her was probably not the time for her to freak out.

"I don't know. I've heard about these, but never seen them—we might need Khirson back down here." Pela rolled more machines over. "They are very old and aren't used anymore. At least not in the Commonwealth."

"I got back as soon as I could." Khirson was out of breath as he entered the lab.

"Can you look at these?" Pela stepped back from her screen. Khirson's swearing wasn't a good sign.

"Yes, damn it. They were a design that our government forbade. They were originally created to repair tissue, but they were misused by the rebels." He looked over to Vas. "I can help you get them out, but this is going to hurt. A lot."

Deven took Vas' hand. "We need to get them out. Are we sure that they are trying to make a bomb?"

"That was the most common form. They destroy as they move about and then they explode. Now you know what we were facing. Since it looks like Enforcers were after you and that they had these, I think we know where my people went when they fled our home world. And not the good ones."

Vas wanted to mention that the ones he thought were good had turned out to be bad too, but a wave of pain crashed through her. Deven didn't let go of her hand and put his other on her forehead.

"We need to tie her down." His voice was soothing, but Vas felt the tension in him.

Pela got straps around her arms and legs, then opened Vas' shirt. Vas winced as the cloth was pulled from the dried blood.

"Not the way I wanted to spend my first day as a blonde." She muttered as the wave of pain eased.

"Funny but save your strength." Pela switched out the IV tubes and then went to consult with Khirson. Out of Vas' range of sight or hearing.

"You'll be all right." Deven kept brushing back her hair like one would soothe a child awoken by bad dreams. "You *have* to be all right."

Vas felt his fear, it was as palpable as the pain that started building again. "Promise me that if it can't be stopped, you'll put me in that damn little ship and jettison me. Save the ship."

"Vas—"

She cut him off. "Promise."

"I promise." There was a look in his eye that Vas would have questioned but a wave of pain struck her. Her back arched and it was a good thing her hands and feet were tied. Her side felt like it burst into flame.

"We can't knock her out, not completely. But we can use a local anesthetic on her to help. I already have one running, but we can increase it." Pela looked to Deven. "You're going to have to try and keep her calm. From inside." The tone of her voice was clear; Deven would have to reach Vas on a deep telepathic level to keep her calm.

"Vas?" He was asking her permission. And Vas knew he'd follow what she said. She still wasn't fond of the idea of anyone being in her head at that level, even someone she loved. But she also didn't want to die just yet. She had too many people who needed payback.

"Do it."

Pela nodded to Deven and he nodded to Vas. Vas felt his presence on a level she'd never felt before as they merged.

"This is a healing trance. I'm entering it and bringing you along. They need you completely calm right now."

Vas couldn't nod but she felt he knew her intentions. A calmness flowed over her, and the pain faded to an annoying background feeling.

"Are you okay?" The voice was Deven's, but it wasn't his voice as much as a feeling of him formed into words.

"I don't hurt as bad. This is a nasty one, isn't it?"

Fear, worry, and concern flowed over her. "Yes. My people don't use nanites. Even the Asarlaí didn't. There are too many ways to misuse them."

"Just remember your promise."

Guilt preceded his words. "I remember."

"And you have no intention of following through. You must. If they can't stop this, I'm dead anyway."

A feeling of being loved so thoroughly she almost couldn't breathe flowed into her. "I know. And I will follow through. But I'm going with you. That's not negotiable."

Vas settled into the cocoon of him. "You're too stubborn."

"Likewise."

Pain jolted her out of her calm state, and she felt herself scream. But it was far away. Words, yelling from others outside of her, were nothing more than vague sounds.

"Come back, you have to come back to me." Deven's internal voice calmed her and she pushed away the pain. The voices faded away.

"Don't ever leave me." Vas was rarely scared, but she was this time. Not only for herself, but of what could happen if the nanites finished their work and destroyed the ship. She had no idea how many of her people were still on the planet below them, but they would be stranded—and the rest of her friends would be killed.

Comforting bands tightened around her. "It's fine. It's all fine. Remember the time we were trapped twenty miles behind enemy lines in Foxworth? Just ten of us. No supplies and the lines moved. We made it." Deven went through years of close calls for them and the company. All while reminding her how much he loved her. How much he needed her. Eventually the comfort relaxed her, and she went into a deep sleep.

———◆———

Stabbing pain broke into her peaceful rest. And there was no soothing Deven voice to block it for her. She forced her eyes open to see Terel standing there with a toothy grin.

"Glad to see you chose to stick around. I'd hate to have to send someone into the afterlife to bring you back."

"You were on the planet." Vas' mouth felt like she'd been chewing on sand. A lot of it.

Pela came to her other side and held up a glass. "Drink it slowly. It might taste weird, but you need to get things back to normal."

Vas looked over the glass and took a sip. It was clear like water but far…goopier. "Oh gods, that tastes awful. What's in it?"

"Drink it all. It has all the nutrients those damn nanites tore out of you while they were trying to rearrange your insides. You're on the way back to normal now, by the way." Terel was standing so close to her that she could probably see every drop in the glass.

Vas drank it down and wished for a whisky chaser. "Damn, you made it taste like that as payback."

Terel laughed and took the glass. "For what?"

"Something, I'm sure. Where's Deven and Khirson?"

"They left hours ago. Well, Khirson left once he helped

neutralize the nanites. That was about fifteen hours ago. Deven left two hours ago because Sedari called an urgent meeting and wouldn't let him send someone else. You've been stable and sleeping like a baby for the last ten hours."

"I've been out for that long?" Vas couldn't recall ever sleeping for that long—maybe being almost dead made for a good sleep. She started to roll out of the cot. She was no longer on the gurney and no longer tied down. But Terel pushed her back into the cot with a single finger.

"Nope. Don't care how you think you feel. You are recovering very well. Khirson and Deven helped massively for that. But you need to let your body build some strength back first. Nothing's going to happen without you, don't worry."

"You said Sedari called Deven down, that's something. And the conclave was supposed to have started by now." Vas didn't try to get up again, she really didn't want to be tied up.

Flarik came in with a smile. "Actually, Deven convinced Sedari that the health issues of Lisha as the result of incomplete security for the participants meant he had to send for his other second-in-command who had been recovering from a fight she won against sixteen Coveten. You are now a bigger badass than either Vas or Lisha, enjoy it. Oh, and your new name is Talria. Don't blame me, Deven had to come up with something to add to the contract."

"Shouldn't you be down there?"

Flarik shrugged. "Not much going on. Sedari is meeting the crew and apparently Wavians make her nervous. Deven picked up on it and sent me back up here for now." Her grin showed a lot of teeth. "I'll have my fun with it later on."

"Can this thing go up a bit?" Vas patted the sides of the cot, looking for an adjustment button. "I'll stay here for a little longer, but I'd like to sit up to see people."

Pela came over and adjusted Vas into an almost sitting position. "Want me to go down to the planet?"

Terel nodded. "Yes, please, who knows what will happen with no medical support down there."

Pela nodded and left.

"Anything new? I almost died, yes. But I didn't and we do have a few things to take care of."

Flarik pulled up a rolling stool. Terel did the same. "You were right about the comm block. They have an almost perfect circle of serious comm interference three clicks out from the camp. Random areas not working for comms is one thing—this is intentional. Deven mentioned that you had problems in the cave and Sedari shrugged it off and said some of the planet was naturally blocked by things in the rocks." Flarik rolled her eyes. "So, we know who set it up."

"Damn it, why? All to capture me? Any more on the warrant by the way?"

"Not much. Janx was right, it's not circulating in the normal areas, dark lanes only. And extremely vague. Even more odd, there are none out for the rest of us, only you. Oh, and it does say alive preferred, but head required."

"Well, that's different." Vas wasn't sure what she thought of that. Usually, it was dead or alive. "Then those Enforcers on Janx's ship wanted me, but probably didn't care in what state. How and where is Janx anyway?"

"Agreed on the assessment. Khirson can't figure out what they were doing either, but he's not happy the only people of his we are coming across are assholes. My theory is it may be a species thing and he's actually the aberration. Janx is on the deck chatting with Hrrru and Gosta. We moved her dozer a bit away, so it wasn't going to be picked up by anyone on the planet. It still flies but will need some work. Gosta thinks he can tractor it with us when we leave."

"Captain? They said you were awake?" Gosta called

down from the ship-wide comm.

Vas realized that medical gowns didn't have comms and looked around for hers. Terel handed it to her with a sigh.

"Yes, Gosta. I'm here. What's wrong?" He had his excited but not in a good way tone.

"Nothing vital, we're all okay. But I did a check and there is a growing communications block up here in orbit. It hasn't hit us yet, but it seemed to start where Janx's dozer was. Any ships in lower orbit are going to have communication issues and it's spreading around the planet."

"What the hell is Sedari doing? This can't just be for me or us. Does she really think no one will notice?"

"It is subtle, and most of the ships are higher up. For now."

"Do we know what's causing it? Either the block up here or the one on the planet?" The communications block would cause issues. If it grew into something else, something like Gosta's weapons blocker, it could be fatal for a lot of people. Sedari was looking at something bigger than a warrant.

"Nothing so far. Hrrru and I are searching, but it doesn't match anything we've seen before."

Vas let out a breath. She wanted to find her answers, help Aithnea... "Is Aithnea on the comms?"

"She is."

"I'm going to pick her brain. Have Janx do some dark web surfing and see if she can find anything about this conclave, the area, and any government that might want to take out a bunch of pirates."

"Janx here. I'll do my best."

"Thank you, Janx. Vas out."

"Aithnea? You're in the comms?"

"Vas. Yes, I'm not on them all the time, but I can monitor things with them. What's wrong?"

Vas quickly told her what had been going on and her

suspicions.

"Very good that you didn't die. I agree this is bigger than just you, but a warrant for you that was issued that quickly is extremely suspicious."

"True. Can you sense anything odd about the planet below us? The comm breakers have to be somewhere, but we can't tell what she's using."

"You're certain it is this Sedari woman?"

"I think if she's not behind it, she knows what's going on. Not to mention who in the hell hires six dozers for ship clean up after a peaceful gathering?"

"No one, and you know it. Give me some time to search the library database. I'll contact you once I find something." Aithnea clicked off.

"How long do I need to stay here?" Vas tried her best to look healthy.

"That look won't work. The monitor behind you says you're still not ready." Terel brought out another glass. "Drink this, let me get some food into you too and then if the nice monitor says everything is back to normal, you can escape."

Vas glared at the glass, but she knew it was a losing battle. She started drinking.

———————

A few hours later, after she'd gone through anything she could think of involving the pirates of this sector in the data files of the Commonwealth library, which wasn't much since the Commonwealth didn't think anything outside of the Commonwealth was worthy of great study, Terel declared her mostly recovered.

That was also after four more glasses of the mystery liquid.

Vas stepped behind a screen to change clothes. "What was in that drink, anyway?" She was grateful to be up again, usually being mostly dead took a longer recovery.

But that drink wasn't like anything she'd ever had before.

"It's something both new and old. Finding Khirson and his people got me to thinking about older remedies. This was one created to help recover from a wasting sickness that was defeated a hundred years ago. But parts of what it did addressed issues that you faced when those nanites were running loose. I modified it, of course, but it really helped your cells recover. I'm certain there will be other applications for it."

Vas came out from behind the screen while Terel was in mid lecture. "I was your experimental subject."

"It helped you recover quicker. Faster recovery, when sound, is much better for the patient as continued—"

"I didn't need to know that much." Vas cut her off with a laugh and looked at herself in the mirror. She hoped she didn't have to stay like this too long; it was really disturbing seeing someone else looking through her eyes. And blonde wasn't really working for her. "I'm glad it succeeded, we don't have time for a long recovery, but I think now Deven's new second, Talria, should get down to the planet." She left before Terel could get started again.

The command deck was quiet with most of the crew down on the planet. Janx was sitting at a computer station and Gosta and Hrrru were quietly debating something on a screen. "Have you people slept?"

Janx jumped and rubbed her eyes. "Sorry, I fell asleep."

Vas looked at the other two. "Did you give her a room?" They didn't have many extras, but there were a few. The bags under Janx's eyes said she hadn't slept.

She got to her feet. "They did, I got involved." She yawned. "Haven't found much yet but getting closer."

"And it'll be even closer once you've rested. My ship, my rules. Get some food from the galley if you haven't eaten, then go to sleep."

Janx started down the corridor, but already looked dead on her feet.

"Okay, so you two?"

"We have found some interesting information." Gosta quickly threw an image up on the front view screen. "There seems to be more incursions from the Lethian Assembly. All happening about the time the Asarlaí clones were taking over the Commonwealth." He high-lighted an area. "This was where the Lethian Assembly called home as of two years ago. Pretty large number of planets, but far out there as you can see." He tapped a button and a second screen settled in over the first. "This is a few months ago."

The light blue of the Lethian Assembly was almost half again as close to the Commonwealth.

"What are those neutral colors?" There were several large areas of space that the Lethian Assembly appeared to be avoiding but going past.

"Those are the worlds they haven't taken." Gosta shook his head. "I'm not sure why, but it doesn't appear they even tried. There's no evidence of attempted aggression. They swallowed smaller systems and kept moving."

"At the same time that the Asarlaí clones were taking over the Commonwealth. Do we think there's a connec-tion beyond the fact they figured the Commonwealth wouldn't object?" As far as Vas knew, the Commonwealth government kept to its own borders, but something had kept the Lethian Assembly from moving forward in the past. That was a damn fast expansion.

"Those are excellent questions, Captain." Hrrru nod-ded and added some more screens. "My theory is that some of the Asarlaí clones were active in parts of the Lethian Assembly years ago. Their moving out to go after the Commonwealth might have given the Lethian Assembly the ability to expand."

Vas looked at the screens. There were connections here she was missing. But the last thing she wanted to do was go into the Lethian Assembly zones to investigate.

It was looking less and less like they were going to get the information they needed here but going deeper into that pit wasn't an option. Not yet anyway. She wanted to make sure they had a damn good reason to go there before they risked it.

"Keep finding more theories. Any signs of new ships coming in? Or our friends in the silver ship?" She went to a science station and brought up the disturbingly round Racki ships and confirmed they hadn't moved. Just because Sedari claimed she couldn't see them didn't mean they weren't working with her.

"Two more ships have come in since we arrived. A Huxilan, which landed a bit out from the camp, and a Trothia vessel. It's staying in high orbit but sent down two large shuttles. Nothing on the silver ship." Gosta said the last bit with relief and Vas didn't blame him. They still needed to get the schematics for the weapons on Home back; it might take Ome and whoever he was working for a while but eventually they could break the code. But she wasn't up to dealing with them yet.

"Talria?" Mac's voice sounded unsure of the pronunciation. Which was fine, Vas wasn't sure either.

"Yes, Mac?"

"The captain wanted me to call up. We think we might have a lead on that missing pirate."

"What? Where?" Vas wasn't happy. Their comm lines should still be secure—Gosta was one of the best—but Mac was still talking in an open camp.

"From the Huxilan group who recently came down. There's a woman who wants to speak to the Mother." He was being cagey, but he also sounded confused.

"Who in the hell would know about her? She's dead."

"Yup, she seems to know that too. I'm in one of our shuttles, by the way." That would cut down on what others could hear.

Vas paused. "Do you have a name?"

"Lady Jasiel. So she says. She looks like a pirate or merc though."

That name sounded familiar, but it wasn't close enough that Vas could attach it to a specific memory. "Hold on." She tapped over to Aithnea. "There's someone asking for you on the planet."

"What?" Surprise was rare for her and Vas wished she'd been down in the holosuite to see it in person.

"Someone from a Huxilan group of pirates approached Mac and asked about you. Said her name is Lady Jasiel?"

Aithnea was silent for so long, Vas was afraid she'd disconnected or passed out.

"Lady Jasiel is dead. She died before we did. She was on a mission for the order and was captured, tortured, and murdered." There was a catch in her voice. "I saw the vid."

"Hold on. Mac, can you get an image of this woman?"

"Aye. Hold on." He came back and sent up an image. Vas didn't recognize her, but the gasp from Aithnea said she did.

"She died. I know she died."

"So did you, but you're still floating around." Vas didn't want to bring a stranger, no matter who she was supposed to be, on her ship. But Aithnea needed to see this woman. "Gosta, can you work out a holo-emitter in the shuttle?" They'd played with adding them during the last round of updates, but the benefit was lower than other needs, so she had postponed it.

"I believe so."

"Then make it happen. Mac, ask our friend to please wait, I'd like to speak with her. Aithnea, I'm coming down to the holosuite."

Gosta and she both took the lift, but he stayed on to go to the shuttle bay after she left.

Aithnea was pacing as Vas entered the holosuite.

"That can't be her, but it looks like her. Even looks

a bit older." She ran her hands through her short hair, spiking it up. "She was killed six years ago but had been on missionary work for many years prior to that. That can't be her."

"We can't be sure of anything, least of all how she could be who she says. Also, no matter who she is, how did she know you were here? You are dead, after all. I'm pretty certain that the destruction of your entire order was news even out here."

"True. There are things we don't know about the universe, and that is fascinating. Is your friend finished fixing the shuttle yet?" The pacing continued and Vas was about to see if she could tackle a hologram if she didn't stop.

"He'll notify us when he's done." Vas sat on a chair, hoping it would get Aithnea to settle down as well. "How do I know her name? Her image isn't that familiar, but I know that name."

Aithnea laughed. "We would use her name to scare all the novices. Jasiel was part of a ruling family, one she left decades ago. She was the fiercest of us all and could fight like no one else. She actually started this incarnation of the order."

"She's over eight hundred years old?"

Aithnea laughed. "Amazing isn't it?"

"Vas, I have the holo-emitter online. It's basic, but it will work. Just transport Aithnea in a chip, put the chip inside the emitter, and she'll appear in the shuttle." Gosta was far faster than Vas had expected, but it was good. This way she didn't have to figure out how to shut Aithnea's program down temporarily out of annoyance.

"Thank you, Gosta, we'll be right down." Vas held up her hand as Aithnea went for the door. "You do realize you won't exist out there, right?"

Aithnea spun around. Vas was impressed that a hologram could look embarrassed. "I lost myself. Jasiel was a good friend. While I don't understand how that being down there is her, I am so very hopeful that I am wrong."

Vas held up the chip and transferred Aithnea's program into it. Gosta was still by the shuttle when she got down to the docking bay.

"The holo-emitter shouldn't have any issues, but it will be clear she is a hologram."

Vas nodded. "If need be, we can explain that Aithnea is on our ship and can't come down right now."

"Is it really a surviving nun?"

"Not sure. Aithnea's not sure. I've given up guessing at this point. Hopefully, even as a hologram, Aithnea can tell who this really is."

Gosta nodded. He clearly had more questions but was willing to hold them.

Vas got the shuttle up as soon as the docking bay doors opened.

The contact on the planet called up quickly. "Approaching shuttle, identify."

That was different. No identification had been needed before, but then again, they were expecting the shuttles at that time.

"This is second-in-command Talria, with the *Traitor's Folly*. Captain Fhailson is expecting me."

Silence came from the comm, so Vas slowed the shuttle's speed.

"Aye, shuttle, you are cleared for landing."

Vas went to say thank you, but they had already cut communications.

The area around the center of camp looked busier than before, but it was evening now and perhaps pirates preferred the dark. It couldn't be good that the conclave had been delayed twice.

Vas locked up the shuttle—she'd had to land a bit further from their camp—and walked up. Divee was standing out front and while not visibly armed, was clearly keeping watch.

"I'm sorry, but we're not hiring on." He'd glanced at Vas, then continued his visual sweep of the area.

"That's good, your captain might be upset if you did that." Vas kept her voice low.

He gave a start. "Cap-Lisha-Talria, I'm glad you've recovered. Mac is waiting near the shuttle."

Vas shook her head. It was good to know that her disguise worked on her own people. Hopefully, it would fool anyone looking for her.

The rest of her crew must have had more of a heads up. A few slightly startled glances gave way to nods as she walked through the tent area.

"Good to see you up and about." Bathie nodded to a cloaked woman sitting by herself near the closed shuttle door. "She hasn't said anything since Mac told her you were coming down."

"It's been a rough day. I'll check on Mac, then we'll be going back to the shuttle I landed in."

"Want me to come too?" Gon had come up silently. Still extremely armed, he looked like he was planning on staying that way.

Vas started to shake him off, then nodded. "Couldn't hurt." She ignored the woman sitting there and checked in on Mac inside the shuttle.

"You can come out now."

"Ah! Good to see you." Mac motioned for her to shut the shuttle door. "I feel like she's looking into my soul. She asks questions that have too many layers to them. Know what I mean?"

Vas understood. There had been a few of the older nuns who gave that feeling, even without speaking. "Don't worry, Gon will go with me. I have a holo-emitter set up in the shuttle we came down in so Aithnea can see who this is. Stay here and keep everyone together." She hadn't walked that far, but there was also an underlying level of tension around the camps. Not surprising, but not something she wanted to get her crew involved in.

"Deal. I'll wait in here until you're gone though." Mac settled back into his seat.

Vas went back and approached the cloaked woman. "I believe you wanted to find an old friend?"

The face that looked up was haughty, the light gray eyes did seem to see right through you, but the smile softened it. "And I know you are not she."

"Nope, I'm not." Vas almost gave her name then decided against it. If she were a nun, she would know the name was a lie. Better to keep things close until Aithnea saw her. "If you follow me, I can bring you to her."

The woman watched her for a few moments and then gave a small smile. "I believe there is a different face you usually wear. Don't worry, no one listens to me unless I want them to." She got to her feet. "Lead on."

Vas led the way to the shuttle, unlocked it, and walked inside. Normally, she would have offered first entry to a guest, but she wasn't sure it would be accepted. She was wary of this woman, and that feeling seemed to go both ways.

"Where is Aithnea?" The woman dropped her hood, but Vas had already seen most of her face.

"How do you know her? The name you gave was from a long-lost and very dead nun."

She smiled. "The same could be said for Aithnea. She and the rest were all killed protecting someone. I want to know who was that important." She slid out a nasty-looking knife about a foot long. The edges were jagged and there was writing on the blade.

"I haven't done anything to threaten you. Why are you holding a qualic knife?" Vas had her hand on her blaster. Those were vengeance blades; the drawing of them requiring the spilling of blood. She was looking more and more like the real nun, but she also looked like she wanted to gut Vas.

CHAPTER TWENTY-EIGHT

———◆———

"NOW WHERE IS AITHNEA? I know she is here somewhere. I have touched the edge of death and can see beyond it."

Vas took a step back to the console of the shuttle and flicked on the holo-emitter. She'd put Aithnea's chip in there when she left the ship.

"You didn't touch death, you old Ilerian slug, you died. Just like me. Why are you threatening Vaslisha?" The voice came first, then a nice, but still transparent, Aithnea came into view. A pissed one.

"Aithnea?" The knife wavered but didn't drop completely. "Where are you? This is Vaslisha? That child you told me about?"

"I haven't been a child for a while now."

"Vas, holster your blaster. Jasiel, you better give that blade some blood and put it away." She folded her arms and gave a scowl Vas remembered all too well. "Now, ladies."

Vas shrugged and put her blaster away. Jasiel looked back and forth between them, then sliced the knife across her own arm, said a few words to appease the blade, and put it back into the sheath Vas saw strapped to her hip.

"Where are you, Aithnea?" Jasiel now sounded sad instead of angry.

"I'm dead, my friend. The convent was under siege, I had no choice. But we died well and took many enemies with us."

Jasiel looked to Vas. "If she is dead, am I interacting with a recording?"

Vas sat in the pilot's seat. This might take a while and she'd been mostly dead recently—she was a bit tired. "It's far more complicated than that. She doesn't need to sit, but you might want to." She motioned to one of the passenger seats.

"Vas has always been the smart one. But it is complicated. Since you came to seek me, I will tell you my tale first, then you must tell me how you survived when I saw you die."

Vas already knew Aithnea's story, so she watched Jasiel as she listened to the end of their order.

"Then they are all gone, you're gone." Jasiel shook her head. "I had heard the rumors, but Commonwealth news travels slowly out here. I have never heard of nuns coming back from the dead however, in any form." She frowned. "Although it is good to talk to you again."

"The same. I saw you die." Aithnea was blunt, but even in the hologram, Vas saw the pain there.

"I almost did die. I'm harder to kill than they thought, so when my heart stopped, they assumed I was gone and froze my body to use against the rest of you as a bargaining chip. Horrible way for one of us to die. No glory. Then at some point, I assume after they realized I would be useless to them, they dumped my body. A young man found me on a rubbish heap and thought to steal anything I carried on me. I'd been in a trance and scared the hell out of him when I sat up." She grinned.

"Why didn't you come back to us?"

"I would have. Unfortunately, I woke up a few weeks after you were destroyed." The sorrow in her voice was echoed by Aithnea's face.

"I am glad you found me. Us. As I said, the rest of the convent is in the ethereal plane. My hope is that once we get the Universe back on track, and our order reestablished, we can move on."

"I'm not sure what to do now. I came here looking

either for you or revenge. Found you, but unlike me, you all died with honor and no revenge is needed."

Aithnea looked to Vas.

Vas sighed. "You can stay with us until you sort things out."

"I would be grateful. Can my friend come as well?"

Aithnea pulled back. "Friend?"

"Thomas, he's the one who rescued me. He's waiting in our ship. We followed the Huxilans down to the planet."

"The one who tried to rob what he thought was your corpse?" Vas said it, but she only beat Aithnea by a bit. Aithnea narrowed her eyes at her friend.

Jasiel laughed. "We all do what we have to do. He was starving and trapped on that planet. Once he realized that I was alive, he shared what he had with me. Between us, we got a ship and fled. The ship we liberated is in awful condition and not much larger than this shuttle. I can't abandon him now."

Vas rubbed her face. Who knew how long Janx would be staying with them, and now two more? "There went the last two extra spots on my ship. But any friend of Aithnea's is a friend of mine." Vas smiled. "I need to find out what's going on with Deven and the conclave. Can I leave you two here to reconnect?"

"I will guard this shuttle with my life." Jasiel smiled, but the promise was sincere.

"Thank you. Aithnea is strong, but she's still dead." Vas nodded to them both and left. She trusted Jasiel because she trusted Aithnea. But she also disabled the shuttle's ability to lift off and had the missing piece in her pocket.

She also told Gon to stay out front, just in case.

Mac was on guard now at their camp and he nodded as she approached. "The *captain* came back, he's in the shuttle." He looked around but didn't ask about Jasiel.

Vas went to the shuttle. Deven had the door shut but not locked. He was sitting on two of the passenger seats that were extended, and his eyes were closed.

"You wanted some private time?"

"Not right now." He got to his feet and gave her a long kiss. "I still don't like this look, but it's you inside there." He rubbed her arms.

"You're exhausted." She pushed him back a bit to get a good look. "You haven't slept since before you saved me."

"Got me in one." He ran his hand through his hair and didn't even try and fight the yawn that followed. Even with his dyed blue skin and tattoos, Vas would know him anywhere. "Sedari has sold out this entire group of pirates to someone with deep pockets. Might have only been trying to make some money off one group, not us though, but she's tossing everyone in." He yawned again and settled back in his seats.

Deven could be one of the least stressed people she knew, and he was exhausted, but this was a bit much for the news he shared.

"And we aren't running out of here immediately for what reason?"

"Easy. She can't do anything without a set of codes whoever she's working for gave her. I took the original and scrambled the copies. It looks like the Foli pirate crew are behind the attacks on the Dackon Industries ships, but there are crews within crews, so we might not want to push the contact I found harder. And we have a lead on the pirate, or rather someone who might be able to narrow down where the Pirate of Boagada last was. I thought we'd get our answers for both issues, get out of here, hide for a bit, then hunt down the pirate's last home."

"You were very busy." Vas shook her head. "But I don't like playing it that close. There are way too many things indicating a major attack. One we might not get out of if we wait too long. *Traitor's Folly* has decent weapons, but nothing like the *Warrior Wench*."

"I know, and it is a risk. But I believe it might be worth it. Considering one of the ships coming in is my brother." He was too tired to give a good snarl, but he did grimace.

"Are they listed to come in?"

"No. They are riding in behind a pack of dozers. Good ploy. The dozers are so big they block visual and a low scrambler is blocking the tech. Gosta and Hrrru spotted them while you were off talking to the scary lady, as Mac called her."

"Okay, so we have them, but if they're hiding behind the dozers, how are we going to stop them?" Vas sat in a seat. "I want those schematics back before they find a way to break them, but our ship against that thing? Not a chance."

Deven adjusted in his chairs and stretched out. "Khirson and I are working on that. I think we all agree getting the plans back is going to be impossible, so we have to destroy the ship that has them."

"Oh, just that. Great."

"On another note, was the woman who she claimed to be?" He had his eyes closed now.

"Aithnea said yes. By the way, we're giving her and her rescuer temporary shelter." Vas told him Jasiel's story.

"Then she's the last nun. Can she find this pirate?"

"I intend to ask Aithnea that when we're alone. Jasiel had been a wanderer and unconventional nun even before I sought shelter with them. She might be able to help, but I have a bad feeling that it's still going to fall to me and that whole Keeper training."

"Most likely." Deven was fading fast.

"You have all of the codes Sedari needs with you, right?"

He nodded but didn't open his eyes.

"Then I'm going to lock you in here for the night."

"Hmmm."

Vas kissed his forehead, dimmed the lights, and locked

him in. She'd seen him be awake for days with less exhaustion than this. Most likely that trick he used keeping her calm and alive during the operation took more out of him than he was willing to admit.

About half of the crew was asleep, or at least resting. The other half were awake and cleaning their weapons. Even though Deven was acting like he wasn't worried, she noticed the standard job behavior of her crew. Two of her people happened to be cleaning their weapons by the two back entrances and she knew without asking that they'd set up guard rotations.

She went up to Mac. "Anything?" It was still early in the night, but there were few people out, and the camps around them were disturbingly quiet. They might not know exactly what was going on, but they knew something was up. She was honestly surprised they were all staying in place.

"Not a thing." He held up a pair of long-range scanners. "I've been watching our friends. Gosta adjusted these to see them. They haven't moved."

Vas knew he was talking about the Racki. "They are still out of phase?"

Mac nodded. "Never heard of anyone keeping it up this long. Those phase shifts are a pain in the mechanical ass for a ship. Longest I've heard of is a few hours."

Vas held out her hand and looked through the scanners. "Yup, damn things are still there." She switched it back to normal and looked again. "Can't see the dozers though."

"Naw, Gosta says they're pretty far out. But I'm watching." He grinned. "Gosta is too. Do you think we'll have to fight our way out?" He was too excited about that option.

"Hopefully not. We've got enough on our plate without having to fight out of a trap for a bunch of pirates." A ship started coming into range, actually more than one but they were coming from different areas. "Damn it." She tapped her comm. "Gosta, can you identify these new ships? Coming in slowly from 2.345 through 4.567." They were so far out that she really couldn't pick up much with the scanners. Improved or not, they were still limited.

"I've got them. No, I can't get what they are. But I think...hold on." Gosta muttered the last part as he saw something.

"Gosta?"

"They aren't close enough to identify yet. I'm tracking the dozers, so it's not them. I'll call once we have a better idea. Oh, and there's been an increase in chatter between some of the crews and their ships in orbit. A lot."

While he was able to track that, Gosta wouldn't be able to track what was being said. Unless Vas ordered him too. It wasn't a safe thing to do; ships could track the breach back to them too easily, and right now there wasn't the call for it.

"Can you send down a list of the most active ones to my pad? That long nap I had meant I'm not sleepy right now."

"Aye, Talria. And we'll keep an eye on our incoming."

"Thanks, and please do. The captain is wiped right now, so send everything through me. Talria out." Vas took one more look through the scanners, then handed them back to Mac. "Thanks, Mac." She went back into the tent and found Flarik. She wasn't asleep but also wasn't cleaning weapons.

"Talria." Flarik nodded to her and kept her voice low. Many around her were sleeping and her eyes glowed golden in the darkness.

"I was wondering if you might want to go for a bit of a walk? I want to check on our newest guest. And a few other things." She'd gotten the intel for Gosta and wanted to check out the crews of those heavily communicating with their ships. She doubted they were asking for bedtime stories.

Flarik silently rose and joined her. Vas quickly filled her in on the recent issues, including Jasiel.

"If we have a nun, couldn't she find the pirate?"

"I haven't confirmed it, but I doubt it. Right now, we'll treat her and her friend as guests and let Aithnea call the shots on that end."

Gon was still standing guard and he lifted his weapon at their approach. "Ah, good to see you two. The lady inside asked for her friend to come over, but I wasn't sure what to tell her. His shuttle is quite a ways out."

"I'm going to have him come to our camp. Wait a bit, I'll want you to escort her back. Flarik and I have some errands."

He gave a sharp nod and went back to watching everything around them. If Gon wanted to know what their errands were, he clearly wasn't going to ask.

Vas unlocked the door to the shuttle. She wasn't surprised to hear soft talking.

"Vas! We were catching up on your adventures from when you lived with us." Aithnea sounded too cheerful, so those were probably embarrassing stories.

"Great. Jasiel, this is Flarik. We are looking at a quick bug out sometime soon, so I'd like to keep folks together. This shuttle is further out than I'd like."

"You're bringing her to your camp," Aithnea said with a shrug. "We probably would have spent the entire night talking anyway."

"What about Thomas?" Jasiel asked.

"Can you reach him?" Vas nodded to the wrist comm now visible on her arm.

"Yes, but it's difficult. Something is muddling communications." She tapped her comm. "Thomas?" Static. "Thomas, please respond?" She looked up. "He checked in a half hour ago."

Vas shook her head. "That anti-comm range is growing. Gon will escort you back to camp. Flarik and I will find your friend. I'll need something to let him know it's okay to go with us though."

"Here." Jasiel handed over a necklace. "This can only come off me willingly. But what of Aithnea?"

Vas turned to the hologram.

"Give my chip to Jasiel. She'll keep me safe."

Vas wasn't sure she agreed with Aithnea, but she disconnected the chip and handed it to Jasiel. "I have a bad feeling about things, so take care going back." Premonition or not, she felt a chill cross her soul right then. They went outside. Gon was either sensing something on his own or picking up on Vas' vibe, he had his blaster raised.

"Gon, escort her back, but keep an eye out."

He nodded but didn't look toward her. "Something is wrong. More wrong than it was before."

"Agreed." Vas looked to Flarik. She wanted to send her back to guard the tent, but the way Flarik was looking out into the darkness, she didn't think she'd go.

"If we're not back in one hour, wake up the captain." The plans to check out the camps of the communicating ships were set aside. There were two that were in a direct line with where Jasiel's shuttle was, but beyond that she wanted to get this Thomas back to the camp. They might be bugging out without getting the information Deven wanted—the bad feeling in her gut was growing.

"There's a chance that Sedari isn't as in charge as she thinks." Flarik kept her voice low as they walked toward the first camp.

"My thoughts exactly. Deven would have picked up on her feelings but if she's lying to herself, that wouldn't come across. But why now? It has to tie to the Lethian Assembly expansion."

"I agree. They aren't here yet, but their recent interest in new areas and visits to the Commonwealth can't be coincidence."

They had been whispering, but both dropped it as they approached the first camp on Gosta's list. There were no guards on duty that Vas could see, and the entire compound was dark. The surrounding camps had lights and voices inside, but this one was silent.

Vas held up her hand to Flarik, then motioned that she was going forward. Flarik nodded and took out her blaster. She faded into the surrounding darkness.

Vas crept forward, waiting until she was certain that there was no sound from inside. Then she pushed aside the fabric covering and stayed low as she entered. There was no one there and judging from the amount of supplies they'd left they'd taken off in a rush. She'd have to ask Gosta to track ships that left. There was no shuttle in this camp right now, but the indentations in the ground notated where it had been.

She scanned the entire area onto her pad—maybe Gosta could pick something out of the mess—then crawled back out and told Flarik.

"Taken?" Flarik kept scanning the area around them but put away her blaster.

"No idea. I scanned it on the pad. They had a shuttle, but it's gone too." She nodded down the path a bit and started walking to the other camp along their path.

It also had no one on guard and no signs of activity. Again, Flarik covered Vas with her blaster as she crept up. The smell of blood hit her before she pushed back the fabric.

Swearing to herself, she crept forward to the scene of a massacre. Someone had brutally murdered this group. It had been fast, violent, and silent. While she noticed a few hands reaching for weapons, none had them out. Something killed them that quickly. The only people she knew who could do that without making a sound were the nuns. Who were all dead but one.

Vas shoved that thought aside as she scanned this camp

as well. At this point, she couldn't risk them being seen out here, and her crew would be much harder to be taken unaware if Jasiel wasn't on the side they thought she was. She doubted a single nun could have done this, no matter how well trained.

She went back to Flarik and briefly told her what she'd seen. Flarik kept her blaster out this time.

They found the shuttle in question. Jasiel was right, it was in crappy shape and quite possibly might not be able to get off the planet on its own in its current state.

The door was open, but inside was dark.

Vas went in. While it was ransacked, there was no blood. Either this Thomas had left on his own, been taken alive, or maybe he didn't exist and Jasiel used him as a distraction.

"I see drag marks." Flarik's night vision was better than Vas' and her eyes glowed softly as she started away from the shuttle.

Vas kept her blaster out as she followed.

There wasn't much out this way, but Vas figured they were still at least a click in from where the cave had been. The comm blocker was extending both outward, as they originally knew, and inward. Vas hit her comm. "Mac? Do you read?" She kept her voice as low as possible, but if they were losing their comms she wanted to know before they had an emergency.

"Aye?" Mac sounded a bit off, but not sleepy.

"Just checking. And have someone watch Jasiel closely."

"Will do. When should they be here?"

Vas shared a look with Flarik. "Damn it, a while ago. Gon was with her. Don't send anyone out to look for them. Wake up Deven and tell him what happened. Oh, and I'm sending two images to your pad, show him those. These were two of the camps that Gosta tagged as having an excessive amount of recent off-world communication. Flarik and I are tracking something, then we'll be looking for Gon and Jasiel. Out."

Vas cut the comm. Whoever grabbed this Thomas person might also have taken Jasiel and Gon. Gon would never go without a fight though, and Jasiel would be a formidable opponent even if she was over eight hundred years old.

Unless *she* took out Gon.

Vas ran her fingers through her hair. Too much was happening.

"Keep tracking the marks, but then we go back and find Gon." If Jasiel was with him and a victim also, Vas would mentally apologize. Right now, she had to treat Jasiel like a suspect. Gon was either already dead or a prisoner.

Flarik picked up her speed but stayed quiet. The trail had originally been heading away from the camp, then it turned on a rocky bed. Vas wasn't certain she would have seen the turn but Flarik did.

It ran along the back side of the camp area to a larger ship. Still smaller than the *Traitor's Folly*, it was larger than most of the ships that had landed.

And it wasn't one Vas had noticed before.

There were screens covering the windows, but they still let out some light. Flarik stood back, letting Vas lead. They moved in, watching for guards but there weren't any. There was something going on inside though. The ship muffled any sound, but the flickering images through the shades indicated a lot of movement.

Flarik touched Vas' arm and held up a small round device about the size of her palm. It took Vas a moment to recognize one of Gosta's toys. A listening device that Vas had acknowledged when he invented it and then mentally set aside. It only worked attached to the wall and was a pain to get off once triggered.

Vas nodded to Flarik. If they couldn't get it off after this, let whoever found it try and figure out where it came from. Like all of Gosta's inventions, it had nothing identifiable on it or in it.

Flarik reached up and slapped it on as high as she could. The ship's nose was rounded and hopefully that was the command deck. It was definitely where the action was.

Two long cords came out of the listening device and Vas and Flarik each held one to their ear.

"What you want doesn't matter. I'll kill both of them and set you up for it. We need to get off this damn planet." The voice was slightly familiar, but he was pissed and talking fast.

"I told you I need more time." The speaker wasn't familiar but sounded young and female. "I have control over the two, and I can break this one as well. Think of what we can do with one of their own. Your brother won't know we have a mole."

Crap. Vas had a feeling she knew who the brother was. She still didn't recognize the voice, but that didn't mean much.

"You're cocky now, but you won't be when they get back. We were supposed to get intel on how to crack that damn code off that bitch Sedari, not keep taking people. I should have never let you grab these two." That was definitely Leil.

How he and possibly more of his silver ship group got down here unnoticed, Vas had no idea. They must be running more than one ship—had the silver ship entered this system, alarms would have rung all over the *Traitor's Folly*.

"I can do so much more with these two, at least with her. She is the last Clionea nun. Do you know what power that gives me?"

"Until she breaks free of your control and fights back. Where is that chip?"

"I don't know." The female voice growled. "She hid it in a moment that she regained free will while I was working on overpowering her guard."

"And you don't think that means she's fighting back? You used her memories to try and win the other over. She didn't trust you either."

"She can't beat me. I have more power than all of them. I will—"

"Sorry, you're not helping the cause. Die." A blaster shot rang out and all hell broke loose on the ship.

CHAPTER TWENTY-NINE

V AS AND FLARIK PULLED THEMSELVES away from their earpieces and ran to the landing ramp. Whatever else was going on, Gon was in there. Jasiel and Thomas as well, was her guess.

Without the earpieces it was hard to hear what was going on. But more blaster fire would have been noticeable. Either Leil was a really bad shot, or the owner of the female voice was damn hard to kill. The landing door opened and a young Pilthian woman came running down the ramp. Vas thought the voice sounded too young for Loxianth, and she was right. The woman was limping and looking behind her, but there was no blood that Vas could see. She ran out into the night.

Leil came running out after her, and Vas held back to see if there were more coming out. When no one followed him, she shot him in the leg. She ran over to him as he stumbled and kicked at his blaster, but he had a tight grip on it. "Drop it now, or the next shot goes into your back."

Flarik ran to her. "I'm going after our Pilthian." She didn't wait for an answer before she left.

Leil stayed down, but the blaster was still in his hand.

"I can keep shooting you in non-vital places until you bleed to death. I seriously doubt that anyone would miss you. I've heard too much about you to think otherwise. Now slowly slide that blaster away from you and get down on your stomach."

"I recognize the Wavian, even with the different colored feathers, but not you. You're with Deven's ship." He flung the blaster out and went face down. "How did you find us?"

Vas forgot for a moment how different she looked— nice to know it fooled Leil. She kicked the blaster out of his reach. "I have my ways. I don't like assholes who steal from my people. Where are the disks you stole from us?"

He was silent for a bit and Vas figured he was trying to figure out how to play things. Conmen were always looking for a way out.

"I left Ome and Loxianth a while ago, they kept the disks. Well, they dumped me. My girl and I were hoping to hook up with some pirate crew for work. We had a fight."

Vas kicked his wounded leg. "Wrong answer. Well, them dumping you would be a good business idea, you're sort of a worthless piece of crap. But what, or rather who, will I find in your ship?"

He moved toward something in his pocket and she shot him in the arm. "I know you wouldn't be thinking of trying to shut the door." She turned and shot the control panel for the landing ramp—nothing was closing now. The fact that Gon hadn't come out or yelled meant he was either unconscious or worse.

"My friend better be sleeping, or you will pay. Tell me what you and the young lady were really doing. Start with her being able to control people."

Leil was silent.

"If Flarik and your friend get back here before you talk, I start shooting again. We only need one of you."

"Fine. Ome thought this would be a good planet to find out more about what tech you had. We picked up on that new ship you are running, the one you weren't supposed to still be alive in, by the way. And he found that nun woman and her friend a few months ago. Kept them in a time stasis pod until he could figure out how to use her. He sent us ahead."

More noise than Flarik would ever make on her own came into the area. Flarik had one hand on the back of the Pilthian woman's neck and was holding her tight. "She's got some weird mojo, but it doesn't work on Wavians."

"Is she a danger to me?"

"Not if she wants to live. It's some sort of tech advancement rather than a mutation, which means she has to consciously use it. I explained that I could snap her head off before she could try. You did want to question her, right?"

Vas glared at the woman, but she was a lot less fierce with Flarik an instant away from breaking her neck. "What can you tell me that will keep you alive?" Vas put her foot on Leil's back when he twitched.

"I can tell you that that he is an idiot and ruined a great plan that had been years in the making. I can tell you—" Her words were cut off as a blaster shot came from the entrance of the ship. The shot went wide.

"Whoever is inside, come out with your hands up and move slowly. Still figuring out who is friend and who is foe here." Vas knew Gon was a friend, but whatever this woman had done to Jasiel and possibly the mysterious Thomas person meant they couldn't be trusted immediately.

"Your friend is unconscious. We had to hit him hard to bring him down. I'm not under her influence anymore, but I know everything I did when I was." Jasiel came down the ramp slowly. "The blaster is on the ramp."

"Where is Aithnea?" Vas was seriously thinking about shooting her and letting them find each other in the afterlife.

Jasiel patted her hip. "I've kept her safe. Most of what was said before was my story. I was almost killed; Thomas did rescue me. But then we were captured by an Etia pirate crew. They knew who I was. The nuns have a reputation for a secret holding of weapons and massive amounts of wealth. They figured as the only one left, I could take them there. They kept Thomas alive as leverage, even though I kept telling them there was no such place."

Vas knew there had been a Clionean nun storehouse, but it was weapons and books—not wealth. And it had been in the Commonwealth.

Leil started to move again.

"You are really getting on my nerves." Vas took out the large dagger she carried, flipped the hilt around and smacked him in the head with it. She turned to Jasiel after he passed out. "Okay, if you're really on our side, tie these two up."

Jasiel walked forward, unwinding a long line of rope from her outfit as she did. Some people worked garrotes into their outfits, Jasiel worked an entire section of Theiam steel into hers. She quickly bound Leil's hands and then looped the cable around his ankles. She snapped the line off with a cutter but didn't move toward Flarik or her prisoner.

"Could you cover her eyes? I'm far more aware than I was when they captured us, but the implant in her right eye could still cause problems."

Flarik covered the Pilthian woman's eyes with her free hand. "If she so much as breathes wrong, I'm snapping her neck and we will still have one prisoner to question."

Jasiel grinned and moved forward to quickly tie up the woman. "It might be better for now if she were unconscious as well. At least until your doctors can take out that implant. It's a nasty piece of work."

Flarik shrugged and adjusted her grip on the woman's neck. The Pilthian tried to move her arms, but Jasiel was damn good with tying things. A minute later the Pilthian collapsed when Flarik finished pinching her neck. She was alive, but would have a hell of a headache when she woke up.

Jasiel stepped forward and kicked her. "That's for every-thing you did to me, Thomas, and our guard." She looked to Vas. "I'm afraid I didn't hear his name."

"Gon," Vas called over her shoulder as she ran up the ramp into the ship. The interior was in shambles; the fighting they'd heard had been going on for a while before they arrived. Gon was laying on his side in the middle of the deck along with another unconscious person.

Vas ran to Gon. He was battered and bloody, but he appeared to be breathing. She went to roll him on his back when he grabbed her hand and pulled her down.

"It's me! Gon! It's me!" Gon was a gentle giant and uncommonly strong. Right now, the gentle part wasn't showing.

"You don't look right."

Vas dropped her voice. "Because I'm in disguise, remember? You saw me like this a few hours ago."

Gon narrowed his eyes then finally let her go. "It's been a rough time. That nun jumped me."

Vas started untying him. "It appears it wasn't her." She held up her hand before he could respond—Gon took things at face value. "I mean it was her, but she was under the influence of another. Are you okay to stand?"

He moved slowly, but nothing appeared to be broken. "I'll take your word for it, but I'll feel a lot better when the captain looks at her. He can get into heads."

"This may be a tech thing, but regardless, remain wary." She walked over to the other body who had to be Thomas. Human, but wasn't much bigger than Xsit. Also beat up but still breathing. Normally she'd ask Gon to carry him back, but Gon was still looking groggy. Not to mention if she asked, he would agree to do it whether he was seriously hurt or not.

"Hello? Thomas?" She lightly tapped his face, but he

wasn't responding yet. She glanced up and saw Jasiel looking down. "He's not waking up."

Jasiel knelt and put her hand on his chest. After a few moments she smiled. "He will be fine. I assume you want him to walk back to your ship?"

"It would be easier. Sorry, leaving the ties on for now."

"Understood." She held out her hands. "You should bind me as well. I was compromised."

Vas wasn't going to, then nodded and took the Theiam steel line and tied her hands. "Although I don't want the other two awake and we can't carry you all."

"They have a shuttle cart in the back. That's how they moved me around."

"That'll work." Vas found the shuttle cart and drove it out of the docking bay area and around to where the bodies were. She and Flarik got Leil and their unnamed Pilthian loaded in first. Next was Thomas, who was conscious enough to stumble about, but not too much else, and then Jasiel. Vas found a tarp to cover them. "Sorry about this."

Jasiel smiled as she was covered. "Trust me, I've been in far worse situations."

Flarik and Gon took the passenger seats and Vas took the driver's and they went to their camp. Although she couldn't check the rest of the camps on their list, she did observe all of the ones they drove by. The images of the abandoned camp and the slaughtered one stuck in her mind.

CHAPTER THIRTY

T WASN'T LATE BY ANY standard, especially for mercs or pirates. Yet most of the area was quiet and with few people out. Vas went to the back of their camp, nodding when Marwin lifted his blaster, then lowered it with a nod once he saw Vas.

Vas and Flarik escorted Jasiel and Thomas inside, handing them off to Divee. Then they carried the other two in. Gon was supposed to rest but he clearly wanted to help.

"Not until you've been checked out. Now go inside and talk to Pela." Vas all but chased him in. She walked back the way they had come a bit, just to make sure there was no one following, but she couldn't see anyone.

Deven was there when she came back and from the look on his face, he'd been waiting. "You found friends?"

"Yes, your brother again."

Deven swore and marched over to where Leil was unconscious. "This bastard—"

"Might be useful later." Vas stood by the woman. "She's more interesting. She was controlling Jasiel through some implant in her right eye."

Pela had been examining Gon, but she perked up at that. "Mental control through an ocular implant? Oh, Terel is going to want to look at her."

Deven looked at his brother once more then stepped back. "Those vids you sent weren't good. There's no sign anywhere that this conclave is under attack, but clearly we are."

"I have a feeling more groups will be eliminated before

morning."

"Agreed. Sedari isn't as in charge as she thinks, or she's sloppier than I thought. I might have overestimated how vital those codes of hers were."

Vas nodded. "Flarik said the same thing."

"So, we bug out? Or we fight?" Mac came up but still looked ready to fight. He wasn't normally bloodthirsty but like all her crew he was used to fighting.

"Maybe both? Who was the connection to the Pirate of Boagada? Which camp?" Vas went to the map they had all the camps on.

"This one." Deven gestured to a spot in-between them and Sedari.

"And the person who had intel on the people robbing Dackon Industries?" That job might have been a way for them to get here, but she still wanted it resolved.

"I found that one. A woman Ilerian talked way too much about them to not be involved." Divee pointed out a camp just past Sedari.

"And we really want to know what Sedari is up too, right?" Vas looked around the sea of confused faces.

"What are you thinking?" Deven folded his arms.

"We use our borrowed shuttle cart and grab all three of them, then get the hell out of here." Vas' smile was still met with confusion. "We have a brig on that ship, we can't stay here, and we don't want to lose the intel they might have."

"I like it!" Mac was bouncing. That alone was almost enough for Vas to rethink things. But she needed to stop thinking Commonwealth and start thinking out here— laws only mattered if you got caught and most people weren't going to care about a few pirates being kid- napped.

Deven watched her, but then nodded. "Risky, but I think we might not have an option."

"Captains?" Gosta's call came through both Vas and

Deven's comms. "We have a situation. The Racki ships."

Vas nodded to Deven. Their ruse at this point was less important, but they'd stick with it until they got off this planet.

He tapped his comm. "What about them? Are they preparing to attack?"

Vas really would love to know what in the hell those ships were up to, but she also wanted to get out of here before they moved. There was no way they weren't up to something. They'd risked staying here long enough.

"No…I don't think so. The sensors say they are still there, but no matter what changes we make, they won't appear. Could we get Aithnea back up here?"

Jasiel handed over Aithnea's chip and Vas put it in her pocket, but they couldn't waste a shuttle to take her up to the ship yet. Vas hit her comm. "In a bit. We have to deal with some things. Code oh-seven-nine." That was a compromised-bug-out code. Used when the shit hit the fan but they didn't want their enemies to know they knew. Like now. Gosta would have them prepared to leave orbit immediately. And if Vas and Deven didn't get up there within the hour, his orders were to leave.

"Understood. We'll keep scanning and be ready. Gosta out." Gosta sounded closer to being upset than she'd heard from him in a long time.

"Okay, folks, so we go with the plan?" Vas looked around. They'd been discussing it in a small group, but she knew her crew was listening. Most were packing up their things.

Deven nodded. "Let's do what the lady says." He separated part of the crew into small strike groups of three people each. The plan was to drive by each camp, separate out the person they wanted to take, drug them, and shove them in the shuttle cart. All before daylight.

"The rest of you, pack up camp without being noticed." Vas held up her hand at the start of protests. "You heard that code. We're only keeping the people we need down here and one shuttle. Get packed and bug out immediately." She spread her glare around. Having a bunch of people on this wouldn't help, just make things worse. They understood that, but that didn't mean they were happy about it.

She went to Divee and handed him Aithnea's chip. "I need you to get this up to Gosta. You'll also be taking Jasiel and our two unconscious guests up. Pela, make sure they stay unconscious if you would."

Jasiel waited until the others started packing up then came next to Vas and dropped her voice. "I'd like to stay here if I could. I can fight, you know."

"I know you can, trust me. You might not have been in the convent when I was, but many of the women you trained kicked my ass for two years."

"And you became one hell of a fighter because of it." The smile was as if she was solely responsible.

"I did. But right now, I need you safe. I have fighters, plenty of them. But we only have one Clionea nun." Vas shrugged. "Two if we count Aithnea, but she is incorporeal, so let's say one. Please don't make me have to drug you."

There was still a fight in Jasiel's eyes, but it faded. "No, I'll be good. Your medic's name was Pela, I believe? I can help her get ready." She shook her head then took Vas' shoulder. "Be careful. There is danger coming."

Vas patted her hand and smiled. "Been that way for a while, but thank you."

Jasiel didn't return the smile. "It's shifted. The Commonwealth is a controlled system, one you know well. Just being out here for a while changes you. And there's a lot more going on now than when I came out here twenty years ago. Be careful." She nodded in emphasis and walked over to Pela. Vas knew the nuns avoided repetition—the second "be careful" would equate to another person's yelling it. She watched Jasiel and Pela for a few moments, then turned to grab her pack. One advantage of not being down here much, almost nothing was out of it. She changed into darker clothing and pulled a black cap over her dyed hair. Hopefully Gosta could figure out more about the bounty on her, and how they could take it off short of turning herself in. She was grateful to Janx and was sorry if those attackers on Janx's ship were there because of her and not Janx. But she really wanted her old appearance back.

Deven came up to her. "I've got three groups of three. I figure that you might want to lead the group getting Sedari? Even if someone sees you, they won't know who you are."

"Good thinking." She stepped into his arms. "You make a damn fine captain."

He gave her a brief but still passionate kiss. They'd had little time alone together the last few days and they both felt it. "I do. Been following this redhead and copying her moves. Don't tell her though, she gets jealous."

Vas looked up. "As long as you don't tell that big, golden-skinned guy. I kinda like the blue you have going." She rested her head against his chest for a bit.

"What are you thinking?" They were keeping their voices down and her crew was professional enough to ignore them in these situations.

"A brief thought of you and me flying away. Maybe pick up a dozer. Start traveling around without people trying to kill us."

Deven tilted her face up. "Really?" The blue made his face softer somehow.

"Yeah, no. Not now. But someday." She sighed and pushed away from him. "Let's do this. Sun will be up in three hours and we need to be far from here when that happens."

"Agreed on both." Deven kissed the top of her head,

then went to hurry up the crew who were leaving. They wanted those two shuttles safe in the docking bay of the Traitor's *Folly* before they hit their targets. They only had one shuttle cart, but Mac would be driving it and collecting their unconscious victims. Everyone on the ground crew traded most of their weapons for stunners but kept one snub-nose blaster just in case. Some blasters could be switched between stun and full blast. Vas only had a few of those herself. She didn't trust them completely.

Vas wanted the three they were grabbing alive and in a talking mood.

Once they knew they were leaving, regardless of what they wanted to do, her crew moved quickly. They gathered silently, split between the two shuttles, and lifted off at the same time. Vas hadn't told them to do that, but it was less disturbing to the people in the camps around them. Anyone with a scanner would know there were two lift-offs, but people half asleep should only hear one.

Mac was already in the shuttle cart. Like the rest of the ground crew, he was in all black and had a skull cap on. That bright red hair of his would have stood out as bad as Vas'—both her own red or the currently dyed blonde.

Deven had his two crew members, they would be grabbing the first person on the route, Glazlie had her two, Vas' group would take the third. Vas, Marwin, and Roha would be taking Sedari. Vas really had no problem if the woman got a bit banged up along the way. She knew nothing about the other two except that they had information they needed. But Sedari had set up all the pirates in the area. Vas might only be a pirate right now in name, but betrayal like that in the quasi-criminal community wasn't good. Not to mention, her own crew could have been killed. And she'd tried to drug Deven to have her way with him. The personal level sucked.

"Ready, Talria?" Marwin asked quietly.

Vas would have told him they didn't need the fake

name, but she was impressed at his dedication. "I think
we can head out." She walked to the tent flap. To keep
up the ruse that they were still in camp, Vas was leaving it
behind. Mac had the shuttle cart dark, but it was waiting
up the road. She didn't see Glazlie or the two with her so
they must have gone inside to get their victim.

"Let's head out. You two take out the guards, I'm grabbing our target. Use your blaster only if you don't have
a choice." Some species weren't affected by stun weapons—Vas didn't want to kill people she wasn't paid to,
but if it were them or her people, she'd pull the trigger
herself.

Once she saw them both nod, she led them out. They
stuck close to the other camps so their dark shapes would
be less noticeable. Roha was hard to miss with her height,
but Vas took her fighting abilities as a major plus against
the slightly more noticeable shadow she cast.

The camps around them were silent, but Vas refrained
from checking to see if any were empty or dead. Hopefully, they were sleeping but she didn't have time to check.

Sedari's large tent was set up quite simplistically. The
front was for meeting with others and was grand and
ornate—for a tent—while the back held the sleeping and
eating areas.

Roha silently stepped past Vas and took out a pair of
guards with her stunner. She caught both as they fell
to mitigate the noise and let them slip to the ground.
Marwin darted to the left a moment later but vanished
behind a screen. Vas glanced to Roha, who nodded and
stayed where she was.

There were no other guards in the back, a stupid
mistake for someone who was betraying all the people
around her. Vas froze when she heard a hushed argument
ahead of her.

"I've done what you told me to. Now get me out of
here." Sedari sounded pissed with a strong wave of panic

thrown in. There was a gurgling sound, but Vas didn't think it was coming from Sedari or whoever she was speaking to.

"They are dead. I have four guards who will escort me to the pickup zone, everyone else is gone." A thudding sound, like a solid kick, put an end to the gurgling. "I didn't betray you, the codes were damaged. No one knows who is behind this. Tell me where to meet you. I'll go without my guards. Just tell *me*." The last was hissed with fear. "Thank you. I will come alone." The call clicked off and Vas turned the corner before Sedari could.

Sedari had a pack over her shoulder and was reaching for a blaster. Until Vas shot her twice with the stunner. Once would have dropped her well enough, but Vas was getting pissed at the level this woman would go to.

Sedari crumpled to the floor with a grimace.

Vas grabbed the pack and the blaster and scanned the room for anything else of worth. It was well picked over but there were four bodies scattered around. People who had been working for Sedari. She pulled the comm device off Sedari's shirt, pocketed it, and started dragging her out. A soft ticking sound came from the back of the bed. Vas got a better grip on Sedari and ran. That was a very distinctive sound. A timed explosive. Whoever Sedari had been working with, they were ending things the hard way.

"Marwin, Roha, there's an explosive counting down in her room. She killed the rest of her people. Help me get her out of here." Roha picked Sedari up like she was nothing, then they all ran.

Mac was halfway between this stop and the next.

Vas ran ahead to him. "Explosive in her tent."

Roha was behind and threw Sedari into the back of the shuttle cart on top of their other prisoner.

Vas hit the shuttle cart. "Move!" Mac took off, past the final pickup, and Vas led the two with her away from

Sedari's place. They were almost to cover when the explosion hit.

CHAPTER THIRTY-ONE

V AS HAD SHOVED THE OTHER two in front of her, but it didn't matter as the explosion was strong enough to knock all of them to the ground.

Shouts came immediately from all around them—at least some of the camps were still intact. Vas scrambled to her feet and motioned for the others to follow. They couldn't go back the way they came; from the noise there were a lot of people out there. It took her a few seconds to orient herself from where they were to where the shuttle was. The first two teams were supposed to meet there, with the third team riding with Mac and guarding their catch. She darted down a narrow lane between two camps with the other two right on her tail.

They had a close call when someone came running out the back of a camp as they passed. They all froze, but if he looked the wrong way, he would see them.

A woman's voice came from the main road. "This way! Sedari is trying to blow everything up." The yell got the man near them to run back toward the front, but left Vas shaking her head. Who would blow up their own tent to destroy others? But if the others believed that, it worked in their favor.

Vas counted to ten, then led them back toward the shuttle. It was dark out here and she kept pushing them away from the camps. No one stopped them as they ran.

Deven peeled himself away from the shuttle's shadow as they approached. He also lowered his blaster. His stunner was nowhere in sight.

"What happened?" He was the master of a powerful

whisper. Vas heard him, but anyone else might not have.

"Sedari was supposed to meet someone who was going to get her out of here and might have tried to blow her up. They were upset she didn't have the codes. Her tent had a delayed explosive in it. Either they really wanted to cut her loose or she was destroying evidence." Whatever the situation was, they needed to get out of there fast.

Deven nodded but stayed outside as the other two went into the shuttle. Vas smiled and switched her stunner for her blaster too. If anyone came out this way after them, they didn't deserve to be stunned.

The main camp was brightly lit as huge spotlights started coming on. There was a lot of yelling, but no weapon fire yet. And also no shuttle cart.

"Did you have any trouble?" She kept her voice low and her eyes on the camp. Mac and the others should have been right behind them. Unless they got caught because of the mess with the explosion.

"Not at all. The idiot we wanted was on guard. Took him out and had him in the cart in thirty seconds." Even with his blue skin, Vas could tell he was scowling as he looked down where the cart should be coming from.

"They would have had to take a longer way around. Hard to be stealthy with that going on." Vas nodded toward the yelling mass on the main road. "You know, I trust Glazlie and the people she's with."

"But Mac is one of those people." Deven finished for her and holstered his blaster and grabbed a stunner. "You want us to go after them."

"Yeah. Normally he can get the job done, but this might have messed them up." Vas stuck her head inside the shuttle. "Deven and I are going after the others. Roha and Marwin, stay outside. Bathie, if people get out this way and there are too many to shoot, get everyone inside and take off." She holstered her blaster and grabbed the stunner.

Roha opened her mouth to argue, about which point Vas wasn't sure. Probably all of them.

"No. My orders stand. Be ready to take off in either case." Vas gave a solid glare, then she and Deven jogged toward the mayhem. One advantage of sneaking up on a lot of chaos, being quiet wasn't as important.

They were a few camps away from the back of the tent Mac should have been in front of when two female Ellines and a male Wavian came toward them.

Ellines were often used as guards in the Commonwealth, fierce, stubborn, strong—and not always bright. These looked far more feral than the Commonwealth variety. They had thick gray skin, stood about seven feet tall, with wide stocky bodies and round faces with snouts and lower tusks. The Wavian stayed back. He looked like a fighter, but he wasn't stupid. Getting in front of an annoyed Elline could be fatal.

"Who are you with?" The first Elline waved her blaster rifle in the air.

"The Hothial crew. Who are you with?" Vas stepped forward, kept her blaster out and growled out the first pirate crew she could think of who wasn't actually here.

"The Eighty-First legion. Do you know what happened?" The Elline stepped forward.

"No, we're trying to find out, heard something blow up." Vas stepped forward again. They were close enough to start hitting each other with their fists if they wanted to.

"Did you do it?" The Elline didn't step forward this time but leaned closer and narrowed her eyes.

Vas leaned forward as well. "Why would we be running toward it if we did it?" Ellines were bullies. There was no doubt even just one of them could destroy Vas in a fight, possibly Deven as well. But they admired guts.

The Elline gave a snort that echoed through her snout. "Agreed. Carry on. Might want to find your people and flee. There's going to be a fight soon." The implication was there—Vas and Deven weren't strong enough to fight, but gutsy enough to respect. This time. Next time they saw each other things might end differently.

Vas gave a sharp nod and jogged around them. Deven ran alongside her. "Nice posturing. Unless I'm wrong, the Eighty-First legion was a paramilitary troop in the Commonwealth. One that went missing a few years ago."

"Yup. I'd say they went AWOL, but I'm not going to tell on them—you?" Vas was keeping watch as they closed in on the tent they'd been looking for.

"Not on my life." His words were cut off as a shuttle cart, firing at a mass of people chasing after them, almost ran them over. Vas and Deven dove out of the way, but she saw Mac's wide-eyed face as he and his full shuttle cart raced by.

"Damn it." Vas rolled to her feet and started firing her stunner at the mob running after Mac's cart. Deven did the same.

"What are you doing?" A short Ilerian who hadn't been stunned yet skidded to a halt with his hands up and dropped his blaster. The few beings behind him did the same.

"What are we doing? Your friends there were trying to kill us. You're all lucky we're on patrol so had stunners instead of blasters."

"They aren't my friends. But those people in the shuttle cart killed a bunch of people in Sedari's tent, blew it up, and set another tent on fire." He took a sidestep toward his blaster on the ground.

"Not a good idea." Vas stunned him and waved her stunner to the others. More were coming their way, shouts and the crackling of flames pointed out that something had happened with the last pick-up.

"Any of you want to try? No? Good idea. We'll go after them. You go help put the fire out." She pointed toward the tent with flames coming out of it.

The ones still standing collectively nodded and turned away.

Vas turned the way Mac had gone and started running.

"I hope Mac didn't screw things up too badly." Since Deven's legs were a good eight inches longer than hers, he loped alongside her easily.

"So do I. What was he thinking, starting a fire?" This job was supposed to be subtle—well, as much as it could be. Instead, Mac made it a circus. "At least we know he didn't kill Sedari's people. But he better still have her in that cart."

The yelling from the camp behind them grew louder and it sounded like blaster fire was joining the noise. Lots of it.

Vas and Deven both picked up speed. The shuttle was still dark when they ran up, but the empty shuttle cart was next to it.

Deven slowed down as they passed it. "They took some hits."

Roha stuck her head out of the shuttle. "I've been watching. Everyone is here, no major injuries. Mac wants to know if we can leave now."

They ran inside the shuttle. Her people looked fine, even the three unconscious bodies tied to seats in the front looked okay. "Get us out of here, Mac." Vas buckled in next to their prisoners. Deven took the navigator seat. It was also the weapons console.

The shuttle lifted awkwardly, and Mac started swearing.

"What is it, Mac?" He was a pain in the ass, but he was also a damn fine pilot. The shuttle felt like it had been on a weeklong bender and bounced around in the air.

"I don't know, damn it. We're taking fire from the ground." A wave of flame shot around them and the shuttle rolled away from the fire and the explosion that followed. "They got the shuttle cart."

Deven fired back, but toward the sky not the ground. "Hostiles above us and on the ground. Punch it, Mac."

"I'm trying to do that."

Deven physically grabbed Mac and switched seats. "Shoot at everything that moves." He ripped off the console, grabbed a bunch of wires in one hand, and the shuttle shot forward.

They missed being incinerated by a nearby fighter by less than Vas wanted to think about. The shuttle kept moving like a wild thing, but now it seemed like a wild thing with a purpose.

Mac swerved in his seat, fired, and the fighter near them exploded. "Yes!" He spun and grinned but Vas shook her head. She'd upgraded her shuttles, but there were a lot of big, nasty ships out there that could smash this shuttle with little effort.

"Keep an eye out, Mac. We're not close enough to our ship to be that cocky." Vas held onto the armrest as the shuttle rolled. Deven got it back in position, but something was seriously wrong with this shuttle.

"Captain, we've got two cruisers closing in. You need to get here faster." Gosta's voice wasn't the most helpful thing to hear.

"Gosta, right now we need to not crash or get blown up. Be ready to get the hell out of here the instant we're on board and the bay doors are shut." Vas trusted Mac and Deven. There was nothing logically she would be doing differently than them right now, but it was taking everything she had to not run to the front and replace one of them.

Her mind-doc called it serious control issues and was trying to get her through it.

Deven started swearing and the shuttle lurched then shot forward. That would have been great but there were two more fighters coming that way. Mac shot the first one, but they were going to crash into the second.

With one hand on the wires he'd pulled and one on the control stick, Deven lifted them up enough to clear the fighter. Mac fired a few parting shots, and they were almost to the *Traitor's Folly*.

"Damn it, that was too close."

"And it keeps getting closer." Deven hit his comm. "Gosta, we're coming in with no fuel and little control. Have everyone clear the docking bay level and arm all fire suppressants to hit us once the doors close."

Vas shot Deven a questioning look, but this was something he could fill her in on later—if there was a later. "And Gosta, I still want us out of this sector the moment we're in." She caught Deven's look as he fought to keep the shuttle intact. "After we get fully fire suppressed, that is." She couldn't tell what was wrong with the shuttle, but something seriously was.

The shuttle stopped most of the bouncing but was still speeding up erratically as they approached the docking bay. Deven fought until right before they entered, then he released the wires, and they went into the bay. Their speed cut the moment Deven released the wires and he navigated a dead shuttle into the bay. They bumped a bit but didn't hit anything too hard. They just stopped when the doors slammed shut and the entire bay was filled with foam.

CHAPTER THIRTY-TWO

———◆———

"IS EVERYONE OKAY?" ALL POWER in the shuttle was gone now, including lights. The thin emergency strips marked the way to the hatch but seeing anyone in the shuttle would take better eyes than hers.

"Mac smacked his head, he's out." Deven grunted. "And I might have burned my hand on those wires—we'll need someone else to move him.

"My team and I are fine." Glazlie checked in from the dark.

The rest all checked in as well. Mac appeared to be their only serious injury.

"Everyone stay seated, let me get the hatch open." Vas unbuckled and slowly made her way to the hatch. She freed a small service lamp from where it hung next to the hatch. The thin burn line along one side of the hatch that it illuminated was a bad thing. She hit the hatch release, but nothing happened. She tapped her comm. "Terel? Can you and a few strong people with tools come down to the docking bay? We're trapped." She peered out through the front window. "Might need to have someone clear the suppression foam first though."

At first there was no response, then a few words came through. Or parts of them. All Vas could tell for sure was communications were down. The shuttle jostled a bit—it really couldn't go far with all of the suppression foam—but something was going on outside.

"We must be under attack." Deven came alongside her and took a look at the scorched hatch. He was holding his right hand carefully as he leaned forward.

Vas held up the lamp and motioned for him to raise his hand. Red angry marks crossed it and movement was obviously difficult. "Damn it, why did you grab those wires?" The flesh looked angrier the longer she looked.

"Something was blocking communication between the column and the steering. We were going to crash or be shot down. And it wasn't accidental."

Vas swore. She'd left Jasiel in the shuttle. Gon had been there, but he wouldn't have been looking for her to have sent a bug. Jasiel either didn't know she'd done it, or the bit about being taken over was a ruse. Neither was a good scenario.

She pushed Deven toward the front. "You get the med kit and do something with that hand. Marwin and Glazlie, I need you two to gently move Mac to one of the adjustable rows. Make him comfortable but secure him in. We don't know if that foam will protect us from a serious hit."

Deven turned as she pushed him forward. But she shook her head. The light helped and she saw what he was about to say before he said it.

"No. You're hurt, and that injury directly impacts your ability to be helpful." She gently pushed him back into the pilot seat. "Except for your brain—that you can use." She kissed him on the head and turned back to the rest. "You all too. We need ideas, folks; it might be a while before anyone can get down here and get us out."

Bathie stood up and moved toward the panel to the right of the navigator seat. "The communications issue might be us as well as them. I'll do a thorough check."

One by one the crew started taking apart the inside of the shuttle to figure out how to fix it. The shuttle rumbled a few more times as the *Traitor's Folly* took more hits. Damn it, Gosta should have gotten them far from anyone following. Unless of course Jasiel had actually been the traitor.

Vas kept trying her comm, but unlike her first attempt with Terel, she got nothing from anyone. She brought out the tool chest from its side wall compartment and started working on the hatch. Soon three people were helping, and they were stripping down the hatch like a science project. The regular interior lights came on and that sped things along.

"Xsit? Thank gods, we've been trying to get—" Bathie swore into the comm she'd wired through the shuttle's system. "Damn it, stay safe. We'll find you." She disconnected the comm. "Xsit said pirates boarded the ship right as we came in. They took most of the crew and sent them adrift in a shuttle. She, Flarik, Pela, and Divee are in the holosuite and have it barricaded. Oh, and Flarik is unconscious."

Vas rocked back on her heels. No part of that was good news, but Flarik being unconscious was almost the worst. Unless locked in hibernation, Wavians were almost impossible to knock out. "Someone knew exactly where we were going and used us to get on board. Gosta and everyone would have been focused on us. I wish I knew if it was the same bastards who broke into Janx's ship."

The power in the shuttle dropped, came back, then dropped to half.

"I think we can force open the hatch." Deven hadn't moved from his seat but was watching the progress as well as something on a pad in front of him. "But we need to get rid of the foam first. My guess is that Gosta was attacked right as he was releasing it. There is a lot out there."

And it didn't look like it was going away either. Normally suppression foam dissipated on its own. Vas felt like they were buried in a snow drift.

"Cold." Mac didn't open his eyes as he spoke but he moved a bit.

"Can someone get him a blanket?" Vas was buried

under pieces of hatch and others were closer to him.

Mac's eyes opened before Marwin could put the blanket on him. "No. Use cold from the shuttle to melt the foam. Rig outside to freeze." He winced and closed his eyes again. "My head really hurts."

"You hit it hard." Deven adjusted some controls in the front, then smiled. "I've never tried either removing foam or freezing the hull of a shuttle, but I can make the freezing part work. Everyone should probably move into the center of the shuttle though."

Marwin helped Vas out from her collection of hatch debris and everyone except Deven huddled together in the center. It took a moment, but fog grew on the front window and the foam outside started shrinking. The ceiling of the docking bay became visible.

The foam continued to shrink, and Vas found some insulated gloves and moved back toward the hatch. She held up her gloved hands. "I'll need two more people to get gloves on and help me move this hatch the moment that foam is low enough. We need to be moving before whoever took this ship knows we're free."

"Captain, I have Aithnea on the comm." Bathie had gone back to her panel and held up her comm. It was still connected to the shuttle's system and judging by the way she kept tossing it back and forth, was pretty damn cold.

Vas went over. With her gloves on it wasn't cold at all. "Aithnea?"

"Yes, things have not been good here and it appears that has impacted you as well. I can't believe Jasiel turned on us. But we can deal with that once we get her and the others back. We have a bigger issue. From what I can pick up, the pirates have left the ship. They also locked some people in here and have the ship set on self-destruct."

Vas swore. "Can you tell how long?"

"Nine minutes and forty-three seconds."

"Damn. We'll get you out after we get that shut off."

"Either way, it was good being with you." Aithnea cut the comm.

Vas handed the comm back to Bathie. The foam was knee-high now. "Come on, folks, we have nine minutes to shut off the auto destruct. Cassil, stay here and protect our prisoners. They should stay unconscious, but we don't want any surprises." All three were not only unconscious they were gagged and tied.

It took a lot of grunting and swearing, but she, Roha, and Marwin got the hatch open. Mac tried to follow the others out, but he could barely stand. "Either we succeed, or we all die. But right now, you shouldn't be up."

That he went back down without arguing said something about his injury.

Vas waded through the foam with the others behind her. They all had their blasters out. Aithnea wouldn't lie about the pirates being off the ship but she might not have all the information. Vas couldn't understand why they would force their way on board, strand most of the crew, then not even keep the ship.

She held her hand up, fist closed, as she checked the first corridor. Then she motioned Roha and Marwin to go past her. They stopped at the next junction, then gave the all clear sign. They kept that up all the way back to the command deck. They used the narrow winding stairs that would get them there without using the lift. Whether the invaders had actually abandoned the ship or not, they weren't in the corridors Vas and her people went through.

The command deck appeared empty as she came around the corner. Deven was right next to her and blocked her from moving forward with his good hand as a blaster shot rang out.

CHAPTER THIRTY-THREE

"Look, I KNOW THIS SHIP is going to self-destruct, you really want to go with it?" Vas stayed back behind a wall and all of her people did as well. But the only answer was more blaster fire. Wild blaster fire.

Vas turned to Deven and pantomimed crawling. Whoever was out there was firing too randomly to actually hit anything except by accident. Deven nodded and she holstered her blaster and crawled forward.

"Look, we don't want to die and I'm sure neither do you. They left you behind, didn't they?" Deven was using his soothing voice.

Vas found herself slowing down just from hearing him, but then shook it off and kept moving forward. The self-destruct had two control stations—the captain's chair and the navigator's console—both of which were right where the blaster fire was coming from.

"They tricked me. Yup. Then tied me up here and drugged me. None of us are going anywhere."

Vas paused, that voice sounded familiar. Or it would have if the speaker didn't sound totally drunk. She crawled a bit closer, no more blaster fire but he was now singing to himself.

Vas crawled up behind a console then went up on her knees. Yup, Thager, the one who'd given Terel the note back on the planet. "I saved your ass, and this is how you pay me back?" She could see him, but as he was still looking where Deven was. He probably couldn't see her.

A round of blaster fire echoed.

"Stop blasting up my damn ship!" Vas still had her stunner and switched to it, rose to her feet, and shot him.

"Who the hell are you?" Thager looked at her in wide-eyed shock, then fell over, and his blaster clattered to the floor.

"Damn it." Vas ran over to him and kicked away his blaster. "I forgot I'm not looking like me. We have to find out about that idiotic warrant, I can't stay made up forever."

The rest of her people came forward and Deven took the navigator's seat. Vas circled the deck, making absolutely certain there was no one else around, then took the captain's chair.

The countdown was at two minutes and three seconds. Vas took a deep breath and nodded to Deven. They both entered the code at the same time and the countdown stopped.

Vas leaned back in her chair. "I would have thought setting another ship's destruct code would have been impossible." She knew it was pretty damn hard, that had been one of the first things she tried to get Gosta to do when he first joined her crew.

"It should have been. Once we get Gosta and Hrrru back, the three of us will find out exactly how they did it." Deven was pale from pain. While he was playing off that his injury wasn't bad, there was no way he wasn't lying. Unfortunately, she couldn't send him to the med bay like she wanted. He did have it fully wrapped, so that was the best she was going to get out of him at this point.

"Agreed. We need to make sure it doesn't happen again. But, we still need to search the rest of the ship and get our people out of the holosuite."

"Plus track down where they sent the shuttle with everyone else." Deven was already entering information into his station. Even one-handed he was fast. "And find out how they got in and where their damn ship is."

"You do that. Bathie, you stay here and keep an eye on

our friend and anyone else who pops up. Everyone use a stunner if possible, blaster only if you have to. There's something off about this entire situation and I'd like to get some answers. Can't do that if they're all dead." She wasn't sure what they were going to do if they found many more—she only had four cells in this brig.

"I'll keep an eye on the people in the shuttle too." Bathie had both her stunner and her blaster out as she settled at a science station. She pulled up the camera of the docking bay.

"Thanks." Vas sent everyone except Marwin in teams to search the rest of the ship. Luckily, this ship was a hell of a lot smaller than the *Warrior Wench*.

She and Marwin did the same pause, scan, and move forward routine they'd done coming in. They didn't see anyone on the way to the holosuite. Vas paused before peering around the final corridor. The hairs on the back of her neck were raised—someone was there even though she couldn't see or hear them. She motioned for Marwin to stay back and remain still. He didn't look happy, but he gave a sharp nod.

Vas came around the corner slowly. This might be her ship, but this corridor was enemy territory right now.

She ducked and rolled into a short doorway an instant before a blaster shot went over her head. Actually, the trailing color of the beam as it passed was from a stunner. Great, they were trying to capture not kill.

"You're out-numbered. Give us the location of Vaslisha Tor Dain and we'll let you live."

Vas could see Marwin hanging back down the corridor. He hadn't moved, and the person or people facing them couldn't see him. But he looked far too ready to jump out. Vas shook him off.

Someone set up this entire thing to get her? Only they didn't realize they already had her in their sights.

"That woman died a day ago. Took a hit and didn't

come back. What did you want her for?" She closed her eyes to listen to the enemy down the hall after she spoke. Shuffling of at least three, possibly four. One of them was swearing, or at least that's what the sharp whispers sounded like. They'd set this up but had no clue what to do if their target hadn't been in that shuttle.

Amateurs.

"She was on that shuttle. Thager told us she'd be on that shuttle." This voice was different and sounded more concerned about their situation.

"You mean the meat bag we whacked on the deck? Wasted your time. We might let you live if you give up the coordinates where our shuttle was sent off to."

More shuffling. There was only an access exit back where they were—nothing that would get them anywhere safe. They'd trapped themselves. This was looking less and less like a professional hit.

"We didn't do anything. The crew jumped ship as soon as we came on board. Pirates, after all."

Vas shook her head. These were mercs or military, and either way really bad at taking over ships. They got onboard; she'd give them that. But they were pretty bad.

"Wow, so who paid you to come after us? And no, I don't believe the crew left on their own, so one of you better start spouting coordinates unless you want to be spurting blood."

More shuffling, swearing, and what sounded like an argument.

Deven came on her comm. "We found their ship. Well-hidden but it's hanging near where they forced their way in. Very similar to the way Janx's dozer was boarded."

Vas hit her comm and kept her voice low. "Anyone on board?"

"Not a soul. Permission to blast it?"

"Agreed. We have three, maybe four hostiles here in the

corridor blocking the holosuite."

"Roha and Glazlie came back. I'll send them down."

"Thanks." Vas cut the call. This standoff could go on far longer than they had time for—there was no way to know the condition of her missing crew. "Here's the deal, one of you tell us exactly where our shuttle went in the next five seconds, or we blow up your ship. After that we start killing you."

She wasn't surprised that none of them stepped up, but she did hear more muttering. She was braced for the nearby explosion; from the swearing, they weren't. One form, wearing the same suit as the ones from Janx's ship, actually tumbled into the corridor and she shot him twice with the stunner.

"Well, your ship and one of you are down. Come on. You have no ship. You're trapped. Surrender and we'll leave you stranded on a planet with air."

"You're not the captain. How do we know you mean what you say?"

Vas sighed and tapped her comm. "Captain Fhailson, could you explain to these idiots that we will leave them alive if they surrender and tell us what we need to know?"

The ship-wide comm crackled and came on. "This is Captain Fhailson. My second in command, Talria, is act-ing in my stead. Yes, if you surrender immediately, you'll be kept alive as long as you answer our questions and get our people back. And in case you didn't realize, yes, your ship is space debris now."

More rustling and the body of the one she shot started to be pulled backward.

Vas shot right above it and was rewarded by a yell. "Seri-ously, there are already troops in the corridor behind me, and more on the way. You were set up and lied to. Give up now."

Another heavily armored person came forward, started to drop their weapon, then fired toward Vas' location. She ducked back even further. No part of her was showing, but a numbness spread over her.

"Marwin! Take them down!" Her stunner tumbled from her fingers. She fought back but couldn't move as Marwin, Roha, and Glazlie all ran forward.

A brief firefight later and Marwin came next to her. "We got them, all stunned like you asked. What did they hit you with?"

"That's what I'd like to know. Tie them all up and dump them in one of the cells in the brig. I should be fine in a few." The numbness had been brief and was already wearing off. But Vas didn't know of any stunner that could work around corners. "I want whatever they used. Once we get our people back, I want those weapons looked at." She pushed herself against the wall and got to her feet.

"Vas, I think I found our shuttle," Deven said. "Drifting in space a system over from here. If we're secure, I'll head us over."

"I believe we are secure, and I'm going to get our people out of the holosuite." She shook her legs out to get the last tingles taken care of, then went down the hall.

The door to the holosuite was jammed and after a few moments, she blasted the locking mechanism. They could fix it later.

Xsit jumped out of a heavily forested hologram with her blaster up.

"It's okay, it's me, remember?" Vas held her hands up.

"Thank the stars." Xsit lowered her weapon and turned off the hologram. "We heard the blasters and Flarik is still out."

Pela and Divee stood aside and showed where Flarik lay. Vas ran to her. Still breathing, no external injuries. Just not waking up. "Did either of you see what they did to her?"

"Some weird blaster, Captain." Divee shook his head.

"Never seen the like."

Pela looked pissed. "I need to get her to the med lab. They chased us down here and shot Flarik when she attacked them. We barely made it in here and locked the door. Then they trapped us."

"Like this?" Glazlie stuck her head in and held up an oddly shaped blaster.

"Is that what hit me?"

"Pretty sure. And if Flarik took a direct hit, I think we know what it does."

"But normal stunners usually have no effect on Wavians. Let's move her to the med bay. We're getting the rest of the crew back." They'd started moving Flarik, but she turned to Pela. "Did Jasiel work with the attackers?"

"Not that we saw. But we were down here when the attack came," Pela said. "Aithnea stayed in the system in case they broke in."

Vas went to the panel. "Aithnea? Are you okay in there?"

"Yes. I'm still pissed about Jasiel and what happened on the planet, but I'm intact. I had the computer run a full diagnostic on my program once we got back. Before the attack."

Vas weighed an idea. Yes, people had used Aithnea to get into their system before, but Gosta and Hrrru had done a serious tightening of the way they'd gotten in. Aithnea having full access to their ship could be more of a help than a risk. "I'm going to authorize full access for you—once we get Gosta and Hrrru back."

There was a bit more silence than she'd expected, but Vas could almost see Aithnea pacing as she thought things through. She wouldn't agree to it if she thought she might be a risk—having been so the one time would have been shocking by itself.

"I agree if I were in the rest of the system, it might help protect us all." She appeared in hologram form. "I would like to have a chance to speak to Jasiel once you bring her back."

Vas recognized the strained look on her face—when she'd been growing up it had been directed at her enough. "Agreed." With a nod, Vas left the holosuite.

Everyone except Pela gathered on the command deck after Flarik had been taken to the med lab. Bathie was at navigation and Deven was in the captain's chair. He rose as Vas came on the deck, but she started to wave him off. Then she shook her head and went up to him.

"You need to go down and have that hand looked at. I think your lowly second in command can handle the deck for a bit.

"Fine. Only because I know fighting with you is point-less. Bathie can show you the intel on where we're going." With a nod, he left the deck.

Vas was glad he went but it wasn't a good sign that he gave in so quickly. His hand must be extremely painful. She waited until the lift doors shut and called down to the med lab. "Deven burned his hand on a cable in the shuttle, and he's coming down *without* an argument."

Pela sighed. "Thanks for the warning. We'll fix him."

Vas called the shuttle. "Cassil? You and Mac still okay?"

"Aye, Captain. But the prisoners are starting to stir."

"I'll send down some help to get them to the brig. Then I want you to escort Mac to the med bay—unless you don't think he can walk that far?"

"I hit my head, not my legs. I can walk." Mac sounded more like himself than he did before.

"Excellent. Cassil will still escort you there once the prisoners are secured." She was glad he sounded better, but she knew blows to the head could be tricky.

Once things were settled, she leaned back in her seat. "Xsit, try to reach the shuttle once we get to their sys-tem." Bathie was getting them to the gate that would take them there, but Vas wanted to wait until they were closer before reaching out in case anyone had tapped into their communications. Gosta had gotten them free of the Nhali system before they'd been boarded, so chances were good that no one from the pirate conclave was still tracking them. But better to be paranoid and safe.

While they flew toward the gate, Vas looked over the logs. Her shuttle came in, and Gosta immediately took off toward the closest gate. Then the ship came under attack and they were boarded. The attackers came from the planet itself or nearby. She pulled up images of the ship they'd come in. Yup, same design as the attackers on the dozer. Khirson had called them Enforcers. Were they seriously still just after her? It would have been smarter to have grabbed the shuttle. And more importantly, how in the hell were they boarding ships with that much ease?

"Captain, we're in the system and I am picking up the shuttle." Bathie scowled at something on her screen that she then sent up to the main screen. "They have explosives attached to it."

"Damn it." Vas swore as she looked at the image. Five claerin mines, all looped around the shuttle. "What the hell is wrong with these people? If they are after me, trapping my people isn't going to help bring me in."

"Unless they weren't sure you would be on the shuttle, even though the ones here believed it to be so." Aithnea's voice came over the comm. "I feel…"

Vas gave her a few seconds, then prompted her. "Feel what? We have to get those mines off the shuttle, get our people, and get the hell out of here before more people come after us." They were going to need to hide for a bit until they figured things out. Once they rescued the people in the shuttle.

Aithnea continued as if Vas hadn't interrupted her thoughts. "I feel Jasiel in my mind, she's reaching out. And I now believe she didn't betray us." She paused again. "We can get rid of the mines quickly. Vas? You will need to come down to the holosuite."

Vas got out of her seat. "Bathie, you have the deck. I'll be down in the holosuite." If she thought about questioning Aithnea's demand, she wasn't going to show it.

The door to the holosuite was slightly ajar, but she'd blasted it well, so that wasn't shocking.

Aithnea was pacing in what looked to be a holographic representation of a prayer workout room. Sparse and covered in elaborate floor mats it was used both for silent prayer and equally silent training. But it was only for the highest-level nuns and the Keepers.

Vas stopped right inside the door, but didn't go further in. "What did you need me for?"

"I need you to come in. This wasn't how I imagined your first Keeper training, but then again, I would never have thought you'd become a Keeper." Aithnea's hologram appeared, but not in her normal clothing. She wore her ritual Gi, the embellished uniform of the Mother Superior—when she was about to kick some serious ass.

"We don't have time, Aithnea. We have no idea how the crew is inside there—at the very least there are far too many of them in that thing to be doing well." Vas stayed where she was. "Now what was your idea for getting them out quickly?"

She smiled and held out her arms to encompass the holosuite. "This. The three of us can remove the mines. It wouldn't work if I were actually alive, or Jasiel weren't inside the shuttle, but we can do this." If her grin got any larger, Vas was going to see if she could reboot her program. This was not normal Aithnea behavior.

"There is a spiritual component to what the nuns do, there always has been. It can transcend the physical in extreme cases. Look in your mind, the blue book—page 1009, I think, near the bottom."

The moment she said that the image hit Vas' mind. Four nuns and two Keepers. Moving a mountain to save a village. A small mountain, but still.

"They were all trained. There were two Keepers and four nuns. We have an untrained Keeper, a trapped nun, and a dead nun. I don't see how this is going to work."

"Knew you'd be stubborn." Aithnea charged forward and made a surprisingly solid kick to Vas' head.

Vas scrambled to her feet. "What in the hells? We have people trapped, maybe dying—" Her words were cut off as Aithnea charged forward again. This time Vas was ready and blocked the kick and the blow that would have landed after.

With moves she'd never done before.

"Damn it! Are you in my head?" Vas shook herself off, but an energy and power came from those moves. "Come at me again."

The grin was different this time, but Aithnea flashed it then flew toward Vas. Aithnea was showing more of her skills and power this time, but Vas still got a few blows in before she was slammed to the padded wall.

"This is great, really, but how are we going to help the crew?"

Aithnea sat down on the floor next to her and took her hands. "Focus on going beyond this ship. Space is open. I'll lead, Jasiel will be our focus."

Vas didn't have a lot of hope this would do anything, but she did feel different.

"You see what to do now?"

The view opened and Vas *saw*. They could remove the mines. With their minds. That was terrifying and something far beyond what she knew of the nuns.

"Yes, it is. It is our secret. Novitiates are never taught that this even exists until they take their final vows. You will not be able to speak of it to anyone, not even Deven or Therian. The words simply will not come out."

This was definitely weird, but at this point whatever worked was good. Vas would sort things out later. "I guess we do it then."

She felt Jasiel's presence join the two of them and then the focus was on the mines—more importantly the small power source for them. Aithnea, Jasiel, and Vas simply drifted between the connections on each.

Vas opened her eyes, and she and Aithnea were back in the holosuite. "But we didn't stop them?"

"Captain?" Bathie called down. "The mines are powered down and are breaking free from the shuttle. I still can't reach anyone on it though."

Vas turned to Aithnea. "Are we done for now? I'd rather be on the deck." Already the power she'd felt was fading.

"Go, but we'll work on this again." Aithnea seemed extremely tired, especially considering she was only a hologram. "Oh, and Jasiel said that everyone except her is unconscious—they have valid life signs, but they are knocked out."

"Got it." Vas hit her comm as she ran out of the holosuite. "I'm on my way up, Bathie. Move us closer to the shuttle, those mines should be dead now." As long as no one asked her how she knew that or what was done, everything was good. She trusted Aithnea when she said she wouldn't be able to speak of it. Sneaky nuns.

"The mines appear dead, but are we sure we want to bring the shuttle in with them?" Bathie didn't even look over as Vas came on the deck.

Vas trusted the nuns—Aithnea most of all—but one of their first lessons was always be prepared for the worst. "We need to get them free first. Marwin, can you take out the last still functioning shuttle and you and Roha pull those mines off? We can blow them up when our shuttle is back here." Leaving explosives around, even ones that were theoretically disarmed, was something Vas never did. Unless she was fighting someone. Too easy for innocents to get hurt.

"Aye, Captain." Marwin and Roha left the deck.

"Pela? How are our injured?"

"Mac is fine, but I want him under observation for a bit still, so no, he can't leave. Get back in that cot, or I will tranq you." Pela was not amused. "I think I've found the frequency they used to knock out Flarik and she's slowly coming around. Deven is already heading back up to you." There was pure annoyance there. "I did what I could, but when he heard about the explosives he took off."

Vas sighed. Pela must have said something comforting to him like "this isn't too bad". Never a good idea to say that to Deven.

The lift opened and Deven came out. His hand was now in a full swaddling of protective wrapping. Clearly, he felt this was enough to come back on deck. "What happened?" He called up the shuttle on his station. "The mines are nullified. How?"

Vas shook her head. She'd chew him out later. "Aithnea was able to do something, not sure how." Which was the truth. Vas might have been involved in whatever they did, but she had no idea how they did it.

Deven shot her a narrow-eyed look as he tried to sort out what she really meant, then turned back to his screen.

The second shuttle launched and approached the first one. It took a few minutes of tense maneuvering, but the string of mines was removed.

"Now how are we going to get them back if no one is conscious?" Vas said out loud as she was out of ideas.

"Captain?" Gosta's voice was weak and groggy, but a welcome sound. "Jasiel woke me. The air is short in here, but I think I can get us back."

Made sense, there was about three times the normal occupancy for that sized shuttle. Being over-capacity for a short while would have been fine, but not for longer than that.

"Okay. Marwin, stay close to them as they come in."

The two shuttles slowly came toward the ship and got secured inside.

"Now, someone blow those mines up and let's find another system to inhabit immediately. Pick one, Bathie, just get us the hell out of here."

CHAPTER THIRTY-FOUR

"GLADLY." DEVEN HIT THE WEAPON bank with his good hand. The mines triggered each other in a nice, albeit brief, show.

Bathie quickly moved them to another system. So far, no sign of followers.

"Bathie, keep jumping systems and leave drones behind. I'm going to go help with our rescued crew." Vas motioned for Deven to sit back down in his chair. "And you are not." She pointed to his injured hand. "Seriously."

"I still have one perfectly good hand."

"And I still need someone to stay on deck." The rest of their reduced crew, except for Xsit, silently headed for the lift.

"Seriously, how is it?" Vas came over to him.

"Pela wants Terel to look at it, when Terel has recovered. There might be permanent nerve damage. Wasn't one of my brightest ideas." He grinned, but worry was hiding around his eyes.

"You did manage to save us, you know." She leaned down to kiss him. "I personally appreciate not being blown to space dust while looking like this."

"Good point. I'm sure the rest of the crew appreciates not blowing up as well." The look in his face said that while he knew something odd had gone on with the mines, he wasn't going to push it. Not yet anyway. "Okay, Xsit and I will keep track of things up here. Go drag everyone else to the med bay."

Vas nodded and jogged to the lift and down to the shuttle bay.

The battered shuttle she'd come in on had been pushed far into a corner to give more room for the people being helped out of the rescued shuttle. Jasiel stood to one side watching.

"Shouldn't you go to the med bay also?"

"Do you send prisoners there or the brig?" She held her head high, but her eyes were sad.

"You helped save everyone. Aithnea doesn't believe you betrayed us."

"I also was unable to stop the attack. A nun of my standing should have been able to. I believe I have been compromised by my near-death situation and imprisonment. I froze."

"That happens. I don't know about nuns, but it does to everyone else."

"Captain? We have a problem." Glazlie was normally calm, but she didn't sound so now. "The prisoners are missing."

"Sedari and the other two that we took from the camp? How?"

"No. Deven's brother and that woman. They were in the brig, but we're putting Sedari and the other two in and they're gone."

"Damn it. Was this entire thing just to get them? And how did they get away?"

"There were two ships when they first attacked." Deven called down from the deck. "I reviewed the vids. The first one took off as we were trying to figure out how to get out of the shuttle. If they had two teams, one could have grabbed Leil and that woman and taken off before they even finished getting the rest of the crew in the shuttle. By the way, they knocked out the crew to get them in there. We really need to look at those weapons they used on you and Flarik."

"Among everything else. Then we assume these Enforcers are working with Ome and Loxianth?"

TRAITOR'S FOLLY   349

"Or against them, and they want Leil and that woman for something else," Deven said.

"There could be answers there if you find out which is true." Jasiel definitely spoke like a nun when she wanted to.

Vas looked around. There were too many things all running into each other. They needed time to sort them out.

"Glazlie, make sure the new prisoners are extremely secure—including our three Enforcers. Deven, start searching as to how those damn Enforcers keep getting on board. Once Janx is recovered have her work with you—she had a way to blow the ship off when it tried to come back and latch on. Maybe we can modify something."

"What would you have me do?" Jasiel still looked haunted and turned away when they carried her friend Thomas out.

Vas had no idea what Pela was planning on doing with so many unconscious people. Even the med bay of the *Warrior Wench* couldn't have held them all, and the one in this ship was a quarter the size.

"Can you help heal?" Vas knew some of the nuns had healing abilities. She seriously doubted someone who had basically been the equivalent of a nun-spy-assassin would, but it was worth a shot. Pela needed help and Jasiel needed a focus.

"I have some skills. Nothing on the level of most of my late sisters, but I can comfort, and I know what to look for regarding complications." She smiled. "Where would you have me?"

"Excellent. Go follow the line of injured and tell Pela I sent you to help. Tell her to take over whatever space she needs." Her crew looked fine, not even any bruising. It was as if they were all asleep.

Jasiel bowed and followed them out.

Vas helped carry some of the crew in. Pela had a seriously extensive triage going and was managing to keep eyes on everyone. Or almost everyone. Flarik was off in a former meeting room along with an annoyed Mac sitting up in a cot near her.

"How are you feeling?" Vas stuck her head inside but kept her voice low.

"I'm fine. I keep telling people, I'm fine. Pela has me watching Flarik, she's trying a treatment that might tie into what happened to the others. She's administering some liquid." Mac might be sitting up but didn't look like he was going to try and go beyond that. Pela could be more vicious than Terel when she was stressed—she'd probably terrified Mac into staying in the bed.

Vas walked over to Flarik's side. Seeing the fierce Wavian down like this was scary. She turned away, then back around when a movement caught her eye. "Her eyes are opening. Flarik? Can you hear me?"

Flarik's eyes narrowed and with great effort she opened her mouth. "I will kill them." She was furious.

"But you moved! Keep working on that. I'll be right back." Vas passed through the gurneys to find Pela. She finally found her in a corner checking on Terel. "Flarik is conscious, whatever you're doing is working." Vas knew how Terel would have handled this—one test subject to start. From the look on Pela's face, she'd done the same. And Flarik was the test.

"Thank gods. Their heart rates were still going down." She gave Terel a shot, then nodded to a table behind her. "Doses are all loaded. I still want to know what in the hells did this, but let's wake them up."

Vas grabbed a few more crew and within a half hour the ones from the shuttle were groaning like thousand-year-old Ilerians. But they were awake.

An hour later everyone had recovered and Terel was ripping apart entire sections of the ship to find the contagion that had taken then out.

"Damn it. Whatever they used left no trace."

"I told you, they had weapons. They were firing a charge of some kind, not chemical." Vas had told her that as soon as Terel was upright. But Terel insisted the reactions the crew had must have been based on chemicals, not electrical. She finally looked ready to admit defeat.

"Do we have those weapons?" Terel replaced the floor plate she'd taken off with a sigh.

"Yup. Walvento wanted to take them apart as soon as he recovered, but I told him you might want to be involved." Vas leaned against the wall and folded her arms.

"Nice of you to think of that." Terel dusted off her hands and stalked down to Walvento's weapons room.

Vas shook her head and went back on deck. "Please tell me we're closer to finding out what those Enforcers are after and we've made sure they can't get on our ship again?"

Gosta nodded. "We're not sure what they are after. You are part of it, but it's more than that. Their communications when they were on this ship were extremely basic. I'm not even certain the ones who were here knew what they were doing beyond the limited instructions they'd been given."

Khirson looked up from his science station. "There's no way to tell how much they changed in fifty years, but they were grunts back in my day. There's some very big higher ups behind them."

"And finding them probably won't be easy," Deven said. He'd managed to avoid Terel about his hand for now, but Vas would be selling him out if he didn't go down on his own. Pela was damn good, better than doctors in hospitals in the center of the Commonwealth. But Terel was simply the best.

"On a positive note, Janx and I have looked at making it impossible for them to latch onto us again." Walvento was rarely on deck and looked awkward sitting next to Janx. His weapons room really didn't have room for two—not with all of the upgrades he'd added before they left Home.

"It's running now." Janx pulled up a screen to the front. "We're basically electro-charging the outer skin. I use a simpler version on Betsy, but Walvento made it stronger and permanent."

"Excellent. Now let's get some answers."

"We have to go to ground before we do that." Deven pulled up the scans. There was an increase in traffic from where they'd been. "Too many people out here are looking for us, we need to hide. Plus, this ship needs repairs and the crew needs time to recover."

Janx took a deep breath. "I know where we might be able to hide. Another cousin of ours has a run-down space station. He needs someone to run his bar for a month or so."

Mac's eyes narrowed at her first words, then he started swearing. "No. No. No. Seriously, Vas, Gerl is a loser."

Vas turned to him. "And do you have any other options beyond going back into Commonwealth space? We can't keep cruising around while we interrogate our prisoners, and none of them appear to want to make this easy. Not to mention we're not sure what went on at the conclave—avoiding being questioned about it would be a very good idea."

Mac shot a pleading look toward Deven. "Seriously, he's like Leil."

"We don't have a choice," Deven said. "Either we find a bolt-hole for a bit or we go back to the Commonwealth. It's not safe to be roaming out here with that damn silver ship after us. Not to mention whatever those Racki ships have been up to. And now these Enforcers."

"He's really not that bad, Mac." By the way she scrunched up her nose, it didn't look like Janx completely believed her own words.

"Ha! He didn't trick you onto a freighter, knock you out, and have you wake up two systems from home when you were sixteen! It took me a month to get back home."

Vas fought to keep from laughing at Mac.

Deven didn't even try. "You know, compared to some other family, yours isn't too bad. And I promise to get you back if he tries that again."

Mac looked appeased. He clearly missed the "get you back" part. Deven wouldn't stop any shenanigans, he'd just track him down at some point after they'd happened.

"Fine. But I'm not contacting him." Mac folded his arms and leaned back in his seat.

"I can," Janx said. "Gerl liked me better anyway. There should be enough room to hide this ship and Betsy in the shipyard. The station has a small, enclosed docking area."

Vas nodded. "Get a hold of him immediately."

"Sensing something?" Deven didn't look toward her, but she heard the smirk in his voice.

"Maybe. Or it could be the ships that showed up three jumps ago." Vas watched as the ships came into view from the drone Bathie had dropped. Gosta wasn't the only one watching the drone footage. Either their friends had a better idea where they were going, or they found them without hitting the first two systems. Neither was good.

CHAPTER THIRTY-FIVE

———◆———

"I WAS ABOUT TO POINT THAT out," Gosta said. "I don't see anything on the first two drones indicating they went there first."

Deven pulled the drone footage to the main screen. There was Ome's silver ship as well as one of the oddly round Racki ships. "Damn it, I didn't know those two were working together."

"We need to find out what in the hell is going on." Vas studied the footage, but there were no clues. The ships weren't near each other, but they must have been aware of each other.

"But if they can find us like that, why are they three jumps back?" Janx peered at the screen.

"That's a damn good question." Deven flipped through a series of screens quickly, finally swearing. "We're leaving a trail marker. Not constant, but something they can pick up."

"How? We scanned the entire ship before we started jumping." Khirson's people might be looking less like the major problem in their lives, but he was still taking things personally.

"Maybe it's not from our ship." Gosta started muttering under his breath as he ran through screens at his station. "There might be a tag on one of our prisoners." He sent one of his screens to the front. "This is a class five bio-marker. One of our newly gathered prisoners has it embedded under the skin. But I can't tell who yet."

"But not the Enforcers?" She figured the Enforcers wouldn't need to use those trackers, but better to narrow it down.

"No. They are clumped in a pile. The reading is being bounced by the shielding in the single cells. It's one of the three you grabbed on the planet." He looked up. "It could be all three from the way these readings are acting. Most inefficient."

"They could be after whoever you grabbed." Janx was watching the screen, but also the copy of it on her monitor. "Maybe they're not after this ship."

"Either way, it's not good." Deven got to his feet. "That level of tech is expensive as hell and painful to have put in." He hit his comm a second before Vas could. "Terel, could you meet us in the brig? Bring heavy sedatives."

"If they aren't after us specifically, I'll send them an apology." Vas followed him to the lift. "Mac, work on a new series of jumps no one can follow. Gosta, see what you can do to increase our shielding against this marker." She winced as the drone feed from the main screen burst into a show of sparks. That took care of that.

Marwin and Gon were standing watch outside the brig. Their three prisoners should still be unconscious, but Vas wanted medical support and heavy sedatives to make sure they stayed that way. These type of bio-trackers were painful as hell going in, and even more coming out.

"Any issues from the Enforcers?" Vas looked over to the larger cell. She had no idea what they were going to do with them. Maybe if they found more, she could trade them for Leil and the woman.

"Not a one," Marwin said. "They're still unconscious. Pela gave them a nice sleeper earlier."

Terel came down the corridor with a full mobile med kit trailing her and an annoyed expression. "I wasn't sure what all was needed since no one felt it was necessary to tell me what was going on."

Deven grinned. "What would be the fun in that?"

"We are being tracked through a bio-tracker. I'm

guessing one of our new prisoners, most likely Sedari. Whoever she was working for didn't trust her."

"From what I've heard, no one should trust her." Terel rubbed the back of her neck.

Deven's grin dropped. "Are you okay?"

"Yes, I think it's the lingering aftereffects from being knocked out and stuffed in a reduced oxygen shuttle for a few hours. That and being cramped over in the weapons room trying to get information. Walvento hasn't even cracked the casing yet." She grimaced. "I hope we do find the survivors—whoever took Leil and that weird Pilthian woman would do. I have many things to *discuss* with them." Her look was one Flarik would have approved of.

"When we find them, they're yours." Vas nodded to Marwin and Gon as they entered the brig. For a smallish ship, it had a good-sized brig. There were only the four cells, but even the three smaller ones were large enough that they could be split up if needed down the line.

Vas shook off that thought. This was a temporary ship, and they were on a job. Once they got things sorted, they'd finish and go back to the Commonwealth. She missed outright fighting as opposed to subterfuge and slinking around.

Gon and Marwin both stepped a foot further into the brig but kept their backs to the doorframe.

They still weren't sure what had been used to take out the crew so quickly, but it wasn't going to happen again if Marwin and Gon could help it.

Terel marched ahead. "So? Which one do I start with?" The cells were solid glastial and frosted on the inside. They could see in, but the prisoners couldn't see out. And the components of the glastial meant they couldn't break out either.

All of their prisoners were on their cots but looked awake. "Might as well start at the top. Sedari knows our personas and most likely it's in her. I'd like to keep the other two guessing as to what's going on for a while if we can." Truth was, she wasn't sure she wanted to deal with them just yet. From what Deven and the others had found, both had intel they needed. The first encounter was always crucial in any negotiations.

Sedari looked over as they opened her cell door and went inside but she didn't move off the cot. "I knew you were lying about who you were. You can't get any money for me; my people won't pay." She watched Terel as she came forward with the medical scanner. Hopefully she didn't see the look Deven and Vas gave each other.

That Sedari was important enough to someone that her first thought was that she was a kidnapping victim wasn't at all expected.

"Who are your people?" Deven stepped forward. Unlike Vas, who was still hiding from the warrant, Deven could have changed back to his normal self once they fled. Vas was glad he'd held off.

Sedari sat at the edge of the cot. "I will talk to you. Not them." She folded her arms and glared at Terel and Vas.

Deven folded his arms as well, accenting his extremely developed biceps, and stared down at her. "You'll talk to whoever I say you'll talk to. Assassins are not always quick about killing someone."

Vas took a step back to give Terel room, but Sedari looked to her with wide eyes.

"I'll talk. I will." She obviously had momentarily forgotten that Deven was claiming to be a retired assassin.

"Much better stance." He moved back again and motioned Terel to go to her. "But first, we need to run some tests. And I do want to hear everything about your people."

Vas grinned. "And the ones who were supposed to pick you up. But betrayed you."

If Sedari had a blaster right now, Vas would be dead. "They were going to save me and would have if you hadn't kidnapped me."

"Did you plan on leaving a bomb in your place?" Sedari could have left it herself to hide the evidence, but the way her face dropped to a very pale blue said probably not.

"Why would I do that? No one would have been around to find anything; an explosion would just draw attention that I didn't want."

"Then your friends were planning on ending you. I saved you. You're welcome."

Sedari looked to Deven and at his nod she turned even paler. "They needed me to pull this off. And they'll still need me afterwards." Her voice rose sharply.

"Obviously, not as much as you thought. You betrayed all of the pirate gangs at that conclave. A number of ships got off planet and will be spreading the word of your betrayal—many died down there. You're a liability to them. Whoever they are." Vas looked over to Terel as she finished her scan. Then repeated it with a scowl, finally stepping back and shaking her head. Damn it, Sedari wasn't the one being tracked. One of the two unknowns was.

"I was important! Am! I am important!" Sedari got to her feet and Deven stepped forward, but she wasn't attacking anyone, she was pacing. And looking wild.

"Is she frothing?" Vas wasn't a doctor but there seemed to be a thin layer of foam coming from her mouth.

"Damn it." Terel ran forward with a loaded hypo-spray and shot her in the neck. "Grab her and we need to get a suit on her." She hit her comm. "Pela, we need a full containment suit down in the brig, now."

Deven put Sedari on the cot and quickly stepped back. "How much trouble are we in?"

Vas watched Terel. She was upset, but not hysterical. This was a worry more than an attack.

"Not sure, she could be having a seizure of some kind.

The sedative will help with that. She's not the one with the tracker, but that doesn't mean that whoever she's working for didn't leave other surprises."

Pela and Gon came charging into the cell and quickly got Sedari in the suit. Terel was doing full scans of the air in the cell.

"She's secure and her nervous system is settling down. There are no contaminants in the air, so it hopefully was just directed at her." She turned to Deven. "Which does mean we can't ask her anything until I neutralize whatever is inside her."

"Damn. Tell me when she's clear." He peered down at her face. "Maybe Khirson will recognize something if he studies her while she's unconscious. You can see where her facial tats were."

They left the cell. "Which one next?"

Vas stood between the two cells. The man was the one with information on the thefts involving Dackon Industries. Early intel put the Foli pirate gang behind the thefts. She didn't know anything about that gang, but they'd be finding out soon.

The woman was the one with connections to what happened to the Pirate of Boagada and hopefully a lead on the missing scrolls. She was supposedly a low-ranking member of the Ohfina gang. Which probably meant there was a lot more to her than that.

"What's the woman's name again?"

"Delimara." Deven nodded. "Her first?"

"Yeah. Someone else might be aware of what she knows."

The three of them went in. Delimara was a Kantari, a species with heavy jaws, long canines, and nasty claws. Their fur made them look soft until you saw them in action. She'd been taken unaware, but Vas was still impressed that they'd brought her in. Unlike the other two, she was chained to the side of the cot. She could move a bit, enough to go to the toilet, but that was it.

Vas made sure the three of them stayed beyond the reach of that chain. Kantari were known for being temperamental.

"Delimara? We have some questions." Vas stepped to the edge of the safe zone.

Terel did as well, but she was on the other side of Deven and was running her scanners.

"Let me go. My people will find me. They will destroy you." She didn't even sit up, and her words were directed to the ceiling.

Vas watched her, then changed tactics. Bluntness worked better with some people. "That's nice. What do you know about the Pirate of Boagada? I say he's a myth, my second here says he's not."

Delimara jerked and turned her head. "That name is sacred and not to be spoken by unbelievers. I could kill you where you stand."

"Your chain doesn't reach that far, and we could blast the hell out of you before you got off that cot. Tell me what you know and we'll let you go."

Delimara sat up slowly. "Or my people are already coming for me and they will tear your ship apart and feast upon your bones." She glared at all of them.

Sounded more and more like she had the tracker. Vas looked to Terel for confirmation, but again she shook her head.

Seriously? Damn it. "We'll be back for questioning. I believe our Wavian lawyer in particular might want to speak to you." Kantari did not like Wavians.

The result was a snarl, then a flop back down to the cot.

They left and Vas glared at the final cell. "She's going to be fun to deal with. We don't get many Kantari in the Commonwealth, thank the gods."

"There aren't many since the Wavians almost slaughtered all of them a thousand years ago." Terel didn't look up from her scans. "Good call threatening her with Flarik, her blood pressure shot up with that—she might be more agreeable later. I can't believe neither of them are our tracker carrier. The type used would show, but neither woman has it."

Deven paused in front of the final cell. "Looks like it's our guy then."

"Which means there is probably more to him and the low-level thefts than we thought." Vas ran her fingers through her hair. There was a red tinge in the strands that hadn't been there before. "Different topic, any clue on that warrant for me? I know we've been a bit busy, but this disguise is starting to break down and Janx has her kit on that dozer." They were towing the dozer behind them. The dozer was mostly functioning on its own, but there were too many systems that had been compromised by the Enforcers' attack.

"You are looking a bit more you-ish." Terel gave her a critical look. "You may need to take it all off and stay away from anyone not on this crew."

"Agreed." Deven held open the cell door. "After you two."

Hjan was a human. Or mostly human. Someone down his family line had been a Xithinal and he had the short stature and bird-like face to support that. He also had some of their behaviors and jumped to his feet the moment they came in. "I didn't do anything." He had a hunch to his back that Xsit got whenever she was feeling guilty about something.

"We'll talk about that later, but yeah, I think you did." Vas studied him. His hair was actually yellow feathers made to look hair-like. He didn't want his Xithinal side to show. "Right now, I want some simple questions addressed. How long have you been with the Foli gang and what was your job?" Pirate gangs were often organized like merc gangs. Hjan looked like an accountant, but a small gang like the Folis probably wouldn't need one of those.

"I'm not with them." He gave a small smile. It was the "now-you-can-let-me-go" look.

"Oh? We took you out of their tent, my people saw you with them, and you have their tattoo on your wrist." Vas knew that Xsit mentally shut down if she became extremely frightened. Hjan didn't look completely freaked out, aside from the huge eyes and bad lying. But she'd bet he was.

"Fine, I'm with them. Navigation. Five years, two months, seven days. The captain never tells me anything about our jobs because he doesn't trust me. Which is fine, I wouldn't trust me either."

Vas glared at him until he stopped rambling.

Terel gave a short nod.

"Here's the deal, for a non-important member of a non-important pirate crew, you have some seriously important, annoying, and illegal tech in you. My doctor will be taking that out and I have a feeling you'd rather be unconscious when she does."

She wasn't certain whether Hjan was really an unsuspecting idiot in all this, or very sneaky. The lack of shock or fear at her words indicated the latter.

He covered a moment later and tried looking worried. "What do you mean? I don't have any illegal tech in me."

Terel walked closer to him and held her scanner. "A T-134 tracker. High end, very expensive. No one would waste one on a nobody."

Hjan's eyes changed. He didn't move a single muscle, but his very stillness gave away a great deal. Vas shoved Terel out of the way as Hjan leapt for her.

CHAPTER THIRTY-SIX

D EVEN CAUGHT HIM IN THE air with his good
hand, pinned his arms, and started squeezing. "If
you're wondering if I can crush you like this—the answer
is yes. Stop fighting now."

Terel scrambled to her feet, punched Hjan hard in the
face, then stabbed him with the loaded hypo spray. He
was out in two seconds.

"Damn it. We really misjudged this one." Vas dusted off
her hands. She'd taken both herself and Terel to the floor.
Hjan was a lot faster than she'd expected. "Who brought
back the intel on him?"

Deven stepped back to her after securing him to the
cot. "Flarik, but all she did was report that he'd been
shooting off his mouth. We didn't get a chance to pull up
full background information."

Terel brought her med equipment forward and started
prepping him. "It's located right under his left scapula.
Where his wings would be if he were a pure Xithinal."

"I'm sure that wasn't by accident." Deven leaned over
to look at the scans. "The nubs of wings are under the
skin; it would have been a very painful place to put it."

"Which means whoever he's working for doesn't like
him much. But if that's the case, why in the hell was he
fighting to defend them? And I don't see the Folis doing
that. Those things are expensive."

"I don't see them taking out the Dackon Industry ships
either." Deven stepped back. "They're a strictly small jobs
crew."

"Someone hired them or is using them. I think we

need further detail on these attacks against Dackon. Beyond what they told us officially." There were a lot of things wrong out here, and they might be connected. The Dackon people had been very insistent about her and her crew getting out of the Commonwealth quickly. Then that bit with someone destroying Khirson's ship. "Damn it."

Deven looked up. Terel kept doing her med prep but Vas could feel her listening.

"I just realized that we might have been set up, but I'm not exactly sure for what yet. Once we get to this space station, I want you, Gosta, and Hrrru to do a massive search for Dackon, both out here and in the Commonwealth."

"You might be on to something." Deven leapt forward as Hjan jerked. He held Hjan down.

"He's out. Should he be moving like that?" Even with Deven holding him down, Hjan was still twitching.

Terel scowled. "No. But whoever put this bio-marker in him is an ass. They tied it to his nervous system."

"You can't get it out?"

"I can. It's going to take longer than expected." Terel looked up. "I'd like Deven to stay. Even one handed he's strong enough to keep him restrained. Maybe get Marwin in here as well." The look she shot Vas said two things: Vas didn't need to be there and Terel would be dragging Deven down to the med bay when this was done.

"I think I'm needed on the bridge." Vas looked at her hair. "Once I do a quick change. Call if you need anything."

Terel was already focusing on her patient, but Deven gave a nod.

Vas left the cell. "Marwin, can you go inside and help Terel and Deven? Gon, call Roha or Glazlie down to join you. I want two guards at the door at all times. And keep knocking the Enforcers out if needed."

There was a sleeping agent dispenser near the cell door. Vas noticed it still was half full. For now, they needed to keep those Enforcers unconscious.

Vas went to the deck. The screen showed no one in pursuit. Which didn't mean as much as she'd like it to. "Any signs?"

Gosta shook his head. "The two ships are following, but still a few jumps behind."

"Which is not my fault." Mac was entering more jump commands.

"Where are we now?" Vas could recognize many of the systems in the Commonwealth. But being as they hadn't had time for much traveling when they'd been out here before, she didn't recognize anything out here unless she had a chart up.

"The Lembari system. We came in through an old gate that's not near the main planets." Mac was far too smug about his choice.

Vas hit her comm. "Terel, any idea when we'll have that tracker removed?"

"Not yet. This thing is really embedded. We want him to keep the use of his arm?"

Vas knew she was saying that to make a point. It was hard for Terel to not help someone—whoever that some-one may be. "That might make him more likely to be accommodating once he wakes up, so yes, please."

"Then keep cruising around—it might be a while." Terel cut the comm.

"Okay, you heard the lady, we keep cruising. Until that tracker is out, we can't hide in the space station." She sat back in her chair. "Did you reach your cousin, Janx?"

"Not yet." She turned away from her monitor. "I have left some messages. He might have already found some-one to take the job. We could still hide there, but he'd charge us a hell of a lot. Let me try again." She spun back to her monitor.

"Options for if we can't work a deal with this Gerl person?" Deven was her best brainstorming partner, but Terel hadn't sent him up yet, and she'd sounded tense enough that Vas didn't want to push things. But they needed to go to ground once they disabled that tracker. Part of her debated running back to the Commonwealth, but if someone was setting them up, they might be waiting for that. She'd kept her contact with Ragkor and everyone in the Commonwealth down to nothing to make it harder for any of the pirates to trace them. Since that was no longer an issue, she headed to her ready room to contact them. At the very least she'd let them know what was going on and where to look for them if things went completely to hell.

The room was still as small as she recalled, but her crew were trying to figure things out, and she didn't want to distract them. She called Ragkor directly, always more awkward than having Xsit do it, but again, better leave her crew to what they were doing.

"Captain?" Ragkor's voice was groggy with sleep as well as a bad connection.

"Sorry, Ragkor. Didn't have a chance to calculate the time there."

"Is everything okay?" He woke up with alarming swiftness, but the connection was still bad.

"Not so much. We have leads on our projects, but there have been some issues. I'm sending you a file." She uploaded everything they had compiled so far since they'd left the Commonwealth.

"What do you need me to do?"

"Are there updates on the attack on that Pilthian ship?" The connection was getting worse.

"No...any...here."

"Damn it, you're breaking up bad—not sure if you can hear me. But here's where we'll be staying—hopefully. I'll try and reach you again in a few days."

"Roger, Captain. I—" The call was cut.

Vas hoped the files she sent got to him. They were secure, so the chances of anyone else getting them were slim. But she wanted him to have the information. Something was making her edgy.

"Aithnea? Are you around?"

"Well, I can't really go anywhere, now can I?" The words were curt, but the tone wasn't.

"True. Do you sense anything?" Vas felt weird asking, she really didn't go for things beyond what she could see. But something was wrong. It began when the call to Ragkor started being choppy.

Aithnea's sigh told her a lot. "Jasiel and I were discussing that. It's good you felt it, you're tapping into the mystical side of the nuns. But it's not good as three of us feeling it confirms the reality. Something is seriously wrong."

"Tell me if you two can narrow it down any. All I'm getting is a skin-crawling feeling. Like a trap." Problem was, she wasn't sure what the trap was.

"Understood."

Vas went back to the deck. Everything looked the same. "Any chatter on what happened to the conclave?" She sat in her chair but stayed on the edge of it. If they were on a planet, she would have sent scouts all around them.

"Nothing I can pick up, Captain." Gosta's brows were lowered, a sure sign something was bugging him.

Vas hit the ship-wide comm. "I'm feeling like we're about to be dropped into an ambush. Is anyone else feeling odd?" She wasn't happy admitting to it, but if the others were picking up on something as well, that would be telling. Half her deck crew nodded or raised their hands and calls were coming in from the rest.

Deven called up privately. "Vas, there is something seriously wrong. Terel got the tracker out and Hjan should live. But I'm feeling intense pressure from outside the ship."

"Like we need to run?" Vas finally narrowed the feeling down. Impending doom with a side of get-the-hell-out-of-the-area.

"Yes, I'm coming up on deck."

Vas knew Terel wanted to look at his injured hand; the fact that she wasn't stopping him meant she felt it too.

"Mac, where is the nearest gate?"

"I've been staying on the edge of the system, but the gate we came through isn't that far away."

Vas stood. "Can someone put up a map of us and the original conclave planet. Show our jumps." She had a bad feeling.

Deven made it to the deck by the time Gosta and Hrrru got the map up on the screen. He came to stand next to Vas.

"That doesn't look right." He shook his head at the huge screen.

"Nope. It doesn't. We had two people picking gates, random jumps, yet someone has been herding us." Vas invented a few new swear words as the pattern emerged. "They didn't have to track us because they were pushing us where they wanted us to go." Once all of the jumps were entered it was as if someone had been giving them instructions.

"Mac, without thinking, where would you have gone to next?"

Mac popped up a system.

"Yup, I think they are trying to send us here." Deven circled an area on the screen. And we're going further and further from the Commonwealth border."

"Okay, change of plans." Vas looked at the chart. Mac's next jumps would have also taken them further from Gerl's space station. "Mac, go through the gate but hit these two immediately after." She selected two gates that were away from the one that was calling to them and closer to the space station. They'd have to move quickly if someone was controlling them.

"But...I think we need to go that way." Mac could whine, and often did so. But this didn't sound like him.

"I agree that direction feels wrong." Gosta looked like he was fighting to get the words out.

"Deven, you and I will take over. Everyone else stand back from their stations." Vas felt the wrongness as she and Deven took over navigation.

"Keep working, Vas, you're breaking through." Jasiel had silently come on deck and nodded as Aithnea called up from the holosuite.

"Keep going. Channel the nuns who came before you."

Wrong choice of words as Vas almost lost her concentration to point out she wasn't a nun, and therefore there were no nuns who came before her.

"We can do this." Deven held her glance and smiled.

They made it through the gate to their destination. The pressure didn't lessen.

In fact, the two Enforcer ships waiting for them increased it.

CHAPTER THIRTY-SEVEN

"EVASIVE MANEUVERS, NOW!" VAS' SHOUT shook her crew out of whatever had grabbed a hold of them, and they resumed their stations.

Both Enforcer ships were smaller than the *Traitor's Folly*, but they appeared to be ready to fire.

Mac moved them out of the way.

"They are tracking us, Captain." Walvento called up from his weapons bay.

"Fire at the lead ship." Vas normally gave a warning shot unless they were in a battle. This wasn't the time for niceties though.

They hit the first ship, but both ships moved away and started sending a charge toward the *Traitor's Folly*.

"They're trying to connect, but the skin you put on is working." Khirson might not have had access to weapons on his console, but the gleeful way he pounded the arm of the chair said he wished he did.

The two Enforcer ships could outmaneuver the *Traitor's Folly*.

"I need a Flit squad out there now. Fire when you can." Sending the Flits out could balance things a bit since she couldn't fire at both of the Enforcer ships. They'd sent one more round of the odd electrical charge before the Flits left the bay.

The Flits flew straight out from the bay, bypassing the Enforcer ships.

"Enforcer ships stand down. We just want to pass through." Vas figured it couldn't hurt to try.

"We want our prisoner. Vaslisha Tor Dain is wanted by

the high counsel for crimes against the Pilthian nation."

Khirson clicked on the ship-to-ship screen and got to his feet. "Under what orders? I've been with this crew; they have done nothing. Since when have the Pilthian people dropped so low?"

"Who are you? Where did you get those markings?" The Enforcer on the other ship still had his face mask on, but they were Pilthian.

"I am Lord Khirson. Been missing for a bit. Look me up. Whose orders are you working under?" He was almost snarling now.

The Enforcer pulled back for a moment, then shook his head. "Things have changed, *Lord*." At the last word he fired missiles at the *Traitor's Folly*.

Vas cut the communication with the other ship. "Everyone, fire at will!"

Mac spun the Tr*aitor's Folly*, forgetting they were towing Janx's dozer. It broke loose and spun into the lead Enforcer ship. Two Flits followed up and ran a line of weapons fire down the side.

"Sorry, Janx! We'll get it back." Mac didn't sound sorry; he sounded like that was his plan all along. But he did extend the tracking arm and grab the dozer.

Two strikes hit the shields and the deck bounced. The alarm that followed wasn't great. "Seal anything that pops. We need to get the hell out of here." This was a new fear. While the other had been general, this was very specific.

"You are right. More are coming. They didn't expect you to come this way." Jasiel was still standing, but she had one hand out and her eyes were closed. "Not this time." A charge came from somewhere on the *Traitor's Folly* and slammed into the second ship. Walvento wasted no time sending missiles along the same path. The Flits spread their weapons between the two then came into the shuttle bay.

"Captain, incoming from that other gate." Gosta threw

the image up on the main screen. The gate near them was inactive but this system had two fairly close together and there were a lot of ship signatures coming through.

"Mac, jump. Head to the Gael system." Vas knew nothing about it, but it wasn't here, and it wasn't the direction they'd been following before.

The first Enforcer ship blew up. At least five ships more came through the far gate, and Mac punched them through the closest one.

"That was too close. Janx, is your cousin ready for us?"

Janx was pale and Vas had a feeling it was from more than seeing her dozer being flung about like a rock. "Aye, he's only charging a hundred credits, since I told him the crew would work the pub and intake for the station for a month."

Vas nodded. "That's fair. And I have a feeling we'll need that long. Get us to that station, Mac."

Two jumps and they were on the edge of nowhere. Not near any space lanes, at least none that had been in use in a hundred years. The station was old enough that it might have been built during Deven's grandfather's time. It still functioned, but the lack of ships around it, there were currently only two, didn't speak well of it. Vas didn't care. This cousin of Mac and Janx was open to hiding them for a bit, and he definitely had the space. That ambush and the way they'd been herded pointed out that as much as she hated the idea, they needed to hide.

"Station Zqui, this is the *Traitor's Folly* requesting berth for us and the dozer we're towing." Gosta was formal about it, even though it had sounded like Gerl ran the entire station, not just the bar.

Static came first, then an annoyed male voice. "You have the ten thousand credits?"

Gosta looked to Janx who scowled at the dark screen. "We have the funds I promised, Gerl. Come on."

"Eh, I was kidding, Janxie girl. Any friend of yours

and all. Sending the coordinates now." He sounded less annoyed, but not by much.

Mac flew them into a cavernous, enclosed repair station and docked next to a ramp. Four smaller vessels were docked at the far end, but still not much for a station this size. The dozer settled in behind him. Staying inside for any length of time wasn't a great idea; it would be too easy to become trapped if someone did find them. But right now, Vas needed to get away from those Enforcer ships. And the Racki. And anyone else looking for them. She'd move into an open orbit in a few days if nothing followed them. They still had to get some answers out of their growing collection of prisoners and a nearly abandoned space station might be the perfect place.

Once both ships were secure, Vas, Deven, Janx, and Mac went down to meet their host. Vas left instructions for everyone else to remain armed and ready for anything.

Gerl was an ugly man, no way to get around that. He was short, like Mac and Janx, but years of hard living had left him with a permanent scowl and narrowed eyes.

"Nice to be meeting you. Talria and Captain Fhailson. My station is your station."

Deven stepped forward and shook his hand. "I thought you just owned the bar?"

"Started that way. Now the entire thing is mine. Have a full block of rooms, a restaurant, my bar. I can put your entire crew up for a nominal price if they don't want to stay on the ship. And of course, ship repairs." He held his hands out toward the hangar. "It's not much, but it's a living. Your crew not coming down?"

"They will be. We want to view the area first. Besides, they need to get their things together." Vas forced a smile. Instincts couldn't always be listened too, but right now hers were saying to kick this guy's ass and run. Unfortunately, their options were extremely thin.

The station looked as run down as it had from the

outside. But it looked solid, and they couldn't be choosy.

"Here's the bar I'll have you fine folks run. Not much going on right now but a few Kantari ships will be through in a bit—always good money and I currently don't have a crew to run it."

The bar was the best spot on the station. Clean and relatively up to date, it had a massive space window. Those were damn expensive. Clearly, Gerl got this place from someone who had actually cared.

Janx had been looking at something on her small tablet, then finally looked up. "They are calling the dozers to clean up an accident on the planet we were on. If I don't show up…" She let the rest drop. If she didn't show up, she wouldn't get future jobs and there was a good chance whoever was chasing them would go after her. Whatever was going on, there were a lot of edgy people involved.

She didn't look any happier than Vas felt. From the brief intelligence Gosta had found, those Racki and Assembly ships had still gotten a number of pirate ships. She wished she knew why they wanted to wipe out a bunch of pirates that weren't even in their system.

"Is your dozer in good enough shape to go?" Vas didn't want Janx lumped in with them if she could help it. But if her ship couldn't go on its own, she was stuck.

"She and I can get it running." Mac had perked up at seeing the bar, but he cared about his cousin and clearly wanted to get her free if at all possible.

Deven nodded, still maintaining his captain role. "Get her up and out of here, Mac." He smiled at Janx. "Thank you for all your help."

"Anytime…Captain." She bobbed her head to both Vas and Deven and followed Mac out.

"So, you guys have run a bar before?" Gerl had gone behind the counter and started pointing to various areas. "Pretty simple really. Here's the drink mixer, extras, glass, mugs, troughs for some of the larger races. I have a few errands to run, so you'll be on your own for a bit. Shouldn't be long, I can't get far in my shuttle." There was a bitterness to his comment.

"You don't have a ship?" Vas was looking over the bar.

"Nope, lost it in a card game a while back." He leaned forward. "It's up to you folks, but I wouldn't recommend running card games." He pointed out a large office and his communication station—lots of room, but cheap equipment. Most likely there had been another one for the station elsewhere but he'd moved it over when he took over the entire station.

"I'll be heading out, call if you need me. The Kantari should be here in a few hours—they drink well." With a nod to both of them, he left.

Vas looked into every cabinet behind the bar. "That was too easy. Think he's setting us up, or planning on getting more funds out of us at a later point?"

Deven was checking out the bar itself and moving around a few tables and chairs. Terel still hadn't done everything she wanted to do about his hand, but it was protected enough for him to use it. "Most likely both, but I think we can stay on top of him." He tilted his head, then moved another table and chairs further out.

"Are you now a designer? Or were you a bar owner in a prior life?" Vas watched him as he shoved a few more chairs apart.

"Neither. Okay, I have worked as a bouncer at a bar before, long before I came to the Commonwealth. And I know Kantari. They like to fight for no reason and it's better to give them space."

"Like to fight, as in we keep our people on the ship?"

Deven looked to be weighing that then shrugged. "Not necessarily. Kantari are fighters, but not assassins. Mostly hired to fight, and often mercs."

They spent another hour going over the area and the surrounding offices. Vas wasn't planning on staying here any longer than necessary, but best to know what the options were. Once she was sure there were no traps, she called for the crew to head in. Except for a security detail that would stay on the ship and be swapped out in a few hours. There were very few people on board, but better to be safe than sorry.

Mac called up. "Captain? We have Janx's dozer up and running."

"I'll be down to say goodbye. Someone is still arranging furniture." She nodded as Gosta and Hrrru came into the bar with a bunch of the crew trailing behind them.

Janx and Mac stood by the dozer as Vas went down.

"Thank you for making me a blonde." Vas pulled at her hair. "And for being smarter than those jerks who tried to take us. If you ever need anything, contact us and if we can, we'll help."

Janx darted forward and gave Vas a quick hug. "Thank you. I like a simple life, but this was an adventure." She stepped back. "And don't trust Gerl; Mac is right, he's an ass."

Vas smiled. "Gathered that. But this is keeping us out of sight for a bit, so we'll take our chances. Take care."

Janx nodded, gave Mac a hug, then jogged to her ship.

Mac and Vas watched her leave, then shut the doors behind her. "She's a good kid. I hope she's not going to run into trouble cleaning up that mess." Mac left and went out to the bay and Vas headed back toward the bar.

Most of the crew had settled around the bar, a few had gone to look over the limited stores in the tiny promenade.

"Who is going to monitor the ships coming in? We're running everything, right?" Gosta was sitting at the bar but didn't look comfortable.

"Would you like to? You and Hrrru could use the setup in that back room, bring what you need from the ship, establish a full communications and recon area?"

She knew neither one was big on drinking, and it would be good to keep things looking like a functioning space station.

"I could join them?" Xsit had been looking around the bar. Knowing how bad of a drinker she was, Vas nodded.

A few more of the crew went with them. Vas told them to take what they needed off the ship, but only what could be quickly put back in. They'd all already gathered their personal belongings, but there was enough equipment they could use down here that wouldn't make the ship unusable.

"You look like you need a drink." Deven went behind the bar and started searching.

Vas leaned against the bar. Now that Janx's disguise had finally been removed, she felt exposed again. If they were going to be on an open space station, there might be people coming in. She slipped her eye patch back on.

"That really doesn't disguise you much, you know." Deven finished mixing a drink and started to slide it to her but stopped. "For a kiss."

Vas leaned over the bar and kissed him. "I've missed this."

"Me too." He kissed her again, then leaned back and scowled at his arms. "I really need to change back as well. This blue is getting to me."

Khirson came in and sat near the bar. "I think the blue looks good, but I am biased. While we're here, I'd like to see about finding my people. There are too many Pilthians running around out here to be coincidence." The look on his face said he wasn't hopeful at what he'd find. They were here, but they'd changed in the past fifty years.

"I don't see why not. We'll be here for a month at least, let things die down and people forget about us. I think—"

Vas' words were cut off by an alarm. "Mac? What the hell is that?" It was habit; if there was an odd sound, he was most likely involved.

"We're being boarded!" Mac yelled over the comm.

"We're an open space station, people land here all the time—who has to board us?"

Deven pulled up the station schematic and found a way to turn off the alarm. "People who don't like normal entrances." He tapped the screen where fifteen dark dots were now coming toward them.

"Again, who invades an open space station? They would have done better to pretend to be customers, then attacked us." Vas folded her arms and shook her head. She hated idiots.

Khirson looked between Vas and Deven. "You don't seem concerned?"

"They don't seem to be too bright. And there are only fifteen." Vas checked the charge on her blaster and wished her blades weren't in her room.

"And we might have a bit more of a problem." Deven didn't sound concerned though. "They are Kantari."

Vas swore. Kantari weren't always the brightest but they were damn good killers. "And not the nice ones we were expecting? We can assume they are here for Delimara. I'm not ready to let her go until we get some answers. Have they changed direction?" They'd secured their prisoners in the station's brig. Low tech, but solid.

"It appears that the ones Gerl said were coming in are delayed. But, no, these haven't changed direction yet." Deven handed an extra blaster to Khirson. "We probably want to guard the brig."

"Agreed. Roha, you, Khirson, and Gon lead the others to the brig. Deven and I will wait for our friends."

Roha nodded and started out. Gon paused. "Captain? Are you sure? Fifteen of those…things could be trouble."

Vas shared a look with Deven. "Thank you, Gon. But Deven and I will be fine." She rolled her shoulders. "It's been a long, irritating trip. I'd like to get some of my frustrations out."

There was an extremely slim chance that the Kantari were just on the station for some down time—Gerl had said some of them were due in, maybe he got the wrong ship. But expected people didn't break in through an airlock. And that they happened to come in through a little used access portal instead of the large gaping bay. Vas shook her head and turned to Deven. "Shall we?"

"You want to meet them in the halls? If we fight them in here, we have more control."

Vas looked around the bar. He had a point. If they were looking for their missing person, they'd have to go right past the bar. "How did they track her though?" She looked up at the map and those shapes didn't waver once. They knew exactly where they were going.

"They must have a bio one that Terel didn't know to look for. We were looking for the ones pulling along ships, like what Hjan had."

Vas tapped her comm. "Terel, we've got some visitors. Deven and I should be able to stop them here at the bar, but we have a large group back down at the brig on the station. Can you, Flarik, and Pela keep the ship secure?"

"Flarik isn't happy that you're fighting without her. Jasiel isn't either. But we will keep things secure here."

"Thanks."

"And I'll help as well." Aithnea popped up on a table. "Well, this is odd. I got into a holo-system for this station. I can't fight, but this is an excellent chance for some training. Now be a good girl and put away the blaster."

"What? This isn't a training. Those Kantari mean business and they want someone I still need. We can train when this is over."

"Deven?" Aithnea jumped down from the table but didn't go far. "Can you talk to her? The targets will be here soon."

Deven shook his head. "I'm not getting in the middle

of this." He turned to Vas. "However, I do know that your fighting is always better in real situations. You are going to have to become a Keeper eventually, you know."

Vas glared from one to the other. "I… Fine." She put away her blaster. "Does Deven get to keep his?"

"He's not training to be a Keeper. But it would be best if he stayed out completely." Aithnea's grin was far too familiar. This lesson was going to hurt.

"I don't argue with deceased mother superiors. It's always been a policy." He put his blaster into his holster and took a seat at a distant table.

"They are coming down this corridor—any words of training before I get my ass kicked? They will be using blasters, you know."

Aithnea closed her eyes and then opened them with a smile. "Not anymore. All of their charging cores died. Not that it's that big of a deal for Kantaris. They see blasters as a weak weapon, and all have short blades. As for words, think of the book. Focus on it."

Vas swore as booted feet echoed down the corridor leading to them. She had no idea what part of the book, but she knew Aithnea meant the blue one. She briefly shut her eyes and images hit her hard enough to make her stagger forward. She opened her eyes and waited.

"Just remember, it is far more difficult to disable an opponent—or opponents—than it is to kill them. The Keepers can easily kill, but they rarely do so." Then her hologram vanished.

Kantari came in two forms. More civilized ones, like Delimara—still scary as hell but they at least could function in society—more or less. Then the ferals. They weren't really feral, but for many of the Kantari, becoming throw backs was an honored way of life. Claws and fangs were untrimmed. They wore space suits, but old ones. If they were disturbed about not having blasters, they didn't show it.

Deven stayed at one of the tables. Vas knew despite his promise to Aithnea, if she got in trouble, he'd jump in. Aithnea reappeared on the table next to her.

"Not a good way to think. You must control the entire situation." If the Kantari cared about, or even noticed the hologram floating around the tables, they didn't show it.

"We need our leader." The first one who stepped forward was bulkier than the others.

"Sorry, she's staying with us for now. Now I can offer you drinks on the house if you'd like." A calmness flowed over her. Even as she made the offer that she knew would be rejected, she was notating where all of the Kantari stood.

"Remember. Not killing is harder than killing. The Keeper is in full control." Aithnea's hologram drifted over to Deven.

The first Kantari charged forward. He hadn't pulled out the short blade he wore, and Vas was vaguely insulted. She grabbed an arm as he ran at her and spun him into the far wall. If Aithnea didn't want her to kill them, she'd do her best. It wouldn't be her fault if one of them landed wrong. The one she threw got to his elbows, then collapsed. One down but not dead, fourteen more to go.

She felt almost like she thought Deven might feel when he fought. Calm and collected, the claws and teeth flying at her were just more to move around. She could like this if this came with being a Keeper. She misjudged her spin and got clocked by a pair of Kantari fists. She plowed through a few chairs and slammed into a table headfirst.

Aithnea drifted down alongside her. "It's great you were feeling the moment, but you are also in a fight with seven beings who would like to kill you."

Vas shook her head to clear the ringing. Seven was good. Much better than what she started with.

Two more charged her and this time they had blades. One of the ones she'd taken down was near her, so she grabbed his short sword. Since Aithnea didn't object, she figured that was okay.

Taking another deep breath to clear her head, Vas waded back into the fight.

———◆———

"Vas? Can you hear me?" Deven's voice was too close, he wasn't supposed to help. She twitched and fought her eyes open. The entire side of her face hurt, and her head had started to pound. She held up her hand and noticed a fair amount of blood. Mostly hers, since the Kantari had a more blueish color.

"What happened?"

Deven pulled her up slowly, but didn't try to make her stand. "You fought like a nun. A serious, bad ass nun. You might have taken a few hard hits though."

She tried looking around but her one eye kept closing. "Did I kill any of them?"

Aithnea dropped down next to her. "Only three and it wasn't intentional. Your people took the survivors, dropped them in their ship and hauled them to another system."

Vas knew she felt like crap, but it was the expression on both of their faces that drove home what she must look like. "Is all Keeper training going to be like this?"

Deven slowly helped her to stand.

"No. Well, mostly not. We'll talk later." Aithnea flashed a grin and vanished.

"It's not fair she can do that." Vas leaned into Deven's arms.

"You need to see Terel."

Vas paused and looked down at herself. "Nothing is broken, even my head. I think I'd rather spend some time helping my favorite guy become less blue." Deven could work some level of healing through his telepathic abilities. And sex was an excellent vehicle for him to do so.

"Let me see your eyes." He bent down and peered at her. "I believe you're right about nothing broken. But you are going to be sore."

She gave him a long kiss. "Then I'll need lots of care, won't I?"

The rest of her crew were going about their business, and actually cleaning up the bar. Deven escorted her to their room. A high-end expensive rental room, it had a bed almost as large as the one on the *Warrior Wench*. Between his bandaged hand, and her injuries, getting undressed was a bit of a challenge. But Deven kept taking it slow and the trail of kisses he left as he removed her clothing made her feel better already.

"I haven't started healing you yet."

Vas pulled back. "You can read my thoughts again?"

"Only vague emotions like contentment. You're still injured so we need to take it slow."

Vas and Deven were falling asleep when the comm buzzed.

"Captain, we have a serious situation." Mac had been in the ship checking out what more they could bring down.

"Can it wait?"

"The giter is malfunctioning. I can't stop it; it's going to cascade." There was suitable panic in Mac's voice and both Vas and Deven jumped out of bed. The giter was a small, simple piece of tech. That could literally blow up a ship if it cascaded through the engine drive. Like this one was about to.

She almost questioned Mac, but if anyone knew about parts of a ship it would be him. "Get everyone off the ship. Grab as much as you can."

"I'll go take it out away from here." Deven was already dressed and almost to the door.

Vas pulled her boots on and followed him. "I am the captain—I go down with the ship if it's required." She winced as a dizzy spell hit her. Damn Kantari, she should have at least killed the one who almost split her head open.

Deven steadied her with his good hand. "We're a pair, falling apart like old Ilerians. But the fact is, dizzy pilots make mistakes. I only need one hand to fly."

"Damn you." She pulled him down for a long lingering kiss. "You dump that ship and take the shuttle back to me. Or so help me, I'll have Aithnea bring you back from the dead." He was right and she knew it. Didn't make things any easier.

A low-level klaxon rang in the bay as her crew came into the station hauling anything they could. Deven pulled up the ramp.

The *Traitor's Folly* lumbered out of the bay. Vas watched until he'd moved away from the entrance, then she went to the bar to watch it on Gosta's monitors. They'd done a great job gutting the ship, she'd be surprised if Deven had a seat right now.

Vas watched as the shuttle came back in. A giter converter malfunction could take out a ship far bigger than it. She hoped it was far enough from the space station if it blew.

"The last shuttle has docked. The ship is clear." Gosta called out.

Vas tried calling Gerl again. He'd said he was holding off leaving for a few days but wasn't responding. She'd finished checking everyone off on her list except for Mac and Deven when he finally responded.

Gerl called down to the bar just as Deven was coming in. Vas thought Gerl was still on the space station, but when he opened the vid, she saw they'd been played.

"Yes, *Vaslisha Tor Dain*, I have your ship." Gerl was on the deck of the *Traitor's Folly*. "The Enforcers might not want you anymore, but someone might be willing to pay for your location. And I have wanted to get out of this hellhole for a long time. A Commonwealth registered ship should be just the thing."

"You won't get far. The damage wasn't made up." She'd seen the specs; that ship was an explosion that just hadn't happened yet.

"You mean the giter converter?" He held up a box of parts. "It took some work to make it look good enough to get you all off this thing. Do say goodbye to Mac for me. I had to knock him out on my last trip up here. He's in the bay in a circuit closet."

Vas leaned into the screen. "I will find you."

"No, I don't think—" Gerl's comment was cut off as a silver ship sliced through the *Traitor's Folly*.

The flash was bright but happened so fast the silver ship was gone from the quadrant by the time Vas and the rest of the crew recovered.

"That was Ome and Loxianth. Damn it, I really hoped we'd gotten away from them." Vas watched as her former ship, now split into two pieces, burned. It was far enough away that there was little threat to the space station.

"On the plus side, if they think we were on board, they'll be surprised when we find them." Mac came up behind them, rubbing his head. "I told Janx that Gerl was an asshole."

Vas leaned against the main window of the bar and watched as the *Traitor's Folly* continued to burn. It hadn't been her ship for long, but it still was hard to lose any ship.

"That's a good point and at least we got everyone and everything we could out." Deven dropped his arm around her shoulders. It was nice to see him back to himself instead of blue.

She slid her arm around his waist and leaned in. "True. Sorry about Gerl. Not that he seemed like a good guy, but I would have liked to kick his ass a bit before he died stealing my ship. Guess we call for a rescue."

"Captain?" Xsit didn't sound happy.

Vas turned. They'd created a makeshift communications station, based on the piece of crap Gerl had, in the main office. Both Xsit and Gosta were standing at the doorway and neither looked happy.

"Why do I think this might be worse than our ship being stolen and then destroyed?"

"It is." Gosta finally stepped in when Xsit didn't speak but stood there looking ill. "The Commonwealth just closed their borders. Military patrols all along the rim. Ragkor sent us what info he could, but communications are extremely dicey too."

"What? Why?" She strode toward the office.

"The Commonwealth is interpreting the actions of the Lethian Assembly and Hive as an attack against them. No one in or out—even people or ships from the Commonwealth." He looked to the dying ship filling the viewscreen. "Even if we had a ship, we're stuck here."

THE END

DEAR READER,

Thank you for joining me on another adventure with Aisling and the gang. As always, I appreciate you for coming along on the newest escapade. The next book in this series will be out in 2022, if not before.

If you want to keep up on the further adventures of any of my characters, make sure to visit my website and sign up for my mailing list.

http://marieandreas.com/index.html

You can also sign up on Amazon to follow me and they will keep you updated.

https://geni.us/NZ6jX0o

If you enjoyed this book, please spread the word! Positive reviews on are like emotional gold to any writer. And mean more than you know.

Thank you again—and keep reading!

ABOUT THE AUTHOR

MARIE IS A MULTI-AWARD-WINNING FAN-TASY and science fiction author with a serious reading addiction. If she wasn't writing about all the people in her head, she'd be lurking about coffee shops annoying total strangers with her stories. So really, writing is a way of saving the masses. She lives in Southern California and is owned by two very faery-minded cats. She is also a proud member of SFWA (Science Fiction and Fantasy Writers of America).

When not saving the masses from coffee shop she-nanigans, Marie likes to visit the UK and keeps hoping someone will give her a nice summer home in the Forest of Dean or Conwy, Wales.

Made in the USA
Monee, IL
19 March 2022